PENGUIN BOOKS
THE SIMOQIN PROPHECIES

Samit Basu is twenty-three. He is currently working on the sequel to
The Simoqin Prophecies.

The Simoqin Prophecies

Samit Basu

PENGUIN BOOKS

Penguin Books India (P) Ltd., 11 Community Centre, Panchsheel
Park, New Delhi 110017, India
Penguin Books Ltd., 80 Strand, London WC2R 0RL, UK
Penguin Group Inc., 375 Hudson Street, New York, NY 10014, USA
Penguin Books Australia Ltd., 250 Camberwell Road, Camberwell,
Victoria 3124, Australia
Penguin Books Canada Ltd., 10 Alcorn Avenue, Suite 300,
Toronto, Ontario M4V 3B2, Canada
Penguin Books (NZ) Ltd., Cnr Rosedale & Airborne Roads,
Albany, Auckland, New Zealand
Penguin Books (South Africa) (Pty) Ltd., 24 Sturdee Avenue,
Rosebank 2196, South Africa

First published by Penguin Books India 2004

Copyright © Samit Basu 2004

10 9 8 7 6 5 4 3 2 1

Typeset in AGaramond by Eleven Arts, Delhi-35

Printed at Chaman Offset Printers, New Delhi

Prologue

*T*ake an orange, Sambo (if your name is Sambo), a nice round juicy orange. Now take a knife—yes, any knife—and cut it. Cut it anywhere; just make sure you cut it so you divide it into two pieces. I don't care if they're equal halves or not. Good.

Now take one of the pieces, Sambo (is your name Sambo? It doesn't really matter). Yes, the bigger one, if you must. Now imagine it isn't an orange. What was the point of taking an orange, then? None—it could have been any round object. An orange isn't a perfect sphere? Oh, Me!

Do shut up, Sambo.

Now imagine the thing you're holding is a world, Sambo. Yes, a world, full of oceans and trees and rocks and people and other things. Why isn't it round? It could be round, Sambo, it could be. You might have just cut off a little bit at the tip . . . The point is that if you were living on this world, you wouldn't know it was round. All you would know is that it could be.

Yes, this world does exist, as far as I remember. The problem *is, I don't remember where I put it. It's a shame, I quite liked it. Excellent lighting.*

What would I call this world? Does that matter? What does matter is what the people living on the world call it, Sambo. And remember that in most worlds, people assume their world is the only one that exists, so why bother to name it? Call it the world, or earth, or something like that. You could, perhaps, call it Slice-World, or Misplaced-World, or Cut-Orange-World, or Maybe-Round-World, to tell it apart from all the others. It's really irrelevant.

Why am I even talking about this world? I don't remember . . . perhaps something important was supposed to happen there. Or not. Just look around for it, won't you, Sambo? Whatever it was, it was going to be quite amusing.

What's that? Speak up, please. Did I create this world? I think so, yes. I'm not quite sure, though. I remember saying a Word, though I've completely forgotten what the Word was . . .

'Lights!'

Someone poured a bucketful of water on the Alocactus. The dry, shrivelled plant started swelling, growing and glowing, a mild light that slowly grew into a dazzling white brilliance that lit up the huge and musty cave. It lit up the wet, bloodstained walls, and the rocks behind which the imps crouched. It lit up the young, handsome, loincloth-clad man standing in the centre, holding a large, shiny, rune-covered sword and a round, battered shield. His noble, square jaw was clenched. His muscular arms held the weapons with practiced ease. He was in the classic warrior's stance, alert and watchful, his face contorted with a mixture of fear and aggression. He was staring at the long, hollow tunnel to his right. He looked like he was waiting for something. Something big and fierce. Something that liked to fight with and eat young, handsome, muscular, loincloth-clad men.

'Chimaera!!'

Ortant, one of the imps, flew up from behind a rock, his wings flapping incredibly fast like a hummingbird's. The imp was bright blue, about a foot tall not considering his huge, saucer-like eye, which was another foot across and clamped tightly shut. He flew straight towards the hero, stopping behind him and hovering in mid-air, facing the cave, which was now glowing red. The shadow of some monstrous creature could be seen, walking out of the tunnel slowly. The imp opened his eye.

The imp's eye was round, white and bulbous. The tiny black pupil moved from the centre of the eye to the edge, and then suddenly began to move, fast, clockwise around the rim of the eye. As the little black circle became a blur, the whole eye began to shimmer until it suddenly shone, a glowing, circular mirror. If one looked into the eye, one could see a reflection of the warrior, shifting his weight from foot to foot, getting ready for the deadly battle that was about to begin, and in front of him, the tiny circle of fire that was the tunnel, and a sinister black shape coming out of it.

'Eye rolling,' whispered the imp.

'Action!'

The chimaera walked out of the tunnel. Its head and forelegs were those of a lion—hideous snarling face, long drooling fangs, graceful sinewy smooth limbs ending in gigantic talons of death. Goat-like were its hindquarters, its huge, ugly, cloven-hoofed feet. Its tail was a fire-breathing serpent, lashing back and forth, angry flames spewing from its venomous mouth as it reared up and glared at the warrior.

A lesser man would have dropped his sword and run out of the cave. But our warrior laughed defiantly in the face of death and raised his sword in insolent greeting. 'I fear you not, hell-cat,' he said.

The chimaera shook its mane angrily, threw back its head and opened its mouth to roar.

'Baaa-a-a-a-a-a-a,' it said.

Many people tend to forget that chimaeras are one-third goat. This particular chimaera's name was Nimbupani.

'What do you mean, baaa-a-a-a-a-a-a?' said the warrior.

'Shut it!' came the voice from the mouth of the cave.

The imp closed his eye and buzzed back angrily to the rock. The actors, warrior and chimaera, glared at each other.

'What do you mean, what do I mean?' asked Nimbupani angrily. The serpent-tail stopped breathing fire and began to cough hoarsely, smoke billowing from its sizzling mouth.

'You were supposed to roar,' said the warrior.

'I did roar, Ali.'

'You bleated.'

'It was the goat's turn to roar,' said Nimbupani, wounded. 'Everyone picks on my goat.'

'It was going all right, Ali,' said the man sitting in the shadow at the entrance to the vast cave. 'The audience doesn't hear what we do here, remember? The sounds come in later.'

Ali looked embarrassed and bowed. 'Your pardon, Badshah.'

'Never mind. It's your first time. Ortant, take whatever you saw and show it to the Picsquid. And get back here as soon as you've smoked, all right?'

'Yes, Badshah.' The imp bowed and flew out of the cave. Ali, who had never acted in a Muwi-vision before and didn't know what a Picsquid was, or what the imps really did, looked confused and miserable.

'Can we try that scene again, then?' asked the Badshah.

'I'm sorry, but I can't do any more tonight. My serpent's burnt again,' grumbled Nimbupani.

'Ah well, can't be helped,' said the Badshah. 'Off with you then. Go get some rest.'

The chimaera trundled off into the tunnel.

The Badshah looked as if he had a lot to say, but just then there was a loud buzzing noise and a black scarab flew into the cave and landed on his shoulder. He ignored it.

'There's a lot you won't understand about Muwi-vision in the beginning, Ali,' he said. 'But keep going. You must excuse me, I have some work to do.' He rose.

The Badshah pressed the scarab's head and its shell popped open, revealing a neatly folded scrap of parchment with two or three lines written on it. He strode out of the cave, extracted a magnifying glass from the folds of his robe, took the parchment out, and read it.

He stood still for some time.

This would be interesting. Very interesting. Of course, if things went wrong tomorrow . . . but things rarely went wrong when the sender of the scarab took charge. He wished he could have been there, in far-off Avranti, when it happened. On the other hand, he didn't like watching people die. And he could always imagine the good bits . . .

BOOK ONE

I n a hole in the ground there lived a rabbit. What is a rabbit? A rabbit (*Bunihopus bobtelus*) is a small, white mammal that loves good food and is anxious when it is late for appointments. This particular rabbit was off on an expedition to the forest. He planned to wander around for a few years and then return home and write a book. *There and Back Again: The Adventures of One Rabbit,* he planned to call it. He popped out of his burrow and looked around, sniffing the air delicately.

He saw a man with a sword standing next to a tree, looking up. 'Afternoon. Set out. Description of Forest. Many trees, leaves, green. Tension in air, palpable. Man, one, standing next to tree, looking up,' the rabbit noted in his mental journal. Attention to detail is the key to holding a reader's attention, he thought smugly.

'They'll be here soon,' the man said.

The rabbit took a look at the long sword the man held casually. Forward, to danger and glory? He wondered whether

a travel writer's job was what would bring out his inner rabbit.
He went back into his hole.

'Are you sure this is the place?' came a voice from above.

'Yes. Three generations of princes have died here, at the
feet of this very statue.'

'Is everyone else in position?'

The man with the sword looked around. The road that
ran through the forest was flanked by tall trees on both sides.
In front of him, however, was a small, circular clearing. A
marble statue of a man, proud-faced, tall, bird-dropping-
streaked, stood in the middle of the clearing, for no apparent
reason. People coming up the road from the south would
see the statue and wonder why it was standing alone in the
middle of the forest. They would not have seen any green-
cloaked, sword-bearing men, and that is what our tree-
climber, the Silver Dagger, the great and mysterious leader
of a small and mysterious band of men, was concerned about.

'Yes.'

'Good.'

'They will be here at sundown. The march is timed very
precisely. The prince will be beheaded exactly when the sun
sets.'

'I'm glad there's an element of tradition involved, Vijay.
And thank you. We will take care of everything. Your prince
will live.'

The voice was keen and hard, the voice of someone used
to having orders obeyed promptly and unquestioningly. But
that was what the Dagger was. Secret agent, thief, assassin,
right-hand man of the Chief Civilian of Kol, master of

disguise, weaver of complex webs of deceit and intrigue, known and feared all over the world. One of those people with more pies than fingers. No one knew his real name. No one except the Silver Phalanx—his loyal band of elite warriors, thieves and spies—and a few select others knew what he looked like. He moved through the land like a shadow, quietly and ruthlessly executing every dangerous and delicate task he had set out to do. Not like your standard hero, who would usually send a few cronies to the most popular inns and dhabas a few days before visiting a town, to say 'Rumour has it that the Great (fill name here) is heading this way'. Sitting on the high branch, the Dagger saw Vijay peering through the leaves, trying to get a glimpse of his face. Fool.

'I will stay, my lord. The men you are about to slay are like my brothers. It is fitting that we fight together.'

'There are two flaws in what you just said, Vijay. First, people on my side tend to stay alive after fights. Second, if you saw my face I would have to either trust you or kill you. Since I know you as someone who sold secrets for money, I cannot possibly trust you. So thank you for all your help and goodbye.'

'I did what I had to do, my lord.'

'You did a very noble and dangerous thing. Which is why you are still alive. And I'm not a lord.'

Vijay left.

What he did with the rest of his life does not concern us.

'These Avrantics are crazy.'

'Quiet, Hihuspix.'

'Of course, the Civilian's crazy too. "The prophecy demands that he enters the human city in a cart driven by a

11

stranger half his height." I mean, is that even true or is she just saying it so that . . .'

'Quiet, Hihuspix.'

'Sorry.'

The Dagger and his men waited, silent on tall trees in the still afternoon. They were used to waiting. The forest was quiet. It waited too.

An hour passed. Nothing happened.

Another hour passed. Many things happened to the twenty-one people who rode into the large circular clearing at the end of that hour. Twenty died. But one lived. And whatever happened to him for the rest of his life concerns us. Deeply. For he was Prince Asvin of Avranti, the Hero of our story. The Chosen One. A Person to Whom Things Happen. Many Things.

2

History tells us that some things never change. One of these things is: history bores a lot of people. And when young spellbinders at Enki University, Kol, were bored, they tended to do something about it.

'Put that thing away, Borphi,' said Chancellor Ombwiri, his eyes never leaving the blackboard.

The Boy Genius put the inkatapult away. How did old Ombwiri do it? But then again, he was the Chancellor of Enki University, the most famous centre of magical studies in Kol, and, indeed, the world, and so he was someone whom you'd expect would have a few tricks up his sleeve. The Chancellor, however, was not using magic on this particular occasion. He was using another potent force—habit.

Ombwiri hardly ever took classes for first-years. He didn't like telling shiny-eyed young students who had been dreaming of coming to Enki from the day they had discovered that they could use magic that their wands would be useless, that unless they were exceptionally gifted they probably wouldn't be able to work magic at all. He didn't like telling them that it was mostly physics, chemistry, biology and astronomy, with liberal doses of mathematics thrown in everywhere. He hated the looks of disillusionment on their faces when they were given white coats instead of blue robes with stars and moons drawn on them, or pointy hats. Magic, like so many other things, was just not what it used to be. But there were always the few who could actually make every spell work, and they made it all worthwhile. For the rest, it was chemicals in huge glass tubes, bodies to dissect, and wires and mirrors to play with.

Many first-year students dropped out and went to Hero School. Not that that was any better, thought Ombwiri. Bunch of mercenaries, really. How could anyone go there from Enki? Enki was where it all began. Enki was what made Kol what it was—the greatest, most powerful city in the world.

Ombwiri's classes were always full. This was because he never stuck to his subject, and he used a large number of thrilling and usually dangerous spells in all his lectures. Explosions, injuries, love potions—all of these were standard ingredients in an Ombwiri classroom. The Chancellor never had to take attendance.

'Early spellbinders used wands to absorb and focus the energy of the magical field around them into one concentrated beam, to make their spells more effective,' he continued. 'So the wand was an essential part of spellbinding even three hundred years ago. It was when the ravians taught the spellbinders of Kol how to do the same focussing through intricate hand movements that the wand or staff ceased to be even necessary. However, many spellbinders are superstitious even in this Age, and so the wand has not died out even now, and spellbinders with little or no ability often believe that buying a wand is the answer to their problems. Before we move on, any questions?'

Ranvir raised a trembling hand. 'Please, sir, what's a ravian?'

Ombwiri started. 'You don't know what a ravian is? What is this? Good heavens! Soon I'll be hearing that people don't know what a dragon is!'

The students who thought it was their sacred duty to laugh, no matter how bad the teacher's joke was, laughed dutifully. Ombwiri looked at them lazily, and they were suddenly silent.

Ombwiri rattled off a list of nine books. 'Essential reading,' he said. 'I must say I'm very surprised. Who will tell Ranvir who the ravians were? Borphi?'

Borphi stood up, dropping various small and valuable magical toys and tricks to the floor. He would have to pick them up carefully later on—the Stuff was very expensive.

'The ravians were an immortal race of powerful warriors and great and wise sorcerers,' he said. 'Chief enemies of the rakshas Danh-Gem, ruler of Imokoi, who tried to take over the world in the Age of Terror. They lived in a hidden city called Asroye, somewhere in Vrihataranya. It was a secret, enchanted city—uninvited people crossing its borders on one side would emerge at the other, as if the city was not there at all. After the Great War, exactly two hundred years ago, when Danh-Gem had been vanquished, the ravians disappeared from the world mysteriously. No one knows how, but their passing is known as the Departure, and there are many songs and plays about it. And after they left, the dragons disappeared and so did many other magical creatures.'

'I see you've been working,' said Ombwiri. 'Good.'

The Boy Genius sat down, flushed with pride.

'And, Borphi,' continued the Chancellor, 'I know the Stuff, as you call it, is all the rage among teenagers, but I would appreciate it if you handed me that rat-in-the-box you have concealed in your desk.'

Borphi's smile vanished, but he had to obey. What an amazing eye for the Stuff Ombwiri had.

'I wish you students would stop buying these silly toys and jokes,' said Ombwiri, feeling slightly guilty about the rubber hippo in his own desk. 'Anyway, that's not the issue; if you want to spend all your money buying silly things you could have made yourselves, go ahead. All right, what were we talking about? Ravians, yes. In case Ranvir's curiosity is not yet satisfied . . . Black Leaf, name the two most famous ravian heroes.'

The young centaur moved forward. 'Isara and Narak. Isara was the name of the princess of Asroye, the Hidden City, and Narak, also known as the Demon-hunter, was her husband. They sacrificed their own lives to slay the Enemy, the great Rakshas, and end the Age of Terror.

'Their marriage was a source of great discord in the ravian world. Her clan had been against the marriage— Isara had been betrothed to another ravian lord, Simoqin the Dreamer, whom Danh-Gem murdered. What was worse, apparently Narak was not high-born, and no one even knew which clan he belonged to. So they refused to let Princess Isara marry him. But she did, anyway, and was banished from the city. They lived in the forest, ceaselessly hunting the servants of the Rakshas and plotting his downfall. Narak was . . .'

'That's all Ranvir will remember at present. Thank you, Leaf, that was well put,' said the Chancellor. Leaf trotted back to his corner and stood there proudly.

Ranvir, however, had another question. 'My mother hadn't wanted me to come to Enki this year because, she said, this is the year of the Simoqin Prophecies. Is this Simoqin the same one Leaf talked about? And what were the prophecies?'

'Your ignorance astounds me, Ranvir. No doubt you are destined for great things,' said Ombwiri. 'Well? Who wants to tell him?'

No hands went up.

'All right, Peyaj, you can tell him.'

Peyaj of Potolpur, known to teachers and students alike as the Textbook Case, looked smug. Of course she knew.

'Before we come to the Simoqin Prophecies, sir,' she said breathlessly, 'as a future gender activist I'd like to take a moment to discuss Princess Isara, who, in my considered opinion, is a fascinating example of female empowerment in ravian society. May I?'

Chancellor Ombwiri looked mildly amused. 'Please, go ahead,' he said courteously.

'Princess Isara was the wisest, bravest and most beautiful living being that ever walked this earth,' said Peyaj fervently. 'Fortunately for her, Simoqin the Dreamer had a sufficiently progressive outlook, and agreed to a long betrothal so she had enough time and space to decide whether she wanted to marry him or not.'

Seeing that the interest of the class was waning, the Textbook Case abandoned whatever she had planned to say about gender issues in Asroye and hurried to the point. 'Unfortunately, Isara's many virtues caught the eye of Danh-Gem himself. He was completely infatuated with her—and please note, class, that he was not aware of her many talents, it was an attraction based solely on Isara's physical appeal.'

Someone at the back of the class said, 'Woo-hoo.'

Peyaj ignored him. 'The Rakshas even sent a proposal of marriage to Isara's father, who rejected it angrily. After that, Danh-Gem hunted Simoqin down and tortured him in the pits of Imokoi.'

Peyaj paused and made contemptuous faces inside her head, deploring the fact that the mere mention of revenge and violence had made her sadly immature classmates sit up and listen. 'It was Narak the Demon-hunter who went to Imokoi and made a daring rescue. But it was too late. The Rakshas had already done whatever he had intended to. Narak brought Simoqin back to Asroye, where he died in Isara's arms. On Simoqin's chest was found the first of the Simoqin Prophecies. It was a poem that we call Danh-Gem's Warning. Danh-Gem had used some brutal method of torture to write this verse in tiny black letters on Simoqin's chest. This is how the verse runs . . .'

'Well, Peyaj, I'm sure he can read the Warning later, and . . .' began Ombwiri, but Peyaj quelled him with a look. No Man could stop her saying what she had decided to say. She cleared her throat and recited:

Lay this sweet young fool to rest and heed the words
    that burn his breast,
For pain unbearable he felt when these same words were
    written.
I am Danh-Gem whom you hate, Danh-Gem rakshas
    wise and great
And on his thin dark ravian skin my bitter quill has bitten.
For even as you blindly grope in long dark hours for
    rays of hope
My great scheme, my one true dream, moves close to
    realization,
I will have all that I desire, for I am Death and Dragon-
    fire,
I am the Darkness and the Light, Destruction and
    Creation,

My banner bright will be unfurled in every corner of the
world

And though the rumours of my death will bring you
passing joy,

In ten-score years I will return, and all you love will bleed
and burn

For what Danh-Gem does not desire Danh-Gem will
destroy.

Though most of the young spellbinders-to-be were
smiling bravely, as they always did when Peyaj was in full
flow, the atmosphere in the room had suddenly become
strained and tense.

'Thank you, Peyaj. Now . . .'

'The second of the Simoqin Prophecies was, the legend
goes, made by Simoqin himself, to Isara, just before he died,'
continued Peyaj calmly. 'He told her that while he was being
tortured, he had lost consciousness and a dream had come
to him. He had seen a clear, shining mirror in front of him,
where his face was clear even in complete darkness, and he
had heard a little voice in his head. It had told him not to
despair, for if Danh-Gem ever returned, a Hero would appear
in the same year, who would be his chief enemy. This hero
would be of royal blood, and would return from the dead.
He would wield the mightiest weapons in the world and
wear the strongest armour. He would be brought to a human
city by a stranger half his height. Of course, the second
prophecy is also written in the form of a poem in the book
I read, sir, but given the fact that the words of this prophecy
were the last words Simoqin the Dreamer ever uttered, and
the fact that he was seriously wounded, and, indeed, dying,
I find it highly unlikely that he expressed himself in the

form of a poem as complex in metre and rhyming pattern as the one in the library. Which is why I took the liberty of telling Leaf the second Simoqin Prophecy in colloquial prose. Personally, sir, I am quite sceptical about these prophecies. Danh-Gem declared several times that he did not believe in dreams and prophecies, and often played very cruel tricks on those who did. Therefore I find it very strange that he would believe in, and, furthermore, tell the world about his supposed reincarnation. And the second prophecy, sir, seems to me to be a message of hope for the people who believe in the first out of ignorance or superstition, even two hundred years later. The reason your mother was worried, Ranvir, is that this is the year when Danh-Gem is supposed to return. However, I am quite certain that no such return will take place, since I personally subscribe to the Organic Decomposition school of thought. Is there anything else?'

Ombwiri looked at Ranvir, who looked as if he'd bitten off much, much more than he could dream of chewing, and asked him gently whether there was anything else that he wanted to know. Ranvir shook his head. Ombwiri looked at Peyaj with a certain reluctant admiration. She hadn't needed to take a single breath pause.

'Very well done indeed, Peyaj. You must remember, however, that there are certain scholars who might not be entirely convinced that the last words of Simoqin the Dreamer are best understood by a first-year spellbinder. But I beg you not to let this affect you in any way.'

A bell rang.

'That would appear to be enough for today. I will see you in class, next year—those of you who survive at least.'

Ombwiri gathered up his robes and swept out of the classroom regally.

3

svin woke up. The first thing he saw was a ceiling. A simple wooden ceiling in a simple wooden room. The bed was comfortable though, he thought, after looking around and seeing a simple stout wooden door, bolted from the other side. His weapons and armour weren't there, and he couldn't see any other way out of the room, so he lay back, enjoying the feel of a pillow under his head. What was even more satisfying was the fact that his body was still attached to his head, which, given the last few things he remembered, it might easily not have been.

So he looked at the ceiling and tried to piece the last few days together. The memory of the grand ceremonial farewell in Ektara still brought a smile to his face. They did things with style in Avranti. The air thick with rose petals and the heavy scent of jasmine, the struggle to get the many marigold garlands off, the people of the city cheering him on, the drums, the elephants lined up to salute him as he walked by . . . the music, the deafening blasts of the giant conch-shells, the flower-strewn path to his chariot, the surprisingly sad face of his sister-in-law as he stepped into the chariot as proud and radiant as the Sun God himself . . . his friends smiling as the crowds laughed, cried and got drunk, his brother, Maharaja Aloke XII, smiling far more than he had expected him to, for after all it was Asvin's day, not his—it was Asvin going on the asvamedh, wearing the holy armour, armed with a dazzling array of weapons; it was Asvin the city was cheering for.

So what if the last three princes who had gone on an asvamedh had failed? He was bound to succeed. It was his destiny. Had not the old priest said he was born under the most favourable set of stars possible? And had he not trained all his life under the strictest gurus, and had they not said there was something special about him?

He had to admit he had misjudged his brother, though. He'd expected Aloke to be jealous that his younger brother was so well loved but his brother had just offered him the greatest glory possible—asvamedh!

The first three days had been immense fun. His bodyguards were all old friends of his—they had been guarding him for ten of his twenty-one years. They rode behind the asvamedh horse, Asvin's chariot leading the others. They were all well trained in the arts of war, twenty-one strong, dashing, bold men . . . Who would dare challenge them? The gods were smiling on them—Asvin remembered thinking it would take a whole army to conquer that intrepid group of friends.

But the gods weren't smiling. They were sniggering.

Asvin and his men had started southwards, towards Shantavan, the Peaceful Forest, having decided that they would pass from Avranti to the Xi'en Empire in a great arc through the forest, so as not to anger their friendly neighbour,

Durg. Shantavan was shared territory—Asvin had thought they would ride swiftly through it, so there was no possibility of conflict until he reached the Xi'en Empire. Singing merrily, they had raced south from Ektara, waving at awestruck villagers, and reached the forest.

Then his friends had suddenly fallen silent. Some of them seemed to be praying. When Asvin had asked them why— for they weren't even in the dangerous part of the forest— they had ridden on silently. Then they reached the statue of Aloke VIII.

Arjun, his best friend, had suddenly put his sword to Asvin's throat and told him to get off his chariot. Stunned, he had descended, the world buzzing furiously around his ears. Arjun had started talking about some secret brotherhood, some ancient tradition—he hadn't understood anything— he had just stood there blinking back tears as his friends looked at him with cold eyes and drawn swords. He was to be beheaded at sunset, they told him, for his arrogance and insolence. His sword and armour were taken from him. They'd made him kneel at the feet of the statue. When the last rays of the departing sun fell on his face Arjun had raised his sword . . .

And had fallen stone dead with an arrow through his heart. Asvin had watched in silence as a group of green-cloaked men swung down from the trees and the air was suddenly thick with arrows. The attack was swift and deadly. He had snatched a sword and struck a blow or two. Then it was all over, and his bodyguards lay dead in the gathering darkness. Then one man had stepped up, taller than the rest, his face hidden by a hood. 'Drink this,' he had commanded, holding out a small vial filled with a clear liquid. Asvin had drunk it quietly and then the whole world had turned on its head and he had fallen gracefully to the ground.

'Did you sleep well, Prince Asvin?'

The door opened and a khudran came in.

Asvin had seen khudrans before—he'd once gone to a khudran village with his father when he was very young. He'd liked the little people then—the taller ones had been about his height—and he liked this one. The khudran had a winning smile and big, bright eyes. Unlike the khudrans that Asvin remembered, this one had short, straight hair, and wore no earrings. He was also tall for a khudran, being all of three and a half feet high, and quite wiry and slim. He was now sinking into a very formal and correct bow, and Asvin smiled, remembering the quaint mud huts and clay toys that he'd always associated the little people with.

'I'm Amloki,' said the khudran in a surprisingly deep voice, 'and I have been sent by the Chief Civilian of Kol to escort you to our fair city. I am her page, and have been brought here by the Phalanx—the Silver Dagger's men—to be your guide and, hopefully, your friend. Your asvamedh horse is being taken care of, and will be returned to you later, if you ever choose to carry on with the quest. Also . . .'

'Wait, my dear fellow,' said Asvin, pleased but quite lost. 'Can I speak to one of the men who rescued me yesterday? There are many pieces in this puzzle that I cannot see, and many things I need to know before I go anywhere.'

'The men you seek are no longer here. They bore you to this inn from the forest. You have been sleeping for three days now—the potion they used must have been quite powerful. We are still in Avranti, but a day's journey should see us past its borders. The Silver Phalanx left yesterday on some other urgent errand. But I think I know what questions trouble you. And I will be delighted to give you all the answers you seek, but we do not have much time. Your guards were not your only enemies in this country—if their bodies have not been found yet, they will be soon—and many will search for you. We must be out of Avranti as fast as possible. In any case, sir, you have sworn not to return to Ektara until you have conquered the world. The Civilian offers you shelter and help. I was told to tell you that she has matters of the utmost importance to discuss with you, matters that concern not just Avranti but the whole world. It would not be very wise to refuse her—not after her men saved you from your "best friends".'

The greatest politician in the known world, Lady Temat, the Chief Civilian, had made the city of Kol what it was. She had kept it, and all the Free States, from falling under the dominion of any of its 'friendly' and immensely powerful neighbours—Artaxerxia, Avranti, Xi'en. She was supremely skilled in the subtle games she played, and her iron will and brilliant intellect were respected and feared in every land. She was cold, ruthless, proud, stone-hearted and immensely powerful. An offer of 'shelter and help' from her was, to put it simply, an offer you couldn't refuse. Even thinking about it for too long was a stupid thing to do.

'Very well,' Asvin said. 'I will come to Kol with you.'

4

'He looks so peaceful, doesn't he?' asked Middlog. 'He's going to wake up soon,' said Rightog. 'He opened his eyes a few minutes ago but the hangover knocked him out again, I think.'

'What was it, his first Dragonjuice night?'

'Yes. The young fool took on Maya. He of all people should have known better.'

'Why didn't you stop him? I would have, but I was mixing and he had already drunk four when I saw him.'

'I didn't see him either. Anyway, *he* was the one Kirin asked, and he doesn't care, does he?' Rightog said, nodding towards Leftog, who was taking a nap, and, by the look on his face, not having pleasant dreams.

'*You* don't talk. *You* don't have to spend the whole night next to him. Grumble, snap, butt, bite . . .'

'I know. He's getting worse and worse.'

'Anyway, who won the Dragonjuice challenge? Maya, I presume.'

'That's right. Kirin was good, though. He had nine before he hit the floor.'

'*What*? Nine Dragonjuices on his first try? I'm telling you, that kid's talented.'

'I know. We should mix them stronger from tonight. Look, he's waking.'

'Oh dear,' Middlog said, turning as far away from Leftog as possible.

'Not *him*, idiot. Kirin.'

Kirin opened one eye. The world was still spinning, but only about once a second now. Some kind soul had also removed the white-hot maces that someone had been pounding ceaselessly against the inside of his skull. The hideous beast that had been trying to strangle him all night was, he perceived with some difficulty, his cloak. He was still alive, and the headache, though still fierce, had abated somewhat.

'He's going to say "Where am I?"' whispered Rightog. 'I just *know* it.'

Kirin opened his other eye. He wondered whether or not to get up, tried, and found he couldn't—the floor seemed to be attached to him. He saw the ogre looking at him with a concerned expression and counted the heads slowly swimming into focus. One, two, three. He was all right.

'What year is it?' he asked, shaking his head slowly.

'Damn,' said Middlog. 'I could've made some money there.'

'What do you mean, what year is it?' asked Rightog.

'Seriously, what year is it?'

'The two hundredth of the New Age, the same as it's been for the last few weeks,' said Rightog, puzzled. 'Why?'

'Just asking. Never mind. Where's Spikes?'

'Somewhere. Tell me, kid, why on earth did you do the Dragonjuice challenge with Maya last night?'

'Oh, so that's what happened. I don't remember a thing since last evening, actually.'

'Now *that* they all say,' grinned Rightog.

The internationally famous three-headed ogre (collectively) known as Triog hauled Kirin to his feet, walked to the bar and started working. Triog was the barman-owner of the Fragrant Underbelly, Kol's most violent and therefore most popular bar. He started vigorously wiping dishes and setting mugs upside down behind the counter where, every evening, he mixed his mysterious concoctions, exchanged pleasantries with patrons and fought off excessively friendly and unfriendly customers—six arms and three heads were barely enough to run the Underbelly. At present his left head was taking a nap, Middlog was washing plates and Rightog, who liked Kirin most, was still chatting with him.

'I don't remember why I started drinking Dragonjuices,' said Kirin. 'Her bragging must have annoyed me.'

'She has good reason to brag, that girl. I've never seen anyone like her. At eight o' clock, when Spikes was throwing out everyone who was sleeping, and you were snoring and twitching about under the table, she got up. Stood up, the girl did, after nine Dragonjuices—I'm going to mix them stronger from tonight. Straight off to the University she went. She told me to tell you to wait here tonight—apparently you said things to her that she wants to talk to you about.' Rightog tried to look coy and bashful and made a series of extremely horrible faces.

Kirin closed both his eyes with a shudder. The mace-pounder, whoever he was, had returned and was making up for lost time inside his head.

'What?' he groaned.

'Oh come on, boy, I know it all—you may act like she's

28

just your friend, but'—the ogre actually simpered, a most gruesome spectacle—'the truth is you *love* her.'

'Go away, Triog,' said Kirin, feeling around for his bag. It wasn't there, and he was suddenly wide awake. 'Where's my bag?'

'Spikes has it. And your money. I don't know where he is. I think he's cleaning up the dance floor. A pashan was sick on it, and that means gravel everywhere.'

The dance floor had recently been shifted from the roof to the cellars after fifteen extremely inebriated pashans, while doing an energetic Stone-boy Stomp, had crashed through the whole building, injuring many and killing the Rani of Potolpur's pet flamingo.

Triog had travelled all over the world before settling down in Kol and establishing his inn, which was now flourishing. Triog's ancestors were, like most ogres, from Ventelot. They were a very highly respected family of ogres, who had eaten many of the famous knights of the Almost-Perfectly-Circular Table, in the forgotten days when Ventelot was the mightiest kingdom in the whole world.

There was more to the inn than the Fragrant Underbelly. Triog's travels had convinced him that the best thing in life was food, and Too Many Cooks, on the first floor, was the finest restaurant in Kol, patronized by the very rich and famous. Cooks from all around the world scurried around all day in the vast and aromatic kitchen, and customers who had enough money could buy whatever food their hearts desired, be it Avrantic or Durgan biryani and kababs, Xi'en noodles, Potolpuri roshogollas, Skuan roasts, Olivyan pastas or the bland fare of Ventelot. The waiters looked inscrutable and wore white, the food was excellent and Too Many Cooks was nearly always fully booked a week in advance. The Chief

Civilian of Kol herself had eaten there a few times. The carpets were incredibly thick, and music was played loudly all the time to provide atmosphere, but more importantly, to help the customers pretend not to hear the raucous shouts and occasional screams emanating from the Underbelly, which was right below.

First-time visitors to Kol were always told that there were monuments, works of art and museums all over the world, but that there was only one Fragrant Underbelly. The Fragrant Underbelly had started out as an Avrantic-style dhaba, where people on the move in the city could walk in for a quick daal-roti or a cup of tea. Triog had not been wholly satisfied with this, and the Underbelly had been, at various points in its illustrious career, a massage parlour, a Xi'en-style pleasure-dome, a Psomedean Poets' Forum, a vaman mini-gymnasium, and even, for one disastrous week, a belly-dance training centre with an Artaxerxian teacher. This venture had failed spectacularly when a group of pashans, not understanding the sign BRING YOUR OWN VEILS, had lugged a full-sized killer whale through the streets of Kol and tried to push it through the door.

Finally, Triog's Ventelot roots and good business sense had asserted themselves, and the Fragrant Underbelly had become a Ventelot-style tavern.

The Fragrant Underbelly was on the ground floor of Triog's inn. There were two floors of guest rooms above Too Many Cooks, and the top floor was where Triog, Spikes and Kirin lived. It was in a large laboratory under the cellar that Kirin made the Stuff, the odd and extremely expensive collection of toys, potions and potentially lethal party tricks that had made him famous in Kol.

He always sat, hooded and cloaked, in the darkest corner

of the Underbelly, with Spikes standing next to him to take care of anyone who was too inquisitive. And there were many things that Kirin didn't want people to know about him. For someone who looked about twenty, Kirin had a lot of secrets. Spikes, of course, knew. And Triog never asked questions.

Not that too many people were very inquisitive—they all thought that he was a spellbinder making some extra money and most people, when sober, were very discreet where spellbinders were concerned—a custom originating not from any ancient tradition but from a perfectly reasonable desire not to be turned into a frog.

All spellbinders were forbidden by their ancient laws to touch any form of alcohol. And everyone carefully ignored the fact that most spellbinders broke one of those ancient laws on a daily basis. There was always some thoughtful pashan who would drag teachers and students back to their hostels in time to catch some sleep before classes began in the morning. Triog made all the necessary arrangements— the spellbinders were his most loyal customers. They spent the most money, cheered the loudest at all the new singers, never killed people and threw the wildest parties.

'Well, good morning to you anyway,' said Kirin to Triog. Rightog laughed.

'Morning? Wake up and smell the rum, Kirin. Go and get your little toys. We'll be opening soon.'

Kirin realized that he had slept all day. He laughed ruefully and started climbing the stairs to his room.

Everyone went to Frags, as the Underbelly was commonly called. And contrary to what most mothers told their teenaged children, nearly everyone also got out of Frags alive. This was because the security pashans at Frags were very, very efficient.

Led by Yarni, their ten-foot tall leader, the men of stone would tramp into the inn every evening. Their sheer physical presence was enough to discourage sober troublemakers. And their brute strength and reluctance to listen to explanations made them very good at dealing with the drunk ones. They would patrol the Underbelly silently, making sure that everyone was still alive. Of course, they never stopped fights—that would have been unsporting. But they always made sure that nearly everyone got out of Frags alive. Of course, if people chose to carry on fighting outside the Underbelly, it was not their problem. Many passing aristocrats had tried to recruit Yarni's Protection. They had offered insanely high wages, but Yarni had turned them down. The reason could be stated in one word: Spikes.

The pashans were fanatically devoted to Spikes. Triog paid them good wages of course, but it was Spikes they always went to for advice and guidance. Not that Spikes was eager or even willing to play mother hen to the lumbering stone-sinewed bouncers. But they never wanted to leave once they had met him. Which was odd, because no one had ever accused Spikes of exuding charisma.

No one knew exactly what Spikes was. He looked like a strange combination of pashan, porcupine, wild boar and yeti. He was shorter and slimmer than most pashans, standing about six feet tall. Barring the huge tusks and the pashan-like eyes, with their reptilian yellow-green colour and vertical lids, Spikes had reasonably human-like features. What set him apart from any pashan that walked the earth were his claws and spikes. When angered—and people saw to it that he was angered as infrequently as possible—

long, curving claws would shoot out of his hands, and long, pointed spike-like quills would rise down his spine, making him look even more menacing. His fingers and toes were also man-like, not the potato-like stumps that most pashans had. But he still managed to be spectacularly ugly. Many a customer, wondering whether they could manage another mug of Triog's strongest brews, had suddenly seen Spikes and decided they had had enough for one night. He was a key character in most post-Underbelly-party-stupor nightmares. No one knew exactly what Spikes was. No one asked.

The reason most people figured he was not a pashan, however, was not physical. Spikes was intelligent. He was ferocious, cunning and extremely hard to trick, as many had discovered and remembered every time they looked at their scars. He liked Maya and, to an extent, Triog. He had chosen Kirin to be his master and followed him with an unswerving and unshakeable devotion.

Yarni, on the other hand, was not intelligent at all but had a very good nose for trouble. He was a huge limestone troll of the stalactite variety. Almost conical in shape, he had narrow legs and a slim waist that suddenly expanded into an incredibly bulky torso.

Now he stomped up to Triog while the other pashans went behind the bar and started cleaning things with surprising speed. The Artaxerxian dune-stone pashans who worked as waiters in Too Many Cooks trudged upstairs to put on their white aprons. It was ridiculous, pashans wearing clothes, but Triog thought it added a touch of class.

'Asur trouble again,' Yarni said. 'Big robbery. Two streets away. Same gang that painted skulls on the palace walls last week.'

'They won't trouble us,' said Rightog. 'Whoever is hiring those idiots will probably be here anyway.'

'I got some more lads today, just in case.' Yarni stomped off unhurriedly. Yarni never hurried.

'Looking for me?' said a voice just behind Triog's left head. Leftog woke up with a start. It just wasn't right. Someone as big as Spikes shouldn't be able to move so quietly.

'Kirin's awake. Upstairs,' said Rightog. Spikes nodded.

'So why the hell did you have to wake *me* up?' growled Leftog. There's always a grouchy one.

A svin was on the plainest chariot he had ridden, clad in the plainest clothes he had ever worn. Amloki was driving very fast—at this rate they would reach Kol in a week. They were moving westwards, on the Grand Kol-Ektara highway, through the famous rice fields of western Avranti. Asvin was glad to find that his weapons and armour were unharmed, though Amloki said the road wasn't dangerous at all. There were very few highwaymen along this route, he explained. They all went to Kol, crime was much more prosperous there. He seemed genuinely shocked when he heard Asvin had never been to Kol and was about to embark on a full-fledged description of the city when Asvin interrupted him.

'Tell me whatever you know about what happened to me yesterday. Why did my guards, my friends, attack me? What crime had I committed? And who is the Silver Dagger, and how did he know exactly when to save me and where to find me?'

Amloki smiled. 'Luckily for you, I talked to the only man

in the Dagger's band of heroes who actually likes to talk. Your bodyguards are—were—a part of a secret society started during the time of the king whose statue stands in the middle of the forest. A very good secret society, too— one that has actually managed to stay secret for over three hundred years. Apparently this king (Aloke VIII, said Asvin) had been imprisoned by his brother (Atanu the Usurper, said Asvin) and had somehow managed to escape and kill everyone who had been part of the conspiracy against him.'

'I know all about him,' said Asvin. 'It was the end of a very turbulent period in our history. For four generations, there had been long and brutal wars between brothers. The Throne of the Tiger was never held by anyone for two years running. It was one of those times when a royal pretender was someone pretending not to be of royal blood. After Aloke VIII regained the throne, this stopped, strangely enough. My country has been free from civil war for three hundred years.'

'After this secret society was formed,' Amloki said.

'I see,' said Asvin. He thought for a while. 'No, I don't see,' he said.

'I'll put it to you another way . . . what happens to younger sons in the Avranti royal family?'

'Well, let's see,' said Asvin. 'I'll count backwards from my uncle, who died while hunting, my great-uncle was killed by bandits on an asvamedh, younger sons before that . . . poisoned mysteriously, died while hunting, killed by bandits on an asvamedh, no younger son, killed by bandits on an asvamedh . . . . Seven generations is all I know. But what does this have to do with anything?'

He thought for a while. 'Oh,' he said, looking like someone whose world had suddenly become a lot clearer.

'Your guards were assassins from the start. It's a secret that is told to the elder son on his coronation day. It is really sad that your holy books require kings to have two children—if the younger child is not an imbecile and if people love him, he is generally killed by his guards, whom he has known for years and trusts completely. These assassins grow up with the prince, make sure he doesn't make any influential friends and then, if the prince is a hot-blooded one, they go with him on his asvamedh and kill him with great solemnity at sundown in front of Aloke VIII's statue. The king generally offers his younger brother the huge honour of going on the asvamedh, which he has been brought up to believe is the greatest thing in the world. You were given many nice and shiny weapons so that even if you managed to escape your friends, you would attract any self-respecting bandit in the forest. Your crime was that you were young, and brave, and that people loved you. Also, you were, forgive me for saying so, naïve. Did you really think you could conquer the world with twenty men by your side? You were being removed from Avranti. Your body would have been carried back into town by your men, nice and shiny weapons intact, and people would have said, "Poor brave handsome Prince Asvin hacked down cruelly by the wicked world, and his poor guards, such friends they were, too. And his poor brother, the king, how he must wish he hadn't allowed the poor brave handsome prince to go on that asvamedh . . . but that's the way life is, pass the chicken, please." A grand funeral, a portrait in the gallery, not a dry eye in the marketplace. And if the people really loved you, a statue in the town square. The divine armour would have lain in state, awaiting the next heroic and popular prince.'

Asvin was quiet for a long time. He saw his brother's smile and his sister-in-law's sad face again. She knew, he thought. 'But how did your Civilian know?'

'The usual way. The society was betrayed by one of its members. Our Civilian has been watching you for a long time. As her page,' Amloki sniffed in a very important manner, 'I get to know most of what happens in Kol Palace. Our spies in your palace picked up one of your guards. (Vijay, said Asvin, so *that* was where he went.) He was persuaded to tell us about their society.'

'Persuaded?'

'Persuaded,' said Amloki with an air of great finality. 'Which is why the Dagger and his men knew just when to intervene.'

'Tell me about the Silver Dagger.'

Amloki's eyes glowed with excitement. 'Ah, the Dagger. The finest man in the land. Also the most elusive. I know he comes to the palace often but I have never seen him. At least, I've never seen his face. Everyone wants to know who he is. Every woman in Kol wants to marry him . . .' He carried on in this vein for about an hour, at the end of which Asvin was thoroughly tired of the Dagger and his exploits.

Nice little man, talks too much, thought Asvin.

Amloki looked at him fondly. 'What a good listener you are. Now I will tell you about Kol. We have a week, but I don't know whether that will be enough. Still, I will probably be with you in Kol after that as well. Let me tell you as much as I can.'

6

S.P. Gyanasundaram flew high above the green sea that was Vrihataranya, the greatest forest in the world. It stretched from the coast of eastern Avranti, running south-west, across north Avranti and the northern Free States to the eastern borders of Artaxerxia. Ages ago, it used to curve back, like a boomerang, across that great barren battlefield, Danh-Gem's Wasteland, to the Centaur Forests in the south. But the Great War had changed all that.

Gyanasundaram was flying towards his home in the northern swamps, in the vast delta where the Holy River, after flowing through Vrihataranya, met the sea. He had just finished a particularly exhausting delivery and was eagerly anticipating a long holiday—basking in his snug nest and stalking the swamps in search of juicy insects. Storks tend to build large communities of nests in single, giant trees and Gyanasundaram knew his neighbours, H. Sampath and I. Narayan, would love a few of the racier stories he was carrying from the mountains.

He knew he was flying over hills, valleys and ravines, but

everything looked the same—an endless, undulating sea of dark green. Hours passed. Sometimes there were silver threads when the streams were wider, but these were rare. Gyanasundaram was glad he was safe, far above the forest where, he had heard, unknown and terrible beings lurked beneath every tree. Praise the Sacred Ibis for the power of flight. He sank in the rays of the setting sun. The sky was glowing maroon, amber and purple, and the forest beneath him looked black and forbidding. He spread his great white, black-tipped wings and flapped vigorously as he soared even higher.

A hundred hideous screams rent the air below him, startling him out of his peaceful contemplation and making him even gladder he was above it all. 'Howler monkeys,' he thought contemptuously, 'evening assembly, or whatever it is those silly beasts yell about.'

He watched idly as the forest birds, who had all scattered, squawking in alarm, returned to their nests in the trees. The trees seemed to swallow them, like the sea welcoming flying fish back. Nice, colourful birds, red, green and blue. He flew slightly lower to get a better view.

It was then that he noticed the crows. There were three of them, flying directly beneath him in a perfect V. There was something odd about them. Their wings were beating in perfect unison, and they flew in perfect synchrony, the distance from wingtip to wingtip maintained perfectly.

Gyanasundaram had always looked down at crows and other carrion-eaters as thieves and rabble, the dregs of the avian world. But he had to admit he was intrigued by the military precision of these three. Not more flight-art fanatics, he hoped. On one of his longest voyages, a delivery to a tiny, uninhabited island far out to sea, he'd met the seagull who had started that load of nonsense. The poor thing was old, practically featherless and starving. His followers, a bunch of thoroughly irresponsible youngsters—airheads, they called themselves—were busy crashing into cliffs and falling dizzily to the rocks beneath. Gyanasundaram had forced some food down the old fellow's throat. 'I will teach you to be free, stork-brother,' the seagull had croaked. 'Let's begin with level flight.' Then he had keeled over and died.

But these crows were different. They were practically marching in mid-air, no 'Whee man' nonsense. They knew how to fly. Gyanasundaram flew closer to get a better view.

Commander Triple-Zero-One 'Kraken' nodded at his henchmen. 'He's noticed us. Commence negotiations.' His trusty wing-crows, Captains Forty-Four 'Yahoo' and Forty-Five 'Maverick' said 'Yes, sir' in perfect unison. Kraken was pleased. Good training always showed. With a stunning display of flying skill, he slowed down in mid-air while his sidekicks streaked ahead, performing perfect barrel-rolls to the left and right respectively. Then they all rose, in a wide inverted V, to meet Gyanasundaram. Maverick and Yahoo flew close to him, perfectly parallel, their wingtips almost touching his, while Kraken zoomed forward, accelerating, until he was right above the startled stork.

'What is the meaning of this outrage?' spluttered Gyanasundaram. The crows were violating his private air-space! And what was more, they were closing him in on three sides, forcing him to fly lower!

'Quiet, stork,' said Kraken imperiously. 'You are commanded to appear before the most high vanar-lord, Bali the Magnificent. I am Commander Kraken, his trusted ally and messenger. You will fly with us.'

'Since when have the crows been vassals of the monkey-men?' asked the stork angrily. But Maverick and Yahoo weren't listening. They were looking down at some large black shape speeding through the treetops.

'We are allies, not vassals,' spat Kraken. 'When the day of revolution comes, we will rule the air while they rule the earth. Now cooperate or you will get hurt, stork.'

The stork made a few more pointed remarks, but Kraken had stopped listening too, and was watching the large black thing hurtle through the black leaves. Gyanasundaram looked down. No doubt it was some fierce creature of the wild woods, and therefore harmless. They were still too high above the forest to be attacked by tree-dwellers. But it was strange, the man-shaped thing moving beneath them. How did it manage to make the higher branches support its weight? And how was it moving as fast as the birds? Gyanasundaram sped up and so did the crows, but the thing kept up with them.

'Now!' shrieked Kraken.

The vanar leapt out of the trees. Gyanasundaram saw, as if in slow motion, the hideous black shape speeding towards him in a wide arc, arm extended, growing larger and larger. Of course it would never reach that high, it was too high, no one could jump that high and . . .

'Good catch!' Yahoo shouted.

The vanar, with the wildly struggling stork tucked under an arm, disappeared beneath the leaf-ceiling. Kraken uttered a wild whoop and dived in.

'Perpendicular, Yahoo!' said Maverick.

The two crows screamed down in a tight arc, entering the forest together, almost vertical. They snapped out of the roll and started flying towards the vanar city.

I t was midnight, and the Underbelly was in full wobble. All of Triog's six arms were busy, pouring drinks, washing glasses, gesturing wildly as his social head, Rightog, made polite conversation. Sitting at his small wooden table in the quietest corner, Kirin looked around and saw all the usual faces. Spikes lurked next to him, looking ugly and menacing in the dim light.

Business had been good. Kirin hadn't had time to make any new Stuff, and had almost finished his reserve supplies; young spellbinders demanding inkatapults and fake scars had to be turned away, bald men had clamoured in vain for colour-changing fast-sticking wigs, and the fireworks were all sold out. Kirin had decided to call it a night.

Smoke and noise filled the Fragrant Underbelly. Well-dressed crime lords, aristocrats, ambassadors and rich merchants kept slipping away from Too Many Cooks to grab quick drinks. One section of the room was occupied by leather-clad vroomer gangs, pouring alcohol down their throats as they loudly discussed vroomstick models, their tattoos and spiky hair standing out even in the dim light. Guards in plain clothes, pickpockets and miscellaneous miscreants roamed around, looking for information, victims and friends; fashionable young Kolis gathered in excited clusters around tables, giggling excitedly as they gossiped. Pashans moved ponderously through throngs of humans; vamans sat on high stools and nursed their hot drinks. A centaur stood near the bar, grumbling as people pushed him around. Spies from various nations listened eagerly to snatches of conversation—the Underbelly was one of the most important sources of misinformation in the world. Wrestlers from WAK, the Wrestling Association of Kol, sat in their tight, spangled costumes and discussed headbutts and supplexes, and men named Abhishek gathered around another table to listen to Houstarr, the world's worst lover, recount his sad tales of rejection and heartbreak. The Teetotallers Anonymous daily meeting was being held at the bar. There were familiar faces everywhere—many Red Phoenix guards from the Civilian's Palace, for instance, haunted Frags in their free time.

But Kirin's eyes kept flickering towards the main entrance, where customer after customer was entering and depositing the more obvious weapons, the broadswords and clubs, into the hands of the security pashans. Where was Maya? He was beginning to get worried. What had he told her? Had they fought? Why on earth had he agreed to a Dragonjuice showdown?

There she was. She was walking towards him. Her short hair was in even greater disarray than usual and the standard inkblot was on her left cheek tonight. As always, she wore a shapeless grey gown, adorned with patches of cloth wherever the holes from whatever dangerous chemical she had been playing with had grown large enough to attract her attention. In spite of all this, however, heads turned wherever she went. She was aware of the attention she always got, and in general she was rather amused by it, but not tonight. She cast malevolent glances around the room, glances that said 'Call me baby and I'll turn you into a cockroach'. And if they had known she was the most brilliant young spellbinder in the city, or that her father was the powerful and extremely eccentric spellbinder Mantric, they would probably have been too scared to even look. She sat down in front of Kirin.

'Put this on,' she said, taking a ring out of her pocket and handing it to him. It was a very dirty ring, with a single, rather grimy, white stone.

'What is it?'

'Just put it on.'

Kirin slipped the ring on his finger. As soon as his hand touched it, the ring started glowing.

'All right. Give it to me quickly, before anyone sees it.'

Mystified, he took the ring off and gave it to her.

'Spikes, be a darling and run down to the Museum and leave this somewhere, please. Don't let anyone see you, because I didn't tell them I was taking it. And try not to kill anyone.'

Spikes looked at Kirin, who nodded. He took the ring quietly and left.

Kirin put the tips of his fingers together. 'No doubt you'll explain someday.'

'How long have we known each other?'

'Six—no, seven years.'

'And I am your best friend, right?'

'You are. But . . .'

'Then why didn't you tell me?'

'Tell you what?'

'Don't pretend, Kirin. Do you know what that ring was?'

'No.'

'I read about it in the library. Not a weapon of any sort, magical but harmless. Jewellery.' She leaned forward, looked around and lowered her voice. '*Ravian* jewellery. It glows when a ravian wears it.'

'So why did it glow when you put it on my finger?' he asked, but he knew that she knew. He wondered how much he'd told her last night. Anyway, he might as well tell her everything. It was the only way she would keep his secret. 'I wanted to tell you.'

'Right. Which is why it took you seven years and nine Dragonjuices to tell me who you were. "And by the way, I'm a ravian," he says, and topples over. My best friend is a ravian and he doesn't tell me! Did it slip your mind?'

'Look, I didn't know how you would react. And you're my only friend. Yes, I know I have Triog and Spikes, but it's not the same. And everyone else is just a customer. I was afraid I'd lose you.'

'Lose me? The last time I read a history book, ravians were heroes. Not something I'd be ashamed of. I just don't understand, Kirin. If I wasn't so angry, I'd have been thrilled. Why didn't you tell me?'

'I was afraid you'd tell someone else, someone like your father. I was afraid I would be taken to people who would ask me questions I didn't have the answers to. It's big news if someone from the lost race suddenly appears—I mean, I don't even know where my people went—I was afraid they would think I was some kind of traitor, that I had been left behind because the ravians didn't want to take me with them. I was afraid that a lot of people would have wanted me dead. And there are other reasons.'

'Such as?'

'Ravians are immortal, Maya. I'm immortal. That changes things.'

'What does it change?' asked Maya. They looked at each other silently for some time. Then Maya spoke, but the edge was gone from her voice. 'So why *are* you here? And who are you, really?'

'I don't know where to start. Or what to say.'

'Just tell me everything you know. And don't forget the minor details, such as you're at least two hundred years old,' she snapped, suddenly angry again. 'I don't know what to ask you, Kirin. I don't know you at all, and you've been lying to me all these years.'

'I never lied to you, Maya. I didn't tell you a few things, but I never lied. I *was* born in the Great Forest. Spikes *did* find me there and bring me to Kol. And I really didn't remember who I was before he found me. Then we came to Triog's, and then I met you. The rest you know. I didn't know I was a ravian when I met you. I worked most of it out in the library, when I read books about the ravians and started remembering things. And then I discovered that I had a few ravian powers.'

'Kirin, this is not making any sense.'

He took a deep breath.

'All right. I'll try harder. When you met me, you thought I was from some tribe in the jungle, and I'd knocked my head on a tree or something and so didn't remember anything. I had told you Spikes had found me lying on the ground in the forest. Which was true, except there was one detail I didn't tell you.'

'And what was this one detail?'

'That I had been turned into stone.'

'You had been turned into stone. I can see why you would forget a little thing like that.'

Kirin smiled. 'Spikes found a stone statue lying on the ground, covered with creepers, outside what he described as a small temple in the forest. He stepped on me, actually, and the stone cracked and I woke up.'

'What were you doing there? Apart from being a stone statue, that is. Exactly why *were* you one, by the way?'

'I don't know when or why I turned to stone, Maya. And it's true; you needn't sneer.'

'What was Spikes doing there? Or did he just stumble upon you by chance? Stumble upon you, heh heh. Sorry.'

'At least you're laughing again. I was worried. Anyway, I don't know what Spikes was doing there, and, strangely enough, neither does he. At the time, I was just grateful he was with me in the forest—I would have had no idea what to do and would probably have ended up as a light lunch for a tiger or something . . . He told me he had been wandering all over the world for about seven years before he found me. And he didn't know what he was looking for, but when he found me he knew it was me.

'The first thing I remember is Spikes stepping on me. I woke up screaming, but Spikes was completely unperturbed. Of course I didn't know then that that was just Spikes being Spikes. He started speaking to me calmly, as if stumbling on statues that turned into people in forests was something he did every day. He said he had looked for me all his life, but he didn't know why. I asked him who or what he was and he said he didn't know that either. He said he'd thought I'd know the answers once he found me, but I obviously didn't.'

'And what about you? What did you remember?'

'I remembered absolutely nothing about who I was or where I was from, but I did remember my name and the names of my parents—I guess being a stone for two hundred years can do things to your memory. But Spikes said that Kol was the greatest city in the world and perhaps we could learn whatever we needed to know there. Besides, he knew Triog. It was Triog who taught Spikes to speak, in some swamp in the far north. Then Spikes brought me here.'

They were interrupted by the vaman Dun Pampo, one of the richest and most feared moneylenders in Kol. It was whispered that he had hired a team of assassins to kill anyone who had ever called him a dwarf. He asked Kirin for a Nose-hair Clippin. Kirin had been telling everyone the shop was closed for the night and they could get their Stuff later, but it was best to give Dun what he wanted. As Kirin and Dun started to haggle furiously, Maya pushed her chair back and sat quietly.

It was Maya who had started making the Stuff, in her very first year at the University. She had been looking for someone to sell it for her, and that was how she had met Kirin. When they had become friends, she had started to get him to help her make it. It was then that she had discovered that Kirin had a natural aptitude for things magical, and could grasp complex spells astoundingly fast, faster than most trained spellbinders. Magic was incredibly strong within him, as it was within her. His powers, though, were different from hers. He had strange powers, powers he was probably not even aware of. Sometimes, doors would swing open as he approached; small objects he reached out for would slide to his hand. Maya had noticed that this mostly happened when he was completely occupied in doing something else . . . Thrilled, she had started smuggling him into the University's huge library, and had been training him in the magical arts for about four years. In four years, Kirin had gone through magical texts and treatises with amazing speed. He now made the Stuff all on his own, though he shared the profits with Maya. He was also the only person she really trusted.

Maya had started putting the pieces of the puzzle that was Kirin together after his stunning announcement the night before. But there was still a lot she didn't know.

As Dun left, somewhat disgruntled because Kirin had pointed out to him that he was not going to sell Stuff cheap to anyone as rich as Dun, Maya leaned forward again.

'So when did you realize you were a ravian?'

'I was reading about them one day, and I suddenly started seeing things—and then I found I could do some of the things ravians could—but I was absolutely sure when I read the histories of the ravian heroes and found my parents' names. And then I remembered many other things, but they were all so confusing—I wanted to tell you, but it was all too much to take, and I was afraid.'

'What did you remember?'

'I remember living in the forest, being trained to fight and hunt by a band of roving ravian warriors. We lived in simple halls, secret and very well guarded, because the woods were full of the Enemy's spies. We never stayed in any one dwelling for more than a month.'

'Were these hunters your family?'

'No. I remembered my mother's face—she was very beautiful, but she was never there—later, I understood why—but I remember her smile. I don't remember my father. The ones who brought me up were my mother's friends and guards. And there was a city, a huge enchanted city, in the forest—which I realized must have been Asroye. I remember being made to stand outside—I was never allowed to enter, but they took care of me at the camps near the gates whenever my guardians had to enter the city.'

'Why weren't you allowed to enter Asroye?'

'You'll understand. Let me finish. I read about the Departure—and I remembered actually being there. I had visions, Maya, of being allowed to enter the city once, seeing a sea of faces—hearing that a great victory had been won, that the Enemy was dead—and that my parents were dead too. A priest came to me—he blessed me, he smiled but there were tears in his eyes, he told me all was forgiven and that we were all going to the next world, a world of peace and plenty that we would never be able to disturb.'

'So if you were there for the Departure, why are you here? Why aren't you with the other ravians in this world of peace and plenty?'

'I don't know, Maya. That's what I'm trying to find out. I remember a bright light, a dome of light, spreading from a great temple in the centre of the hidden city—over castles, roads, avenues, fountains, over great warriors in shining armour and sorcerers standing still. And then the light reached me. The next thing I felt was a great weight on my foot, and I woke up and saw Spikes.'

'Must have been a bit of a shock.'

'Not what I thought the next world would be like, certainly.' Kirin took a deep breath. 'And nearly two hundred years later there I was in the library, reading my parents' names, remembering being told tales about their valour in ravian voices. I've forgotten the stories, but I remember the names.

And when I read them and remembered so many things, I knew I was a ravian.'

'And what were the names?'

'Isara and Narak.'

'*What?*'

'Which is what I said, aloud, in a dark corner of the library and woke up the librarian.'

'So let me get this straight. You're saying you are the son of the Demon-hunter and the princess of the ravians?'

'Straight out of the legends, he walks the earth.'

'You're a ravian prince! That's difficult to digest, Kirin. This is big news. BIG news. This is going to amaze the magical community.'

'Not a prince, Maya, you haven't been studying hard enough. My mother was exiled from the Hidden City when she married my father, remember?'

Maya laughed aloud.

'My best friend is a two-hundred-year-old stone-statue-turned-ravian. And yesterday you were rolling around under the table. Not very ravian-like, you know.'

'Don't remind me. You're not going to tell anyone, are you?'

'I think you should tell my father, he knows more about ravians than anyone else.'

'I don't want to tell anyone, Maya. Now that you know, you have to find out why I'm still here. I've been through so many books about ravians—there was even a book which mentioned me, *Ravian's Peerage* or something like that—but there was no legend or anything about one ravian being left behind. Help me. I keep thinking I'm here for a reason, and I want to know what it is.'

'More research. Just what I need,' said Maya.

'I'll do anything . . . anything. I'm begging here. Name your price.' Kirin grinned.

Maya grinned back. 'Come over to the University tomorrow around lunch time, and I'll let you into the library. Now walk me home or I'll fall asleep on my feet.'

'Thanks, Maya. You're incredible.'

'I know.'

8

Vanarpuri, the great city of the vanars, was about three hundred miles away as the crow flies, and the crows were flying very fast. Some king of a long forgotten civilization had built a magnificent palace of pink marble, of soaring arches and stately domes, in what was now north Vrihataranya. Time and the forest had conquered the city, but the palace was mostly still standing, though covered with creepers, lichens and moss. Right in the centre of the highest dome, now green with moss and cracked open, a gigantic banyan tree had thrust its branches through. Its giant creepers draped over the walls like some grotesquely large octopus and its branches towered above the dome, making it impossible to see the palace even from the sky. The great hall of the palace had also been filled with huge trees but the vanars had cleared the middle. The ceiling, once covered with beautiful frescoes, was now a wild tangle of branches and leaves, which were slowly making cracks in the roof and forever pushing outwards and upwards. In the centre of the hall, in a huge, ornate, moss-covered marble throne set between two mammoth roots of the giant banyan sat the great and terrible Lord Bali, mightiest of the vanars and self-proclaimed lord of Vrihataranya.

The vanar city was a well-kept secret. It had been a few centuries since the vanars had ventured out of the forest and most of the world had forgotten about them. The other inhabitants of the jungle, human and animal, kept away from Vanarpuri. For it lay in the very heart of Vrihataranya, where the Sun God himself feared to tread, where immeasurably tall trees, whose very roots were man-high, strove amongst themselves for possession of the earth.

Into this hall now marched Ulluk the hunter, right up to the throne of Bali, and flung his prey down on the root-covered stairs in front of the throne.

'You asked for a stork, my lord,' he said.

Gyanasundaram spluttered into consciousness and opened his eyes. He counted his toes. All eight intact. Then he looked around and saw the Parliament of Vanarpuri.

The hall was lit by torches in the walls, weaving an eerie web of shadows through myriad creepers and ferns. Trees filled most of the hall, and in the branches of the trees at the outer rim of the circular hall sat monkeys of every kind imaginable. There were titis, sakis, uakaris, wise-faced capuchins, macaques, langurs, baboons, mandrills and hundreds of monkeys and apes Gyanasundaram had never seen before, their eyes glowing red in the firelight. In front of the trees, making a huge border to the cleared circle, sat the anthropoids—orang-utans, gorillas, chimpanzees and gibbons. And guarding the great doors of the hall, sitting in the ring of crudely fashioned wooden seats arranged in a wide circle around the throne and standing inside the ring of anthropoids were the vanars.

The Kol Zoological Society had recently advanced the extremely controversial theory that the anthropoids were the ancestors of men. Vanars, they contended, if they still existed, were what man would have been if he had never come down from the trees.

If, on the other hand, man had been created in any of the nine hundred and forty-two ways documented in the Kol Religion Office's library, the benevolent Creator, when creating vanars, might have given instructions to his assistant (call him Sambo) somewhat like this:

'*Take a man, Sambo, a very hairy man. Broaden his shoulders, shorten his neck, make his muscles large and powerful. Make him stoop just a little bit. Keep the face, make the eyes smaller, make the mouth protrude just a little bit but keep the lips thin. Hold it. The arms slightly longer, I think, and a slightly egg-shaped head. Yes, good. What's that? Still looks like a man? All right, then. Make the fingers really long, and the toes too. Prehensile? Opposable? What? I said long, Sambo. Long, see? Get it? Good. Of course he can hold things like a man, what sort of fool question is that? Still looks human? Oh all right, very well. Make him bigger. A little more. And give him a tail. Yes, Sambo, a tail. Now, next. No, I said next, not necks. Oh, Me!*'

Gyanasundaram saw there were four types of vanar. The orang-utan-vanars were nearly all clad in long flowing robes, the baboon-vanars were hairiest and naked, and the rest wore light steel breastplates and caps above human-like clothes. There were vanaresses too, slender and less hairy, clad in short robes, though some were in armour. Nearly all of them carried daggers, though some of the gorilla-vanars bore huge heavy metal maces. Their eyes were small and cunning. Bali was one of the gorilla-kind. He was tall, broad, immensely strong and ferociously intelligent. A mighty ruler of a mighty folk.

'Then let the great council begin,' said Bali. 'I am glad you are all here, my brothers, because tonight we shall learn a lot that will aid us in the years to come, and give us part of what we need to achieve our ultimate destiny—to be the lords not of the mighty forest, but of the whole world.'

The monkeys started to cheer, and were silenced.

'My sister-son Ulluk and my friend Kraken, lord of crows, have brought into the Great Hall of our fathers a stork. Why a stork, you may well ask. The answer to that question is a long one, but at this great council you will hear it.'

Ulluk dragged Gyanasundaram to the edge of the inner circle. The vanars listened in silence as Bali spoke. He spoke of his secret journeys to the far north, beyond Imokoi to Skuanmark, and of his meetings with the ruthless and fierce Skuan chiefs. He spoke of the gathering bands of asurs, of secret societies in Artaxerxia that he had heard of, of rumours of people in many lands who wanted Danh-Gem to return, and he spoke of his desire to unite them under the leadership of the vanar-lords. He spoke of human prejudice, of the fact that humans did not take vanars seriously, thinking they were dull-witted, like a lowly asur or pashan. As the darkness outside deepened and the torch-fires flickered, he spoke of his alliance with Kraken and the crows, and how every day his winged messengers brought him news of strange and mysterious beasts coming to life all over the world. As he spoke, a strange undercurrent of excitement, of fear and anticipation in the air grew in the draughty old hall. Gyanasundaram felt it too—here was a true leader, an absolute ruler of infinite conviction and resourcefulness, a ruthless visionary, someone who could, and probably would change the world, for better or for worse. Probably for the worse.

He was also beginning to realize what he was going to be asked. And that he would be killed if he didn't provide the answer.

'And so,' said Bali, 'things stand. If I am ever to successfully lead armies that can overthrow the lords of men, it is clear what I must do. I must raise Danh-Gem. We vanars cannot challenge and overthrow any of the human nations through armed might alone. Only Danh-Gem possessed power of that magnitude. Not aligning with him was the biggest mistake our forefathers made. Our objective, therefore, is to bring him back.'

Gyanasundaram looked at the vanar council and saw, with horror, that none of the vanars looked shocked, or even perturbed. Bring back Danh-Gem? Bring back the Age of Terror? Have the War again? That was sheer madness! The great Rakshas had died two centuries ago! They were all mad! He looked around wildly, seeking a means of escape, but Ulluk's grip on his neck never slackened for an instant.

'But until we know how to bring him back, we must ensure that the faithful are united. Humans will help, but will not easily be led by vanars. Not unless the vanars are the ones who bring Danh-Gem back. Is that not so, Djongli?'

Bali looked at the circle of anthropoids and Gyanasundaram saw something he had not noticed till then. Sitting between two immense bull gorillas was a man. He was naked except for a leopard-skin loincloth, and a hunting knife slung across his shoulder with a leather belt. His hair was wild and matted. He stared back at Bali angrily, but said nothing.

Bali carried on. 'Men will only declare their loyalty openly when they see Danh-Gem's other vassals united under us.

Rakshases are waking again, but they do not fight in groups. Dragons died out after the War. Asurs will join any venture that would help Danh-Gem, but they already have a leader and Bjorkun Skuan-lord is in Imokoi, speaking to him. The undead and the ice-giants are of no use. This leaves only the pashans. I told Bjorkun I would get to the heart of this matter, and I will.'

Gyanasundaram's heart sank. He knew what was coming.

'Pashans!' Bali continued. 'Those big, ugly men of stone. None of you have ever seen them, my brothers, but I have. And they seem to have forgotten completely that they ever served Danh-Gem, that they were among his most fearsome followers. They live in contentment with men in the Free States. Some of them, I hear, work for pay—for human masters—in Kol and other such cities. And then, when I was crossing the grey mountains of east Imokoi, I met a pashan and spoke to him at length.

'He was a granite man, hard and black-streaked. He was going to Kol, he said, to earn a living. He had never even heard of Danh-Gem. I was horrified. I asked him why his parents had never taught him the history of his kind. He replied he had never met his parents. I was amazed, and asked him how he was orphaned. He seemed confused. He said the storks had brought him. He would not stay, saying he would be late for work. I met many other pashans during my travels—muddy brown swamp pashans, huge limestone pashans and other kinds—all travelling to human cities to look for work, and I asked them how they were born. They all said storks had dropped them. They knew nothing more, or would say nothing more. When I tried to tell them about Danh-Gem and that pashans had served him, they said simply that he must have paid good wages. Not only were they unmoved, they were unconcerned. But the legends speak of pashans as bloodthirsty warriors, completely dedicated to Danh-Gem. I am convinced that pashans are, in some way, the key to the whole mystery. And once we learn how to unite the pashans we will learn how to bring Danh-Gem back.

'When I returned, a few days ago, I met Kraken. And when I told him the tale of my journeys, he told me a truly strange tale. A tale about storks. I had not taken the ramblings of the stone men seriously, but when I heard Kraken's tale I was intrigued, and I realized that a mystery worth solving had presented itself to me.

'He told me he had once seen forty-five storks flying over the forest, very slowly, in formation, and that the leader of this group was wearing a black sash that bore a strange emblem upon it. And Kraken had seen the same thing happen at around the same time the previous year, and the year before that. Storks and pashans, pashans and storks. Why? So I said to Ulluk, "Get me a stork and I will solve this mystery before the whole council." And here we are today. And here is the stork.

'Well, stork? Your task here today is very simple. Explain to me this whole strange story, this connection between pashans and storks. Or die.'

The vanars murmured approvingly. Ulluk carried Gyanasundaram to the centre of the ring.

Gyanasundaram looked at the wide circle of vicious eyes and weighed his alternatives. Professional discretion required that he maintain absolute confidentiality about his deliveries. On the other hand, was he prepared to die? If he refused to talk, they would catch other storks. Maybe they would even travel north and invade his community. And what would the beautiful S. Padmalakshmi and their loving children, S.G. Raju and S.G. Balasubramaniam do without his tenderness and guidance? Also, he would really be violating his oath. These vanars didn't mean any harm to the pashans, and, once he told them, would leave the storks and their cousins alone. On the other hand, there was the matter of the Oathbreaker's Egg. But then they would never find it. But what if they did? No, the consequences could be terrible. He wouldn't talk about *that*.

'I, Gyanasundaram Stork, son of the venerable Padmanubham,' said S.P. Gyanasundaram, stretching his head forward, trying to look unruffled, and looking into the cold black eyes of Bali, 'agree to tell you of the ancient contract between the storks and the pashans in exchange for my freedom. What do you want to know?'

'How are the pashans born?' asked Bali.

Pashan Family Planning was something Gyanasundaram taught young storks every year before they made their first deliveries.

'What happens, my lord, is that first a boy pashan meets a girl pashan,'—Ulluk's fingers sneaked around his neck—'and anyway, the female lays an egg. A stone egg. And then they hire a stork to deliver it to wherever they want their child to be. This is why all pashans know about their birth is that storks carry them.'

'But why do storks carry them?'

'Because storks can fly. Because the pashans give us food and help whenever we need it. Because pashans cannot be trusted to remember to carry their own eggs to proper hatching sites. And because the safest hatching sites are remote ones, carefully selected by storks to protect the infant pashans from predators in the larval stage, until they become stone-hard. And a pashan always opens a broad path wherever he or she goes, which is practically an invitation for egg-thieves.'

'Make him explain better, Ulluk.'

As Ulluk's fingers tore off a flight feather, Gyanasundaram discovered hitherto unexplored reserves of eloquence.

'In determining what a pashan will be like, location is everything. The storks carry the pashan eggs in their beaks and drop them in the appropriate place: in glaciers for snow-trolls, in swamps for the mud-pashans, in volcanoes for the lava-pashans, in deserts for the dunestones, and in cave rivers for the stalactrolls. The stone egg absorbs certain materials from the surrounding environment and these determine the type of pashan that will emerge when the egg finally hatches. Pashans grow very fast—they reach full size and hardness in a week. This bond between storks and pashans has existed for thousands of years, ever since a pashan in some forgotten age saved one of our forefathers from a hunter.

'In the Age of Terror, however, Danh-Gem brought the pashans together. He somehow found out how pashans were born and hired thousands of storks to bring eggs from all over the world to special furnaces he made in the pits of Imokoi. And there he bred his army of killer trolls, cunning and vicious. Those furnaces were broken down after the War, and normal stork-pashan contracts resumed. We have always kept this secret, partly because we care for the pashans and partly because no one, except Danh-Gem centuries ago, had ever asked us. Until now.'

'Now tell us about the forty-five storks that flew over the forest. What is that ceremony for?'

'I don't know,' Gyanasundaram said quickly.

'You lie,' hissed Bali. His eyes were sharp and piercing, and Gyanasundaram had the uncanny feeling that his mind was being looked at.

Ulluk whipped out a dagger.

Gyanasundaram saw his beloved Padmalakshmi's face float in front of his eyes. She looked extremely annoyed.

'I'll tell you everything,' he squeaked, feeling small and ashamed. 'That was the Oathbreaker's Flight ceremony. Its an ancient and irrelevant stork custom,'—the dagger reached his throat—'which I will now tell you all about.

'When a stork tells a mother pashan that he will deliver her egg, it is a very sacred oath—one that many storks have died to keep. In all our history there is only one instance where that oath has been voluntarily broken. The Oathbreaker family of herons, however, is held in high esteem, because the Oathbreaker, O. Veerappan, sacrificed his honour and his life for the sake of the world. Exactly what Veerappan did no one outside his family knows.' He paused. Bali shook his head. Another flight feather came off. Gyanasundaram hurried on.

'The first pashan the great Rakshas bred was the most fearsome troll that has ever walked the earth. He was said to be endowed with magical powers, and was Danh-Gem's personal bodyguard and most trusted adviser. This pashan's wife laid an egg.

'This egg was the most beautiful stone egg ever, covered with strange, glowing red and green mystic signs. O. Veerappan was hired to deliver this egg to the mountains north of Vrihataranya. What happened after that I do not know.'

'There's more,' said Bali, looking into Gyanasundaram's eyes. 'Keep talking if you want to fly again.'

'The egg was fiery and hot, and Veerappan's beak was badly burned. The egg seemed to have a life of its own—it skipped and jumped about, and he caught it in mid-air several times. Danh-Gem himself came to bid him goodbye as he set off, telling him to be very careful as that egg would hatch a pashan with powers even greater than its father's. This was during the last part of the War—Danh-Gem was slain by the ravians the very day Veerappan started off from Imokoi. That was two hundred years ago.

'As Veerappan flew over the Great Forest, he thought many thoughts, which are all chronicled in the epic poem, 'Death of a Stork', by O. Ganesan. He decided he would not deliver the egg to the mountains, for surely a pashan as deadly and evil as the one this egg would hatch would turn the course of the Great War. He took the egg home. O. Veerappan was so badly burned during the long journey across the Great Forest that he died soon after. The egg stayed with the Oathbreakers—it burned their nest so they moved to a cave—and was an object of great curiosity for all us pashan-bearers. Fortunately for the Oathbreakers, Danh-Gem's followers never found out.'

'There it is!' exclaimed Bali, his eyes glowing. 'Stork, we must have this Oathbreaker's egg! Where is it?'

'Honestly, I do not know. About fifteen years ago, the egg disappeared. No one knows where it went. It just disappeared. Some say it rolled out of the Oathbreaker's cave and down the hills, but the country was searched for miles around and it was not found. Then, the storks guessed that the egg, like the dragons and many other evil things, had simply run out of magic and disappeared. Since then, the Oathbreaker clan flies across the forest once every year, to commemorate the day when O. Veerappan saved the world.'

'You speak like the ignorant bird that you are,' snapped Bali. 'The pashan you speak of must be alive, for the Great Waning happened two hundred years ago—if the egg was to truly disappear, it would have happened then, not now. Is there anything else?'

'I have told you everything.'

Bali looked at him keenly and was satisfied.

'Very well, stork. You may go now.'

'But you said I could eat him, Uncle Bali,' whined Ulluk.

'I did? Oh yes. Yes, by all means, eat him.'

Ulluk dragged Gyanasundaram out of the great hall.

'So there it is, my brothers. Let us find this pashan the bird spoke of. If he is indeed the son of Danh-Gem's bodyguard, finding him could be the solution to our problems.'

'But where will you look for him, Bali?' asked a vanaress by his side.

'That, my dear Angda, is where our friend Kraken will truly earn the rich reward that I have promised him. When the time comes, I will go to Kol. Bjorkun has promised to help me in my quest in exchange for the services of our finest assassins. But of my plans I will speak later. There is the other matter we have to speak of . . .'

The vanars moved in, forming a close circle around the throne and Bali's voice dropped to a murmur. Kraken flew to the throne to hear what was being said. The anthropoids began to shuffle out of the hall. Secret matters were being discussed which were not for their ears. Seeing that the council was over as far as they were concerned, Yahoo and Maverick flew up and left the hall through the great crack in the dome.

'So, he's going to Kol to look for the troll,' Yahoo said.

'All roads, like, lead to Kol, man,' said Maverick.

'Yes, if you can make it there you're going to make it anywhere.'

Yahoo and Maverick began to sing *Kol, the big mango* as they flew through the twisted banyan branches, up above the dark forest to the clear and star-studded sky.

9

Lady Temat, the Chief Civilian of Kol, sipped her tea and looked out at the great city from the wide terrace of her marble palace. To the left rolled the steel-grey waters of the river Asa. She sighed as she looked at the peaceful waters, then rightwards and upwards at the city she ruled.

The Palace was in the heart of the city, and though it was a tall and magnificent building that had once been the dominant feature of the skyline, it was now dwarfed by the massive towers that had risen up all around it, in which the rich and powerful businessmen of Kol sat in offices, running gold and paper through their fingers, plotting exports, imports and investments with as much cunning as their forefathers had drawn battle plans. The objective was still world domination, but the businessmen of Kol intended to do it peacefully.

The city looked as if it had been designed by an architect who had drunk too much Dragonjuice—there were arches, minarets, turrets and domes everywhere. When Kol found that it couldn't extend tentacles outwards and grow more suburbs without damaging fertile agricultural land, it started growing upwards. Buildings were built one on top of the other and they stood on each other's shoulders raising their heads to the skies. The mightiest bridges in Kol now stretched between towers, casting into insignificance the beautifully crafted bridges across the Asa.

The streets of Kol were world-famous. They were always crowded, and very dangerous at night, but above and below ground level there were very few accidents and traffic flow was usually smooth and fast. Huge carts, carrying agricultural produce, traded goods and minerals from great mines trundled through the streets all day. The footpaths were wide, and full of jostling citizens, humans, vamans, occasional centaurs, scurrying asurs, and lumbering pashans. But this was not all that made Kol unique.

The top-most spire of the University of Enki was still the highest point in Kol. On top of this spire, encased in a spherical crystal covered with an intricate golden mesh of sharp needle-like spikes on the outside was a small red ruby given to the spellbinders of Kol by the ravians. This was the Heart of Magic, the stone that had given the spellbinders of Kol incredible powers during the Great War. Now it was used for a purpose slightly less noble though equally awe-inspiring—traffic control.

Magic carpets flew over the streets of Kol, like bees around a hive. The carpets could fly within the boundaries of the city, wherever the power of the ruby was strong enough to hold them in the air.

Layer upon layer of carpets criss-crossed in the busy airways of Kol. Slow-moving Tobaggons (Smooth Flying for the Whole Family) and Caravans (Fly Safe, Fly Stylish) floated across the lowest carpet paths. Fast-flying racing carpets, Ripples (Soar Like an Eagle) and Avalanches (SWOOSH!) whizzed between the highest towers of the city. And in-between, scores of other kinds of carpets, suited for every conceivable kind of customer, flew gracefully over roads, through tunnels, into gateways and around towers. Bright yellow Bumblebee Taxicarpets streaked from building to building, with mahouts blowing horns furiously at one another. Rich young aristocrats, city guards and vroomers tore through the sky on their vroomsticks, heedless of the accepted flight-heights, drawing torrents of abuse. People who were too poor to afford carpets, of course, had to walk, but often travelled in magically hollowed giant tubeworms that wriggled at high speeds through specially constructed underground tunnels in certain parts of the city. This sort of public transport was unique to Kol, and was another stunning example of the fusion of spellbinder ingenuity and vaman craftsmanship. This then was Kol, the Big Mango, a teeming, vibrant, vast metropolis, a bewildering, extremely hazardous three-dimensional maze.

Lady Temat sighed. 'I have bad news for you, Chancellor. Your fears have been confirmed,' she said.

Ombwiri took another sip of tea. It was Avrantic tea, black and strong, just the way he liked it. Of course she had bad news. He'd known she would. But the tea was nice.

'Reports are coming in from all over the world,' she continued. 'Avranti, Durg, Artaxerxia, Elaken. Monsters are reappearing. Rakshases have been sighted in the forests and hills of Durg and Avranti, the undead are multiplying in Elaken and Skuanmark. Strange creatures are roaming the western deserts. I know what course of action to take every time the asurs decide to rebel, but magical monsters worry me.'

A magical monster shot across the floor of the terrace and slithered up the Civilian's body, winding itself around her shoulders. She didn't seem particularly worried as she patted one of its heads. It was Ojanus, the Civilian's pet amphisbaena. The short black-and-gold two-headed snake was, it was said, the only thing that knew what the Chief Civilian was thinking. One of the heads began to nuzzle the Civilian's ear and the other one stared coldly at Ombwiri.

'I apologize, my Lady,' said Ombwiri, 'I should have come to see you earlier. We in Enki were afraid this would happen.'

'Tell me why this has happened, Chancellor.'

Chancellor Ombwiri finished his tea and set his cup down. 'Magic levels are on the rise,' he said. 'The waters of the Vertical Sea are rising again, and the University fountain is flowing higher.'

The Vertical Sea had been created long, long ago, when magic was young and wild in the world. Some well-meaning prophet, the legend goes, had tried to part the seas to let his people cross southwards from Elaken to unknown lands across the southern seas. The immensely powerful charm he had used had worked beyond his wildest expectations. Unfortunately, however, he had been pointing his staff in the wrong direction. He had created a vast passage, not southwards to the unknown world but right across the world in a great circle, and the displaced waters had risen upwards on either side of the vast trench he had created, forming the Vertical Sea and, tragically, drowning the prophet and all his followers.

The Vertical Sea was very magical and very dangerous. Ships could not, obviously, cross it. Explorers had travelled all around the world, but they had never been able to cross the Vertical Sea and find out what lands lay further south.

Storms always raged over the Misplaced Trench, making it utterly impossible to fly over.

The height of the Vertical Sea, above horizontal sea level, was a very good indication of how strong the magical forces in the world were. In the Age of Terror, when Danh-Gem and the ravians scarred and scorched the earth with magical blasts, the Vertical waters had touched the sky. After Danh-Gem's death, the Departure and the consequent lowering of magic levels all over the world, the Vertical waters had come down to a large extent. The University fountain contained water from the Vertical Sea. This water showed the spellbinders of Enki exactly how strong the magic that flowed through the earth air was, and therefore how successful they could expect their spells to be.

In fact, it was a widely accepted theory that the ravians had left after the Great War to lower the levels of magic and make the world a more normal and peaceful place to live in. After Danh-Gem's death, the dragons were running amok, laying waste to many beautiful towns in their anger and confusion. The Departure had lowered magic levels so drastically that the dragons, who required a lot of magic in the air to be able to breathe fire, had disappeared altogether from the face of the earth. Many other powerful monsters that had plagued the world in the Age of Terror were either destroyed or buried deep underground when the ravians left. It was, ironically, only when the ravians departed that the War was won. Now magic levels were rising again, and magical creatures were reappearing in many lands.

The Chief Civilian stood up. Ombwiri looked at her, feeling with his spellbinder's intuition the power of her mind as she looked at the city silently. The two-headed snake slithered down from her shoulders and started making lazy circles around her feet. Her grey-black hair was tied back in a tight bun, her eyes were keen and searching and her movements were graceful and cat-like. In her youth she had been devastatingly beautiful. Now she still left people dumbstruck, but it was mostly out of fear.

'Does this rise in magic affect you spellbinders as well?' she asked abruptly.

'Yes. Spell-casting is a lot easier, and I for one have been feeling younger, more powerful. Our young spellbinders are learning fast. There are benefits to the increase, you know, my Lady. If the rise continues, we could see the return of the phoenix, the unicorn, the griffin, and, indeed, many other noble beasts that aid our arts to no small extent.'

'Yes, Chancellor, but you know that we all have reason to worry.'

The Chancellor knew indeed.

Rakshases.

And not just rakshases.

Dragons.

What if the level of magic grew to a point where the dragons reappeared?

Before the Age of Terror, dragons had largely been wild, solitary creatures. The Northern dragons, who populated the wild, barren lands of north Skuanmark were ferocious and evil; the great fire-serpents of Xi'en, on the other hand by and large, had been peaceful beasts who were revered— even worshipped—in the great Empire. But that was before the Wu Sen monks, enslaved by a fierce mountain warlord, had made the Gauntlet of Tatsu.

The Wu Sen monks had managed to warn the Emperor of the warlord's designs. The warlord had been executed. The Emperor had then ordered the monks to complete the

Gauntlet, in spite of the warnings of his counsellors. The Gauntlet was kept in the Wu Sen Monastery, high in the Mountains of Harmony, and was used by the Emperor every New Year's Day for the Earth-Awakening Ceremony, when he would command the dragons to use their magic to bring harmony and fertility to the earth.

Then the inevitable happened. Danh-Gem, learning of the Gauntlet and its powers, stole it, making bitter enemies of the people of Xi'en. But their enmity was irrelevant, because Danh-Gem now wielded greater power—the dragons bowed to him, and unleashed their mighty powers in a torrent of war and destruction that changed the very shape of the world. With his armies of asurs, pashans and dragons, and doubly fortified by his secret alliances with the Sultan of Artaxerxia and the High King of Skuanmark, Danh-Gem burned his way through southern Vrihataranya, destroying utterly the great cities of the Psomedeans and changing the landscape of most of the southern lands. He even burned his way into the peaceful lands of Elaken, giving the land of pyramids to the Artaxerxians as a reward for their treachery. He took the Gauntlet to the north and found to his great delight that even the Northern dragons, the terrible flying lizards, accepted the Gauntlet-wielder as their lord. With their aid, he wreaked havoc upon the entire northwest, humbling the mighty armies of Ventelot with fire, magic and cavalries of ferocious Skuans.

Xi'en would have opposed him, but could not, because it was torn apart by civil war. The fearless samurai warriors from the islands east of Xi'en were conquering province after province, and the Emperor's forces could not even take part in the war against Danh-Gem. The daimyos of the East had taken over in Xi'en, and though they had never fought for Danh-Gem, they had no quarrel with him, so they refused to take part in the war against him.

But that was all over now, thought Ombwiri. The castles of Ventelot and the fair cities of Psomedea were now broken, burnt ruins in charred, dangerous lands. The dead pharaohs of Elaken slept in their hidden chambers; Danh-Gem had been destroyed and the Gauntlet had been found and returned to Xi'en. But what if the dragons returned?

Ombwiri shuddered. The world was different now. It was a world ruled by common sense, by money and by trade. It was a world based on cooperation and mutual avoidance of warfare. It was a new world, a world where ravians, rakshases and dragons had no place, where 'good' and 'evil' were words used to describe people, not species. It was a world where Artaxerxia had an embassy in Avranti; where asurs and pashans walked the streets of a great human city, the ruler of which, Ombwiri realized with a start, was talking to him.

'When did magic start growing stronger?' Lady Temat asked.

Ombwiri thought for a while. 'Well, the waters rise and fall all the time,' he said, slowly, 'but there was a sudden spurt in the fountain a few years ago—eight years, or was it seven? The waters suddenly rose by about six feet. We watched and waited, and when the news came that a rakshas was sighted and killed in Avranti we thought that that had caused the waters to rise. We didn't realize that the rakshas awakening must have been an effect—and not the cause—of the rise in magic. We failed in our duty, my Lady. I apologize.'

'I did not call you here to lay blame, Chancellor. You came to me, remember, and perhaps we can solve this before any serious damage is done.'

'But the waters have been rising steadily, my Lady. And

we can see no way of stopping it, or of understanding what is going on. Why, indeed, is magic rising? Does it have anything to do with the Simoqin Prophecies? After all, this is the year they are supposed to come true. We have tried to find the answer, but we have failed. Our best spells have done nothing to help us decode the books that were rescued from Danh-Gem's tower. The letters are Ravianic runes, ironically—a little showing off on Danh-Gem's part—but even our best scholars failed to decipher the code.'

'The Simoqin Prophecies. The return of Danh-Gem, and the arrival of the Hero,' murmured the Chief Civilian. 'I had forgotten about them.'

Ombwiri was surprised. He had thought Lady Temat never forgot anything. And the twin prophecies were a little difficult to forget. If Danh-Gem returned—well, the Hero of the other legend had better be good at whatever heroic thing he intended to do.

'May I ask you something, Lady Temat?' he said suddenly.

'Certainly.'

'Why is Mantric not here? Would it not be wise to order him to return to Kol? He may be quite eccentric and unreliable, but he is probably the most powerful spellbinder among us all. Why did you send him to study the bunyips of Bolvudis Island? And why has he been there for the last three years?'

'Let me make this very clear, Chancellor,' said Lady Temat in a voice that would have made burning coals freeze, 'I did not send Mantric to Bolvudis, to study bunyips or other insignificant water monsters. He chose to go on his own, and I do not know why he stayed on—if, indeed, he has— for three years. I shall not order him to return to Kol. And since he is, as you say, eccentric and unreliable, I think he should be left to his own devices. I cannot trust someone who is not completely devoted to the city, no matter how powerful he is.'

The Chief Civilian looked at the Chancellor's stunned face, and her voice became less harsh. 'You, on the other hand, are eminently trustworthy, Chancellor. I believe that is all; thank you so much for coming.'

Ombwiri, perceiving that he had been dismissed, smiled uncertainly and made a hasty exit.

Walking out of the Palace, Ombwiri felt that strange sense of dissatisfaction and confusion that he always felt after talking to the Chief Civilian. The magic thing was worrying, very worrying indeed. But the other things were even more confusing. Why was Temat so angry with Mantric? He'd always thought they really liked each other. Why, when Mantric had turned the Skuan ambassador into a skunk and back 'to see if he smelled any different', the Civilian had done absolutely nothing! And how could she have forgotten about the Simoqin Prophecies?

It suddenly occurred to him, as he got on his carpet and started gliding back to Enki, that the Civilian might not have been entirely truthful about everything.

Lady Temat, on the other hand, seemed to be entirely at peace, humming a little tune as she stood and watched the sun set over the Kol skyline. She seemed to be waiting for something.

A few minutes later a small buzzing black shape flew down from the sky and landed on her shoulder. She pressed the scarab's head and the shell popped open. She took out the small piece of paper inside and unfolded it.

ASVIN ARRIVING TOMORROW, it said. There was a strange, shiny mark on the bottom left corner of the paper. It looked like a little dagger.

10

Bolvudis Island was the northernmost island of the Ossus Archipelago, named after the famous Psomedean hero, Ossus of Kol. The Ossus Archipelago was a cluster of small islands a little distance south of Bolvudis, and was one of the most naturally magical regions in the world. Every island was the home of at least one dangerous monster—there were hydras, gorgons, cyclopses, and strange and beautiful sorceresses, to name but a few. Most of these had reappeared recently as the Vertical Sea grew taller further south, and since all the treasures that these islands had possessed had been taken long ago by questing heroes, mariners stayed clear of the deadly islands, clashing rocks and living whirlpools of the Ossus Archipelago. Bolvudis, of course, had never had any native monsters—in the eyes of the world it had always been an insignificant part of the archipelago, useful only to send captains to when mutinies were taking place.

The islands had been part of Psomedea, but no one wanted them now—they were wild, beautiful and dangerous.

It was Ossus who had first journeyed through these islands on his way back from a war in Elaken. He had lingered in the arms of a beautiful enchantress for many years in the little island he had landed on, and his wife, angered, had gathered a crew of women and searched the entire archipelago, killing monsters left, right and centre until she found him. She took him home to Psomedea and then threw him out of his palace, after which many suitors courted her day and night. The sad Ossus wandered for many years and ultimately settled down in Kol, which was a very good thing for Kol, because he was a key figure in many glorious wars after that. And though the beautiful enchantress of the island joined him there later and they had many children, historians insisted he never found happiness again. Which was why the giant statue of Ossus in Kol faced southwards, yearning forever for his wife to forgive him and take him back.

There was magic in the air and the sea around the island of Bolvudis. It crackled, tingled and sparkled in the moonlight. The dark waters rippled and broke to show lithe shapes that frolicked and sang in the moon-road across the Psomedean Ocean. Bolvudis by moonlight was misty and dreamlike. Imps flew around the cliffs, sometimes swooping down into the Very Blue Lagoon to slide along the giant tentacles of the placid Picsquids. Soon it would be spring, and the selkies would start migrating, returning to the thawing waters of the north.

It was always warm and merry in Bolvudis. An enormous elephant-makara sat on the beach, its dolphin-tail curled beneath it, politely thanking imps for the fruits they had brought it. Mer-people played tail-blowfish, shouting boisterously. The sirens were quiet—they liked to come out after the mer-men, who made ardent but sadly unrefined swains, had returned below the surface. Two picnicking young bunyips loped around on the beach, bellowing happily as they tried to crush lobsters.

Oster the imp was not a part of the moonlight revelry, though. He had work to do. The scene he had just witnessed was one of the best the Badshah had ever directed. The Badshah had told him to fly as fast as he could to show the Picsquid what he had seen, and that was exactly what he was doing.

The Badshah! Now *there* was someone the First Eye had surely winked at. It was whispered that he had once been a renowned spellbinder in the great city of Kol in the north, before he had come to Bolvudis Island and discovered his true calling. It was the Badshah who had started the wonderful voyage of self-expression and discovery they had all embarked upon together and it was the Badshah who, soon after coming to Bolvudis, had learned the powers of the Muwi tree and discovered the magic of Muwi-vision.

Oster heard the rustling of the palm leaves of the Very Blue Lagoon below him and zoomed down, eye tightly shut, navigating through sound like a bat, towards the sparkling waters. Now, to find a clear Picsquid . . .

The Muwi tree was truly the First Eye's greatest gift to the world, thought Oster. The imps did not know why the Badshah had come to the island, but they were glad that he had. The Badshah had ground the leaves of the Muwi tree and burned them for some spell, and had discovered their unique power by sheer accident. If an imp inhaled the smoke of burning Muwi leaf, his eye glazed over and he was able to remember everything he had seen recently in immense detail at least while the effect of the wondrous leaf lasted, after which whatever he had seen would emanate from his eye in a minutely detailed recreation of the real thing, in a beam of light which, if suitably magnified with mirrors and lights, created a truly magical spectacle. Oster loved the feeling that smoking the leaf gave him—the stunning clarity of vision, the vividness of every speck of living, vibrant colour, the way every movement burned little trails in his mind . . .

Initially the Badshah had simply been amused by his little discovery. He had tried to take the imps and some Muwi saplings to Kol, to aid the spellbinders in their studies, and had found out that both the tree and the imps died swiftly and painfully if taken beyond a certain distance from the island. It was after nearly eight months of painstaking and meticulous study that the Badshah had found a way to store the images that the imps saw, by using the Picsquids.

And now the Badshah had hired a team of actors from all over the world. He hadn't needed to hire them, in fact, they just turned up whenever the Badshah had decided to enact a new play. Now various grim historical plays, squishy modern romances and tense action-oriented thrillers were being created that would surely thrill the world—once all the necessary machinery had been built.

Oster skimmed over the sparkling moonlit waters of the Very Blue Lagoon until he found the Picsquid he sought. He flew down, felt it reach upwards and grasp him gently but firmly with its two larger tentacles. Then he felt the cold, clammy sensation that meant the squid had closed its largest sucker over his eye. He opened his eye and saw the scene he had just witnessed rush into the strange multicoloured liquids in the squid's sucker. He felt the squid change colour, from greyish pink to a deep, mottled green. Then he flew, up and away, while the squid swam to join its brethren, both clear and exposed, in the deeper waters near the mouth of the lagoon.

There were now more than thirty exposed Picsquids waiting in the lagoon, the scenes from the Muwi-vision plays changing their ink forever. The Badshah, having realized the Picsquids' ability to store light as chemical energy, was using them as a reservoir, a storage medium for his strange new art form. He was now working on a device that would somehow be able to take the squids' ink and reconvert the ink into moving images. Oster knew that the Badshah would do it, too. There was nothing the Badshah couldn't do.

There was magic in the air and the sea around Bolvudis Island. It spun and streamed through the air, filling the inhabitants of the island with strange, giddy, exhilarating, unrealistic dreams. Udent, Oster's brother, had told him that it was something to do with the pollen of the Muwi flowers—it caused madness. There was something in the air that made shy, reserved men want to wrestle with lions, jump from high buildings, beat up a couple of villainous strangers, sip mango juice with dark, sinuous, exotic, scantily clad women and plant burning kisses on their quivering, upturned lips. The actors, who by and large were not particularly shy or reserved, simply went berserk. And upon eating a little ground Muwi root, these wild men and women performed spine-chillingly dangerous stunts eagerly and brilliantly. Muwi masala, the Badshah called that potent powder, and it was Muwi masala that was was responsible for the incredible acts of daring and bravado which had now been immortalized, captured by imp eyes, the feats swirling in the ink sacs of the Picsquids. They all shared a dream—one day those amazing scenes would compel stunned admiration and applause from audiences around the world, giving the actors the even more exhilarating elixir they craved—stardom.

Wise men all over the world had avoided Bolvudis for ages—the island had no military significance, no one was even interested in claiming it for any country, and most people who went there ended up turning insane. Oster wondered whether the Badshah was mad. He was definitely a little mad, said the actors. But then the actors were mad too. Yes, the Badshah did spend far too much time in his little hut, drawing complex objects, building strange machines, mixing strange potions, reading the books that somehow turned up in his hut—the imps did not know who brought them—and generally behaving like a lunatic, but wasn't a genius supposed to be like that? And Mantric of Kol, whom the imps of Bolvudis called the Badshah, certainly was a genius.

Apart from the years Asvin had spent with his kul-guru in a small ashram in Shantavan, he had lived in Ektara all his life. He had heard that Kol was a big city, but as they said, you had to see Kol to believe it. Not that he had seen much of Kol since he had arrived at dawn yesterday, but the carpet ride from the gates of the city to the Civilian's palace had been a mind-boggling experience.

This, Asvin decided, biting into the dripping phuchka that Amloki had brought for him, was the good life. And not being a prince was so liberating. Not that Asvin minded being the centre of attention, but it was nice to have conversations with pretty young women without knowing that as soon as you'd left, the harem-wardens would surround her, demand to know who her parents were, and try to induct her into the harem. And Kol women were so wonderful, thought Asvin. They looked him in the eye, talked to him as an equal and knew so much more about the world than he did. What puzzled him, however, were the whispers of 'Is that the new one? Very pretty' before they came to talk to him. And one dazzlingly beautiful woman had actually felt the muscles on his arm, winked at him meaningfully and passed on without saying a word! He'd asked Amloki about it, and Amloki had smiled and said that that was how women in Kol talked to handsome men. But it was not just the women. Many men seemed to be smirking and nudging one another as Asvin passed with Amloki at his side. Asvin had almost lost his temper when he had intercepted a particularly snide look from a helmeted Red Phoenix palace guard, but Amloki had told him to calm down. Asvin decided to let it be, since he was enjoying himself otherwise.

He had spent most of yesterday wandering around the Civilian's palace with Amloki. The little khudran had proved to be a mine of useful information. He was also very resourceful when it came to getting food from various parts of the city, and Asvin had eaten ravenously, allowing the delicious flavours of spicy Xi'en and Avrantic dishes to sweep away the uncomfortable memories of the last few days. The Civilian's palace was a wonderful place, and Asvin was perfectly happy roaming through many-pillared corridors and gazing at the priceless sculptures and paintings that filled every hall.

Asvin had been very intimidated by the prospect of meeting the Chief Civilian, but she had been perfectly warm and friendly. She had greeted him in flawless Avrantic, and though Asvin's Koli was perfectly fluent, he loved the Old Tongue much more. They had spoken of Avranti and of Kol, of art, trade and politics, and Asvin perceived that their conversation was not to learn anything about Avranti, for he could tell the Civilian knew the answers to the questions she was asking him. He guessed, correctly, that he was being judged and analysed coldly and ruthlessly under the keen glare of Lady Temat's eyes. Within an hour of meeting her, he had told her almost everything there was to tell about himself.

When Asvin had started to talk about what had happened to him, Temat had told him to forget the events of the last few days, and to look forward, for this was not the time for revenge. What quest she had for him and why she had rescued him, she did not say, and Asvin had been perfectly happy to accept her lavish hospitality and prepare for the days ahead. He knew that the (younger) Sun of Avranti was, for the time being, dead, and was willing to let him lie in peace and see what the future had in store for Asvin, prince in hiding. Amloki said he knew why Asvin had been brought to Kol, but had been forbidden to tell.

Asvin looked at himself in a long mirror in a wide, sunlit corridor. He wouldn't have recognized himself—they had done a good job. His long, flowing hair was no more— they had cut it brutally short, Kol fashion. They had shaved off his moustache—that precious moustache (back home there had been a servant whose sole task had been to oil it)—taken off all his jewellery (he missed the earrings a little), and removed the chandan from his forehead. Asvin quite liked the loose shirt he was wearing—the Sacred Armour of the (younger) Sun had been a little difficult, especially in summer—but the trousers were, well, a little, well, constricting. In spite of all the changes, he looked sufficiently regal, he thought. He wished he were carrying a sword, though.

'Enjoying the view?' asked a soft voice.

Asvin started. The Civilian was standing right next to him. Amloki had disappeared.

She walked up to a statue of a woman carrying a torch and a book. She poked it in the eye. A section of the wall slid back.

'Follow me,' she said, disappearing into the shadows.

He followed her. She pulled a lever and the wall slid back.

'Is this where I finally get to meet my brave rescuer?'

'I'm afraid not. The Silver Dagger is rather . . . shy.'

'Where are we going, then?'

'Downstairs.'

He followed her silently, down stairway after narrow stairway, until it seemed to him that they must be underground. The stairs were completely dark, but there was a faint glow coming from below.

They reached the bottom. A long, narrow passage stretched out in front of them. There were torches on the wall. 'Pick one up,' she said.

It was a maze, Asvin realized, but the Civilian obviously knew the way. As they turned corner after corner Asvin looked at the dark openings to tunnels they were ignoring, and wondered how many thieves had met mysterious and possibly gruesome ends here, and what treasure it was that the Civilian was going to reveal to him.

The Civilian stopped. This was a dead end—there was a wall right in front of them. She walked towards it and pulled a lever. Nothing happened.

'Put the torch out.'

'Why?'

'Because the air in the next passage bursts into flames at the least spark.'

Rocks moved behind them, closing them in, and the wall in front slid back. They stepped forward and the wall closed

85

behind them of its own accord. There was a mild smell in the air.

'It's not poisonous,' said the Civilian, moving forward. They walked down the narrow passage in pitch darkness. Asvin sensed the Civilian stop.

'There's a curtain of mewlips in front of us. You do know what these flowers do, don't you?'

'No,' said Asvin.

'Listen, then.'

The Civilian walked forward, and Asvin heard a rustle as she passed through the fronds. Suddenly there were loud, angry yowls, as if a dozen cats had had their tails trodden on simultaneously.

'Now you know. Step through the curtain, please.'

Asvin felt the fronds brush against him as he walked through the mewlip curtain. The flowers yelled again.

A trapdoor opened in the floor, flooding the tunnel with light, white Alocactus light.

A deep, rumbling voice said, 'Identify yourselves.'

'Mati, it's me,' said the Civilian, 'and Prince Asvin of Avranti. He is unarmed.'

She reached the trapdoor. There were stairs leading down. In the bright white light, Asvin saw a large, square room with two doors, to the right and left. Standing in the middle of the room was a golem.

Asvin had heard tales of these mighty men of clay, but had never seen one before. The vamans made them, and used them for heavy work in their cities and mines deep underground. Asvin knew he was safe, but he still felt a tingle of fear as he looked at the sheer size and obvious power of the giant figure in front of him. A golem could break most pashans with a single blow. Asvin, who had never seen pashans before yesterday, now realized that he was in the presence of something far more dangerous. And who could be a better guard than a golem? They were immortal—well, they weren't even living beings—they were eternally faithful, immune to most kinds of magic, and they never needed to eat or sleep. But he'd never heard of a golem that served humans before. And he'd thought golems could only work under the earth . . . but of course, they *were* underground.

'Where are we?'

'This is Mati's chamber, where *really* good thieves discover Mati a few seconds before he kills them. The door to the left is called the Room of Signs. The door to the right will lead you to the Treasure Chamber. It is where the Crown Jewels of Kol are kept.'

Kol and the Free States had been part of the Kingdom of Kol before Danh-Gem had killed the last king in the War. The people of Kol had waited, going by the general rule, which was that an heir to the throne would appear mysteriously from distant lands in the north, bearing unquestionable proof of his royal birth, but their patience had worn thin after about fifty years—after all, the old king had never even been married, and all the heirlooms which could have proved that his son was indeed his son were in the royal treasure room. The Free States had declared themselves independent, and Kol had become a city-state.

'But why . . .'

'Your restraint has been admirable. Follow me, Asvin.'

The golem poured a little water on a small potted Alocactus and handed it to the Civilian. Lady Temat led Asvin to the Room of Signs. The Alocactus light was faint, and as Asvin walked behind Temat, he saw tables along the walls of the large hall, and strange objects glowing gold and silver as the light fell on them.

The Civilian stopped in front of a huge stone. There was a large, shiny sword buried in it, almost up to the hilt. She was silent for a while.

'Too easy,' she murmured. She walked on.

A few pillars later, they came to a huge cauldron, bubbling on a strange green fire. There was a hideous, slimy green ooze boiling inside.

'Stand near the cauldron.'

Asvin walked up to the bubbling slime and felt its hot green glow on his face.

Suddenly an arm burst out of the cauldron: a fat, black, scale-covered arm ending in cruel red claws. Asvin leapt back with a startled cry. The arm disappeared into the cauldron and came back again holding a great black club. It held the club out of the cauldron, pointing towards Asvin.

'The Lady of the Swamp appears to like you,' said the Civilian. 'Excellent.'

'What, um, what do I do? Do I take that thing?' asked Asvin nervously.

'It's very poisonous, so I would advise you not to,' said Temat. 'But thank her politely. She is very sensitive.'

'I thank thee, O generous one, but I am not worthy to bear thy mighty weapon,' said Asvin. The arm disappeared again and a loud, disgruntled belching sound was heard.

'A flair for words, too. Well, well.' The Civilian walked on. They had almost reached the end of the hall.

'Lady Temat,' said Asvin, 'please tell me why you have brought me here.'

'There are a few things you might have to do, Asvin. Quests, as it were.'

'Tell me, Lady Temat. I am ready.'

'I am not asking for your trust, Asvin. What I am asking for is your patience. All will be made clear to you in a few days. Until then, please do as I ask. For you are not ready yet. Far from it.'

'I understand. Pardon my impatience.'

'Speak no more of it. There is one more test, Asvin, in this Room of Signs. What I will now show you is a weapon you have read about, for it is one of the greatest magical weapons ever made in Avranti. It is a priceless object—Avranti would probably declare war if Maharaja Aloke knew it was here.'

They reached a small stone platform. Temat reached down and removed the black cloth covering it.

Asvin saw a huge bow. It was covered with emblems and mysterious signs. It glowed red, casting long shadows in the room. He gasped.

'The Bow of Fire,' he said reverently. 'This should be in Ektara, in the Temple of the Sun. Death comes to any man who sets arrow to this bow, save the sons of the Sun.'

'Are you ready now, Prince Asvin?'

So this was what he was here for, thought Asvin. He had stared into the face of death and been brought to Kol to look at it again. Well, his life had been saved, and the astrologers back home had all told him how auspicious the time of his birth had been . . .

There were arrows in a quiver by the platform. He picked one up. Your body has been trained, his guru had told him. Let it take over when your mind feels fear. You are a son of the Sun. The stars say so.

He picked up the bow. It was hot, and glowed brighter as he picked it up. He took a deep breath, and set an arrow to the bow.

There was a crack of thunder, and the tip of the arrow burst into flames. The room glowed red for an instant. Asvin smiled, his heart beating furiously, his face flushed with pride and joy.

'Impressive,' said the Civilian, 'You just might be what I am looking for.'

Asvin said nothing. He set the bow down and looked at her questioningly.

'A few days,' said Temat, 'and I will explain everything. Till then, Asvin, explore Kol. I will tell Amloki to accompany you. For now, I will say only this: take care of yourself. You might become very valuable very soon.'

Asvin nodded, and started walking with slow, purposeful strides towards the door of the Room of Signs and the world beyond.

The Civilian looked at him and sighed. Nice boy, she thought. Good Hero material. Never asks questions. Who put the sword in the stone? Why did the Lady of the Swamp have a club? If anyone who touched the bow died, except the hero it was meant for, how did it get into the Room of Signs in the first place? These were not questions that came to him. Fate, destiny, karma. Quests, swords, good, evil. Honour, courage, loyalty. He didn't have the sort of mind that asked questions and listened to answers primarily to search for more questions. He didn't have a mind like hers. Would he live long? She had watched over him from afar for years. Her spies had protected him, guarded him, bled for him. A young boy had lost his thumb for spying on Asvin's archery lessons. Two of the Dagger's men had died in the forest. He didn't know about them. He didn't need to know. But he was a nice boy. No dark corners in his heart. He would do. He would have to.

Unaware of anything except the burning memory of the bow in his mind and heart, Asvin walked on, head held high. He knew there were things he didn't know, but he didn't care. The gods would look after him. For he was a Hero. A Chosen One. A Person to Whom Things Happen. Many Things.

12

'Do you really think Danh-Gem will return?' asked Kirin. Maya had smuggled him into Enki Library in the morning and they had pored over books on ravians all day.

'It all depends on whether he thought he was a Dark Lord or not,' said Maya.

They were strolling down Lost Street with Spikes. Lost Street was so called because normal people never went there unless they were lost, and most of the things that were lost, stolen, robbed or left behind went to Lost Street before they found their new owners. It was considered an achievement to walk through the whole of Lost Street unscathed.

Kirin went there quite often, though. This was because a lot of herbs and chemicals that were magical or dangerous (and often both) were sold on Lost Street, in seedy little shops run by asurs. Of course, it was all illegal, like the weapons stores, the smuggled goods counters, the 'hotels' and the famous asur gambling joint, Your Money And Your Life, Haha. The only legitimate enterprises on Lost Street were an auction house and some law firms.

After the Stuff started becoming popular, Kirin hadn't been able to meet the demand with Maya's supplies alone. Lost Street had gained a new customer, and a good one— one who paid for whatever he bought, and didn't come into a shop with a bunch of club-wielding pashans.

'What do you mean, Dark Lord or not?'

'Well, everyone knows Dark Lords come back. They are killed, then they spend some time hanging around without bodies, generally as dark shadows in places full of dark shadows anyway—it's called camouflage—and then they return, greater and more terrible than ever before, and so on.'

'So if he returns he's a Dark Lord, and the only way we can tell is if he returns?'

'Yes.'

'Thanks.'

'Well, you're the one who was around when it happened, remember?'

'I wish I remembered.'

'But seriously, Kirin, you should tell my father. He knows more about ravians than anybody else. And you can't just sit on a secret like this. You may have forgotten why you're here, but you can't have been left behind by accident. Not the son of the Demon-hunter. There has to be some legend, somewhere. And if anyone knows, it'll be my father. Maybe we should look at the Untranslatable Books. They're in a small room on the lowest level. You know, the one with the Red Phoenix guard.'

'The fat Red Phoenix guard?'

'I know—why do they even bother having him— apparently it's a matter of tradition.'

'But won't we be wasting our time? And don't you need special permission?'

'Kirin, I get you into the library nearly every day. In case you've forgotten, that is strictly forbidden. We might be wasting our time, though. Coming back to the point, you should tell my father. We should go and meet him, wherever he is. I mean, what if, hypothetically speaking, you *were* the hero of the Simoqin Prophecy? You know, last ravian striking the last blow of the ravian war, avenging his parents and all that.'

'Don't be ridiculous, Maya.'

'All right, then, so that *was* ridiculous. But there must be *something*.'

'Poor Simoqin. The hero of his dream walking into an asur shop.'

'I still don't like all this dealing with asurs, Kirin.'

'Don't be silly. A lot of them are perfectly nice. And the city wouldn't run without them. They do all the jobs no one else will.'

They entered Hooba's Emporium, the dark little shop where Kirin got his supplies. Spikes waited outside.

Hooba shuffled forward, rubbing his bony fingers together. 'Hello Kirin, end how is everything?' He looked at Maya suspiciously and spoke to Kirin in Asurian. 'Why did you bring the woman? These are troubled times.'

'It's all right. She's more dangerous than any of *your* friends, and Spikes is outside,' replied Kirin in the same guttural tongue.

Maya had been surprised and a little shocked when Kirin had learnt how to speak the language of the asurs, but had quickly accepted that it was only ancient and deep-seated prejudice that had prevented her from learning it herself. But then Kirin was like that. Perhaps it came from not being human, she thought. She was picking up the language from him now, though her fellow spellbinders, who generally thought of asurs as moving spell targets, would have been shocked.

'Whet'll it be, then? The usuel?' asked Hooba in his strangely accented Koli. Kirin nodded, and put some coins on the counter. Hooba produced a little bulging bag. Kirin took it, and didn't even look inside, which was sheer stupidity when dealing with an asur, thought Maya. But Kirin always said Hooba wouldn't cheat him. And Hooba never did.

Not that Hooba was some pearl among asurs or anything like that. He was a low-down, dirty, smelly, violent, foul-tongued, back-stabbing, two-timing asur. But he never cheated Kirin. Perhaps it was out of fear of Spikes, or perhaps it was because Kirin had learnt the asur language. Whatever it was, it worked.

The sound of an asur voice drifted in from outside.

'Get out of here fast, Kirin,' said Hooba, reverting to Asurian. 'Trouble is heading this way.'

'What's happened?'

'You wouldn't understand. Go.'

'I'm perfectly safe, Hooba. Everyone on this street knows Spikes and me. And speak in Koli. How many times do I have to tell you Maya's a friend?'

The voice was heard again. It was slightly raised, as if it was demanding something.

'Yes, but the trouble I'm speeking of isn't from this street. There ere more of us moving in every dey. The hordes from Imokoi seem to be shifting here slowly. The sewers ere filling up. There's en ermy of esurs gethering in Kol, end I don't like it. No one on this street likes it. The king is coming, Kirin.'

'The king?'

'King Leer, Supreme Commender of the Divine Ermy.'

'The Divine Army?' asked Maya.

'Thet's whet we cell our forces,' said Hooba a little sheepishly. 'Es if you humens don't do it ell the time.'

There was a scream outside, then a thud. The screaming stopped.

'Kirin?' called Spikes from outside. 'Could you come outside for a bit?'

There seemed to be many asurs outside. They were all shouting.

'Get ewey from my shop!' hissed Hooba. 'The northern esurs ere moving in, don't you understand? They don't went to cleen sewers like us Kol rets! Some of them hev never been out of the mounteins before! They come here looking for trouble! End they fight ell dey! End you bring e women to my shop!'

He practically pushed Kirin and Maya out of the shop, and banged the door shut. They could hear him locking and barring the door. Then they looked around them, and saw why.

Lost Street was almost empty, which meant Big Trouble. Usually it meant gang warfare, or an asur-human brawl, or an International Friendly Football match in Kol Stadium. One way or another, when Lost Street was empty, it meant serious injuries all around and a plague of tax collectors' and moneylenders' enforcers the next morning.

The street was empty, that is, except for the ring of asurs that had formed around Spikes, who was standing in the middle, a stunned asur at his feet.

They weren't your average city-bred, black-leather-clad, vroomer-imitating, I-clean-sewers-now-but-what-I'd-*really*-like-to-be-is-a-blacksmith asurs. They were a little taller, about chest-high. Their bodies were covered with dirty, straggly white hair, and their bloated pinkish-grey bellies protruded from under their chain mail vests. City asurs usually dyed their body hair in bright colours. Hooba's, for instance, was green. But the ones around Spikes were danavs from the mountains of Imokoi. They had vacant pupil-less grey eyes, long pointy ears, big jaws, thick drooling lips and small, sharp teeth. Their claws were long and grey (the city asurs always painted theirs). The danavs wore helmets with horns on either side, Skuan fashion. They were all yelling challenges at Spikes and pointing daggers or spears at him.

The sky was full. The vroomer gangs were hovering in the sky, yelling encouragement and abuse at the people on the street and at each other. They were like vultures, thought Maya. They somehow *knew* where the big fights would be.

Most doors on the street were closed. All the windows were, however, open, and there were heads poking out of each one. Living in Lost Street meant free entertainment all the year round. Unless you were performing for this knowledgeable and faithful audience in which case, it usually meant very expensive treatment. If you survived, that is.

There were about thirty asurs around Spikes, more than enough to deal with any pashan. But then, was Spikes a pashan? Even Kirin didn't know.

The asurs hadn't noticed Kirin and Maya yet. But the vroomers had. Three vroomers pointed their vroomsticks at them and zoomed down from the sky, hovering at eye level around them.

'So, is the happy happy couple done on the little bitty city tour?' said one, leering at Maya. All three vroomers were clad in black cow-hide kurtas. Maya looked at them with interest. Their heads were shaved, with a single streak of hair down the middle. Their bodies were covered with tattoos.

On the bed of tattoos they had raised gardens of rings and studs, piercing every possible part of their bodies.

'Now would be a good time to fly away,' Kirin told him.

'Shut up, you. We're talking to the *lady* here. Mmm, a lovely little lady, huh boys?' said the vroomer, sticking out a very pierced tongue.

'Short hair, *just* the way I like it, a-ha. She's *wild*,' said another.

'Dark and *delicious*. Wanna come for a little ride, girlie?' asked the third.

Maya looked at them. She laughed aloud. Her laugh was deep and very, very loud. 'You're funny,' she told them.

The ring of asurs was beginning to inch a little closer to Spikes.

'And very, very stupid,' she continued.

The vroomers pulled out their crossbows.

Maya smiled and held out her hand. She thought about fire.

With a little *whump*, a blue fireball appeared over Maya's outstretched palm.

The vroomers looked at it for a few seconds, then at Maya's warm smile. 'Spellbinder!' roared one. They zoomed up to safety, amidst jeers and catcalls from the other vroomers.

'If you're thinking about saying anything about playing with fire, don't,' grinned Kirin. 'Do you need anything, Spikes?' he called.

'I'm all right. But maybe you should tell these asurs to back off before they get hurt.'

'They speak a different language,' called Hooba from a first-floor window behind them. 'You'll need an interpreter.'

One of the asurs in the ring, a particularly ugly, bowlegged one, stepped forward. The rest fell silent. The leader shouted at Spikes.

'What did he say?' Maya asked Hooba.

'He seid, "Ell those who stend in the peth of the Glorious Revolution will be shown no mercy!"'

'The Glorious Revolution? Is that a gang?'

'No. It's e glorious revolution. When esurs overthrow the yoke of human oppression.'

'I see.'

Spikes seemed unmoved. The leader looked at him, and decided he was standing in the path of the Glorious Revolution and should be shown no mercy. He barked out an order.

'What was that?' asked Maya.

'He seid "Cherge!"'

'What? Speak up.'

'He seid "CHERGE!"'

The asurs charged. And stopped.

With a smooth, silken sound, Spikes had unsheathed his claws. They stood out of his hands, incredibly long, incredibly sharp. With little clicks, the spikes along his spine came out.

The asurs looked at one another. Some took a step or two backwards. This wasn't going the way it was supposed to. They'd picked on Spikes thinking he was a short pashan. Fighting pashans wasn't supposed to be like this. You were supposed to charge, fifteen at a time, jump on the pashan, bring him down to the ground and stab at the eyes and the joints. Claws and spikes weren't in the script.

'Put your claws in, Spikes. Play fair,' said Kirin.

'Oh, very well,' grumbled Spikes.

The leader yelled again.

'"Charge!" again, right?' asked Maya.

'Yes,' said Hooba.

The asurs were evidently a little hard of hearing. They shuffled their feet uneasily. The leader couldn't take it any more. He charged, his spear streaking towards Spikes's head.

Spikes swatted him with one hand. The asur flew several feet, hit a wall, landed and was still.

Three more ran at him, screaming.

Swish.

Dhup.

Swish swish.

Dhup dhup.

Another asur shouted.

'Still "Charge!"?' enquired Maya.

'No. That was "Flee!"'

The asurs fled.

There were hisses, jeers and disappointed shouts all over Lost Street. The vroomers zoomed off. Doors opened and business resumed. Everyone looked a little grouchy. The Big Fight had been a washout.

Maya, Kirin and Spikes walked on.

'What were we talking about?'

'Going to meet my father.'

'Where is he, anyway?'

'I think he's on Bolvudis island. He last wrote about six months ago.'

'What's Bolvudis like?'

'I don't know. None of the other spellbinders have been there. Actors seem to be going there a lot, though. I wonder what he's doing. When he wrote, he said he was studying bunyips, but I know that's not all.'

'Let's see these Untranslatable Books of yours—these are Danh-Gem's books from Imokoi, right?'

'Yes. Though scholars have tried to translate them for years, and failed, and languages aren't my strong point.'

'Let's try them anyway. If we can't understand them, I'll go to Bolvudis.'

'*We'll* go to Bolvudis.'

An asur crouching in the dark shadows in an alley crept out as they passed, clutching a dagger. He ran up behind Spikes and leapt. Spikes never even turned around. His arm moved a bit, there was a *crack*, and the asur ran, clutching his arm and yelping.

'It's been one of Spikes's most peaceful visits to Lost Street,' said Kirin. 'Only six injuries, and no deaths.'

'What do we do now? Frags again?' enquired Maya.

'Where else?'

They walked on.

Back in Hooba's Emporium, Hooba was sweating profusely and trembling with fear.

'They were not my friends, your Highness,' he stuttered. 'They were customers. Good customers.'

'That thing which fought my soldiers—what was it? A pashan?' came a voice out of the shadows.

'I do not know, your Highness. I don't think so. He's too short, and he has claws and things. Also, he speaks like a human.'

'The Glorious Revolution is coming soon, Hooba. We will raze Kol to the ground and rebuild the towers of Imokoi. Danh-Gem is coming. You city-born filth will have to take sides.'

'I am your Majesty's most faithful servant.'

'We shall see, Hooba, we shall see. Maybe I will soon ask you to prove your loyalty.'

'It will be an honour, your Highness.'

King Leer watched as his bodyguards broke a few things in the shop. Then they left.

13

'I dentify yourself,' rumbled Mati.
'It's me, Mati,' said the Civilian, climbing down the steps to his chamber. She had brought Ojanus with her this time, and the amphisbaena was coiled around her head, its two heads standing out, like horns. 'The key to the Treasure Chamber, please.'

Mati gave her a huge key and a small Alocactus pot, and Ojanus, who was not allowed inside the treasure room, slithered off and wound himself lovingly around the golem. The Civilian unlocked the door to the right, entered, and locked the door from the inside.

The Treasure Chamber was packed with precious items. Gold, silver, pearls and precious stones of every shape, size and colour gleamed in the white light. There were weapons, armour, crowns, sceptres, artefacts and jewellery of every possible size, design and weight. Even the greatest dragon of all, Qianzai the magnificent, had never gathered this large a hoard.

The Civilian walked to the middle of the room.

'Are you awake, old friend?'

'Yes,' croaked the unwaba.

The Civilian looked quickly at the place where the sound was coming from. She looked hard, but the unwaba, the oldest chameleon, could not be seen.

'How are you? All right, but I sleep nearly all the time. Do the pearls taste good? Yes. There is something I need from you today, old friend. What is it? You know, old friend. Yes, I know, but I always say that,' said the unwaba, who, being all-knowing, always said everybody's lines in all his conversations.

The unwaba was the most powerful oracle-prophet-seer in the world, all the more powerful because no one except the rulers of Kol knew of his existence. He had lived there since the room had been built, and was very, very old and frail. A sudden burst of sound or light could kill him. The Civilian never came to see him more than once a year, and only when in great need.

It was always very frustrating talking to the unwaba. He knew all the answers, but generally fell asleep before he got to the really important ones. The Civilian opened her mouth to ask a question, and the unwaba started again.

'I'll be brief, old friend. Is Danh-Gem coming back? Yes, he is. Is Asvin the hero of the Simoqin Prophecies? He could be. If he can walk through the Mirror, he is. How do I train him? Your plan is a good one. The vaman and the spellbinder can do it. Can I stop Danh-Gem's return? No. Why? It's very simple, really . . .'

The unwaba, wherever he was, had fallen asleep. The Civilian stood in silence for some time. She was very annoyed. The unwaba would not wake up again for a year, and he had not told her much, except that Danh-Gem would return, which she had suspected anyway. She had known for long that many believed he was really coming back. Now she was certain he would.

The unwaba had been born in Vrihataranya. For centuries he had lived in the forest, contemplating the nature of the Universe, and at some point of time had realized he had prophetic powers. He had spent centuries predicting the weather and explaining the food chain to ungrateful animals, who then went ahead to eat or be eaten.

The unwaba's peaceful if pointless existence had been rudely disturbed by humans long before the Age of Terror. When Prince Amrit the Almighty, another younger Sun of Avranti, tired of explaining to the colonists from Ventelot that they could not civilize a land far older and richer than their own, had raised an army and driven the knights of Ventelot out of Avranti, there had been a huge battle at the edge of the Forest. The unwaba, annoyed at being woken up, for he had loved sleeping in cool shadows even then, had slipped out of his tree and made his way through the blood and gore to Amrit's chariot. He had spoken reproachful words to Amrit, and Amrit, falling prey to common error, had assumed that the little voice he had heard in his head was divine, and not that of the lizard wandering around on his crown. Amrit had stared at the dying and the dead around him, and had been filled with remorse. He had burst into tears, thanked the gods for saving his soul and ordered his men to stop fighting and spend their lives in peaceful meditation and prayer.

The soldiers of Avranti, obedient to a fault, had laid down their weapons, and the knights of Ventelot, the few who were still alive, had begun to butcher them. Amrit, however, thinking that the gods themselves had spoken to him, decided he would not fight. It was then that the unwaba, realizing he should not have said anything until after the battle was over, spoke to Amrit again. The divine words Amrit heard on the battlefield were recorded in the most lyrical, moving epic poem ever written, the *Why War*. The poem was as long as an average battle, was divided into four sections, and was regarded as a holy text in Avranti.

In reality the unwaba had said, 'Stop bawling and fight, idiot.'

The tale had grown somewhat in the telling.

The rest, as they say, was history. Amrit drove the armies of Ventelot back to Ventelot, drove the Psomedeans back to Psomedea, destroyed the Hudlumm hordes and established the kingdom of Kol. Kol went on to become the cultural and financial capital of the world. Amrit established the University of Enki, and, heeding the Voice of A God he heard from time to time, made peace with his neighbours (a peace that his neighbours were only too willing to keep, since Kol had the mightiest army in the world), and opened the gates of Kol to peace-loving (and luxury-loving) people from all over the world.

The unwaba had found he was suited to city life, and discovered that nothing tasted as good as pearls, if your teeth were sharp enough. Many years later, when Amrit, heeding the divine voice again, had given up his life of worldly pleasure and gone to Xi'en (where, under the name of the Shanti-Joddha, he had started a new religion based on peace and love that was now the official religion of the Xi'en Empire), his crown had been laid to rest in the Treasure Chamber.

The Civilian smiled to herself. It was nice to think that so many people were living in harmony because the all-knowing unwaba had thought the cold comfort of the Kol treasure chamber was what would give him true peace and quiet.

The unwaba had been discovered quite by accident, by a former Chief Civilian, when it had woken up and said, 'What year is this? What's that noise? Oh no! He's found me!' years ago. Since then generations of Civilians had tried to keep it awake but had failed.

But Temat did not need prophecies and words of wisdom to run Kol. She just liked having her facts confirmed. That was something that happened often to people with minds like hers. She smiled again. She didn't know if there was only one unwaba in the world. But she did know that the calm voice in *her* head was her own, and not that of a god or an old omniscient little chameleon.

14

Somewhere in the desert of Al-Ugobi, the great desert that covered most of western Artaxerxia, a solitary traveller and his camel struggled through a blinding sandstorm. The young man's name was Hasan. He was sixteen years old, and had set out with his camel to seek his fortune out east, in Amurabad, the Artaxerxian capital. His brother, Ali, had left a year ago—he had wanted to be an actor. It had been a whole day since the last oasis, the sun had been shining as if it had a personal grudge against him, and Hasan was already thoroughly sick of life in general and sand in particular.

The great dunes were shifting slowly, and the air was full of hard, biting, blistering sand. As Hasan crouched, he saw a sudden flash as something glimmered golden and was hidden again. Hasan ran to the dune, heedless of the stinging sandstorm, and plunged his hand in.

The jinn awoke. It was suddenly very hot. Yes, something was deliberately rubbing the walls of its lamp. It yawned. It wondered how long it had slept. Strangely enough, this time it didn't even remember going to sleep. That was odd. The last thing it remembered was watching a particularly good belly dancer in Amurabad. Well, time to get up, it thought.

Hasan rubbed harder, the sandstorm completely forgotten in his sudden, wild joy. A jinn-lamp! This was the stuff dreams were made of! Everyone said a jinn-lamp hadn't been seen for hundreds of years! Hasan saw the future. He saw an almond-eyed, veiled princess—why one, a hundred!—gold, fame, scimitars, subtle wines, flowing silk robes, flying carpets, pliant, amazingly beautiful and barely clad belly dancers surrounding him and pressing ripe grapes into his mouth as music played and he lay back on soft, soft cushions . . .

'What?' asked the jinn, rubbing its eyes.

Hasan looked at it. He'd expected a jolly, fat man with a curly beard and a big turban who would start singing songs about how he would be Hasan's best friend. The jinn was . . . well, it didn't look very *friendly*, for a start. It was a shape, a large, muscular shape, trailing off into smoke near the mouth of the lamp. Sand blasted into it and gave it an outline, a large, muscular outline. Its eyes glowed a brilliant, blinding white. But Hasan didn't care what it looked like. He laughed aloud in excitement. Three wishes! What would he wish for?

'I suppose I can't wish for more wishes,' he said.

The jinn got used to the sand. It had been a long time. It noticed Hasan. Good-looking boy, though a bit thin, it thought. Not as good-looking as the little belly dancer, though. The jinn preferred girls. They were prettier, softer, they smelled good, they fought less.

They *tasted* better.

It was *hungry*.

The boy was saying something.

'Wishes?' asked the jinn. It noticed the camel. Camel bones were *good* . . .

'My three wishes!' said Hasan. 'You will grant me three wishes, won't you?'

The jinn thought for a while. 'Why?' it asked.

'That's what jinns do! Don't you know that? Everyone knows that!'

Three wishes, thought the jinn. What was he talking about?

The camel took a look at the jinn. It started to run.

'I don't know what you mean,' said the jinn. 'Why would I want to grant you three wishes?'

'I freed you! From the lamp!' Hasan looked around wildly for his camel. It was gone.

The jinn had had enough of this nonsense. Freed him from his own lamp, indeed! It flew up in the sky, caught up with the running camel and ate it.

Aaaaaah, fresh camel. *Very* good.

It was still hungry.

It looked around, found Hasan, wide-eyed and trembling, trying to hide behind a dune, and ate him too.

Why? Why had he wanted wishes? He was quite juicy, though.

Then it found the lamp—the handle was sticking out of the swirling sand—and flew inside. Time for a nice nap.

The dunes shifted again in the howling sandstorm. Sand covered the beautifully carved golden lamp.

Inside it the jinn was having trouble sleeping.

What wishes? Why wishes?

Another, very disturbing thought struck the jinn and kept it awake for a long time.

Why *three*?

15

Under the streets of north Kol, a giant tubeworm sped off down a tunnel. The platform was empty, except for a crow loitering on the iron railing, and a man. A blond, bearded giant of a man, with a two-handed sword in a huge scabbard slung on his back. His helmet had horns on it. He wore leather armour and was carrying a large rolled-up object. He vaulted over the railing, off the platform into the tunnel, his long hair flying backwards in the wind rushing down the tunnel. He walked down the tunnel, ignoring the slime the tubeworm had left in its wake. His huge boots made squelching noises as he disappeared into the darkness.

The man who had been following him waited for a while, and then walked on to the platform. That Skuan is insane, he thought, if another worm arrived he would be crushed. But it would be foolish to follow the wily Bjorkun into the darkness, where he could be waiting, broadsword unsheathed. You didn't want to take on a Skuan lord in the dark. You didn't want to take on a Skuan lord anywhere. They were strong, the raiders of the north—strong, cold, vicious and barbaric. And Bjorkun, if the stories were true, was the worst of them all. Pirate, robber, plunderer. Of course, Skuanmark was at peace with Kol—everyone was at peace with Kol. But everyone knew Bjorkun for the bloodthirsty brigand that he was.

The man waited for a quarter of an hour. Bjorkun didn't return. Another tubeworm, nearly empty—for it was very late—arrived at the platform. A few people got off. The worm left.

Well, he's not in the tunnel, thought the man. Must have walked to the next stop, I'll never catch up with him now. Better to get back on the street, walk to the next worm-stop and try to pick up the trail from there. Bjorkun must have realized he was being followed. In which case I'm lucky to be alive. Of course, if I'm really lucky he's lying dead under the slime in the tunnel, but I don't think so. Not Bjorkun.

He looked at the crow, sitting on the railing staring down the tunnel. Stupid bird. He walked off hurriedly, towards the next worm-stop.

After a few minutes, Captain Forty-four 'Yahoo', having made sure the man had left, called out hoarsely, 'All clear!'

Bjorkun flew out of the tunnel on a carpet. 'Where is he?'

'Follow me,' said Yahoo.

They flew over the platform, up the stairs and into the city. Soon they were flying high over the houses of north Kol, heading eastwards.

'He should have just met me in Lost Street,' growled Bjorkun.

'Head for that bell tower.'

As they passed the tower, Yahoo let out a single, harsh croak.

A black shape streaked through the air from the roof of the tower and landed neatly on the carpet.

'Nice jump,' said Bjorkun.

'I have much to tell you,' said Bali.

In a hole in a palace wall there lived a rabbit. It is a well-known fact that rabbits, by twitching their sweet little noses in an endearing manner, can sense danger, even when danger is far away. It is also well known that on sensing danger, a rabbit always runs.

What made this particular rabbit different was the fact that he ran *towards* danger.

This rabbit was fierce, swift and deadly. He was a member of the elite Red Phoenix Guard. He was one of the best bodyguards in the world. His name was Bunz.

Steel-Bunz.

The Civilian had presented him to Asvin. Asvin called him Fluffy.

Steel-Bunz was enjoying his new assignment. There hadn't been any biting to do so far. Asvin and Amloki had left the palace with him at dawn and flown around Kol all day. They had been to many museums, seen an ancient Psomedean play at the Academy of Fine Arts, fed pigeons in King Amrit's Park, walked around Ossus Square, where the huge statue of Ossus of Kol stood proudly, gazing southwards. After the sun had set, they had been to see the fireworks in Little Xi'en and then flown back to the palace. Amloki had been yawning for more than an hour—Asvin hadn't blamed him—the little khudran had been walking and talking all day. So when he had asked for permission to retire, Asvin had readily agreed.

This is one of the nicest bedrooms in the whole palace. Wonder why he's so important, Steel-Bunz thought, looking at Asvin, who was sleeping peacefully. As he paced the room silently, he saw lights in the east wing, where the Civilian lived. It's very late by human standards. Does she never sleep?

The Civilian was in her own bedroom, staring at a magnificent portrait of a fat smiling woman. After a while, she walked up to it and tapped the right side of the frame casually. A tall mirror on the other side of the room slid back, revealing a narrow, dark corridor. The Civilian entered it.

She was in a tiny room, which contained two chairs and a small table with a single flickering candle on it. She sat down, her shadow filling the room, and waited.

Captain Rupaisa, the Civilian's personal bodyguard, was sitting in the library opposite the Civilian's bedroom, reading a book of poems by the Bard of Potolpur. On her right, a large window looked out towards the city. The Palace grounds, of course, were a no-flying zone, and Rupaisa, occasionally looking out of the window, saw heavily armed Red Phoenix guards skimming by on their special Harpoon vroomsticks, looking for assassins and other intruders. The Palace was safe, thought Rupaisa, and returned to her book.

The Silver Dagger entered the room through the window, noiselessly. He jumped down to the floor, drawing in a blackened rope and a black cloth-covered grappling hook.

'Hello,' said Rupaisa, without turning around.

'Is she waiting?'

'Yes.'

'I was hoping she would be late,' said the Dagger, looking at the Captain of the Red Phoenix. She was from Durg, like the Civilian, and she looked every inch a Durgan, tall, athletic, proud, in her maroon and black uniform. Her sword, he noted appreciatively, was drawn. She rose and smiled at him.

'I was too. And how have you been?'

'Busy. And so have you, I hear. How many would-be assassins this week?'

'Four. But only one got as far as me.'

The Dagger looked at her. 'Can you . . .' he started, but then paused. 'I'd better go.'

'Yes.'

He started towards a bookcase. He paused, and looked at her. 'But then again . . .'

A little later, a bookcase slid back, and the Dagger disappeared.

Rupaisa returned to her book, a strange smile playing over her lips.

A little later, a wall slid back and the Civilian said, 'Well?'

The Dagger sat down. 'They have returned. There seems to be a new problem.'

The Civilian sat back. 'Tell me.'

'Before I come to that—the asur situation is graver than we thought. Apparently the pests have a king. His name is Leer and he is in Kol now. Bands of northern asurs, the danavs, are slipping past the checkposts and into the sewers.'

'An underground movement, in short.'

'It's no laughing matter. Right now they're sticking to defacing monuments and the occasional robbery, but there will be riots soon, I'm sure of it. An asur rebellion is not what we need now. I could, um, remove the king, of course, but that wouldn't really help; they would simply crown someone else. And they seem to be absolutely sure that Danh-Gem will be reappearing soon. I, um, interrogated one yesterday— they don't know *how* he's coming back. But they do know that the world is getting more magical. I think you should start evicting asurs who don't have work permits.'

'I will do nothing of the sort,' snapped the Civilian. 'If I do that, there will be protests, followed by riots and a mass migration to Imokoi, where they can build their armies in peace with Koli money. Besides, the city needs asurs. It is the asurs, ironically, that keep the city clean. Let the danavs come. We have room to spare. The city asurs are far from happy about the sudden appearance of their northern cousins. This whole asur movement's sole aim is to provoke me into angering the asurs, and thus uniting them. There will come a point when the city asurs will drive the newcomers out. And remember, the city asurs are the ones with the money. For the asurs to be a threat, they need weapons, armour and wide spaces to run around in. Leer, and whoever sent him, cannot build an army in the sewers of Kol.'

'I see. And who is behind this asur movement? Artaxerxia?'

'I don't think so. The Sultan gains nothing by aiding asurs. And he does not play childish games—not with me. He wants to control Kol, not cripple it. It is Avranti he wants to destroy. Artaxerxia will not take sides unless Danh-Gem really returns. Perhaps not even then.'

'But they served him in the Age of Terror.'

'They gained Elaken in return, and were promised Avranti. But this Sultan is no fanatic. He may aid Danh-Gem's allies in secret, but will not raise his own armies until Avranti gets involved. No . . . Skuanmark is behind this.'

'Which is why that Skuan cut-throat Bjorkun is in the

city,' said the Dagger grimly. 'He entered, in secret, three days ago.'

'He should be watched.'

'He is being watched.'

'But not, I think, by the Silver Phalanx. In spite of all our efforts, we have not been able to uncover the plot to raise Danh-Gem, and now it is time to prepare for his coming. I have certain . . . shall we say . . . assignments for your men in Artaxerxia and in the north. And now, tell me—what is this news you speak of? Why did your men return late?'

'Manticore,' said the Dagger simply. 'The man-lions walk again.'

Very few people had seen the Civilian look alarmed. The Dagger was one of them.

'Where?' she asked.

'Vrihataranya,' he replied. 'My men were riding back from Avranti, and they found a vanar lying on the road, his tail stretched across it.'

'Vanars? Where did they enter this tale?'

'I do not know. This vanar was a young baboon-man named Ulluk. He had been pierced by a poisoned dart, and was dying. Hihuspix asked him what had happened, and he said he had been following a lion with a man's head, three rows of fangs and a tail that shot darts. Hihuspix tried to heal him, but could not. This Ulluk said some other things as well. He cursed Hihuspix and all humans, said the vanars would raise Danh-Gem, and that his uncle would rule Kol one day. Then he died.'

'His uncle?'

The Dagger shrugged.

'I see. And what was Hihuspix's report? Did he meet the manticores?'

The Dagger was silent. 'Hihuspix has not returned. He went into the forest to investigate,' he said finally.

'I see. Well, this is news indeed. Manticores in the forest, shooting vanars who plan to raise Danh-Gem. Another of those . . . unfortunate side-effects of the increase in magic, do you think? Who knows. This was not planned.'

'Should we try to kill the manticores?'

'Manticores are harder to kill than dragons. And the manticores, as far as I remember, served the ravians. Therefore, we will do nothing. There is much here that I do not understand. I will speak to the spellbinder, and see what he thinks. But I suspect the reappearance of manticores is something the allies of Danh-Gem should be worrying about, not us. The vanars, on the other hand . . . I had not considered them. That was a mistake. Yes, something will have to be done about the vanars. Especially this "uncle" who will rule Kol one day.'

They were both silent for some time. The candle had almost burned out.

'What do you think of our hero?' asked the Civilian. 'Is he adequately trained?'

'By Avranti standards, yes. He shoots well, and his swordplay is adequate. He fought well in the forest, when we attacked his guards. But he would not last two minutes against me. He needs an experienced tutor. Also, his knowledge of the world outside Avranti is very limited. We should continue with the original plan.'

'Is he attracting attention?'

'Just his looks, but that cannot be helped. No one has recognized him yet. The spies in the castle see him wandering around harmlessly with a little khudran, and assume he is another of your . . . friends. If they find him alone, they will try to buy him to assassinate you, he will react angrily and will be found out. But they will not find him alone.'

'I would have sent Asvin to Hero School,' said the Civilian softly. 'The School is not what it used to be, but he would have learnt some things there. But that is not possible now. He would be recognized. Are you sure the vaman— Gaam, is it?—can be trusted, though?'

'Yes. He has helped me before . . . unknowingly, of course. And we cannot keep Asvin in the city—sooner or later he will be found out. The only thing is, I do not want to go with them. I think the vaman and the spellbinder will be adequate protection. I could send a few of my men too.'

'Let me put this in perspective, my friend. This is probably the most important task you have undertaken yet. We are sending the young man whom we think is the hero to be trained by the best teachers possible. This will involve sending him on very, very dangerous quests. We thought the last one would manage on his own if he was indeed the hero. He died, and so did the one before him. This time, we cannot afford to take any chances. I want you to be there yourself, to watch over him and protect him.'

'And what if he is not the hero?'

'Then we will have run out of time, and will have to defeat Danh-Gem with whatever we have.'

'And if he is the hero, and I keep him alive until he is ready, you will remember what I asked for.'

'We will discuss that later.'

'No.'

'Very well. Listen to me, then. You cannot retire now. You are far too young, and Kol needs the Silver Dagger. I like to say no one is indispensable, but you come close. And I can see interesting times ahead. Very interesting. We will give Kol a hero, a hero Kol will never forget. I will send messages to the spellbinder, the vaman and the girl. As for your retirement, we will discuss that later. For now, I shall go and get some rest.'

The Civilian left.

'I need some rest too,' said the Dagger. 'A year or two.' But even as he said the words he realized how pathetic he sounded. All the more so because the candle had burned out.

The Dagger sat there in silence for a while. Then he climbed out into the library, took out his rope and grappling hook and swung out of the window. I could have used the stairs, he thought bitterly. I could have worn a disguise or just *walked* into her room. But no, it has to be this way.

Two crows sat on a tower and watched the sun rise.

'How did it go, man?' asked Captain Forty-five 'Maverick'.

'Very boring,' said Yahoo. 'First, they talked about asurs. Bali doesn't want to work with them. Bjorkun said it was absolutely necessary. Personally, I agree with Bali—those asurs *eat* crows. They eat anything they get. Imagine! How uncouth!'

'*We* eat anything we get,' said Maverick, perplexed.

'That's different,' explained Yahoo. 'Anyway, you were right. They don't seem to be heading towards the Revolution at all. Bali told Bjorkun all about the blasted pashan, Bjorkun said he would find out about it, probably from the asurs.'

'And when are we, like, invading Kol?'

'They didn't even talk about that. They kept talking about stealing books from some library.'

'Books? Stealing *books*? Yes, that'll scare the people of Kol, all right. Are they pigeons?'

'I don't know. It sounded all hush-hush, though. Sounds like Danh-Gem had some books in Imokoi that the asurs gave to the spellbinders of Kol when they surrendered.'

'They took books from asurs? What were they, like, stupid?'

'Bali said that too. But Bjorkun said these were very powerful books, and that the spellbinders thought they could use them to help people and things like that. But they could never understand what was written in the books, the idiots.'

'So why are they going to steal these books if no one can understand them?'

'Bjorkun said he hoped these books would have spells which would raise Danh-Gem. If they can read the books somehow, it would be goodbye Kol and we'd be kings of the air, yes!'

'Hey, that would be big, man. But if these books are, like, so important and all, won't they be tough to steal?'

'Yes. Bjorkun wants Bali to steal them since he's being followed and no one knows Bali is here. Bali didn't like that much. Then Bjorkun said he's found a back way into the library—he caught a magician and made him tell or something like that—and he's going to get Bali in.'

'So they're going to steal these books they don't know if they can read, and if they read them, they don't know if they can bring back Danh-Gem, but they hope they will. And that's why they came here.'

'Yes.'

'That's crazy, man.'

'I know. Sometimes I feel like Bali's just using us to find things out, and that the Revolution won't happen at all.'

'That's, like, negative thoughts, man.'

'I know. Don't tell Kraken, he'd kill me.'

'But you know what? I think you're right, Yahoo. We've got to do something about this.'

'Yes. The Revolution has to happen. Otherwise, we crows, we'll be reduced to eating garbage.'

'We *do* eat garbage, man,' said Maverick, perplexed.

'That's different,' explained Yahoo.

16

*E*nki, *Bearmonth 22nd, 4 a.m.*

Proposals for marriage and related activities 4, Number of times caught self looking in mirror, thinking of appearance etc. 3, Dragonjuices 0, Non-lethal drinks 2 (good, am not alcoholic), Lechers quelled 14, Lustful thoughts 2, Interesting facts about ravians many, Answers to unanswered questions 0, Magic 7/10.

Lost my diary again so here I am starting a new one. I'm hopeless. But went to Frags, cured Triog's headache. Poor thing never knows which head has it. Forgotten my New Year's Resolutions, should write them down. Anyway, have broken all of them except the don't-need-a-man one. We played mindball again; Kirin won today. He's getting really good. Oh damn, that whole thing about him being a ravian was in that diary. Anyway, I'm not likely to forget that. Plus I will probably lose this diary too.

Did some good work on the Intulo Paradox today. Got a letter from father, which ran 'Hello Maya I hear you topped University very good are you going to teach if not you can come here help with my research by the way you can act can't you,' and then two pages about bunyip courtship rituals. At least he's still on Bolvudis. I think I will go there with Kirin—it's been a long time since I last went on a holiday. Will just take a shot at the Untranslatables, though. Made a new decoding spell that I want to try. Of course Ombwiri said it wasn't a code, it was another language. We'll see.

Met Amloki, the Civilian's page, flying around the city with a man in a hood. He said hello very sheepishly and flew away.

Prince Kumirdanga of Potolpur wants to marry me. Wants isn't the word, is willing to make the great sacrifice. He came to Enki, barged into my room and was very eloquent and very romantic. 'After all you have finished your studies and it is time you settled down. You need a husband and I am, let me tell you in confidence, considered to be an excellent catch.' Moron. 'And let me tell you something, you know no one wants to marry spellbinders, especially spellbinders from Durg, as they are often disobedient wives; but I think if you cleaned up you would be adequately beautiful, also your (long pause) figure is, if I may take the liberty of saying so, quite excellent. Yes, you will do. I am willing to be your husband and have you bear my heirs, but you must understand my word is law. Always best to make things clear to spellbinders and Durgan women haha, haha.'

I turned him into a slug. He doesn't look very different, actually. Will change him back if anyone misses him. I hope I don't lose this diary before I forget all about this, because no one is likely to miss him.

Need a husband. Moron. Kumirdanga is now in a little matchbox. I was keeping him in an empty bottle but then I realized he would have seen me changing. I wonder if that would mean anything to a slug. I've thrown his royal robes away. Must remember not to be in the same room as him when I change him back.

I suppose it's something to do with finishing the degree. A lot of people in class are falling in love with one another. It's really sad that most male spellbinders, after all they learn here, want housewives. But then it doesn't matter to me either way. The other girls are experimenting with makeup and jewellery. Revolting. I turned my hair blue today by accident. Tiara saw me and screamed. I told her I was all right, but it turned out she was screaming because she liked it. Now lots of people are wandering around with blue hair. I am a trendsetter, heh heh. Like the time I turned myself bald by accident.

Somehow I get the feeling that Kirin is Simoqin's hero. Everything fits. He came back from the dead, in a manner of speaking, he is of royal blood, he did come to a human city. Spikes isn't half his height, though. But that's Spikes's fault, not Kirin's. I'm glad I found out about him. Can't figure him out at times. The whole Spikes issue is bothering me. How did he just find Kirin? Maybe it really is a coincidence. Stop worrying.

Must clean up my room. What a mess. WHAT a mess. Must stop being lazy sloth-type who tries to get away with magic. Must stop being confused and eccentric and become controlled, authoritative young adult. Must buy new clothes, clean old ones and throw away the ones with larger holes, because people look. Must stop wasting money, especially on liver-burning addictive substances. Must stop laughing loudly at people inside my head. AND outside, i.e. aloud. Must stop flirting with anyone I find mildly attractive. Must stop giggling at stupid things said by, and falling stupidly for, handsome muscle-bound men, as am succumbing to image of hero perpetuated by society which places too much emphasis on physical prowess. Or not. All things considered, am fine the way I am.

I'm glad Kirin is my best friend. Wish I could tell people he's a ravian, at least Tiara, who I think really likes him. Which is not so difficult, he's very funny. Good for Tiara, too—she's growing a brain. She was very angry when she saw us hugging in Frags. Of course she would be shocked if she knew I brought him to the library. And if I mentioned he's more than two hundred years old . . .

Must get some sleep now. I think we will hit the Untranslatables tomorrow. If that doesn't work, then it's off to Bolvudis.

Why did father ask me if I could act?

'A world of magic,' said the Civilian, 'is not a world governed by rules. Of course, there are always rules, but where magic exists, these rules create themselves and change by themselves. Look at Xi'en. They worshipped their dragons and used their magic to bring peace and plenty to the land. Then Danh-Gem stole Tatsu's Gauntlet and wreaked havoc on the whole world, using the same power. Personally, I don't like magic. If I had my way, I would have removed it altogether from the world. Unfortunately, people like me—and I might just be the most powerful ruler in the world—cannot change the world. To change the world, you need a hero.'

Asvin stood and watched her pace the library floor. It was morning, and bright sunlight was streaming in through the window.

The Civilian continued. 'The Bard of Potolpur said of heroes, "Some die mediocre, some lose their mediocrity and some have their mediocrity removed forcefully." Not one of his best lines, perhaps, but true nevertheless.

'But what no one pauses to consider, Asvin, is the fact that heroes are made. Heroes have to be trained, taught and protected. Their minds have to be opened and their deeds have to be recorded. This is done by people the songs do not speak of. The Hero School of Kol was set up during the Age of Terror for this very purpose. They would find the brave, the intelligent, the daring and the simply lucky and teach them what heroism was. Then the Age of Terror passed, the ravians killed Danh-Gem and departed and the world was suddenly a less magical place to be in.

'The Hero School went into a decline, because there were no monsters to slay and no quests to go on. The dragons, everybody's favourite monsters, had disappeared and it wasn't particularly heroic to go looking for their gold. In the end, the vamans tunnelled upwards and took most of the dragon-hoards back below the earth.

'The poets finished off their epics with flourishes and They-lived-happily-ever-afters. But no one lives happily ever after, Asvin. The world passed into the hands of people like the Chief Civilians of Kol—people like me—people who believe not in magic but in money, not in valour and banners but in power and control. Swords are not the sharpest weapons, Asvin, minds are. But when magic grows strong, reason is cast aside and swords may be the only answer.

'But that is not what I have called you here to tell you, Asvin. You have waited patiently, and now I will give you the answers you have been seeking. And I suspect you must already know.'

'This is the year when Danh-Gem is supposed to return,' said Asvin hesitantly. 'And you think I might be the hero Simoqin the ravian spoke of. That is why you had me saved and brought here, and that is why you took me to the Room of Signs.'

'Exactly. All the signs say so. You can wield the Bow of Fire, and Simoqin's prophecy describes you accurately. Of course, I brought you back from the dead and ensured Amloki, who is half your height, brought you to this human city. But I assure you, in later ages, the songs will not sing of that—if you succeed. There are people like me behind every hero. They are called luck, chance and fate because their names are not remembered.'

The room had been quiet before, but the silence was now deafening. Asvin felt as if a giant weight had suddenly been put on his shoulders.

'What do I have to do?' he asked. 'Slay Danh-Gem? How?' He sat down, suddenly feeling very lost.

'Danh-Gem has not risen yet,' said the Civilian. 'But I believe he will. And when he does, it is my task to ensure that you are ready.'

'And you say the songs will not sing of you!' said Asvin. 'Even if what you say is true—if my dreams have come true and I can achieve what you think I might—you will be the true leader of the forces of Good.'

The Civilian took a deep breath. 'Two words I hate,' she said slowly, 'are Good and Evil. Try not to use them, Asvin. They are words for fanatics, not for people of sense and reason. Danh-Gem, in my mind, was not evil. He was a Power. If his forces had won, ravians would be cleaning sewers, or worse, like the asurs are doing today. The historians wanted to call him the Dark Lord, or the Prince of Darkness, or the

Lord of Evil, or The Nameless One, or something equally foolish. Did I say I could not change the world? True, but I can change history. Danh-Gem is now called by his true name and treated with the respect that a great ruler and leader deserves. It does not matter if he was a rakshas. At least, that is what I believe. You will not find words like evil in the history books of Kol.

'Yet ask any asur who the most evil person in the world is, and they will say "Temat of Kol". The same Temat of Kol who allows them to work in a city full of prejudice and hate. They did not follow Danh-Gem in madness or fear. They followed him with joy, and they hope desperately for his return. You have been told, I am sure, that Good always triumphs over Evil. What generally happens is that the losers are called evil after the war is over.'

'Will I be joining this Hero School, then?' said Asvin, not feeling very heroic.

'No. I wish you could, for I myself was a student there years ago. But now the Hero School is not good enough. They train economists, administrators, merchants and accountants, the people who run the world today. And there is also the threat of recognition. I did not tell you, but you were seen when you were coming to Kol. Our . . . friends in the Avranti Embassy have told us that the Ambassador recently received messages asking him to hunt for you in Kol. If you stay in Kol, you will be recognized, and I cannot risk Avranti's displeasure in these turbulent times.

'Besides, if you are indeed the true Hero, there is a place you are destined to go, and it is there that I will send you. It is a small, unknown island called Bolvudis. I will not tell you why now—it is best that the guardian of the island tells you about it himself. You are going to be trained, Asvin.

You are going to be trained as no hero has ever been trained before.'

'Who is going to train me?'

'There is one teacher left in Hero School who remembers the old ways, and tries to teach them to unwilling students. He is a vaman, and his name is Gaam. He will go with you to Bolvudis, and there you will meet Mantric the spellbinder, the guardian of the m . . . of the island. They are to be your teachers, and they will prepare you for the task ahead of you. Amloki will go with you, and assist you in every way. There is another person I intend to send with you. She is Mantric's daughter Maya, the most brilliant young spellbinder in Kol. If magic is to be used against us, we will fight it with magic, and no one will be able to do that better than Maya. She will aid you in your quests and share your adventures.'

'What about the Silver Dagger? Will he not aid us? If I am indeed the hero, should I not meet him?' asked Asvin eagerly.

'The Dagger has other work,' said Temat, looking amused. 'It is quite possible, though, that one of the members of the Silver Phalanx will escort you to Bolvudis. Amloki will meet Gaam and Maya, and arrange a meeting. And as for the Dagger, I will say only this—he will turn up when you least expect him. Because that is his job.'

'I will not let you down,' said Asvin fervently.

'I should hope not. Only time can tell, though. As I told you in the Room of Signs, Asvin, you have become very valuable. I will not wish you luck; apparently your stars have already done so. Leave Kol quickly and quietly— meet Gaam and Maya today and leave tomorrow at dawn—there will be no ceremony, no grand farewell. Learn well, learn fast and prepare yourself. I hope—I trust, that if Danh-Gem ever does return, you will be all we hope you are.'

Asvin's heart was beating wildly and his face was flushed with excitement. Things were moving, moving very fast indeed. He was unaccustomed to a life of leisure, because Things always Happened to him.

'May I ask you something, Lady Temat?' said Asvin, feeling dismissed and scared.

'Certainly.'

'Simoqin the Dreamer made the prophecies to Isara before he died. The ravians knew Danh-Gem was going to return. Could it be that they will return too?'

'No one knows where the ravians went, Asvin. And know this—no matter how great and noble the ravians were, they were, like all other living beings, fundamentally concerned with themselves. If they left the world seeking a better one, I do not think they will return, for their war with Danh-Gem was to avenge the deaths of Simoqin and other ravians, not to vanquish 'Evil' or even protect humans. Psomedea and Ventelot had fallen long before the ravians joined the War. If Danh-Gem returns, will we see ravians again? That is another question only time can answer, for the books are silent. We will wait and see.'

17

'And speaking of ravian powers, have you ever tried controlling minds?' asked Maya as she and Kirin walked down the stairs towards the lowest level of the library.

The library was mostly empty—classes were in full swing at Enki University. There were a few final-year students doing research work, but they were mostly in the Advanced Magic section, which was on the top floor of the five-floor library, the only floor above ground.

'Not really. Anyway it's only supposed to work on less intelligent beings, and the asurs do listen to me. Animals, too. And most pashans. But one of the books said only the most powerful ravians could control the minds of humans, and they generally didn't want to.'

'Yes. But do you think you might be exerting some power over the minds of people without realizing it?'

'Do you think so? I don't know. If I do, that is why the Stuff sells so well, I suppose. I think that's why all the human history books speak so well of ravians . . . the sweet-tongued folk and so on. Me, I don't think I've got that much power.'

'True. Anyway, I wouldn't know, since it wouldn't work on me.'

'Smug, aren't you? I'm sure I'm controlling your mind at some level.'

'Rubbish. You're not.'

'I'm sure I am. Doesn't everything I say sound amazingly right?'

'No.'

Kirin grinned. 'You're just being petulant.'

'No, Kirin. And I'll tell you why. Ravian mind control never worked on beings with magical powers.'

'Are you sure? Maybe I want you to think so.'

'Stop annoying me; ravian or not, I'll turn you into a slug as soon as we get out of the library. And you know I'm right about ravians not being able to control magical beings. That's why Danh-Gem stopped sending asurs and humans to attack them and sent rakshases and dragons instead.'

'All right, so I forgot. Let it go. But why were there so many guards outside the university today?'

'I don't know. The Civilian apparently sent them to guard the library. Ombwiri told the librarian, who threw a fit and said he wouldn't allow more than one guard in the library. Good thing for us that happened. Ombwiri is still arguing with the librarian.'

They reached the lowest level of the library. Very few spellbinders bothered to come here—it was more like a storeroom of books. The other library floors were well-lit and airy—here the shelves were closely packed and the room was dark and stuffy. The books here were magical, of course, but they were mostly old books, the kind that read themselves and grew minds of their own. The books about monsters had claws and tentacles, the books about sprites were tied down with string and made annoying squeaky noises, the books about fire-wizardry emitted angry red glows. Over the years, the spellbinders had extracted spells from these books and written them in magic-resistant tomes, so you no longer ran the risk of having your arm bitten off as you read *Griffins of the World*, or being eternally doomed for accidentally tearing a page from *The Unicorn in Myth and Reality*. The whole floor was filled, floor to ceiling, with tattered, worn old magical books, some brooding darkly, some fluttering, others pushing and shoving for more shelf space.

In a dark corner of the library, a middle-aged, wheezing Red Phoenix guard sat on a little chair near a little door and tried to read, pretending to ignore the hisses and whispers from the books around him. He'd had this job for four years now—he was Protector of the Untranslatables—of course, they'd put him out to pasture, he was no use at fighting.

'Stay here,' whispered Maya. Kirin slipped behind a shelf and watched as Maya approached the guard.

'Hello, I just came to have a look at the Untranslatables. Why don't you take a little stroll or something? You must by dying of boredom, cooped up here. I'll find you when I'm done.'

The guard looked up. 'Hello, Maya. I heard there were more guards coming here today. Where are they?'

'Outside, arguing with the librarian. Now come on, get up.'

'I can't leave my post, Maya. The Civilian herself sent word in the morning. I'm to stay on full alert all day and more guards will be sent to patrol this floor.'

'Why?' Maya saw Kirin moving closer, crouching, to her right. He sat down on the floor and closed his eyes. On the topmost shelf behind the guard, a book began to move closer to the edge of the shelf.

'I don't know why. I asked Captain Rupaisa and she said it was a precaution.'

The book suddenly fell off the high shelf, landing with a *clunk* on the guard's helmet. His expression suddenly became very dreamy, and he toppled over and sprawled out on the floor.

'Nice work. We'll have to move fast, before the other guards get here.'

It was dangerous to use magic inside the library, which was why Maya hadn't used a simple drowsiness-inducing spell. The effect of magic fluctuations could have very strange effects on the books.

'Thanks. The control is coming along a lot smoother now.'

They went into a tiny wooden room, lit by a tiny Alocactus. It was empty except for a single shelf on which six books were arranged. Maya closed the door.

'The Untranslatable Books. Possibly Danh-Gem's personal collection,' said Maya softly.

'Not a particularly voracious reader, was he?'

Maya laughed. 'No, the rest of his books were either non-magical or standard magic texts. Rakshases have very powerful magic, you know, and Danh-Gem would have made an amazing spellbinder. These were the books that couldn't be translated. These books were given to Kol by the asurs who surrendered after the War—they were allowed to stay in Kol after that. It's fairly safe to say they were all Danh-Gem's, or perhaps they belonged to some trusted henchman of his, because I don't think visitors to Imokoi had much time to read or write.'

'Well, now what?'

'We . . . borrow them for a while. Get six other books. The guards won't know the books have been changed.'

Kirin picked up a book. He flipped it open. It was written in a strange runic script. It was illustrated, and very obviously a book about torture. Kirin shut it with a snap. He felt slightly sick.

'Are all the books in the same script?' he asked.

'No. Some are in ravian scripts, some in runes. But they're all in the same language, the words sound the same. We can talk about this later. Hurry up and get the books out.'

Unseen by either of them, a large black shape slipped down the stairs. A huge, hairy arm shot out and grasped a book that had begun to growl. The book squeaked and was silent.

So this is the bottom floor, thought Bali. Now, a room in the corner . . .

Kirin picked up the books and one of them slipped and fell at his feet. It was a small, thin black book with silver edges. Kirin picked it up.

The edges of the book started to glow. He opened it. The pages were blank.

'Why is this book glowing?' he asked Maya.

Maya looked stunned.

'It doesn't do that normally,' she said. 'Give it to me.'

She took the book from him.

'This is odd,' she said. 'The edges of the book are made with moongold, the same metal as the ring I put on your finger. But only the ravians used moongold . . . that means this is a ravian book!'

She gave him the thin black book, picked up the other five from the shelf and turned towards the door. 'Come on,' she said.

Then things began to happen very fast.

Before his nearly-two-hundred-year holiday as a stone statue, Kirin had been trained to fight by the ravians. The memories of ravian-style unarmed-combat training had stayed with him, and he had never lost a fight. Of course, Spikes was generally with him, so he hardly ever got into fights. Still, no one ever *dreamt* of not paying for the Stuff. The unique thing about ravian-style fighting was that the ravians not only knew where all the nerve endings were and where a subtly placed finger would stop blood flow, muscle movement and so on, but they also *knew*, in a most uncanny manner, where the opponent's next blow was going to land. Most of Kirin's fighting consisted of not being in the wrong place at the wrong time. His ravian reflexes made him almost impossible to hit.

At that precise point of time, however, Kirin was concentrating on the book in his hand. Even so, he *saw*, in a corner of his mind, the huge black shape crashing through the door, knocking Maya out, and then spotting him. He *saw* the huge fist speeding towards his back. He could have jumped to one side, he could have at least turned around, but there was a slight problem.

It was a tiny, narrow room and there was nowhere to go.

And Bali was very, very quick.

As Kirin slumped forward, Bali scooped up the Untranslatable Books. At the same time, there was the sound of many booted feet on the stairs. The Red Phoenix Guards had arrived.

Holding the books under one arm, Bali looked around wildly. He needed a hostage.

One of the fundamental Laws of Nature is that when a great ape (or ape-man) visits a big city for the first time, he kidnaps a young, beautiful woman and climbs up a tower. The laws of magic can be broken, but no one argues with nature. Bali picked Maya up and threw her over his shoulder.

Kirin opened his eyes and spun around. He pulled a Rope Trick out of his cloak. *No magic in the library, it could implode* he remembered just in time. *What is that thing?*

A guard came out from behind a shelf and saw Bali. He shouted a warning and drew his crossbow, but it was too late. Bali knocked him out of the way and ran. The other guards didn't dare shoot, so they drew their swords and charged. Bali jumped over them neatly and bounded up the stairs.

The guards followed. Kirin got up groggily. He still had that one book; its edges were glowing brightly. He stuffed it into a pocket and ran in pursuit.

A few final-year students were studying peacefully when they saw the vanar with Maya slung over his shoulder, bounding up, a staircase at a time. They ran, scattering their books as Bali practically flew across the huge hall and crashed out of a window. He ran down the street for a while and then took to the air. The guards ran out of a door and gasped.

The vanar wasn't flying. He was jumping, but each bound took him higher in the air, and he was jumping from wall to wall with amazing skill, zigzagging across the street, further and further upwards. The Red Phoenix guards ran to their vroomsticks and flew after him, blowing horns furiously. A few blue-uniformed city guards also gave chase, but Bali was moving much faster than their carpets. He was moving as fast as a speeding eagle, his incredibly powerful legs thudding against the walls. Carpets and vroomsticks scattered as the huge gorilla-man arced through the busy airways.

Far below, Kirin slipped out of the library and watched hopelessly. There was nothing he could do.

Bali practically ran up a tower, and paused for a moment, drawing in huge gulps of air. He was looking around wildly, looking at the skyline and trying to remember the map Bjorkun had given him, trying to remember which way he had to go to get out of Kol. Which was the shortest way? He would have to move fast, they were catching up.

The mighty hunter stood proud and black on the tower roof and smiled grimly. It had been a long time since anyone had hunted him. East, he remembered. He saw the river shining steel-grey far below, the Civilian's palace gleaming white, and several small maroon and black figures racing towards him . . . they were flying faster than the others. Elite troops? He crouched and sprang eastwards.

The palace guards joined the chase, in their Harpoon vroomsticks and Silverstreak carpets. Maya regained consciousness as Bali took off. She found herself flapping helplessly on Bali's shoulder far, far above the street. The world below spun and whirled in a mad blur as Bali leapt from roof to roof. *How does he do it? And what is he, some kind of giant monkey? No, this is a vanar! And they can't shoot him because of me, and he's stealing the Untranslatables!* She would have to do something herself. She saw Captain Rupaisa leading the chase on a carpet, her black hair streaming in the wind, her crossbow aimed at Bali. *I've got to make him let go. He's heading out of the city. They can't chase him if he escapes the city borders. If he gets out with me, I'm dead anyway.*

Maya wrenched a hand free and grimaced as Bali's claws dug deep into her side. She looked at his tail, bobbing and weaving behind him. She winced as Bali slammed into a huge dome, ran to the top and took off again, soaring into the sky. Then she pointed at his tail and thought about fire.

Bali's tail burst into flames. Bali screamed in agony as he writhed in mid-air and dropped Maya. He somehow held on to the books as he crashed into a wall, and then on to a roof. Maya watched the street far below rushing towards her as she dropped like a stone. Then there was a soft noise and she fell into Rupaisa's carpet, which dropped quite a distance, spiralled downwards crazily and then regained control.

'Are you all right?' shouted Rupaisa.

'Yes! He's stealing the Untranslatables! Get him!'

Bali rolled over and got up. He broke into a run as a hail of arrows shuddered into the roof near him. As his tail dragged behind him, he saw with astonishment that the roof had burst into flames. Then it hit him. Spellbinders! Spellbinder fire! It would burn almost anything! It could burn Kol . . .

He leapt on to another roof and that started burning too.

'Put the fires out!' screamed Rupaisa.

Bali was moving fast again, a black blur in the glaring sunlight. Tower after tower was beginning to burn. The guards checked their vroomsticks and zoomed off in search of water and firemen. A few raced after Bali, but he was accelerating, shrugging off the arrows. A few moments later he had reached the edge of the city, and they had to bring their vroomsticks to earth as the magic in the air grew weaker. It was pointless chasing Bali on foot. They shook their fists and showered him with arrows, but the chase was lost. Bali had won.

'I'm all right, really,' said Maya. 'He's got the Untranslatables. Is there any way you can catch him?'

'I'm afraid not,' said Rupaisa. 'Did you see how fast he moves? He can practically fly. No, the Silver Phalanx will have to deal with this.'

Maya looked at her, surprised, as the carpet floated gently towards Enki University. She had always thought the Phalanx and the Red Phoenix Guards were bitter rivals. But then again, they were obviously on the same side. It would have to be the Silver Dagger then, she thought. She wondered who he really was . . .

Behind them, high amidst the towers of the city, firemen and guards were still pouring water on the smouldering fire. Spellbinder fire was very difficult to put out. Bali had burned a straight line to the edge of the city, and smoke was rising in a thick column, like an upside-down waterfall. Maya felt slightly guilty, but she'd had no choice. At least she was alive. She shuddered.

Rupaisa dropped Maya off at the University and flew off to the palace. Maya walked slowly back to her room, where Kirin was waiting.

She was dizzy, disoriented and bruised all over. Her side was bleeding a little and she was in no mood to talk. She cast a few healing spells on herself, cut short his apologies and told him she needed rest and that she would meet him at the Underbelly in the evening. He left quietly and she flopped down on her bed, trying to get the hideous image of the black, hairy, sweating, snarling, supernaturally strong vanar out of her mind.

As she was about to doze off, there was a knock on the door. 'Look, it's all right, I can take care of myself! I don't expect you to protect me!' she half yelled. She got up and opened the door angrily and saw there was no one outside. Then she looked down.

'I saw what happened, and I'm sorry to disturb you when you clearly need rest, but the Chief Civilian has sent me on an errand that cannot wait,' said Amloki, the khudran.

18

Gaam Vatpo was a vaman. One of the few vamans above ground who was not an engineer, moneylender, architect or trade baron. That was not the only thing unusual about him. In fact, in vaman circles, Gaam was considered quite a freak.

For example, if you called a normal vaman a dwarf, he would consider it a mortal insult. 'Height-based slur!' he would shout, produce a large battleaxe, jump up and make you considerably shorter by the simple method of cutting off your head. Gaam, on the other hand, would look mildly annoyed and say, 'I'm the first one you're meeting, right? Because there are easier forms of suicide.'

Again, vamans were proud of their fine, stiff beards, but Gaam shaved. Of course, that didn't help much because his beard grew back again every day, but he never stopped. It might have been a Hero School joke that you could tell the time by the length of Gaam's beard—but it wasn't, because they didn't tell jokes in Hero School, at least not jokes that anyone outside Hero School could laugh at or understand.

Even his name was unusual. Gaam was not a normal vaman name—it was usually spelled 'Gam' but Gaam, believed in numerology and had done so ever since it had saved his life. Gaam had once fallen asleep while reading a book on numerology and missed to a party that had crashed. The roof had fallen in.

Gaam watched his students watch the firemen put out the last few fires. The other classrooms didn't have windows; they'd been filled in ever since the students had said they wanted to remove all factors inimical to perfect concentration. But Gaam had refused to let the masons touch his precious window, and often even encouraged his students to look out and see the world. His students, who had no desire to see the world, thought he was insane.

Gaam was a Mentor in Kol's Hero School. He was a skilled warrior and one of the most knowledgeable people in the world when it came to weapons and military strategies, and the only vaman in the world who was comfortable riding a horse. When the school had been established, everyone in the faculty had been a Mentor. Now he was the only one. He taught Traditional Heroism. It was an optional course. Students generally took it up so that they could catch up with their sleep or finish their graphs under their desks.

He looked at his students, now engaged in a bitter debate over whether the firefighters should be financed by semi-autonomous quasi-public institutions or not. He'd given up trying to remember their names, and had stopped reproaching them when he caught them doing their Koli Economic Development essays in his class. They were just children, he thought, they didn't deserve this. And they would never really need to know about the heroes of the past. They would never need to shoot crossbows, look dragons in the eye or even ride horses. Look at them now, almost in tears over whether the vanars were an example of a Closed Economy without Government or not. They were the heroes of today. They would soon all be snapped up by governments all over the world, become leaders of trade guilds or advisers to kings. Some of them would *be* kings. But something was not right, thought Gaam. How could they have seen that magnificent vanar leaping over mighty domes and towers in the morning without being moved at all? Where were their hearts? Why was he teaching the taxmen of tomorrow?

It had all started in Ventelot, when knights starting out on quests had begun taking squires who were trained accountants, because they'd found that a lot of dragon-gold disappeared mysteriously on their way back home, in roadside inns and other places where bland-faced and surprisingly prosperous people lived. These squires were always paid more than the knights, because they ran twice the risk—not only were they running the risk of being killed by the dragon or other monster the knight had set out to kill, but they also faced the prospect of being run through with sharp lances by their own employers, who were generally irritable and highly-strung men who did not enjoy people harping on about overhead costs when they were dreaming of quaffing and barmaids.

'What do you think, sir?' asked Pasty Face Four.

'About what?' asked Gaam. Once upon a time, he'd cared what Pasty Face Four's real name was . . .

'Do you think the new Xi'en carpets Typhoon and Tsunami, with their many features and low cost of production, can pose a serious threat to the carpet-makers of Kol and Artaxerxia? It's a fascinating case . . .'

'Yes, yes,' said Gaam wearily. 'It's very fascinating. In fact, why don't you go to the Information Centre and do some research. Assume this class is over. Have a pleasant afternoon.'

With joyful faces, the students of Hero School practically ran to the library. Gaam trudged off to his room, feeling disgruntled, tired and very, very bored.

Gaam was a sensitive, progressive and thoroughly modern vaman who deplored the fact that vamans were generally dismissed as avaricious, boorish and mean. Of course, most of the vamans who lived above ground *were* avaricious, boorish and mean, but that wasn't the point. The vamans who stayed at home, in Bhumi, deep below the surface of the earth, were noble and true. Well, most of them anyway.

He entered his room, which was decorated in accordance with the Shanti-Joddhist Principles of Harmony, and was welcomed with great affection by his dog, Queeen, who was called Queen before Gaam discovered numerology. Gaam and Queeen had met when Gaam had been exploring the far north a few years ago, before he joined Hero School as a teacher. She was an extremely beautiful wolfhound. Of course, no other vaman kept pets . . . Gaam sat on his unconventionally soft bed and heaved a deep sigh. He hummed a little tune tunelessly. He could play a variety of musical instruments, but he couldn't sing at all.

Someone knocked on his door. Another prospective student wanting to know how to prepare for the entrance test, he thought wearily. Really, this whole rigmarole of multiple-choice test, group discussion and interview to get the young idiots into the place was ridiculous. Far better to throw a sack of gold into a mud puddle and see who dived first. Reproaching himself for this unbecoming cynicism, Gaam opened the door.

He looked up—it was a habit, looking up—and saw a girl. A tall, thin, good-looking girl, with short hair. Lacks grace, but looks intelligent, he noted. Probably a spellbinder. And she looks most annoyed. I wonder why. *Not* a good dresser, though, ragged grey robes with miscellaneous stains are *so* last year. Gaam was quite interested in fashion, and was often seen not wearing *any* armour.

'Mr Gaam Vatpo, Mentor?' asked the khudran beside her. Pleasant looking fellow, thought Gaam, noting enviously that the khudran was a little shorter than him.

'My name is Amloki,' continued Amloki, 'and she is Maya the spellbinder, daughter of the famous Mantric. We have been sent by the Chief Civilian of Kol to invite you to join us for what may be the most important quest of all time.'

Quest! Gaam's eyes lit up. Finally!

'Do come in,' he said.

Enki, Bearmonth 22nd, 8 p.m.

Number of vanars kidnapped by 1, Dragonjuices 0, Non-lethal drinks 0 (so far, but it's not going to stay that way), Near death experiences many, Magic 6/10.

Memo: Change the Prince of Potolpur back before leaving.

What a day. WHAT a day. Went to the library with Kirin. One of the Untranslatables was a ravian book! How on earth did it get into Imokoi! Then when we were taking the books out, we were attacked by a vanar. He dragged me all over Kol before I set his tail on fire. He dropped me and Rupaisa saved my life. The vanar set lots of buildings on fire and escaped. With the Untranslatables. I wonder who he is working for. The Red Phoenix Guards were furious. They came by this afternoon and asked me many questions. I wouldn't want to be in Lost Street right now.

Just finished packing. And why? Because things happened after that which were almost as strange as being carried around by the vanar. Amloki came to visit me. He told me that the Civilian expected me to go for a quest tomorrow! I was stunned. Apparently the Civilian has found this Avrantic prince who, she thinks, is the hero of Simoqin's second prophecy. She's made sure he meets all the requirements—Amloki was taken to Avranti by the Silver Dagger's men and brought this prince back to Kol. And the Civilian thinks there's a distinct possibility of Danh-Gem actually returning, so she's sending this prince to Father to be trained. And they want me to go with him and help him in his quests. Well, they could have told me before.

I didn't want to do it, initially. Because I want to go to Bolvudis with Kirin and Spikes—and this quest, it's not even a quest, it's like training for quests. But then I thought it could be really interesting. And any other spellbinder would die for a chance to learn the finer points of hex-magic from my father. Also, Amloki said all expenses would be paid, and the Civilian would pay me a large amount of money later, if I wanted it. So, the Civilian thinks I am tempted by money, and the grandeur and nobility of the heroic quest are not enough! She's perfectly right, of course.

Amloki and I then had an argument over whether Kirin and Spikes could come with us or not. Not an argument, really, Amloki said he didn't mind at all—he knows them, he buys a lot of the Stuff—but it depended on what Arjun (is the prince's name Arjun?) said. I said I would take care of the prince.

I asked Amloki what my father, a spellbinder, could teach the prince, a person with no magical abilities, and he said my father wasn't going to teach him, Gaam the vaman Mentor at Hero School was. I asked him why my father was involved in the first place, and he said he couldn't tell me. Apparently all this had been planned a long time ago. Someone could have told me. Then he asked me why I wanted Kirin and Spikes to come, and I said I wouldn't tell him, which served him right.

Anyway, then we went and met Gaam, who was really nice, though he was looking at my clothes a little oddly. I realized there were a few holes in my robe, but why would that matter? I know most vamans are supposed to be a little leery, but Durgan women are safe, because vamans traditionally like fair skin. And Gaam was very funny and charming. I promise to be impeccably dressed from now on, especially since I am going to be hobnobbing with princes. I think he's really bored teaching at Hero School—he's completely wasted there, what a horrible place. Met a student on the way to Gaam's room. He asked me in a supercilious voice if I was from Enki. My fingers were itching to turn him into something but self-restraint won. Am proud of myself. Gaam was very enthusiastic about the whole thing, he was dying to get out of Hero School. He was practically skipping when he ran off to resign.

So I told Amloki to send this Prince Ashish, or whatever his name is, to the Underbelly tonight, and then we could all leave at dawn. Amloki looked shocked at first, and then very amused. 'Why not the Underbelly? We're leaving tomorrow anyway,' he said, more to himself than to me. I like Amloki. And this is why I am all well dressed now and off to Frags.

Yes, I almost forgot—I went and told Kirin all about it

afterwards. He was rather annoyed and said he didn't want to go, or would go alone with Spikes. But I soon shut him up. He was still a little upset about the morning—poor thing, now that he's a ravian and everything he thinks he should use his powers to protect me. He'll come, and so will Spikes. I forgot to ask him whether he still has the book he was looking at.

What a day. Have I written about everything? Yes, that's about it. Now I'm off to the Underbelly, where I have to use my feminine wiles (heh, heh) on Ashish so that he agrees to take Kirin and Spikes with us. The only problem is I don't have any feminine wiles. But I do have a little plan. . .

19

He had been trained in a hidden monastery by the ninjas of Xi'en. He had studied yoga and meditation under an Avrantic guru. His strength, stamina and ability to withstand pain were legendary. He was as silent as a shadow of a black cat in the night, as deadly as a cobra's fang. He moved like a panther, taut and sinuous. He could climb up rock faces with his bare hands and stay underwater for hours without breathing. His skill and luck at love and cards was legendary, and he had *almost* beaten the Civilian at chess once.

He was wondering what to wear.

When in Doubt, Black is the Answer, the dance teacher in Ektara had said.

He dressed, swiftly. It had been a long time since he had worn the original costume. Black silk clothes, padded boots. The cloth around the face, with slits for his eyes. The fire-resistant Xi'en lava-worm black silk cape. Of course, disguises and camouflage were fun, and often necessary, but this was his favourite.

He strapped on his Necessity Belt. He had been all around the world and seen many beautiful things, but *this* was the finest example of vaman craftsmanship he had ever seen. He opened a trunk under his bed and started thinking about his assignment. His fingers, trained by years of practice, began sliding things into the right pockets on his belt.

Into the little sheaths went the darts, the crossbow bolts and the blackened throwing knives. With practised ease his fingers found the little pouches, side by side, one after the other, for the wires, the brass knuckles, the vial of oil, the sachet of poisonous powder and the *shuriken*, the little blackened poison-tipped discs the ninjas used. On his back was the slim bag that contained a little black chalk, his stamp and his emergency scarab. If he was killed or captured, it would fly to the Civilian. The message inside said *Owing to unavoidable circumstances our next meeting will be slightly delayed*. He slung a pouch over his shoulder—it contained his blowpipes, ropes, strangling cords and cloth-covered grappling hooks. Over his other shoulder went the light and specially constructed crossbow. The flat bag filled with what he called his 'special effects' went on his back.

He felt a little naked.

He strapped on little black daggers in sheaths to his left arm and outer thighs. He tapped his left foot thrice on the floor and felt the blade slide to the front of the boot. He tapped again and it slid back to the heel. Love those vamans, he thought. He slipped on his gloves.

Finally, he picked up the sheath that contained his first love. It was the one love he'd always been faithful to, the long, curved, deadly and beautiful Artaxerxian dagger that glittered and shone even in the candlelight as he pulled it out and held it lovingly. It was the only weapon he had never blackened. The Silver Dagger. He attached it to the Necessity Belt.

Now he was dressed to kill.

He looked at the clock. Two minutes. Not bad.

He looked at the blackjack lying on the table. No, *that* would be overdoing it.

He was a little tired. Warm up, he thought, it's going to be a long night.

He jumped on to the table, threw the blackjack up in the air, did a double somersault, caught it and landed softly on his feet. He bowed to his reflection in the full-length mirror across the room. You show-off, you, he thought.

He knew that no matter how good he was, a day would come when someone would find out who he really was. He hoped he could retire before that day came.

He picked up his Nightshade vroomstick with special ink-spray and smokescreen attachments. He got on it and shot off into the night.

The Underbelly was full, but not bulging yet. Asvin walked in, looked around and recognized her instantly. He walked up to her.

'Hello, Maya? I'm Asvin, from Avranti.'

You're very good-looking, Asvin from Avranti. 'Hello, Asvin. You're right on time. Do sit.' *Punctual, too, I like that.*

There was a sharp nip on Asvin's foot. He looked down. 'Oh hello, where did you come from? Maya, I'd like you to meet Fluffy.' He patted Steel-Bunz on the head.

Kind to animals, too. Maya held out her hand and Asvin kissed it. *Charming. So charming. Quite the prince, aren't you.*

Very good-looking. Muscles, too, and nice and tall. Of course, all this means nothing to me. 'Where's Amloki?'

'Packing. He's packing for himself and for me. He told me he had to go meet Gaam the vaman—I haven't met him yet—who is to be my new guru, and organize our departure at dawn. Apparently a member of the Silver Phalanx is also going to come with us. I love Amloki, he works so hard.'

Caring, considerate, respectful. What a nice smile. 'I love him too.' *I love him too? What is wrong with you?* 'I mean, he's very nice. Yes.' *Control yourself, Maya. He's not the first handsome type you've met. Probably really stupid, and never read a book in his life.*

'Yes, khudrans are fascinating, aren't they? I haven't seen any other khudrans in Kol, though. I guess they don't generally like city life. I once went to a khudran village, near our eastern border, with my father. It was amazing, quite unlike the books.'

The books. So, well-read. Knowledgeable, probably ferociously intelligent. Must have travelled a lot, too. But obviously he's special. He's a Hero. Simoqin's hero, no less. I must say he suits the part. 'Is that so?' *Is that so? Is that so? I've read all the books in Enki library on all the known races in the world! Is that so? He must think I'm a silly cow!*

'Amloki and the Civilian have told me wonderful things about you,' said Asvin, feeling intimidated by Maya's glassy stare. *The most brilliant spellbinder in Kol,* he thought, *no wonder she doesn't seem interested in what I'm saying. She's probably far away, in some land where mathematics and magic mingle and sing to her in strange voices.* 'Can I get you something to eat?'

I'm not hungry, not any more. He will be such a good Hero. I can tell just by looking at him. What a nice person he seems to be. Probably witty, too, if only I could stop my tongue hanging out and engage him in brilliant conversation. 'No, thanks, I'm not hungry.' *On the other hand, if he gets up to go to the bar, I could . . .* 'On second thoughts, could you see if Triog has any bhel-puri from upstairs?'

'Certainly,' Asvin got up and turned towards the bar.

Oh, very nice. Must get a lot of exercise. 'Actually, forget it. Triog hasn't met you before, and he always makes strangers wait. And I'm not really hungry.' *Finally, she stops speaking in simple sentences. Congratulations. I can't wait to go on this quest. So, I'm to be his companion and helper. That doesn't sound like such a bad thing. Of course, I must let him know that I'm working with him, not for him. But that can wait. What nice eyes he has. But that's not why we're here. There's something I've forgotten . . .*

Asvin sat down obediently. He was obviously boring her. 'Amloki said you wanted to talk to me about something.'

Kirin! What a bad friend I am. Kirin has to come with us! What is wrong with me?

She looked at Kirin, sitting in his corner with Spikes and a customer. He was looking back at her. And shaking his head. Maya felt very guilty. She cleared her throat, and began the long speech she had prepared.

Maya had met many intelligent, charming and handsome men before. Her reaction to them had never been so strong, though. She was generally very level-headed and analytical, even cynical sometimes. Yes, Asvin was really attractive and dashing and heroic, but Maya was reacting more strongly than she would have in other circumstances. Normally she would have flirted happily with him and then forgotten all about him as soon as she found an interesting book. But as she looked at Asvin, she had a sudden urge to marry him and have six children. Because here she was dealing with more than standard attraction. She was dealing with one of the fundamental Laws: The Hero Always Gets The Girl.

Hooba the asur was trembling. He had been trembling continuously since King Leer had offered his house to Bjorkun the Skuan and his bodyguards. But he was trembling especially hard now.

'Please, my lord,' he was saying, 'don't take away my shop. I've worked all my life for it. The Emporium is all I own, I've proved my loyalty, I've given the men food and shelter, don't turn me out.'

'After the Glorious Revolution there will be no possessions for anyone, Hooba,' said King Leer. 'You are a soldier in the Divine Army of asurs, personally conscripted by the Supreme Commander. Is that honour not enough for you? You will travel to Imokoi tomorrow. This shop is now Divine Army property, gifted by me to Bjorkun, asur-friend and brave-heart of the cold North.'

'Don't do that,' sobbed Hooba as a few danavs started taking objects off the shelves. Others tore off the big 'Hooba's Emporium' sign outside the door.

'Go now, I have no more time to waste on you, I have a council to attend,' commanded King Leer. Hooba saw the spears his guards held and slunk quietly out of the door.

'That little maggot will betray us,' said Bjorkun.

Tungz, King Leer's official translator, translated.

King Leer jabbered a little. One of his guards started out after Hooba.

'His serene highness King Leer, Supreme Commander

of the Divine Army, Sword of Justice, Mace of Destiny, Descendant of the One . . .' began Tungz.

'Tell me what he said, and spare me this rubbish,' snarled Bjorkun.

'He said "I know. The city-rat will not live another night,"' said Tungz hurriedly.

'Shall we begin the meeting, Leer?' asked Bjorkun, striding towards the stairs.

'His serene . . . Yes,' said Tungz a little later, and followed.

Hooba broke into a run. Lost Street was usually crowded and bustling at this time of the night, but after that mad vanar's morning escapade, the Red Phoenix Guards had come and shut everything down, curse them. The street was deserted, pitch dark and eerily quiet. It was not a good time to be an asur in Kol. All day there'd been bad news—asurs were losing jobs all over the city as panic spread. Word had got out that some important things had been stolen, and everyone blamed asurs for everything. All the doors and windows on the streets were closed. The human inhabitants of Lost Street, sensing trouble, had left for the night. Not that the darkness mattered to Hooba for asurs had excellent night-eyes—it was only the city asurs who were completely comfortable in bright sunlight.

Hooba saw the spear-bearing danav come out of the door and give chase. He ran faster, but he knew the guard would catch him eventually. His time was up.

A lasso fell on his shoulders and sneaked under his arms. The noose was drawn tight, and suddenly Hooba was airborne, struggling and flailing his arms wildly as he dangled spider-like in mid-air. Hooba looked back and downwards at his pursuer. He was lying on the street, immobile, dead. What . . .?

The Silver Dagger threw Hooba down on to a roof and jumped off his vroomstick. Hooba, sprawled face down on the roof, mouth full of grime, felt cold steel on the back of his neck.

'Don't even *dream* of turning around,' said the Dagger.

Hooba shook his head obediently and vigorously. Turning around was not high on his current to-do list.

'I don't remember there being only one asur on Lost Street,' mused the Dagger. 'Do tell me what's going on.'

'The other esurs ere all underground, es fer es I know,' croaked Hooba. 'They've been ordered to weit for King Leer's commend. He's in my house, heving a conference with thet eccursed Skuen wolf, Bjorkun. They took my house, I done nothing. Blested northern swine.'

'And which house is that? Point, don't turn.'

Hooba raised a trembling finger and showed him.

'What's your name?'

'Hoobe.'

'Well, Hooba, tonight is your lucky night. I'm not going to kill you. After I hit you, you should be unconscious for about an hour. What you do with your life after that is your problem, not mine. Is that understood?'

Hooba nodded.

The Dagger knocked him out noiselessly and jumped on to his vroomstick.

As assignments went, this was quite a trivial one. The Civilian had told him not to kill Bjorkun or Leer unless he was sure that killing them would positively stop Danh-Gem's return. Since neither the Civilian nor the Dagger ever made assumptions about anything, that meant they were to be left alive. This kind of eavesdropping could have been done by almost anyone in the Phalanx. Still, if you want something done well, do it yourself, thought the Dagger as he reached into his 'special-effects' bag and brought out the Sticky Fingers. That Kirin lad was very bright, he might grow up to be a member of the Phalanx one day . . . It was a shame that the Stuff, like the vroomstick, didn't work outside Kol. When all the magic-glue covered finger caps were in place, he crawled down the walls of Hooba's house, lizard-like, and listened to Bjorkun and Tungz.

'I do not know where Bali has gone,' Bjorkun was saying, 'but the crows will let me know. Until then, I will stay in Kol—they have no proof of my involvement in the theft of the books.'

'Everything else is proceeding smoothly,' said Tungz. 'But my king wants to know what the strike tonight will achieve.'

'I think the books will tell us all what we need to know about bringing Danh-Gem back to this world,' said Bjorkun. 'But Bali insisted that I also find the most dangerous pashan in the city, and take him away with me, by force if necessary. He met some stork who told him there was a magical stone egg that yielded a pashan that would be Danh-Gem's bodyguard when he rose.'

'My king says he does not understand a word of what you are saying.'

The Dagger listened, fascinated, as Bjorkun, somewhat annoyed, told the asurs what Bali had told him about pashan reproduction, the role the storks played, the Oathbreakers, the Oathbreaker's Egg and its mysterious disappearance. This was important. This could be very important. He was glad he had come himself.

'. . . and so Bali thinks this pashan, the child of Danh-Gem's bodyguard, walks the earth today, and finding him will be the crucial step in the resurrection of Danh-Gem,' concluded Bjorkun.

'My king says, could you say all that again? He understands it all, of course, but he thinks you should explain more clearly.'

'It doesn't matter. You don't need to know. The point is that we need to find the deadliest pashan in the world. Crows are searching for unusual pashans all over the world, but Bali says—and I agree with him—that such a pashan would probably find his way to Kol somehow—that's where the best pashans all end up, apart from the snow-trolls. Finding this pashan would help us, I think. What if we do not manage to read the books? Even if the pashan is too stupid to understand his worth, there must be something about him which will answer our questions.'

'You need to know who the most fearsome pashans in the city are? We already know, thanks to our peerless intelligence network. Our city cousins inform us that the biggest, strongest pashan in the city is one named Yarni, and there is another one, which they are not sure is a pashan, called Spikes. Crows have been watching them for the last few days. Strangely enough, both work at a place called the Fragrant Underbelly. We will capture them both and bring them to you. My king has seen the one called Spikes fight. He is very good, but he has claws and spikes, and so cannot be a pashan.'

'I am not interested in things which might not even be pashans,' said Bjorkun, 'and I do not have much time. I have been followed since I entered the city, and I want to leave before the Silver Dagger becomes involved personally. Bali should have done his job quietly. That fool has made Kol an unsafe place for all of us. So my soldiers will bring back the big pashan—the one called Yarni.'

'My king will send asur soldiers immediately. Your soldiers will not be required. It is time the asurs struck back. Too long have we waited. Innumerable atrocities have been committed against asurs this very day. My king says the Glorious Revolution will start tonight.'

'Don't tell your king, but he is a fool. Asurs are good warriors on battlefields, but you cannot overthrow Kol, believe me. You will never reach the Underbelly—I have been there—the security pashans there can handle any number of asurs, and if you get asurs thrown out of the city you will alienate your city kindred. Why do you not understand, you need their money! The first act of aggression cannot be committed by asurs in Kol. We are not ready to strike yet. The number of asurs you would need to send to bring this pashan back by force would be immense, and that would be an overt act of war. No, I will send some of my soldiers. They are trained snow-trolls, and they cannot be identified as Skuans.'

'But asurs have rights, and . . .'

'I agree with your king, but I do not have much time. I have to go west, I have business there. Your day will come.'

He called out in the Skuan tongue, and the Dagger heard the stairs creaking as the snow-trolls thumped their way upstairs.

'Find an asur to guide you to a place called the Fragrant Underbelly. There is a pashan there called Yarni. Bring him to me. Do not reveal the fact that you work for me.'

'Yah,' said a grainy voice and the snow-trolls began to thump down the stairs.

Bjorkun and Tungz began to speak of the glory of Danh-Gem, and how they would humble Kol and burn Avranti.

The Dagger had heard all he needed to hear. Crows and

vanars, he thought. Yarni's too thick to be the key to anything. But Spikes? I will have to keep an eye on Spikes. Even crows are watching. Spikes . . . personal bodyguard of Danh-Gem? And he walks around the city with Mantric's daughter and Kirin, who I'm thinking of asking to join the Phalanx? And I'm sure neither of them has any idea about this. Are they in danger? Does Spikes know he might be the pashan who sprang from the Oathbreaker's Egg? Or is all this totally irrelevant? And why is Bjorkun going to Artaxerxia? Is the Sultan already in league with him?

Who is Spikes, really? Storks? Eggs of stone? The Oathbreaker's Egg? The Civilian needs to be informed about all this.

'Want another one?' asked Maya. She was smiling now, the smile of someone who was totally in command of a situation and knew it. It was the kind of smile sharks smile when, swimming around feeling peckish, they see pale pink legs thrashing about in front of them.

Asvin opened an eye. He saw Kirin setting two more glasses of Dragonjuice down on the table. He opened another eye and suddenly there were two Kirins, both smiling at him winningly. Asvin looked at the Mayas across the table, gulping down their Dragonjuices.

'Bottoms up,' they said.

Asvin closed an eye. He looked at the glass in front of him and sighed.

When Maya had said she wanted two of her friends to come with them on the quest, Asvin had been all smiles. Any friend of Maya, he had said, was a friend of his. He had waved happily at Kirin, sitting in his corner selling the Stuff. Kirin had waved back. Then Asvin had seen Spikes.

Avrantics hated pashans. Pashans were not allowed in Avranti ever since the War, and even Avrantics who lived in Kol avoided pashans as much as they could. Asvin had refused point-blank, saying he would not go anywhere with a pashan. Maya had then pointed out that that was not a problem, because Spikes was not a pashan. Asvin had still not been satisfied.

Then Kirin had come over to the table and struck up a conversation with the prince, and had completely charmed Asvin by showing him the Stuff. He had suggested that they resolve their differences over a game of chess—Spikes would go with them if Maya won.

Asvin was quite happy with that—chess, after all, had been invented in Avranti and Asvin was a skilled player. Kirin had brought a chessboard and Maya had proceeded to demolish Asvin in twelve moves. But Asvin had looked so crestfallen that she had relented, explaining that spellbinders were unbeatable at chess because they could see a little bit of the future. Kirin had known this was completely untrue, but he never interfered with Maya and her prospective conquests, so he had said nothing.

Then Maya had set her master plan into motion. She issued the Dragonjuice challenge to Asvin, saying Spikes would go with them if she stayed conscious longer than Asvin did. Asvin had agreed enthusiastically, thinking that Kirin was laughing out of excitement. They had already gone four rounds, and Asvin's world had started turning purple and spinning really fast a little while ago. Maya, on the other hand, was looking serene and poised.

'It's not such a bad thing, us coming with you,' said

Kirin kindly. 'We're good at fighting, and I can do a little magic.'

Asvin tried opening the other eye again and gave up—it seemed to want to stay shut. 'AnifrenoMaya ishafrenomine,' he said.

'I really don't think he should have any more,' Kirin told Maya sternly. 'We have to leave at dawn tomorrow, remember? We should all get some sleep.'

'But he's still conscious,' Maya pointed out.

'I know. That doesn't matter. You've won.'

'But it's a Dragonjuice challenge. Someone has to hit the floor,' said Maya, slowly, because Kirin was being so obtuse.

'Am I coming with you?' asked Spikes, coming up to the table.

'Of course you are, Spikes, that was never in doubt,' said Maya grandly. 'I'll just wait until he's unconscious.'

'Heshreallyugly. You're reallyugly, Shpikesh,' said Asvin happily.

'I know,' said Spikes, who knew.

Asvin managed to open his other eye and saw two Spikeses. An expression of frozen terror crept over his face.

'Go away Spikes, you're getting him all sober,' said Maya crossly.

'I'mallshober,' said Asvin, grabbing his fifth Dragonjuice and drinking it in one huge gulp.

'Triog's made them really strong today,' said Maya to Kirin, who was looking concerned. Kirin looked even more concerned.

'I'mshorry IwashmeantoShpikesh. I loveyou, Shpikesh,' said Asvin, leaning forward and crashing gently on the table.

'I think I win. You can go and pack, Spikes,' said Maya proudly.

The snow-trolls entered Frags. There were fifteen of them. A particularly vicious-looking one, the leader, walked up to a security pashan and said, 'Which one of you is Yarni, yah?'

'Him,' said the pashan, pointing a stubby finger at Yarni.

The leader walked up to Yarni, who was demonstrating the laws of gravity to a group of unruly Artaxerxian carpet makers by picking one of them up and letting him go.

'You Yarni, yah?' he said.

'Yah,' said Yarni. He looked at the cowering carpet makers. 'I'll be back,' he said.

He turned and looked down at the snow-troll. 'What?' he asked.

'You come with us, yah.'

'Why?' enquired the huge stalactroll.

'We can't tell you. Just come, yah.'

'No,' said Yarni after a while.

The snow-troll hit him in the face. A snow-troll can knock out a young polar bear with a punch. Yarni looked at him, puzzled.

The Fragrant Underbelly was silent. Triog groaned. There were many kinds of silences in the Underbelly.

This was the expensive kind.

Kirin looked at Spikes. 'How bad do you think this is going to be?'

'Not very bad. About level-two brawl, I think.'

'I guess so.'

The silence stopped.

Fifteen pashans charged into the Underbelly. Yarni's security pashans rushed towards them. The leader hit Yarni again.

Some people never learn.

Yarni's punch knocked him a good four feet back. The snow-troll flung his arms around wildly, looking for something to hold on to, caught something but fell anyway.

The something he had caught was a vaman's beard.

In the north they have a saying. The saying goes: Never *ever* touch a vaman's beard.

Some people *never* learn.

The vaman went berserk. His friends pulled out daggers and charged at the other snow-trolls, who picked them up and threw them across the room. On to a table of vroomers.

All hell broke loose.

Violence spread fast in the Fragrant Underbelly. There were pashans everywhere, wrestling, kicking, clubbing innocent bystanders. You could tell the snow-trolls apart because they generally had a screaming vaman attached to the backs of their heads. The vroomers, always happy to oblige anyone looking for a fight, had started to mix it up. They believed in democracy—they attacked everybody equally. The men named Abhishek disappeared under a table as screaming vroomers began to run through the bar. Houstarr, the World's Worst Lover, stopped telling a woman about his skin diseases and dived for cover. Tables, glasses and mugs flew everywhere. The members of Teetotallers Anonymous went on drinking. There was little else they cared about.

Steel-Bunz, who had been sleeping quietly under the table, woke up happy. He loved fights. He whizzed off in a white blur and soon people all over the Underbelly were holding their ankles and yelling in pain. A vroomer stepped on Steel-Bunz's tail and regretted it immediately, as the deadly bunny launched a vicious attack on his kurta.

'No, level five, I think, actually,' said Spikes. He knew

all about the different kinds of brawls in the Underbelly. He ended a lot of them. It wouldn't be level six until Spikes unsheathed his claws.

'I think we should get Asvin out of here,' said Maya, watching Yarni hit a snow-troll. With another.

'Upstairs, do you think? It'll be difficult carrying him,' said Kirin, looking at Triog, all six hands holding clubs, roaring as he bludgeoned one and all.

'I'll manage,' said Spikes, quietly.

'I wasn't thinking about you, Spikes. We don't want him to catch a stray dagger.'

'I'll wake him up, I'm sure he can walk,' said Maya hopefully.

A vroomer came soaring through the air and crashed on their table. Asvin didn't even mumble in his sleep.

Spikes got up. It became a level-six brawl.

'That might be a little difficult,' said Kirin. Asvin dropped peacefully on to the floor as the table cracked and fell apart. He started to snore.

'Look, why don't you go and fight someone?' said Maya crossly, shifting a little to allow an enraged vaman to jump over the vroomer and attack a snow-troll. 'I'll manage.'

She waved at her fellow spellbinders sitting quietly in another corner and sipping their drinks, looking mildly annoyed because service had stopped. No one would bother *them*. Not until level nine, anyway. The young Elakish woman Triog had hired in the morning to be a crooner was hiding behind the bar, which despite Triog's best efforts was disintegrating fast. Humans forgot all issues of race and nationality as the battle lines were drawn between vroomers and non-vroomers. In many ways, the Fragrant Underbelly did its bit for world peace.

The door of the Underbelly fell in. Standing in the light were more snow-trolls. The spellbinders groaned and began to complain. The newcomers joined in the fun. But it was a lost cause—the superior bulk of the stalactrolls, the superior shortness of the vamans, the sheer malevolence of Spikes and the sheer surprise of Steel-Bunz were now working together, and the newcomers were welcomed with stunning blows, sharp stabs and vicious nibbles.

'That bunny should definitely come with us,' said Kirin, watching in admiration as Steel-Bunz accidentally ripped off most of a vaman's beard.

Maya wasn't listening. She was doing some finger-waving near Asvin's head. Asvin's eyes suddenly opened. 'Where am I?' he said.

'What was that?' demanded Kirin. 'What did you just do?'

Yarni lumbered by, holding two snow-trolls under his arms.

'All right, you caught me; it's a spell I invented. Gets you sober instantly.'

'So *that's* how you do it!'

'Look, it's not cheating. The rules for Dragonjuice challenges are stated very clearly, and every possible violation is listed. They say nothing about not using magic.' Maya protested, dodging a flying bottle.

'That's because your spellbinder laws forbid you to touch alcohol!' Kirin yelled. 'It's most unfair!'

Asvin sat up. 'Is it morning? I don't remember a thing since last evening, actually.'

'They all say that,' grinned Maya.

A snow-troll crashed down on the floor near them.

'Get away, monster!' yelled Asvin suddenly. Avrantics really hate pashans.

The troll lunged at him, and he would have been seriously hurt but . . .

'Stop,' said Kirin. The troll actually froze in mid-lunge and looked at him, puzzled. Then he moved to strike again, but Spikes hit him in the back and he fell, stunned.

'It works,' said Maya, impressed.

'You saved my life, you two,' said Asvin. 'And I was actually not wanting to take Spikes! I'm so sorry!' Large tears rolled down his eyes.

'Please tell me he's not always like this,' whispered Kirin.

'No, it's the spell,' said Maya. 'It doesn't do that to me, but non-magical people probably get a little emotional. Not his fault, poor thing.'

Asvin was weeping openly. 'Kirin, we must swear an oath of brotherhood and eternal friendship. You will be my friend, won't you?'

'Yes, yes,' said Kirin, but Asvin bawled on. 'Heroic, isn't he?'

'Shut up, Kirin. It's all my fault. I shouldn't have cast that spell on him—I designed it for myself. So you needn't be mean to him.'

'Can you take it off now? The spell, I mean.'

'I think so,' said Maya, doing things with her hands. Asvin stopped crying abruptly and fell asleep again. 'Tell Spikes to take him to your room, quickly.'

At a signal from Kirin, Spikes picked Asvin up and fought his way to the stairs.

'The party's almost over,' said Maya, watching Yarni's pashans pound the snow-trolls into submission.

'The vroomers are still at it, though,' said Kirin, as Triog threw vroomers out from behind the bar, where the Elakish crooner was still screaming. People were groaning on the floor everywhere and the Underbelly was a complete wreck.

'I've had enough of this nonsense. We've got what we wanted; now let's get some sleep. We've got to leave the city at dawn tomorrow—today, actually. Gaam will be waiting at the War Temple at five. With Amloki, I suppose.'

The War Temple was in south Kol. It had two doors, one facing north and the other south. When Kol was at war, one of the doors would always be open. Inside the temple was a huge statue of a running soldier. When Kol was winning the war, the north door would be opened and everyone saw the magnificent charging soldier, complete with naked sword and tall plumes on his helmet. When Kol was losing the war, the south door would be opened and everyone saw a man running away.

'Do you like Asvin?' Kirin asked suddenly.

'I don't know. He seems nice.'

'Yes. We'll be seeing a lot of him, though. I hope he learns to like Spikes.'

The last snow-troll was thrown out of the Underbelly. The vroomers, loudly protesting that they had only been defending themselves, were pushed out as well. The vamans, of course, stayed—they were all very rich and Triog took care never to offend them. Triog calmed the spellbinders down and gave them a round on the house, which cheered them up. The Underbelly began to settle down. The crooner, asked to croon, broke a plate over Leftog's head and stormed upstairs angrily.

'I'll calm her down, if you know what I mean,' said Houstarr, emerging from under a table and following. When Houstarr got out from under a table, it meant the fight was over. All those craving more violence either sat down and resumed drinking or trudged off dejectedly.

Kirin and Maya walked to Enki. They reached Maya's room.

'Good night,' said Kirin, hugging Maya. 'I'll see you in a few hours.'

'I know—we're actually going to meet my father. It's been a long time.'

Kirin left. Maya sat down on her bed and took out her diary but was too tired to write, so she put it back in the drawer. She suddenly remembered what she had forgotten to ask him. She ran to the door and opened it.

'Do you still have that ravian book?' she called out, but he was gone.

20

Somewhere in the Southern Free States, Griffinmonth 1ˢᵗ, afternoon

Lustful thoughts many, Lasting regrets 1 (forgot to change Prince of Potolpur; still in matchbox in room), Aches and pains from riding for a week severe, Magic 5/10.

Am lying on grass in a very beautiful leafy glade. This is the first time in my life that I'm getting to use the words 'leafy glade', so I'm happy.

I suppose I'd better catch up or I'll end up abandoning this diary, like all the others. After I wrote last, I went to Frags and met Prince Asvin of Avranti, and over a few Dragonjuices managed to persuade him to take Kirin and Spikes with us. There was a bit of a brawl and Kirin saved his life, and they've now become fast friends. Kirin hasn't said anything to anyone about being a ravian, of course.

We were supposed to leave at dawn. Kirin came over to Enki with a carpet and picked me up. He said he hadn't been able to wake Asvin up, and Spikes was going to bring him to the Temple. We flew there and met Gaam, his dog, Queeen, Amloki and Red Pearl.

Red Pearl is a centaur, or should I say centauress. The horse part of her is sleek and glossy, and the human part is . . . well, somewhat spectacular. Even at that hour, there were a few people who had got out of bed and were hanging around just to stare at Red Pearl. She's really beautiful, and has muscles everywhere—I mean everywhere. And she wears really little. Practically nothing, in fact. But then there are the centaurs for you—apparently, when Kol was founded, they had lots of trouble persuading the centauresses that it was necessary to wear clothes at all. Of course, if you look at it, the centauresses have a point—if the centaurs can walk around bare-chested, why not them? But that's the way it is.

What puzzles me is that she's a member of the Silver Phalanx. I thought the very essence of being in the Phalanx was that you were inconspicuous and could take everyone by surprise. But with Red Pearl around, everything else seems to fade into the background. Maybe they use her as a decoy. She's going to come with us as far as Bolvudis Strait, because she knows the southern lands very well—she was brought up in the Centaur Forests.

So we met them, and I had asked Kirin whether he still had the black ravian book with the moongold edges and he said he did—and we all waited for Asvin and Spikes. Amloki was getting very worried—apparently the Civilian didn't know Asvin was all alone in the Underbelly and would be really angry to learn Amloki wasn't with him. Gaam pointed out that Amloki wouldn't be much protection for Asvin if someone *did* attack him, which might not have been the most tactful thing to say at the time, because Amloki looked really upset.

Spikes arrived a little later, and said he couldn't wake Asvin, and that if he tried any harder Asvin would get seriously injured. So we went back to Frags to wait for him to get up.

That Asvin can sleep. Kirin kept looking at me accusingly, because obviously it was the Dragonjuice—and possibly the spell as well—that had done this to him. He finally woke up at about ten, and was really apologetic. He's so nice.

Gaam said that traditionally quests began at dawn or in the dead of night, apparently because then the environment represents the troubled times which necessitated the quest in the first place, but since we weren't really going on a quest but on a training mission it didn't really matter.

Then we all went back to the War Temple, where Red Pearl was waiting with the horses. A small crowd had gathered around her, which dispersed when Spikes arrived. We left the south gate at noon.

Being out of Kol is very disorienting. The most unnerving thing is the silence. Not having carpets sweep by, not having asurs shouting at you, not smelling strange smells all the time—it takes getting used to. I was looking forward to this, actually—being one with nature and so on, but after a week I'm beginning to think I'm best suited to life in the city. I miss Kol. I mean, if the country was all wild and rugged it would be fine, but so far it's been really tame—mostly rice-fields and empty stretches punctuated by dhabas. This wood is nice, though, light green and fresh. The land is slightly hillier now, which gives me hope. We're going to follow the south road until it bends eastwards towards the Centaur Forests and Ajaxis, and then get off the road and cut through the Bleakwood to Bolvudis Strait. It should take around three more nights, including tonight.

Another thing that takes getting used to is the substantial

drop in magic. Even simple lighting spells are so much harder to do out here in the country. Most of us spellbinders tend to forget how closely magic is interwoven with the place you're trying to perform it in. The power of the land, and so on, but of course in Kol it's more the power of the Heart of Magic.

I'm reasonably bored. The last week has been really dull. I mean, there is only so much entertainment you can extract from paddy-fields and bullocks chewing cud. And while this wood is really pretty, watching trees grow takes more time than I'm prepared to give. That's the thing about city life— it shortens the attention span. Kirin and Asvin both spent a lot of their early years in forests, so they're perfectly happy strolling around and smelling the 'sweet, fresh smell of new leaves'. Good for them.

Gaam and I have been talking a lot. He's wonderful— knows so much about heroes, weapons and legends—I must find out more about the vaman city, no one knows enough about it. He told me that most heroes get bored on quests, but of course they never talk about it later, and of course life would seem slow to me, since I am used to travelling really fast. Not that we're travelling slowly now—the horses are big and strong, and Spikes runs amazingly fast. So does Queeen.

Speaking of travelling, Gaam and Amloki both astonished the rest of us when they calmly mounted their horses. I didn't know the little people could ride. And they generally can't—it's just the two of them. Amloki's quite a character, too, and very affectionate. He spends a lot of his time staring at Red Pearl, who, frankly, is beginning to annoy me with her constant preening and look-at-me-I'm-an-amazing-centauress-ness. Gaam, Asvin and Kirin are all practically drooling over her.

These lands are quite deserted. The only animal I can see

is Asvin's pet rabbit Fluffy, who is nibbling the grass near my foot. There aren't too many birds here either, except a crow that has been following us since we left the city. Gaam said I shouldn't be disappointed, but these were among the least beautiful lands around Kol. I wish we were going to Durg. The journey to Bolvudis is not a pretty one. Soon we'll be getting off the road and entering the Bleakwood, which is desolate and full of bandits, but Bolvudis is apparently really beautiful.

So I'm on a journey in the wild. Well, a journey in the tame, soon to be wild, anyway.

I'm glad this is not a proper quest, otherwise I would have been severely disillusioned. I thought that going on a quest would mean incredible hardships and being ambushed every half hour. But we've been speeding down the road, stopping every now and then to eat in dhabas and sleep in inns. Gaam said that the Bleakwood would be very dangerous, so I'm looking forward to that. It's been like a little holiday so far—thankfully no one has started singing, though Asvin has a very melodious voice.

I don't think I am as drawn to Asvin now as I was that night at Frags. He's incredibly nice and attractive, but he keeps offering me his arm, helping me get on and off my horse, opening doors for me at inns and so on, which is a little irritating. I'm not some frail little thing he has to protect in the wild. What is really annoying is not him, though, but the fact that I enjoy the attention sometimes. Not a good thing. I caught myself blushing two days ago when he told me I looked wonderful in the sunset, though later I realized that must be because visibility is lower then. It's very confusing. Yesterday he climbed a hill to get me a wild rose, fresh with the morning dew and everything, and gave it to me to put, he said, amidst my lustrous tresses. I would have pointed out that I didn't have lustrous tresses, but Kirin stopped me with a look. I have no idea what to do with flowers, I generally use them as targets, so I gave the rose to Kirin, who gave it to Red Pearl, who promptly put it amidst her lustrous tresses, which annoyed me even more.

Luggage is not a problem either—no trudging through marshes with heavy packs, there are spare horses carrying everything. But we are going off the road tomorrow, and all the extra blankets I brought will come in handy then. The country is a lot colder than Kol, obviously, and the weather is really nice.

A part of me wishes it would all be like this, a pleasant jaunt out in the country, and after a few weeks we could return to Kol and carry on with life, but I know everything's going to change. If Danh-Gem rises again . . . And what is Kirin's part in all this? Father will know . . . It will be such a good thing for them, the sudden appearance of a ravian. I'm sure Kirin will have something really important to do. I might be getting bored now, but when things start getting difficult I know I'll be looking back at today and wishing I could be back here in this leafy glade—I did it again!— with the warm afternoon sunlight on my back and Fluffy sleeping next to me as I write and watch ladybirds scuttle through the grass. I'm getting positively lyrical. Must be all this fresh air.

Must tell Spikes to stop killing butterflies. They seem to be drawn to him, suicidal little idiots.

Kirin just came and lay down next to me. We're moving in an hour. We won't move far this evening, but we're not getting back on the road again. We're sleeping in the woods from tonight.

He's lying on his back with his eyes closed—he's looking as relaxed as I feel. Which reminds me of what we were talking about, another aspect of quests that the books never ever speak of. Kirin and I discussed this at great length today, and concluded that the only reason that heroes are generally male is not superior strength or cunning (obviously) but the simple fact that males can stay alert and upright, and can even hold weapons, while doing certain things. How many brave female warriors must have been attacked and overcome by cunning enemies when they were looking for a suitably private place to squat in the bushes. It's really unfair. Answering the call of nature in the midst of nature is not something I'm looking forward to. Funny how no legend discusses this. When I write my book on heroines in history, there will be a chapter called 'Bathrooms and Bravery'. When we brought the subject up in front of the others, Gaam was very appreciative, but Red Pearl looked disdainful—what does she care anyway, she's practically a horse—and Amloki and Asvin went bright red. Asvin looked really shocked and sad. I don't think he's very attracted to me at the moment— I'm probably not lofty, noble, graceful and ladylike enough for him. Gaam, on the other hand, has an open, inquiring mind—I'm glad he and Kirin are here.

I think I'll sleep for a while now.

One hour later.

Kirin woke me up. Asvin and Gaam had gone ahead to scout around, and they came back with the news that a reasonably large stretch of barren land lies ahead, separating this wood and the Bleakwood. They think it's best that we don't move any further tonight. Fine by me. Asvin—trust him—has brought a chess set with him and is demanding a rematch—apparently Spikes told him spellbinders can't see the future. Damn. Well, I suppose it's all for the best that he knows—if I am to go on many quests with him, he shouldn't think I have powers that I don't have. I'll beat him quickly and be done with it. Will write more tomorrow. It's getting darkish.

21

The night was dark, as most nights tend to be. Red Pearl was keeping guard. She looked at her fellow travellers, sleeping in the shadows of a large tree. She raised her head and sniffed the night air. She looked at the moon, a thin white curve in the sky above the wood. The stars were shining bright, though.

She trotted away from the sleepers. She was tired of these humans, clumsy, noisy, simple. She was tired of the slow pace they were moving at. But there was always the moon.

Red Pearl held out her arms to the dying moon and walked in the starlight. She revelled in the soft glow, feeling the last quiet rays of the old moon sliding along her glowing skin, caressing her, bathing her. She took a deep breath. Finally, nothing binding her, no one watching her, she was free . . .

'And I thought the stars were beautiful,' said the Silver Dagger softly, jumping down, catlike, from a nearby tree.

Red Pearl sighed. Back to work. 'Save the charm for humans,' she said, but she smiled. 'Or grow a horse's body and a tail, and I am yours. I warn you, though, centaurs mate for life.'

'What a truly horrifying concept,' said the Dagger. He looked around. 'All asleep?'

'Yes. Kirin took a long time, though.'

'That boy is more than he appears to be, I can feel it. I like him, somehow. But tell me, Pearl, does anyone suspect anything?'

'Asvin has been asking me many questions. I don't know when he got it into his head that you were following us. I assured him you weren't, but he wasn't convinced. But he is no threat, and he lacks the skill to see you when you don't want to be seen. I pretended I didn't know where you were, or what you were doing. But I was never a very convincing liar, was I.'

'It must have been something the Civilian said, then. I don't want him finding me out—that would be a grievous blow to professional pride. What do you think of him?'

'He's more intelligent than he seems. His woodcraft is sufficient, but he lacks patience. Which, again, is a good thing if you're a hero.'

'And Kirin?'

'I like him too, and like you, I don't know why. He's hiding something in that little bag of his.'

'We shall find out what it is, trust me. Now listen. Your assignment has been revised a little.'

'Because of the crow? I was wondering if it might be a good idea to just shoot it.'

'It's not just one crow, they're operating in shifts. No, they will find us; killing one will only answer their questions and confirm that Spikes is the pashan they seek. You must watch Spikes at all times, Pearl.'

'I've been doing that. I'm fairly sure he knows nothing

about this Danh-Gem's bodyguard business. He seems really attached to Kirin. If you want to know what I think, in my opinion Kirin is a spellbinder too. He can work magic, I'm sure of it. I tried to find out how he became Spikes's master, but he was evasive. He isn't as drawn to me as he wants little Maya to think. Well, he might be, but his mind is still working clearly.'

'Modest, aren't you. But it's true, what you said,' mused the Dagger. 'I think the vanars will attack fairly soon. If we read the signs right. Perhaps they already await us in the Bleakwood. We have been moving too slowly.'

'Of course we read the signs right. We always do. We are definitely being followed. But we will deal with the attack when it comes. What is my revised assignment, then?'

'If Spikes leaves the group at any stage, I want you to follow him. I will have to stay with Asvin. Spikes appears to be harmless, but don't trust him.'

'I wasn't planning to.'

'I got a scarab from the Civilian today. Almost gave my hiding place away, when it buzzed down from the sky. She said Yarni had been attacked again, so it is imperative that Spikes does not fall into vanar hands.'

'He won't. Not while I'm alive.'

'Stay alive, then. The Civilian also said Bjorkun had left, and was heading eastwards, but that was a ruse—as soon as he finds and kills whoever's tracking him, he'll be off to Artaxerxia.'

'And will he be meeting you there?'

'No. I am to guard Asvin until he is fully trained. The vaman is strong and very clever, but I will be needed, I think. The Civilian herself had not anticipated the vanars getting involved.'

'I would be happier if this whole pashan issue was resolved. There is much that needs to be done in my homeland, and I grow weary of this journey.'

'I think it's a good sign that Spikes is here, and we can keep an eye on him. But beware of him—I do not think he serves anyone other than Kirin, and Kirin trusts no one but Maya. But if he is indeed destined to be Danh-Gem's servant, he must be watched. Do not leave him alone with Asvin. And if you have to fight him, do not engage him in close combat; shoot him from as far away as possible. I know you are immensely strong, but so is he. And I do not want anything to happen to you, Pearl. The centaurs need you, and so do I.'

'I can take care of myself.'

'I know.'

There was silence for a while.

Then the Dagger whispered, 'Someone's coming,' and disappeared.

His ears are sharper than mine, thought Red Pearl, as she turned and saw Spikes walking towards her. Had he seen anything? 'What is it?' she asked sharply.

'I heard voices,' said Spikes.

'We centaurs talk to the dying moon. It's an ancient custom.'

'I think we are being followed. I was looking down the road in the evening, and I saw a black shape slip into the woods. I will stand guard with you.'

'It is quite all right,' said Red Pearl sharply, 'I will wake you if anything approaches.'

They eyed each other warily for some time.

'Is Kirin awake?' asked Red Pearl.

'No.'

'Very nice young man. How long have you known him?'

'Long enough,' said Spikes gruffly. 'Are you sure you don't want me to keep watch?'

'Yes.'

'Good night, then,' and Spikes walked back to where the others were sleeping, quickly and quietly.

After a while, Pearl looked up at the tree, but the Dagger had disappeared. Long enough, she thought grimly. She flexed her arm and watched the muscles ripple in the starlight. Long enough, indeed. I will be keeping watch, thank you, Spikes. And I will be watching you.

A little while later, a short distance away, the vanars were preparing to attack. There were three of them, sitting on a low branch of a large tree, clad in mail vests, longbows in their hands. They were talking to a crow.

'I'm telling you, they're all sleeping, except the centaur,' said Corporal One-hundred-and-two 'Thunderbird'. 'I just went and checked.'

'Did anyone see you?' asked a vanar, taking an arrow out of a quiver.

'The centaur saw me, I think, but I'm just a bird to her. She was talking to the pashan, anyway.'

'No one else saw you?'

'No. They're all sleeping, I told you.'

'Lord Bali will be pleased. We will take the pashan tonight, and the boy, and kill all the rest.'

'I don't think we should attack now,' said another vanar. 'We should follow them, see where they're going.'

'How many times do I have to tell you, our orders do not concern the rest. Lord Bali told me himself,' replied the first.

'Where is he now? Did he return to Vanarpuri after his glorious victory in the city?'

'No. The last crow said he was still somewhere near Kol, and was speaking of having to travel soon. That was four days ago. He's still in hiding; the guards of Kol are looking for him. He sees no one except the crow Kraken.'

'Commander Kraken,' said Thunderbird.

'Yes. So it's settled, we attack now. Shoot the centaur first; centaurs are good archers, almost as good as us. I will kill the sleepers.'

'I don't like this. There is no honour in this slaying. We vanars are warriors, not assassins,' said the second vanar. The third vanar sighed.

'Times change,' said the first, tersely, 'Let's go. Ready?'

'Yes,' said the second.

'Nala?'

The third vanar didn't reply. He wasn't there.

'Where did he go now?' asked the first crossly. 'He was here a second ago.'

No one replied. There was a soft *thud*.

The vanar didn't turn around. He jumped out of the tree and soared to another, fitting an arrow to his bow and looking around wildly. Curse the bird! He had been followed!

'Show yourself!' he shouted, desperately looking around. He saw his fallen comrades lying at the foot of the tree, their bodies twisted at odd angles. They were quite dead.

'They're dead! They fell off the branch!' yelled Thunderbird, flapping his wings loudly as he perched nearby.

'Get away from me,' hissed the vanar. There was a sudden stinging pain in his neck. Curse the wasps! Now was not the time!

He fell dead.

Thunderbird panicked and flew upwards fast, but it was

too late. A dart pierced his wing, the poison spread instantly and he crashed into a tree and slid to the ground.

Well, they won't be looking for other pashans any more, thought the Dagger, slinging the blowpipe over his shoulder. Hopefully this will give us the time we need before more vanars arrive. They shouldn't know we are going to Bolvudis. I will have to make sure our tracks are covered in the forest. They will find us less easy to follow this time. Should I shoot every crow that tries to follow us? Bit of a risk, though. Now, a little sleep, he thought, and melted into the night.

T hey all rose early, and set off further southwards. The trees around them stood scarred in the bright sunlight. They crossed the stretch of charred ground that separated the Bleakwood from the forest they had slept in, and rode among the gloomy trees. Once this had been a lush, green forest, part of western Psomedea—it had run to the borders of Elaken and there it had merged with Vrihataranya, like a river running into the ocean.

Then the knights of Ventelot, long before the Age of Terror, had overrun the land, clearing the forest, fighting the Psomedeans and driving them eastwards, towards the Centaur Forests and their capital, Ajaxis. In the hills the armies of Ventelot had built castles, in the plains great barracks; they had then pushed north and east, conquering Avranti. Then King Amrit had driven the forces of Ventelot back to the west, founding Kol on the banks of the Asa. Years later, far in the north, the rakshas Danh-Gem had driven Ventelot's knights even further away, founding the realm of Imokoi, and freeing the wild horse-men and pirates of Skuanmark. Ventelot still existed, of course, but now it was a minor power holding the lands to the north-west of Artaxerxia and its chief concern was keeping the land-hungry Artaxerxians and Skuans at bay. But it was not during the years of Ventelot's power that the Bleakwood had got its name.

The fiercest battles of the Great War had taken place in the ruined plains now called Danh-Gem's Wasteland. Danh-Gem's dragons and magical blasts had burned their way through the woods of Psomedea, destroying some parts of the forest forever and ravaging the rest with fire. Some tall trees still stood, leafless and black, eternal testimony to Danh-Gem's destructive powers. Some other parts of the forest had grown again in the two hundred years since the Great War.

The trees were tall, but they huddled together as if still afraid of dragon-fire—as the travellers rode under them, the forest seemed to creak and grumble, as if ancient wood-spirits below the earth were brooding over the evils of years past. No light penetrated the thick leaf-canopy. This was darkness unlike the darkness of Vrihataranya—there the forest shut out the sun as a brazen display of power, not to hide whatever lay beneath from watchful eyes. The travellers rode in the eerie silence, not wanting to talk, the hoof-beats sounding jarringly loud and then dying suddenly, muffled by the oppressive air.

On the hills in the western parts of the Bleakwood, they saw the ruins of abandoned castles still disfiguring the horizon, standing jagged and cruel like the teeth of burned skulls—the land remembered bloodshed, treachery and death. The Psomedean Empire had been destroyed in the Great War, and the centaurs now ruled Ajaxis—they had let the Centaur Forests into the great city, where trees and buildings now lived in harmony. The Great Colloseum of Ajaxis was still famous, and people from all over the world gathered there to watch chariot-races and the centaurs' athletic contests. But no one had ever gone back to the Bleakwood. There were parts of that desolate wood that had not seen humans for more than three hundred years.

The northern half of the Bleakwood was completely deserted, though it was said that old ghosts and evil spirits sometimes wandered there, across Danh-Gem's Wasteland, from the pyramids of Elaken or the mountains of Imokoi. But the southern half, through which the travellers were riding, was rumoured to be full of bandits. These were the failures of the criminal world, who had been muscled out of Kol and other cities by the young and the unscrupulous. Led by the famous Tlotlot the Highwayman, they had occupied some old castles and lived there in miserable poverty, dreaming of days when they would move back to rich cities or prosperous trade routes. They had been forced to give up their lives of crime simply because rich people did not come to the Bleakwood. Even the actors who had started coming to Bolvudis Island generally took the longer route, travelling by road to Ajaxis and then by sea. The bandits of Bleakwood were poor, but they were still proud. They had once been criminals of repute. They would not stoop to robbing aspiring actors.

Maya snapped a twig off a dead tree as she rode by it, looked at it and thought about fire. It burst into flames instantly. It was a good day for magic. As she blew it out and rode on, she suddenly thought it had become a little colder. The forest did not like fire—it stirred up bad memories.

They were riding fast through the trees, heading for a little stream some distance ahead. Asvin and Gaam were riding in front; Red Pearl was running behind them. Then came Amloki, with the horses bearing their packs, followed by Kirin and Maya. Queeen was keeping up effortlessly with the horses, and Spikes was running a little distance behind, his heavy feet leaving deep grooves in the grassless earth. Asvin and Gaam were trying to sing from time to time, but faltering as they jerked up and down as the horses galloped over the hard ground. They were discussing Ventelot military tactics—Asvin was quite fascinated by the castles, and was asking Gaam whether Ventelot had used magic to conquer so much of the world.

'No,' Gaam said, 'they were all quite hopeless at magic. Their wizards, called druids, did very little apart from supervising the creation of large circles of monoliths—the largest one is in Imokoi, called the Circle of Darkness. Why they made these stone rings, no one knows—but their magical abilities were very limited. No, what made Ventelot great was the valour of the knights of the Almost-Perfectly-Circular Table. And the fact that their enemies generally stood and laughed at their strange armour right up to the moment they got lances pierced through their stomachs.'

'What was the armour like?' asked Asvin. They had reached the stream, which was running merrily through the middle of the dreary Bleakwood. The waters were quite deep here—they were planning to cross an old bridge a little further downstream.

'Well, it was really comical. Useful for mounted combat on a battlefield, but really cumbersome at close quarters. A nimble asur with a dagger could take a knight on any time. Your standard knight of Ventelot looked like a large, awkward tin soldier. Like that knight standing in the middle of the bridge, look,' said Gaam. He was silent for a moment, wondering what he had just said. Then he looked again. His eyes hadn't been fooling him.

A knight clad in ancient, rusty armour was standing in the middle of the bridge. His battle-stained shield had the emblem of a black cat on it.

They rode up to the bridge. The knight saw them and drew his sword.

'I don't remember him being here,' said Red Pearl, puzzled.

'I'll handle this,' said Gaam, riding forward. 'Hail, Sir Knight!' he called.

The knight stuck his sword into the wooden bridge. He spoke in a deep, booming voice.

'None Shall Pass,' he said.

The words echoed a little, probably because of the armour.

'Who are you, O noble one?' asked Gaam. 'My friend, the centauress, has walked these lands many times, but she has never seen one as mighty as you.'

'Then heed my words, dwarf,'—the Kol-dwellers all flinched and looked at Gaam, but he was unmoved— 'and tell thy woman-horse I am Sir Cyr, Guardian of the Bridge.'

'Sir what?' asked Gaam.

'Sir Cyr.'

'Sir Sir what?'

'Cyr.'

'Never mind. How long have you been guardian of the bridge, Sir Knight?'

'It matters not,' the armour creaked as the knight stamped his foot on the bridge again. 'None Shall Pass.'

'I could challenge him to a duel . . .' whispered Asvin.

'I'm negotiating, be quiet.'

'Right. Sorry.'

'Why are you guarding the bridge, Sir Knight?'

'It matters not,' offered Sir Cyr. 'None Shall Pass.' Stamp.

'Very well. We will just have to take the other bridge, then.'

'The other bridge?' asked Asvin, whose mind was keen and straight, like a spear.

'Ah yes, the other bridge,' said Kirin, whose mind was keen and twisted, like a corkscrew.

'The one with the young girl in a grass skirt who puts a garland around your neck and welcomes you to the south?' asked Maya, getting into the spirit of things.

'The other bridge that's a little way down, just out of sight from here?' asked Amloki.

'There is another bridge?' asked Sir Cyr, suddenly sounding old and weary.

'Yes,' said Gaam, cleverly answering everyone's questions simultaneously.

Behind the visor, Sir Cyr's eyes blinked balefully. Under the armour, his shoulders sagged.

'The reason we came here is that there's always a queue there—you know how it is with young girls and garlands. Now come, sir, you are a knight noble, fair and chivalrous. We come in peace. Let us pass,' said Gaam.

'No one told me,' Sir Cyr said mournfully. 'I have been guarding this bridge since morn. They broke the lock.'

'They broke the lock?' enquired Asvin.

'Never mind. I think he's a little mad, whoever he is,' whispered Gaam.

'Go on, cross the bridge,' Cyr picked his sword up and sheathed it. 'But how is it that brown-skinned easterners walk in the woods of south Ventelot? They broke the lock. It escaped. Beware, men, I see bandits. Open not that door, bandits. Brown-skinned easterners in south Ventelot. The world hath changed much.' His voice was suddenly edged with fear and wonder. He was talking to himself.

They rode across the bridge, watching him warily. Sir Cyr stayed in the middle.

'South Ventelot?' asked Red Pearl scornfully. 'This is the Bleakwood, and Ventelot is but a bad memory in these lands. Where have you been, ancient one?'

'I am Sir Cyr of the Macabre Gard. Sir Cyr, Guardian of the Bridge. The king has ordered us to keep it imprisoned. But bandits came, alas. The cat is out. My men are dead. Deep, deep underground. The south will know the nundu once again. Must Guard the Bridge. None Shall Pass.' He sounded frantic.

'The king? What king?'

'God save the king of Ventelot. Have they returned from the land of Avranti? Cat ate the bandits. Guard the cat. A cat may look at a king. There is another bridge, God save the cat. No one told me. None Shall Pass.'

'He *must* be mad,' said Gaam, looking worried. 'Does anyone know what a nundu is? I don't.'

No one else knew what a nundu was either.

'Let's go, I've had enough of this madman. South Ventelot, indeed. South Ventelot hasn't existed for centuries,' said Red Pearl.

'Let me try one more time. Can you tell us what ails you, Sir Knight? We might be able to help.'

'It matters not. Deep, deep underground. The cat is out. The rest are dead. I am Sir Cyr of the Macabre Gard, Guardian of the Nundu. There is another bridge. Girl and garland, welcome the king. None Shall Pass.'

'No. He's mad,' said Gaam resignedly.

They rode on.

'I could have challenged him to a duel,' said Asvin ruefully. 'Now I feel a little worried. What was he talking about?'

'If you wander in the wilds in this part of the world, you will meet madmen every day,' said Red Pearl. 'Think no more of it, he was babbling. If you want to put everything he said together, he was probably a crazed ex-bandit who found a room with a lock deep underground, found that ridiculous armour and that shield with a cat on it, and then decided he would be Guardian of the Bridge, and a knight of old Ventelot waiting for the king to return from Avranti. You meet dozens of people like him on the streets of Kol. Why, while I was waiting for you to return from the Underbelly a man came up to me and said he was really a centaur who had lost his tail, and invited me to help him find it. The south will know the cat again, indeed! Think no more of it.'

Of course, after that they all thought about practically nothing else all afternoon. But nothing happened.

'You must remember this is not the story of a quest—this is real life, and not everything happens for a reason,' Maya said to Asvin, who was scanning the forest for cats and unknown beings that might, on close investigation, turn out be nundus. Asvin looked mildly disappointed, but sheathed his sword.

They travelled fast through the Bleakwood all day, meeting no bandits, madmen or monsters. They rode for a while even after sunset, until the horses needed rest. They found a little sheltered hollow and camped there for the night. The skies were clear—there was no moon that night but the stars were twinkling merrily. They were all in reasonably high spirits, and they lit a fire, sat in a circle around it and told stories till it was very late. Then Maya, who was telling the others how, in the city, she hardly ever slept, fell asleep in the middle of a sentence. The rest spoke for a while in low voices, put out the fire and drifted off too. Asvin offered to keep watch but Red Pearl would have none of it.

She walked around a little after the rest had fallen asleep, but the Dagger did not come. Red Pearl listened to the night noises of insects and the whistling of the wind through leaves and bare branches. An hour passed.

Asvin was dreaming of Avranti, of elephants and tiger chases in Shantavan, of a beautiful woman he had once seen near a sage's ashram when he was very young. She had smiled at him and vanished, and he had run after her, thinking she was an apsara who had come to distract the sage from his meditation. But she had run away; in later years he had thought she must have been a Durgan warrior-woman. In his dream, he had been running after her, when the trees turned into his guards, his friends, who all attacked him, naked swords in their hands. He was unarmed. Arjun stepped up and swung his sword . . . Asvin woke up.

He sat up. He was sweating slightly, the memory of Arjun's hate-contorted face in the dream still vivid in his mind.

From a hole in the bag he was travelling in emerged a rabbit. This assignment was not all it could have been, thought Steel-Bunz. Bumping around in a bag on a horse was not his style. Besides, Asvin seemed to be well protected. I would have been better off staying in Kol. It's just not fair: They give me all the easy assignments because I'm a rabbit, he mused. I've got to do something to make my presence felt. And the next time that silly wolfhound nuzzles me in a patronizing way she loses her nose.

He saw something moving in the woods, far away. He looked around for Red Pearl and saw her standing motionless in the night, looking the opposite way.

Now here's a chance for Asvin and me to bond, he thought.

He scurried off to Asvin and nuzzled against his palm.

'What is it, Fluffy?' asked Asvin absent-mindedly.

Steel-Bunz gave his sleeve a little tug. Just look that way, something moving in woods, time to investigate with little rabbit friend, isn't it?

'I do believe you're trying to tell me something.'

Do you, now. Will you look up for a moment, please? Look, there it is. Whatever it is, it's moving further away. So hurry.

'You know, Fluffy, I love you, but I wish you were a dog. Dogs understand their masters.'

That settled it. Steel-Bunz nipped his finger sharply. Asvin snatched his hand away with a little cry of pain. Pathetic, Steel-Bunz thought. He stalked off to his bag, and stayed there.

'What is it?' Red Pearl asked Asvin.

'Nothing, really. Now why don't you get some sleep? I can't sleep tonight, for some reason. I'll stand on guard, and wake you at the slightest sound. Please don't say no.'

'Very well, then, wake me in three hours,' said Red Pearl reluctantly, acknowledging and succumbing to charm and tiredness. She trotted up to where Amloki, Gaam, Maya and Kirin were sleeping in a circle. Spikes was standing next to a tree—like centaurs, pashans slept upright—looking like a very ugly, badly carved statue. His tusks were rising and falling gently and his vertical eyelids were shut. Red Pearl stood next to the tree where the horses were tied and was soon asleep.

Asvin got up, picked up his sword and walked around for a while. His dream had made him remember home, and he suddenly felt very lonely and forlorn as he walked alone in the Bleakwood. He had been trained from birth to face and accept things as they came, because it was all karma, but the whirlwind-like life he was leading now was beginning to take its toll. He forced his mind into a state of calm and listened to the whispers running through the trees and the ground. He wished he were back in Shantavan, where the colours of day and night were fresh and vibrant, newly painted, unlike the faded tiredness of the Bleakwood.

Then he heard the singing.

It was coming from far away, a girl's voice, singing a song in a language he did not know. As sweet and melodious as a nightingale's was the voice that sang it, and Asvin felt himself drawn towards the sound, his feet trying to move of their own accord towards it.

Asvin was no fool. He knew that enchanting voices in the Bleakwood would probably be treacherous and belong to strange, hungry monsters singing for their supper. He had heard of the sirens of Psomedea of old, who lured men to their deaths with their songs. But this song was not seductive and beguiling, like a siren's—it was innocent and pure, like dew on leaves, like sunrise over Tiger Hill in Durg, like a mountain spring. It did not overpower the senses, it invigorated them. But Asvin knew he could not leave the camp unprotected. He badly wanted to find the singer, though.

Asvin was not very happy with the way things were going.

He had the feeling that everyone, except Kirin perhaps, was being a little condescending. He knew he wasn't as clever as Maya or Gaam, or as strong as Red Pearl or Spikes, but he was the Hero, after all, and he was willing to learn. And his hunger for adventure was completely unsatisfied. He knew he was being protected, shielded from the dangers that it was his right to face, and he didn't like it at all. He wanted to have an adventure on his own and this seemed like a good opportunity.

He hesitated, wondering whom to wake up. Red Pearl or Gaam would not let him go, Maya would want to come with him. Spikes scared him. Kirin, he decided. Kirin wouldn't mind.

There was a sudden noise behind him. He whirled around, swinging his sword.

It was Spikes. He caught the sword with one hand and pulled it out of Asvin's grasp.

'Careful,' he said quietly, 'you could hurt people with this thing.'

Asvin looked at the sword in Spikes's hand. Spikes looked as if he could break it like a twig. He took a step backwards, shaken. It wasn't fair, someone as big as Spikes shouldn't be able to move so quietly . . . He looked at Spikes. His eyes were glowing pale green. Asvin felt a stab of fear. Avrantics didn't *like* pashans.

'What's that noise?' said Spikes after a few moments of silence. He gave the sword back to Asvin.

Asvin breathed again. 'I don't know,' he said. 'I'm going to go look. Will you keep watch?'

'It could be dangerous,' said Spikes. 'There are many things in this forest that do not love humans. Perhaps I should go.'

'No, I will go,' said Asvin, suddenly remembering how clear and sweet the song was. 'If I don't return in an hour, wake the others.'

'Very well,' said Spikes. 'Remember I warned you.'

But Asvin had already gone, threading through the trees, towards the enchanting voice far away. The magical voice had woven little webs of melody in the air, and was drawing him in like a spider.

Wake up, Kirin, said the voice.

Kirin sat up hurriedly and looked around. Everyone else seemed to be asleep, though Spikes was prowling around the camp. He shook his head groggily. He had a headache.

Take the book out, Kirin.

Who was it? The voice seemed to be *inside* his head. And it sounded strangely familiar . . .

'Who . . .' he said slowly. His head was really aching.

Take the book out, Kirin. Quickly. I do not have much time.

With a little start, Kirin realized why the voice was familiar. It was almost exactly like his own.

He took the book out of the little bag stuffed with rolled-up clothes that he had been using as a pillow. As he touched it, the edges glowed bright in the night, almost as bright as a little Alocactus. Light to read at night, thought Kirin. Very clever. Too bad the book is empty.

Open it.

'Who are you?' whispered Kirin.

Open it.

He opened the book. In the glow of the moongold, he saw the pages were still empty.

Then a faint black line appeared on the page. As Kirin watched, it curved, another line appeared below it, curving up to meet it. Little spiky lines shot out. A circle formed in the middle. Kirin realized he was looking at an eye.

It winked. Another eye appeared beside it.

Then a nose, then a mouth, then the rest of the face, in fine black lines, as if sketched by a very good artist. The lines drawn were thin and spidery, as if there was not much ink.

Kirin looked at the face. It was his own.

Then a scar appeared on the left side of the face, from beside the eyebrow all the way down to the jaw. Kirin noted that the face looked older, the jaw was stronger, the eyebrows were a little thicker and the lips were a little thinner than his own. It was not his face. But it was the face of someone who looked very like him.

'Who are you?' he whispered again.

I had many names, said the voice in his head. *When I sold magical toys in the streets of Asroye as a child, they called me the Trickster. When they threw me out of the hidden city, they called me Outcast. When I prowled through the pits of Imokoi, slaying left and right in the darkness, they called me the Shadow. In the dungeons of Danh-Gem, when they tortured me, they called me the Silent One. When I brought Simoqin back to Asroye and returned to the War, they called me the Avenger. But the name they used most often was Demon-hunter.*

Demon-hunter. The words burned a bright streak of recognition down Kirin's brain. It couldn't be.

My true name is Narak, and I am your father.

There was a faint silvery glow ahead of him. Asvin walked towards the light stealthily. The song was louder now, and clearer. And even more beautiful. It was as wonderful as a morning raga, a song of youth, beauty and love, a song that had words but didn't need them. Asvin had the sudden feeling that he was floating towards the music, his feet weren't touching the ground any more. Then he hid in the shadow of a tree and looked.

He saw her shining in the darkness, glimmering, radiant, beautiful.

His heart stopped. His eyes bulged.

He was in love.

Shut out the joy. Shut out the pain. Think, Kirin. So he says he's your father, and the book is a ravian book. But it's one of the Untranslatable Books, it's from Imokoi, it was probably written by Danh-Gem himself. It could be a spell-book of Danh-Gem's, something he used to look into the minds of ravians, to find their thoughts and desires and thus trick them. Do not believe it.

'Why should I believe you? Prove it,' he whispered.

I did not expect you to believe me, Kirin. It would have been foolish to trust a book from Imokoi, would it not? Perhaps I am a creation of Danh-Gem, you are thinking. I do not blame you. And I will give you proof, Kirin, but I cannot now. This wood you are in is an evil place, Kirin. It saps away my powers, and I must conserve my powers, for I have much to tell you. The pain you are feeling is mine, Kirin. Get out of here fast, Kirin. You are in deadly danger.

The voice was anxious, fervent; it was either telling the truth or it was the best liar in the world. The pain in Kirin's head was blinding. He was seeing straggly little white shapes floating around him.

'What do you want me to do?'

Get out of this forest in secret. Take your pashan with you. Tell no one. That is of utmost importance. Tell no one. You are in deadly peril, and so are those who travel with you. You are being hunted, and you must live, Kirin, for great and terrible deeds lie before you. There are some things only ravians can do. Take your things, and leave tonight. Leave now. I need some time before I am strong enough to prove I am indeed your father. But the longer you stay in these woods the weaker I will get. And you need my guidance, son.

'I cannot do that,' whispered Kirin. 'All that you say is fine, but I will not abandon my task without proof.'

Understand this, Kirin. You were left behind for a purpose. You were left behind by me, to finish the task that I began. You are the Slayer, son, the one the Prophecies do not speak of. When Danh-Gem rises, you are the one burdened with the task of killing him. You are the only one who can. And I must guide you. Please. I beg you, listen to me. Do not gamble with the lives of those dear to you, for danger will seek you out wherever you go. I will explain everything. I am your father, Kirin, trust me.

The face on the book was twisted with pain, and the lines were growing thinner.

Kirin wanted to believe him, wanted to hold on to him, part of his mind was screaming at him—to obey, to take the book, his bag, and Spikes, and disappear quietly. This was the ideal opportunity. But Kirin was not a hero.

'Save your strength, if you are indeed my father,' he said finally, as great lumps of pain forced their way into his brain. The world was a black blur. His head was throbbing wildly. 'I am going to meet the most powerful spellbinder in the world,' he said, with difficulty. 'And Simoqin's hero is my friend. Save your strength, and we will work together to destroy Danh-Gem.'

There was a dry laugh in his head. *So you will not believe unless I show you. Son, if human heroes could save the world, I would not have cast the spell that caused you to be left behind.*

But you will not trust me. You are indeed my son. So be it. But beware, for danger lurks beneath the boughs of this evil wood. I will save my strength indeed. Sleep now—you will need it. Tell no one.

The face faded, and so did the pain. Kirin fell back to the ground, exhausted. He managed to shove the book into his bag before he lost consciousness.

Asvin watched, wonderstruck, as she sang.

She was the most beautiful woman he had ever seen. Her features were serene and perfect, her eyes were large, blue and bright. She looked like the pictures of Skuan goddesses Asvin had seen in Kol. Her hair was shimmering golden in the night; her skin was fair and glowing softly. As she sang, Asvin's heart soared—he felt as if he was flying high, above clouds and mountains in a snow-covered land. Her red lips called out to him, her slender arms seemed to reach out for him. He was enchanted.

Flowers grew at the maiden's feet, even in the scarred earth of the Bleakwood. Vines grew magically, entwined around her, sprouting leaves in strategic places covering her beautiful nakedness. Just like the paintings, Asvin thought. Of course, he had not even noticed that she was naked, for Asvin had always been a Good Boy; he had just noticed in passing that she was slender and incredibly graceful—he was lost in her eyes, her shining face and her glimmering hair.

The sky was growing lighter.

'Where is Asvin?' demanded Red Pearl angrily.

'He heard noises in the forest and went off to look,' said Spikes.

'What? You let him go off alone?'

'Why would I want to stop him? He's not a child, he seemed to know what he was doing.'

'What a fool I was, to sleep in the Bleakwood! Which way did he go?'

Spikes pointed.

'You made a mistake letting him go, Spikes. If I do not find him, I will blame you,' said Red Pearl, and galloped away into the forest.

The maiden suddenly stopped singing and looked around. She has sensed my presence, thought Asvin, I must speak to her. I must find out who she is. I must make her mine.

He stepped forward, young, tall, noble, handsome.

'Nightingale!' he said.

She looked shocked. She leapt out of the vines, nature's chaperones, and ran naked through the forest. Asvin shut his eyes gallantly. After a while, he opened them, but she had gone.

Nightingale? Nightingale? Of all the stupid things I could have said or done, stepping out of the bush and saying 'Nightingale!' was probably the stupidest, he thought. Now, where am I, exactly?

The sound of hooves thundered through the forest, and Red Pearl was upon him.

'This was a very irresponsible thing to do, Asvin!' she yelled. 'You might have been killed! What were you thinking?'

'I apologize for making you worry, Red Pearl, but I was in no danger. I can take care of myself.'

'No danger? I cannot think of anyone in this group who is less in danger than you! Except Amloki, perhaps.'

'That is unfair, Red Pearl. It is time, I think, that you began to trust me,' said Asvin gruffly.

'Brash young fool!' thundered Red Pearl. 'Abandoning us as well!'

Asvin drew himself up regally. 'I am a prince of Avranti, Red Pearl, and possibly Simoqin's Hero. I am quite capable of taking care of myself and facing the consequences of my own decisions. I would advise you to treat me with respect. And I did not abandon you—Spikes was on guard all the time. And you may doubt his ability to protect you, but I do not.'

'I should not have spoken so harshly,' said Red Pearl, softly but sternly, 'and I understand your need for respect, and I do respect you. But you must understand, Asvin, that I am in charge of your safety until you reach Bolvudis, and that the decisions you make are likely to affect the whole world if you are indeed Simoqin's hero, and that many people might suffer a horrible fate if you throw your life away rashly. You are more than a prince of Avranti now— you may be the world's greatest hope. You might feel we are being overprotective—but I assure you, we need to be. The Bleakwood is an evil place. I will speak no more about what happened this night. It is a new day, let us forget the night and journey on.'

'I understand now. I am sorry,' said Asvin, feeling guilty.

They walked back to the camp in silence.

Asvin felt very unwanted. Gaam was looking annoyed, Maya was ignoring him and trying to wake Kirin up. Even Fluffy was refusing to come out of his bag. The only ones who seemed pleased to see him were Amloki and Gaam's dog Queeen, who welcomed him back with hearty handshakes and enthusiastic licks respectively.

'We should move swiftly,' said Gaam. 'I want to reach Bolvudis Strait at dawn tomorrow.'

They packed quickly and rode off. Asvin soon forgot about Red Pearl and thought instead of the maiden in the Bleakwood. I will probably never see her again, he thought. Who was she? A dryad? A goddess? A lost princess? A part of my heart will always remain here . . .

The sun rose and shone and saw them riding through the forest. It grimaced when it saw Spikes running behind. Then it rose further and began to cast away the darkness in Artaxerxia. As its first rays filtered into the great city of Amurabad, it noticed a white-robed man riding a camel into the city.

23

The Sultan of Artaxerxia sat up and raised a thin eyebrow.

'What is it?'

The young woman by his side adjusted her veil.

'I crave your pardon, O Exalted One,' said the Grand Vizier. 'But Omar, chief of the Desert Patrol, brought something in the morning that I felt craved immediate attention.'

'Indeed? Fascinating. How are your daughter's stories coming along?' said the Sultan. 'I really must listen to her one day.'

May that day never come, thought the Grand Vizier, suppressing a shudder. 'It would be a great honour for her, Exalted One.'

A casual observer could have been forgiven for wrongly guessing which one of the men in the room was the Sultan. The Vizier was short and plump, while the Sultan was thin, tall, hook-nosed and inscrutable. The Vizier wore an expression of harassed bewilderment that was usually the defining characteristic of good-natured Sultans who were being manipulated and plotted against by their cruel, sinister and scheming Grand Viziers. This particular Vizier, however, looked anything but sinister. Of course, he *was* extremely cruel and scheming, but that was because he had to be—you couldn't be Artaxerxia's Grand Vizier unless you were. And very few people who knew the Vizier's true nature were alive . . .

The Sultan, therefore, by the Shanti-Joddhist principles of cosmic balance, should have had a heart of gold under his cold and extremely sinister exterior. But he didn't.

Compared to the Sultan, the Vizier was the soul of kindness.

'No doubt you will tell me, at some point of time, what it was that was so important,' murmured the Sultan.

'This,' said the Vizier, holding the lamp forward.

The girl gasped.

'I will send for you later, Rupina,' said the Sultan. 'Run along now.'

The girl almost ran out of the room. Her name wasn't Rupina, but she didn't care, she had escaped, she was alive.

'A jinn-lamp,' said the Vizier. 'Omar said he saw the jinn, eating an entire horde of desert bandits, two days ago. He hid behind a dune and waited until the jinn went back into the lamp, then he crept up to it and stuck a jade bead into the spout. Apparently that prevents it from coming out when it wants to—I didn't know. Omar is quite a storehouse of information on these things.'

'What an energetic young man he is, is he not?' said the Sultan. 'Most useful. But I fear his restless spirit will make it difficult for him to achieve his true potential in the army.'

Find something important for young Omar to do, noted the Grand Vizier. Something nice and rebellious.

'What does this mean, Exalted One?' he continued.

'Only yesterday the sorcerers came to me, saying their spells had suddenly become more powerful. And there are rumours that a Zu has been seen in Elaken.'

'And a jinn-lamp suddenly appears. Interesting. Of course I had no idea.'

How does he get to know all this? Has Omar been talking to him directly? But he couldn't have—he entered Amurabad this morning, and came straight to me, thought the Vizier. But why am I even surprised? Of course he knows. He always knows.

'Is not your daughter very knowledgeable about jinns and other such things?' enquired the Sultan, enjoying the little flicker in the Vizier's eyes.

'No, Exalted One. Her tales are but fairy tales for children, where jinns are kindly spirits. She would be shocked indeed if she knew the truth about the being that dwells in this lamp. What should I do with it?'

'I do not know,' said the Sultan, looking bored. 'We do not even know whether there is a jinn inside it—Omar might simply have had a bit too much to drink. Put it somewhere, take it home, give it to your lovely daughter . . . I do not care. Do with it as you please.'

The Vizier nodded. Top security. He would have to keep it in the little underground chamber under the Sultan's bedchamber. He wondered if it would be safe enough. The Sultan never bothered to look this bored unless the matter was really important.

'And when the Skuan arrives, tell him I will not meet him, since it is suspected that he is hatching plots against our friends in Kol.'

The Vizier groaned inside his head. He *hated* the barbarians. But now he knew what to do with Omar.

24

Whoever had named the Bleakwood the Bleakwood had got it just right, thought Maya as they raced through a particularly desolate cluster of dead trees. The day had been uneventful. Apart, of course, from what Kirin had told her that morning.

It was now evening, and the shadows were lengthening. To the east, they could see the beautiful green hills that marked the beginning of the Centaur Forests, and Red Pearl in particular was dying to return to her own lands. They were drawing closer to the Psomedean Ocean and there was a sea-tang in the fresh breeze that rustled through the Bleakwood. It cheered the travellers, reminding them that Bolvudis Island would be green and beautiful.

Amloki and Red Pearl had been to Bolvudis before. But they had never stayed there. Amloki had, in fact, accompanied Mantric when he had first come to Bolvudis; they had taken the longer route through the Centaur Forests and it was then that Amloki had first met Red Pearl. Maya smiled as she remembered Amloki describing their first meeting to her—

apparently Red Pearl had thoroughly intimidated both Amloki and her father.

They had travelled fast and far that morning. When they had stopped at a brook to let the horses drink, Kirin had quickly and surreptitiously told Maya what had happened to him. Maya was still finding the whole thing hard to believe, but she had to admit it made sense to a certain extent. Of course, it would be unwise to trust the book, but if it was telling the truth, this was wonderful news. Narak was the greatest of the ravian warrior-mages of old—his guidance would be invaluable. After all, he had already defeated Danh-Gem once . . . and it would also explain why Kirin had been left behind. It still did not explain Spikes, though, or why this book had been with the Untranslatables, but the voice had said it would prove its claims. And as for the threat of deadly danger, and the scornful dismissal of humans . . . well, Narak had always been disdainful of human abilities, unlike Simoqin, who had loved humans and had taught them so much magic. And if Danh-Gem rose again, deadly danger would find her and Asvin anyway. It wouldn't even need to find them, she thought, they would probably seek it out.

Maya had even taken a look at the book, but the pages were blank and lifeless in her hands. It would take very powerful magic indeed to create a such book. But then, Narak the Demon-hunter had been very powerful. She had told Kirin to take the book to Bolvudis and show it to her father. Kirin had agreed, because that would mean taking it out of the Bleakwood as the voice had wanted. He was still forcing himself not to believe it, though he really wanted to—his heart had leapt in joy when the voice had said it was Narak. Kirin had never really known his father.

They had had to stop talking about the book because

Asvin had fallen back and had begun riding with them, and had told them the tale of his own adventure. He had been trying to tell Gaam earlier, but Gaam had been most unenthusiastic—he had told Asvin never to do such a thing again, and that he was probably lucky to be alive.

As he told them of the maiden's amazing beauty and magical voice, Maya was all smiles and encouraging nods, but inside she was very, very annoyed. She knew she was not very good at hiding her thoughts from Kirin, and she saw him casting several curious glances at her. Kirin, on the other hand, was sympathy personified. When Asvin got to the point where the maiden had run away and he had gallantly not looked, Kirin asked him to tell them the whole story again. And Asvin, of course, readily and happily did so.

Red Pearl, galloping in front, suddenly noticed a man hiding behind a tall branch, watching them. Bandits, she thought grimly. She saw a little circular clearing ahead, bare earth encircled by close-growing tall trees. Perfect for an ambush. Bandits were probably waiting for them there.

'Halt!' she cried. She set an arrow to her bow with incredible speed. She pointed it at the tree. 'Come down, and I will not shoot you,' she said. There was no response— the bandit was either confident about his hiding place or a slow thinker. Red Pearl sent an arrow up into the tree. It came down a few seconds later, attached to the leg of the bandit, who hit the ground hard and rolled around, clutching his other leg, which had broken in the fall.

'We have neither the time nor the desire to kill you and your comrades,' said Red Pearl. 'But we will, if we are attacked.'

'Stand and deliver. Your money or your life. Hand over

them beauties, missy,' said Tlotlot the Highwayman, riding, riding, riding out from behind a tree. But there was no snap, no life in his voice. This wasn't even a highway, and he knew, looking at the travellers, that he and his men would probably not be able to overcome them. But a highwayman had to do what a highwayman had to do.

'Tlotlot, isn't it?' said Amloki. 'I'm Amloki, remember me? We met on the Avranti–Durg road four years ago.'

Tlotlot looked relieved. It would not have to be a fight to the death after all. He looked at Spikes in the fading light and shuddered. Then he smiled a dashing smile.

'Why yes, it's the khudran! Come out, boys! They're friends!' shouted Tlotlot, keeping a wary eye on Red Pearl's bow, which was casually pointing in his general direction.

There were half-hearted shouts of 'Dang, we woulda got' em', 'Yer lucky stiffs', and then the bandits emerged from behind the trees around the clearing. Apart from Tlotlot, Maya noted, they were mostly past their prime—thin, gloomy, tired-looking, unwashed ruffians wearing faded leather armour on which they had painted, in red, slogans like 'StAnd aND dLivER', 'ShOOt 2 KIL', 'BaD Momma', 'BAD 2D bon' and 'Yer MONIer Yer LIFF'. So these were the famous bandits of southern Bleakwood, thought Maya. I'm shaking with fear.

Tlotlot was telling his men how Amloki had found him lying wounded on the Avranti–Durg highway, healed him and then given him some money. Of course, Tlotlot was claiming that he had forced Amloki to do it all, but his men were saying 'You sure showed him, boss!' in mildly sceptical voices. There was much merriment and shaking of hands. Most of the bandits were staring at Red Pearl, open-mouthed. One particularly disreputable, scruffy old fellow sidled up to her and said, 'Howdy there, purty lady,' in an intrepid voice. Red Pearl made his day with a little smile. He thought of sliding a friendly arm around her waist, but decided against it. He was bold, but he was not suicidal.

Kirin was not smiling, though. He had been feeling uneasy for the last half-hour or so—some nameless fear had crept into his mind. His ravian senses were alert, searching the trees, the earth and the sky for a sign of danger.

He looked at the tree where Red Pearl had shot the bandit down. In their excitement, everyone had forgotten about him. The poor man would bleed to death if someone didn't take care of him, thought Kirin. He looked at the spot where the man had been a second ago. He wasn't there now.

There was a puddle of blood under the tree and a huge, bloody paw print on the ground beside it.

Kirin's ravians reflexes took over. He *felt* the great, brooding black shape crouch and prepare to spring. He *saw*, in his mind, the giant black panther-shape flying through the air, straight towards Maya. Then he saw the fiery eyes, glowing like burning coals. As he dived at her and grabbed her, knocking her off her horse, he felt the nundu's hot breath, a whisker away from his body.

The giant cat leapt right over Maya's horse, landing on and killing two bandits.

There were screams and snarls as it whirled and struck. More bodies fell. The travellers and the bandits scattered, like drops of water when a stone splashes into a river.

It was the most terrifying thing any of them had ever seen. Twice the size of a full-grown lion, the black panther was snarling over the bodies of six fallen bandits. The rest were fleeing desperately. Queeen fled. The horses bolted, carrying Asvin, Gaam and Amloki away. Leaving Maya and Kirin on the ground, with Spikes standing over them.

Red Pearl moved in a blur, trying to get far enough to shoot her deadly arrows into the beast's heart. But the nundu was too quick. One giant paw knocked her weapon out of Red Pearl's torn hands, another knocked her senseless. The panther snarled and raised its paw, claws shining in the light of the setting sun, to finish her off.

Then it yelped as Spikes dug all his claws into the beast's flank. He grabbed it by the tail, to spin it around like a discus. He was moving incredibly fast, his stone sinews groaning as he applied all his strength to the panther's body.

But he could not move it. It was too strong, too heavy even for the mighty pashan. The nundu struck him, hard. Spikes almost broke. His body sagged, his spikes retracted. The beast shook him off and he crashed into a tree, breaking it.

The nundu turned around to finish Red Pearl, but just then it felt blinding pain.

It was Asvin. He had leapt off his horse and run back to the battle. Even as Spikes flew through the air, he buried his sword to the hilt in the beast's heart. He would have died a second later, as the enraged panther turned on him snarling and screaming, but before it could strike the hero down to the earth with one deadly stroke a new assailant entered the fray.

Maya's arms were moving like pistons as she hurled fireball after fireball at the demon cat. The blue missiles sizzled and crackled as they landed in the black velvet coat and scorching flames spread swiftly on the nundu's back. Fur in flames, bleeding badly, the beast struck blindly but Asvin managed to spring back unscathed.

The nundu knew it was beaten. It ran. It streaked off, a

wailing black blur, after the fleeing bandits. The whole attack had lasted less than two minutes. Then Gaam and Amloki rode back, white-faced, and found Maya casting healing spells on the motionless Red Pearl. Gaam fished out healing herbs from his pack and took over, while Kirin and Maya tended to Spikes.

After some time, Red Pearl opened her eyes. Amloki was tying bandages on her arm swiftly and efficiently. It would be some time before she could wield a bow again. She was badly bruised and still bleeding where the talons had entered her flesh, but she could walk. She hobbled around for some time, and pronounced herself fit to go, but she was limping, and she almost swooned after getting up. Gaam told her to rest for a while. The screaming of the panther had stopped, and they knew it was either dead or far away, cooling itself in a stream.

Spikes, on the other hand, woke up snarling and angry. He had suffered no damage, except for a few broken spikes on his back where he had cracked the tree trunk. He wanted to go after the nundu, but accepted graciously enough when he was forbidden to do anything of the sort. He was silent for the rest of the day, glowering angrily and snapping when spoken to. He had never lost a fight before.

Gaam vaulted on to his horse again, and rode off in search of the other horses.

They waited for a while, until darkness set in, keenly scanning the woods for any sign of the giant panther. Kirin and Maya sat under the dark boughs of a tree, talking in soft voices.

'You saved my life,' said Maya.

'I did nothing,' said Kirin. 'I did nothing today, I did nothing in the library. I pushed you off the horse when I saw the thing jumping, that's all. Even Amloki could have done that. And you saved everyone with your fireballs after that.'

You are in deadly peril, and so are those who travel with you.

'But I saw you conjuring up a fireball too, Kirin. Why didn't you throw it?'

'Well, Asvin had stuck his sword into it and you had already hit it. It would have been like flogging a corpse. And what is worse, somehow I feel it's my fault that it attacked in the first place. The book warned me I would place the ones I care about in deadly danger if I stayed. Maybe I shouldn't be here.' *Do not gamble with the lives of those dear to you, for danger will seek you out wherever you go.*

'Rubbish. The knight warned us, remember? Before the book said anything. There's absolutely no reason for you to feel guilty.'

But Kirin was silent, looking at Red Pearl stalking around, pretending to feel no pain; at Spikes, brooding under a tree, flashing his claws from time to time, and at Asvin, who was walking towards them.

'That was a very brave thing to do,' said Maya to Asvin. 'You saved Red Pearl's life. She will not forget that.'

Asvin smiled and sat down next to them. 'I wish I could have pulled the sword out. It was very dear to me, and was supposed to possess magical powers.' He sighed, leaned back against the tree and looked upwards. 'The south will know the cat again. I wonder who that man on the bridge was, and what he was talking about,' he said. 'Maybe one day we will come back here and find out.'

'He was talking about bandits killing his men and freeing that thing deep underground,' said Kirin. 'And he thought he was in Ventelot.'

'And he was quite mad,' said Maya.

Amloki walked up to them and sat down as well.

'Unless . . .' said Asvin, 'unless he was the Silver Dagger in disguise. I have long suspected that he is following us secretly. I have heard he is a master of guile, and that could have been his way of warning us.'

They stared at him, surprised. 'Surely he could have left us a little note, or told Red Pearl or something,' said Maya after a little while.

'The old man on the bridge?' asked Amloki. 'The Silver Dagger in disguise?'

'What do you think?'

'I have never seen the Silver Dagger,' said Amloki. 'But I have heard his voice once, and it was not the voice of the knight. Of course, the Dagger is supposed to be a wonderful actor, but I do not think it was him. He would have warned us more clearly.'

'When did you hear the Dagger's voice?' asked Asvin. And regretted it immediately, because Amloki started telling them a long and involved story about the Dagger. Asvin remembered the week he had spent listening to similar stories while coming to Kol, and Kirin and Maya smiled as they saw his expression. The little khudran prattled on.

An hour later, Gaam returned with bad news. Asvin's horse and one of the spare horses were missing, and they now had no blankets. They had initially planned to travel to the very edge of the Bleakwood, where Mantric was supposed to have sent people to wait for them. But Red Pearl was in no condition to gallop, and they had lost some time. They rose, and travelled for a while in silence, Asvin sharing Amloki's horse, the horror of the nundu still fresh in their minds. But they soon realized it was impossible; it was very dark,

Red Pearl was stumbling and falling, and Spikes was lagging behind. Kirin looked at him, then at Maya and thought about Bali in the library and about the giant beast leaping towards her, fangs gleaming. It was all his fault. *Get out of here fast, Kirin. You are in deadly danger.* They stopped.

As night fell, no one seemed to be in the mood to talk— Kirin and Spikes had both withdrawn into their own shells, Gaam and Asvin were walking around worriedly, keeping watch, listening carefully to every noise, every whisper echoing through the Bleakwood, and the spells Maya had cast on Red Pearl had made her very sleepy. She was sitting on the ground now, her magnificent muscles slack, her head bowed, and the sight of her saddened them all.

It was midnight. Spikes was awake, standing tall and menacing over the huddled forms of Amloki and Red Pearl. The horses, tied to a tree, were restless and tugging at their ropes from time to time. Kirin was sitting with his back to a tree a little distance away, thinking.

He took the book out, and it glowed as he touched it, but the glow was dim and remote, and the page was blank as he opened it. There was no voice in his head. *But you will not trust me. You are being hunted, and you must live, Kirin.* He closed the book and put it away.

I cannot risk more danger to Maya, he thought. I have been nothing but trouble for her all these years. That creature could have killed us all.

Seconds later, a warm, slender body crawled under his cloak.

'I'm cold, and I can't sleep,' whispered Maya. 'Talk to me.'

'What do you want me to say?'

She put her head on his shoulder. 'Nothing. Just stop worrying about me. And stop blaming yourself for everything.'

He put his arm around her. 'And what would Asvin say if he saw you here?'

'Why would he say anything? For all you know, he's running around after more singing women even as we speak.'

'Jealous?'

'A little.'

'But that's not why you're here.'

Maya laughed. 'It's the cloak,' she replied. 'I'm just a girl trying to get a little sleep.'

They sat in silence for a while. He sensed her smile in the darkness. 'What is it?'

'I am your best friend, aren't I?' she murmured.

'Yes.'

'And you do love me very much, don't you?'

'You know I do.'

'And you're not going to run away tonight, are you?'

He said nothing.

'Kirin?'

He looked at her and met her eyes.

'I'm not awake,' he said.

'Good,' she said, 'neither am I. But promise me you'll come to Bolvudis.'

'I will come to Bolvudis.'

'All right, then,' she hugged him. He held her, thinking of long afternoons in the library, midnight walks in the streets of Kol and exploding crucibles in the Fragrant Underbelly. A little while later, soft, regular breathing told him she was asleep.

Yes, I will come to Bolvudis. Maybe I will even come

tomorrow. But first let me hear what this book has to say. If it is lying to me, I will join you soon. I will come to Bolvudis. But not with you, he thought, looking at her. Not until I am sure that all the terrible things that have happened to you over the last few days were not because of me. But I know in my heart that they were. *You were left behind for a purpose. You were left behind by me, to finish the task that I began.*

He picked her up and carried her to where Amloki and Red Pearl was sleeping. He laid his cloak down on the ground and set her down upon it.

He was no hero. And he knew she could take care of herself, but the memory of the springing panther was still fresh and painful. He had been warned, and she was dear to him. *I am your father, Kirin, trust me once.* And if he carried danger with him, he would carry it alone. No, not alone. With Spikes. He did not trust the book, not yet. But he had wanted proof, and he had got proof. Not proof that the voice was telling the truth—that would have to come later before he could trust the voice. But enough for him to believe that he should listen to whatever it had to say. *Get out of this forest in secret. Take your pashan with you. Tell no one. That is of utmost importance. Tell no one.* If he went to Bolvudis, they would make him stay.

'Come, Spikes,' he whispered.

He looked at Maya, sleeping with a serene smile on her face. He looked at Asvin and Gaam, with their backs to the sleepers, sitting and talking about Avrantic politics. He sighed, bent, kissed Maya on the forehead and walked away. Spikes followed him silently.

Suddenly a thought hit him—what if I never see her again?

Don't be ridiculous, he thought. Of course you'll see her again. And stop being melodramatic and sentimental, it's sickening. Why, next you'll be kissing her forehead tenderly.

Wait a minute, I just did that.

It doesn't mean anything. She's just the only friend I have. Apart from Spikes, of course. Excessive dependence arising out of loneliness and lack of female companionship. I wish I could take her with me.

Why not? She's the best spellbinder in Enki—I'm sure I'll never need to protect her. But you're leaving her so that she doesn't have to meet giant panthers every day, remember? Saving her from danger and all that. How noble.

But I'm not noble at all. I'm just very scared. Time to go, then. In case we don't meet again, Maya, goodbye. Should I go and kiss her forehead again? No, she might wake up. Besides, Spikes would think I'm crazy.

I'm not even human, he thought. She knows that. It could never happen. And of course it's Asvin she likes—who wouldn't. He runs bravely into the jaws of death and sticks his sword into monsters' hearts. I don't belong here. I shouldn't even be here. I should be with the other ravians, wherever they are. I wish I felt a little older, though. It's supposed to bring wisdom, age.

Well, time to go then. Wait, wait. Which way do I go? Bolvudis to the south, days of the forest to the north and west—anyway I don't want to go to Danh-Gem's Wasteland, or to Elaken. Eastwards it is, then. Red Pearl said the Centaur Forests were pretty. And close by. Good.

He clutched the bag containing the book close to his chest and walked eastwards, into the whispering night. Spikes followed him.

Red Pearl waited a little while, and then opened her eyes. How considerate of them, she thought. They knew I wanted to go home. She smiled grimly.

25

When the rest awoke, they found Asvin and Gaam sitting and looking at Spikes's footprints, leading eastwards. Maya wanted to follow them and find out why Kirin, Spikes and Red Pearl had gone, but both Gaam and Amloki said that Red Pearl had told them not to worry if she disappeared suddenly, because a call for Silver Phalanx work could come anywhere, any time—they had ways of finding her. As for Kirin and Spikes, said Gaam, they were not directly involved with the quest, they had only come along as Maya's friends and were perfectly free to leave whenever they wanted—and if they had gone to the Centaur Forests with Red Pearl they would be perfectly safe. Besides, it was only a short way to the coast now, and they could always send search parties later if necessary, and whoever Mantric had sent to wait for them would not wait indefinitely, so it would be wise to move on.

Maya had to admit he was right, but she was very worried. Why had Kirin left? Had something else happened? Had the book said anything? He had promised to come to

Bolvudis. But he was the most intelligent person she knew, and if he had gone, he must have got the proof he was looking for. He was not one to be swept away by emotion. She looked at Asvin. Or by strange voices, she thought, and actually grinned. She had decided to forgive Asvin for the maiden in the forest. After all, it was not as if he was supposed to lavish all his attention on her, and everyone knew that for some strange reason, Avrantic men were obsessed with fair skin.

Asvin was very worried—he kept looking for paw prints, and asking if Spikes could be trusted, and who Kirin really was, and why he had come in the first place. Maya said she couldn't answer his questions, but he could rest assured that Kirin would never be an enemy, and that he always knew what he was doing. Asvin, who thought Maya knew everything, seemed to be satisfied with that.

They set off. It was a two-hour ride to the coast, and now that Red Pearl and Spikes were no longer with them, they rode even faster. The Bleakwood was less forbidding now, as the fresh sea breeze in their faces swept away the evil memories of the last two days. The horses ran faster, sensing the change in the air, eager to be out of the old wood that was gloomy even under the morning sun. Even the trees around them seemed to accept that there was happiness outside the Bleakwood—at the edge of the Bleakwood, there were a few defiant young trees that thrust their green boughs into the faces of their forbidding elders, fortified by the irreverence that the sea breeze inspired in them.

As they left the Bleakwood, Asvin scanned the skies. Red Pearl had told him to beware of crows. But there were no crows anywhere, not above the Bleakwood, not above the green hills that marked the beginning of the Centaur Forests to their left, not high above in the sky. The ground was rocky now, and they rode through huge boulders, hearing the roar of the sea up ahead. The ground was sloping upwards, and they knew that they would see the sea in a little while, and the thought gladdened their hearts as they galloped up the rocky slope.

Then suddenly, the Psomedean Ocean, blue and sparkling, vast and beautiful, stretched out in front of them. They tore down to the beach, revelling in the sight of the bright, clean sand. They galloped eastwards for a while, and soon they saw Bolvudis in the horizon, small and green under the sun. There was a mist around it.

They all looked at Asvin, riding ahead, the wind in his hair, tall and straight on the brown horse as it streaked over firm sand, and knew in their hearts that he was a Hero. If you looked *that* much like something, chances are you were it.

Gaam called a halt. They stopped, watching foam-crested waves charge and hammer against a cliff in front of them, watching the beach run westwards for miles, a bright, endless yellow river of sand. They rested a while in the shadow of the cliff—it was here that Mantric's men were supposed to meet them. They had planned to travel by night, so as to reach Bolvudis before dawn in secret. But they had been delayed, and if there had been a boat waiting for them, it had gone.

'Is there any way we can send a message to Bolvudis?' Gaam asked Amloki.

'They send boats across occasionally, when they see a lot of actors have arrived, but that's all,' replied the khudran. 'We'll have to wait and hope they see us—Mantric has made a powerful telescope, so we shouldn't have to wait long.'

'You won't have to wait at all,' said a voice behind them. They turned, but there was no one there. A large, soulful-looking seagull was sitting on a rock, looking at them.

'I'm Irik Seagull,' he said, 'former Airhead from Freegull Isle far away in the north. My interests include sky-diving, fishing and script-writing.'

'Script-writing?' asked Gaam.

'Light romance,' said Irik. 'The Badshah sent my brother Stivin and me to welcome you last night. But you're late, you know. The boat's gone. But Stivin's gone to get another one—always one for action, doesn't talk much, my brother.'

The travellers introduced themselves to Irik and started pulling packs off their horses. The horses were trained— they had journeyed through the Bleakwood before, and knew what they had to do. They would return to higher ground and move along the edge of the Bleakwood until they came to the Centaur Forests, where they would be taken care of.

Amloki, sad to see them go, for he had grown attached to them, patted each of the horses and spoke to them softly in turn. How good he is with animals, thought Maya affectionately. Then the horses sped away, leaving a fine spray of sand in the air.

'So what is it that you write scripts for?' Asvin asked Irik.

'For the Muwi-visions, of course, what else is there?'

'The what?'

Irik looked shocked. 'You don't know what Muwi-visions are? The Badshah told me you were the best actors in the world! He said he was even thinking of paying you!' He looked deeply suspicious. 'Asvin of Avranti, Gaam the vaman, Amloki the khudran and Maya of Kol, right? Because otherwise you're not on the list.'

'Of course we know about Muwi-vision,' said Gaam quickly, silencing Asvin with a look. 'It's just that . . . well, it's our first time here, and though, as you say, we are the world's best actors, we thought we would like to learn all about it

225

while we wait . . . the boat is coming, yes? . . . from one who is so obviously . . . one of the most important people involved.' He tried to look meek and humble.

Soon they were listening spellbound as Irik explained the wonders of Muwi-vision to them. Amloki had told them that Mantric was called the Badshah of Bolvudis, but Mantric, in his messages to the Civilian, had said nothing about Muwi-vision. So enraptured were they in Irik's tale that they didn't notice another seagull, a large, inscrutable-looking wide-winged seagull, until he flew down next to Irik and said out of the corner of his beak, 'Boat's coming.'

'Skuan frigate, like yesterday?'

Maya looked at Asvin, seeing sudden suspicion forming in his mind. No, it couldn't be a trick, she thought. But for all the seagull's tales of imps and choreographed dances in artificial streets, she was not going to get on board a Skuan frigate. Not unless she saw her father on it.

'No. That's busy. They're watching *The Bear That Came In From The Cold* today. They're sending the Dead River boat,' replied Stivin.

'But that's really slow,' said Irik.

'Dolphins,' said Stivin laconically and flew up into the air. He was a restless bird.

They sat in silence for a while, trying not to feel confused. Soon they saw Stivin again, sitting on the prow of a long, thin, flattish boat heading towards them. There was a man standing at the far end, a tall, thin man—or was it a man?—clad in a flowing black robe. His head was covered in a black cowl, one like those of the monks of Ventelot of old. He held a pole in his hand, perhaps an oar, but he didn't appear to be rowing. A very sinister and gloomy sight was he, looking completely out of place in the bright morning sunshine. Add a mist, thought Maya, or a swamp, make it evening, and he'd be really scary. The Dead River boat, nice name. But how was it moving? Dolphins, she remembered, looking at the boat skimming across the water towards them—dolphins must be pulling it underwater. Ingenious. Trust her father to come up with these things. Of course, when it reached shallower waters . . .

The boat came closer. The man stuck an arm out from beneath his robe. Maya heard Asvin gasp, for it was not a human arm. It was a skeleton's arm, one bony finger pointing towards them. The dolphins must have stopped swimming, because the boat was not moving any more, bobbing up and down dangerously as waves threatened to topple it over. The man finally stuck the pole into the shallow waters, found bottom and pulled, propelling the boat forward to the beach.

'Ab-abandon all hope, f-f-or I am D-d-death,' the man said in a sepulchral voice.

Maya saw Amloki smile, and she knew he had noticed it too—the robe had slipped back a little, and his real arm had appeared, clutching the bony toy and waving it about.

'We can see your arm, Death,' she called.

'D-d-damn,' said the man, and fell over.

He got up, spluttering. His cowl had fallen off, and a crab was attached to his straggly hair.

He pushed the boat over to a huge boulder in the shallow blue waters, and they waded up to it and stepped gingerly into the boat, which was very wobbly. D-d-death clambered on, nearly upsetting them all, and Irik perched on the prow. D-d-death's pole sent the boat into motion again, and soon it was moving fast as the hidden dolphins started pulling again. Asvin, who was sitting nearest the front, sometimes saw a sleek grey body coming close to the surface, and was filled with joy, for he had never seen a dolphin before.

'So, this Death, he's an actor?' Gaam whispered to Irik.

'Yes, and not a very good one,' said Irik, 'which is why we're training him as much as possible, sending him to pick people up and so on. He's getting scarier, though—he only fell into the water once this time. You must remember he's a very new Death.'

'A new Death?'

'The old Death died.'

'The old Death died?'

'He was a *very* old Death.'

Bolvudis grew larger, a beautiful little island covered in a mist that was lifting fast under the hot sun. They saw, on a cliff, huge letters, carved out of wood, painted white: BOIUDVLS, they said, shining in the sun.

'People lost jobs over that,' said Irik apologetically.

They all stared open-mouthed at the strange island. Smoke was rising from some parts of the island—Irik said the Badshah had made an artificial Volcano in the Natural Disaster Valley—and they could hear the sound of many drums in the Square Forest where, under the watchful eye of an imp, the warrior-dancers who served Tupshi, Queen of the Jungle, were beginning their martial arts routine, which consisted mainly of gyrating wildly, shaking hips and spears and trying to ensure that their tiny costumes, inexpertly knitted together from reeds, stayed on.

'You are now entering the Very Blue Lagoon, and we hope you had a pleasant journey,' crooned Irik as the travellers stared in wonder at the Picsquids, the imps buzzing around, eyes winking merrily at the newcomers, and the giant crocodile (trained, of course) basking in the sun.

Mantric was standing on the shore, bald head gleaming

in the sun, a huge smile spread over his dark face. He looked a lot like Maya. He was clad in maroon robes, and was clean-shaven, unlike most spellbinders (Chancellor Ombwiri's beard, for example, reached his waist). Nimbupani the chimaera stood by his side, roaring a welcome.

'Thank you so much, Death, and we were all terrified,' said Maya sweetly, shaking his bone-hand warmly.

'It's a pup-pup-pup,' he replied, gracefully hitting the water, upsetting the boat and giving our intrepid heroes a very wet welcome.

'You must forgive him,' said Mantric, as they waded out of the water, completely drenched. 'He's a very new Death.'

'We heard,' said Gaam, grimly, for there were seaweeds in his beard and an unidentified wriggling object down his back.

Mantric hugged Maya and shook everyone else's hand affectionately. He welcomed Amloki as an old friend, and called Pygmy Lion, a pashan, who took their dripping packs from Asvin and walked off.

'I'll take you to the village later,' said Mantric. 'But first, you must blow the casting conch, to win the favour of the gods who preside over the performing arts.'

'The casting conch?' said Maya incredulously.

'They all think you're actors,' hissed Mantric. 'Do it.'

They all sounded forlorn blasts on the huge conch-shell that an imp handed to them, in turn, ceremoniously.

'Welcome once again to Bolvudis,' said Mantric loudly and warmly. 'In the hut over there you will find costumes, to wear while your clothes are wet, and then I will take you to the village—it's a short walk. A song has been composed in your honour, for it is not often that we get world-renowned actors in this little-known southern paradise. A feast awaits. Follow me.'

26

He was tired and completely out of breath, but he was still running. They had run all day, no food, no rest, no stopping to admire the beauty of the Centaur Forests. When they had crossed into the Centaur Forests just before dawn, a little bit of ravian hand-waving had brought a large branch crashing down on the centaur who was standing on guard at the western border, looking for strange things coming out of the Bleakwood. Strange things like us, thought Kirin. The centaur wasn't going to tell anyone about that little episode—getting knocked out by falling branches wasn't exactly going to win him favour with his superiors—which meant their entry in the forest would not be noticed. For a while, at least.

The ground was still hilly and getting rockier as it sloped gently upwards. Kirin knew that the hills would get higher and higher, but very gradually, until they suddenly rose sharply far in the east to mark the western border of the Xi'en Empire.

They'd thought they would be followed soon, and since Spikes was leaving deep footprints in the fresh, damp earth, they decided speed was of the essence. But though Kirin was very fast indeed, as fast as the fastest human, he could not keep up with Spikes, and would certainly not be able to outrun a centaur. Luckily, they thought, Red Pearl, who would be the one sent to follow them if anyone was, was wounded and would not be able to gallop at full speed. And, Kirin thought, it was unlikely that she'd send other centaurs after them—after all, they hadn't stolen anything. Besides, Red Pearl *liked* him.

But the soothing smell of damp earth and green leaves was very, very good, thought Kirin, as he raced after Spikes, especially after the Bleakwood. Old memories were simmering in his mind—he was trying to remember days, long ago, when he had run in forests with his ravian guardians, learning to hunt, fight and hide.

They reached a sparkling stream, which gurgled merrily as it flowed swiftly towards a little waterfall a short distance away. They were crossing the stream, when Kirin suddenly had an idea. They waded downstream for a little while, then Kirin climbed on to Spikes's back and they jumped down the waterfall. They waded to the edge of the little pool it had formed and climbed up again, on the same side of the stream. Kirin knew it wouldn't deter a skilled tracker for long, but it was the only ruse he could think of at the moment. It was evening, and they began to hunt for a place to sleep. Spikes found a little cave—it had paw prints all around the entrance, but was empty—and they moved in. The original inhabitant of the cave didn't return as night fell. It must have either abandoned the cave long ago, or seen Spikes on its way home, decided the neighbourhood was going downhill and moved to a more prosperous locality.

Night fell softly over the Centaur Forests. Spikes was

sitting near the mouth of the cave, out of the pale light of the new moon, listening intently. Kirin was sitting on a rock near the end of the cave, with the book glowing softly in his hands. He was turning through the pages, one at a time. They were all empty.

He set the book beside him on the rock. It stopped glowing when his hand left it. Then there was a rustling noise in the darkness as the cover flipped open on its own.

Late, but not too late, thank the stars. Thank you for coming, Kirin.

Kirin grabbed the book. In the soft white glow he saw Narak's face emerge in expanding ripples, as if it was coming out of water. The eyes opened. The lines of the face were dark, much darker than they had been in the Bleakwood. The face looked stronger, harder, even younger. The scar looked deeper.

'I still don't believe what you said,' said Kirin, 'but we were attacked yesterday. It was probably a coincidence, but I'm going to give you one chance to prove that you really are my father.'

Very well. I will give you the proof you seek. But before I begin my tale, let me say this. I am still weak, and you will have to keep me here with the force of your own will. As my power fades, you will probably feel the pain I feel. Do not be alarmed. Even if I disappear suddenly, I will return as soon as I have gathered enough strength. But pay close heed to whatever I say, because I will only say it once, and I will not have the strength to speak to you often. I created this enchanted book more than two hundred years ago, and I have several things to explain to you before I can rest in peace. I have a task, a great and terrible task for you to perform, but I will guide you through it, and you will find help in the unlikeliest of places.

The voice was much stronger and clearer now than it had been the previous time. Evidently, getting out of the Bleakwood really was good for it, Kirin thought.

Let me first state my claim, Kirin. I am Narak, Demon-hunter, ravian cast out of Asroye, husband of Isara, princess of Asroye, slayer of the body of Danh-Gem, and you are my son. I do not ask you to trust me blindly—I just ask you to hear what I have to say. Whether you believe what I tell you or not, whether you carry out the tasks I set for you or not—these, and many other decisions I will leave to you.

Kirin nodded. The voice was speaking swiftly and crisply. It sounded even more like his own now. 'I'm listening,' he said.

If I guess right, you have learnt about your people from human books and your own dim memories. Is that not so? Kirin nodded. *Very well.*

You have spent your life among humans, and you know what they are like—as greedy, violent, and selfish as the lowly asurs. And yet some of them are bold and wise, savages with hearts of gold. You know what humans do to the world they live in. They settle in a region, suck it dry of all its beauty, cut down trees to build their machines and their towers, mine rocks out of the earth and slay one another over them. Ravians, on the other hand, are gentle and wise, friends of the living earth. They are strong, yes, strong as rakshases, but they hate warfare and bloodshed, and do not seek more land than they need.

Unfortunately, the ravians also possess powers that are both a blessing and a curse—magical powers, Kirin. And magic can be used to create many beautiful things, but magic cannot be controlled. When the ravians enter a world, it becomes magical. And if it was magical to start with, anything can happen. Evil creatures suddenly find powers they never knew they had, and use these powers to maim and plunder. And when the ravians find that they are responsible, however indirectly, for ruin and devastation in the world they live in, they move on. But while humans leave desolate wastelands in their wake, the ravians try to heal the wounds they opened. Which is why the ravians joined the Great War against the rakshas Danh-Gem.

'You know,' Kirin said slowly, 'I really didn't run away from my friends for a history lesson, no matter how fascinating.'

You will listen to what I have to say, son. The voice was a bit harsher.

'I thought you would leave the decisions to me.'

True. Narak laughed, a dry laugh. *The long years have made me talkative. I never thought of myself as old before. I apologize. You are much like me, son.*

Suffice to say that the ravians came to this world because they felt they had hurt the last one they were in, and they left this one because they thought the consequent lowering of magic in this world would heal all its problems. They knew this would work to an extent at least—the dragons, most rakshases and many other terrible monsters would disappear, or at least become weak enough to be dealt with by humans, after they left. Danh-Gem, however, was the wiliest adversary they had ever met in all the worlds they had passed through. Danh-Gem, seeing he could not defeat the ravians in the War, decided to hide in some form until they had gone, give his allies two centuries to rebuild their armies and then return more mighty and dangerous than ever before.

'Where do you arrive in this tale?' asked Kirin.

I was one of the first ravians sent into this world to find out whether or not it was suitable for us. I was very young then, an apprentice warrior-mage. Only low-castes made the first journey—it was considered less of a loss if they died in a hostile world.

'Low-caste? The ravians had castes like they have in Avranti? But that's horrible!'

But you have learnt about ravians from humans, Kirin. Humans met them very rarely and thought they were perfect. And the ravians who loved humans—Lord Simoqin, for example, were all gentle, mild-mannered souls, skilled in the arts, noble, high-minded. In truth—and I tell you this as one who has suffered more than most—they were as proud and rigid as any other race when it came to imposing social distinctions. But I thought you did not want history lessons.

'But you said you were a warrior-mage. That doesn't sound like a low-caste profession to me.'

I became a warrior-mage. I was low-caste by birth, not profession. And so they sent me and others of my kind here first, to be killed if the world was too dangerous. They even tried sending those who were not wholly ravian, but they died while travelling between worlds. My family had no name, no clan. I stole books from libraries and learnt magic. I learnt to fight on the streets. I sold magical toys for a living. And when I became richer, it mattered no more. Then I bought all the training my heart desired, and no questions were asked. I became the most powerful warrior-mage in all of Asroye.

'I don't understand . . . those who were not wholly ravian?'

It is not relevant to your quest.

'Nevertheless, I want to know.'

As you wish, son. Ravians, like some other magical races, can mingle bloods and have children with other, similar beings. Did you not know this?

'No,' said Kirin. And neither did Maya, he thought.

Have you not heard of the half-rakshas heroes of Avranti of old? The rakshases of this world have that power too. Be that as it may. I have wasted too much time. Do I have to tell you the whole story, Kirin? Do you not believe me? Will you not do as I say?

'You still haven't proved anything yet, you've just told me things about ravians. And you were getting very expansive, why are you suddenly in a hurry?' said Kirin, aware of a sudden, slight headache. 'Are you in pain?'

A little. It matters not. Come, I will answer your questions, one by one. Ask, quickly.

'Well, you haven't really explained anything, have you? The book, my mother, the Simoqin Prophecies, Spikes . . .'

Very well. I shall carry on. After we came to this world and found it habitable, the other ravians arrived. The city of Asroye was founded, deep in the heart of Vrihataranya. The ravians lived in peaceful isolation for years, never venturing out of the forest, except in disguise, when they wished to learn more about the world.

Then the inevitable happened—the world outside discovered us. Danh-Gem the rakshas, who lived in Vrihataranya then, saw Isara, ravian princess young and beautiful, as she walked in the dark woods. He wanted her; he grew desperate to have her. He tried to abduct her, but she was skilled in magic, and would have killed him, but did not—for she was kind and wise, and believed that the rakshas was only doing what his brutish nature forced him to.

But Danh-Gem was even then a powerful rakshas-lord, and his armies were beginning to make war in the north. Years passed, and his power grew greater and greater. Vrihataranya, once a green paradise, became full of evil birds and beasts, ever watchful, ever spying on the ravians, ever trying to find the hidden city.

Finally, Danh-Gem could wait no more. He came to Vrihataranya from his newly established realm in Imokoi, and, catching a ravian in the woods, gave him a letter to bear to the king, Isara's father, asking for the hand of his daughter in marriage.

The poor fool. He thought that the fact that he was lord of many lands, rich beyond compare, the wisest and most dangerous of rakshases, and a mighty sorcerer as well, would make the king accept him. Narak laughed again, a rather unpleasant laugh. *I could have taught him better.*

The king sent him a reply—it was the head of another rakshas, one that had attacked ravians a few days ago. That was uncharacteristically savage for a ravian, but the king had thought Danh-Gem would not understand anything less than a direct, even threatening insult. Which was foolish. For Danh-Gem wanted to be a friend, and now became a bitter enemy. The most powerful enemy the ravians could have made in this world.

The king, of course, thought that no ravian would turn traitor. He was wrong again. Danh-Gem bought the loyalty of some ravians with dragon-gold—he had stolen Tatsu's Gauntlet some years previously—and found out that Simoqin the Dreamer, human-friend and tutor to the spellbinders of Enki, was betrothed to Princess Isara. Not of her own volition, mind you; but she had not objected, for her father and the customs of her land were very dear to her, and Simoqin was a very noble ravian indeed. But her heart, though she knew it not then, was already given elsewhere.

'I was wondering when you would enter this tale.'

Princess Isara and I had first met long before the War, when she bought toys from me. We were both young, and though I was a low-caste, I fell desperately in love with her. And she returned my affection, though she would always say I was nothing more than a dear friend to her—she would have been quite happy with Simoqin, I admit. So while the Hidden City prospered and the ravians made merry amidst the mighty trees of Vrihataranya, I spent the years that followed learning the arts of magic and war like one possessed, so that one day I could be the greatest hero the ravians had ever had. So great, indeed, did I dream of being, that in my vision of the future, the king himself would declare me unbound by the barriers of caste, the betrothed of his daughter, heir to his throne. So when the enraged Danh-Gem captured Simoqin the Dreamer and bore him back to Imokoi in his chariot, I saw my chance to win Isara's hand. I entered the pits of Imokoi, slew many of Danh-Gem's evil monsters and returned with Lord Simoqin.

'This is a very nice story,' said Kirin, 'but do tell me—how would bringing her betrothed back from Imokoi help you win her hand?'

I admit it was naïve, but it was the right thing to do. Simoqin however, had been cruelly tortured in Imokoi, and did not live. A year later, Isara and I pledged our troth in secret. By that time I was truly the greatest hero in Asroye—no one wielded the sword or cast the earth-tearing death spells better than me. I had become Danh-Gem's chief enemy, and there was a great price on my head. Those were the darkest days of the Age of Terror.

'Why did they make you leave Asroye, then?' asked Kirin. The headache was getting worse.

Emboldened by my success and the favour of the king, which I thought I enjoyed, I returned to Asroye—I had slain a dragon at the very edge of the Great Forest—and asked for his daughter's hand. The king was enraged, and banished me from Asroye in spite of the pleas of all his generals—even the high-caste ones, I am happy to say. But he would not listen.

I left Asroye with a good number of warrior-mages and hunters, and lived in the forest ever since. The princess left with me as well. One summer's day, under the shadow of the grey mountains of east Imokoi, under the cool green leaves of the Great Forest, we were married.

You were born exactly a year after that day. That year had been a particularly tumultuous one—dragons and rakshases all over the world were marching to the Great Forest, and there was scarcely a day when swords did not ring and flash in the webbed sunlight under the trees. But even as I roamed the barren valleys of Imokoi and slew the servants of Danh-Gem, my mind kept going back to one thing—Danh-Gem's Warning.

Danh-Gem was hatching a plot for his own return, I thought, a plot that I had to foil. A plot that he had had in readiness for years, I thought, for why otherwise would he boast brashly of his return? He had burnt his challenge on his rival's breast— fire is very sacred to rakshases—and I knew in my heart it was no idle boast. The War was tearing up the land—a War that we were winning, but a War that would eventually ensure our departure, for we had scarred the land, and we would not stay . . . I decided to make a plan of my own, to ensure that if Danh-Gem did indeed return, that he would not be able to wreak havoc upon a world whose magic we, the ravians, had removed when we left. That is where you come into the story, son.

Kirin said nothing. He gritted his teeth, to shut out the pain in his head, and listened intently.

What if, I thought, Danh-Gem managed to stay alive in spite of our best efforts? Or if, as he himself foresaw, he died apparently, but somehow rose again after two hundred years? There would be no ravians left in the world then. My task, as I saw it, was to ensure that at least one ravian was left behind when he reappeared.

I started preparing the most powerful spell that has ever been prepared in this world, at least by human or ravian. I decided you would be the one left behind—you were a mere infant then, and I saw you whenever I could, and every day I fed you a drop of a potion that I concocted which would turn you into stone the moment the ravian-portal to the next world appeared, and keep you alive until you were woken.

I bitterly regretted having to do such a thing to a helpless infant—I kept it secret even from your mother, who would not have allowed me to do such a thing—but I had to, I was driven mad by my desire to defeat Danh-Gem. The Demon-hunter's heir completes the Demon-hunter's task; I thought, it is as it should be.

Once I had finished the charms I had to put on you, I was in a quandary—what should it be that woke you up? And who would guide you, who would tell you of the great and terrible task you had to perform? For even if I told you what you had to do when you were growing up in the forest, I could not be sure that you would not forget once you turned into stone.

When I sat awake one night, on guard, unable to remember when I had last slept, the answer suddenly came to me. I began to write this book. I poured out my heart in it, so that one day I could return to guide my son through the terrible things I would make him do. From the bottom of my heart, son, I crave your pardon.

'I still don't understand,' said Kirin. 'Why me? Why did you not stay back yourself? And why on earth did you make Spikes wake me up? And how? Spikes wasn't even alive then!'

I could not cast it on myself, because I was too old, and resisted magic too well. I could not stay back myself because I was not sure I would survive—I needed to choose someone who was protected well. As you were. And as for the other questions— patience, Kirin. I will explain. The story is far from over.

Your mother, Isara, was also immensely powerful and skilled in the use of magic, as I have already said. We hardly ever met in the years that followed. There were hurried trysts at secret places where we had walked together when we were young—but Asroye was forever shut to us, and the forest was full of danger. Our friends brought you up—we hardly ever got to even see you. But I have often watched you training in secret—you have it in you to be a mighty warrior, Kirin.

'But I have forgotten all that, Father,' said Kirin. 'I do not even carry a weapon. How am I going to fight the mighty Danh-Gem?'

You cannot imagine how much happiness it brings me to hear you call me father, Kirin.

'Slip of the tongue,' said Kirin sullenly. He was quiet for a while, so was the voice in his head. 'Go on, then,' said Kirin, his voice shaking a little.

Yes. Your mother hardly ever met you either—we were busy protecting the city we had grown up loving, the city that had cast us out, but we cared not. As time passed, I completed the spell that would keep you here when the ravians departed.

I then bent my mind to deciphering what Danh-Gem's plan was—how would he return from the dead? It would take magic more powerful than any I had ever seen. I had fought with the undead in the marshes of Imokoi and in the deserts of Elaken, Kirin, and they were all mindless bodies, animated by the wills of others, or by resentful spirits. What, then, was Danh-Gem's plan? He could not do it all alone—the very essence of his plan was giving time to his followers to regroup, to do whatever was necessary to bring him back, to grow strong in his absence and yearn for his rebirth.

Who, then, was Danh-Gem close to? Men he had never trusted. Dragons, other rakshases and other monsters would disappear or diminish after the ravians left. That left only two races—the faithful but witless asurs, and the pashans.

Danh-Gem had bred a strange race of pashans in the furnaces of Imokoi. They were eternally loyal to him, but they were also vicious and ruthlessly cunning. But how could I, a ravian, find out what went on in the minds of Danh-Gem's most loyal servants? To answer that question, I hatched my most desperate scheme yet. I would have to go to Imokoi myself and find out.

Of course you would, thought Kirin, overcoming an urge to laugh. And Maya thought *her* father was crazy.

I bade farewell to Isara and told her I was going to Imokoi, and that if I did not return in a year, she would have to avenge my death. Tearful was our parting, as we remembered our childhood days together in the Hidden City. Isara began preparing her most powerful spell ever, a spell she should have cast years ago—a spell to slay Danh-Gem. There was no other being in the whole world who could have made that spell, Kirin. Not even me—I had spent a lot of my magic on you, and the book, which I took with me.

I went to Imokoi, and there the whispers about a silent killer in the night spread almost instantly. The number of asurs I killed with sword and spell cannot be counted, Kirin, I boast not. And then I allowed myself to be captured and brought before Danh-Gem.

He could not give me much of his attention, as the greatest battles of the Great War were being fought even then. But he left me to the tender care of the only living thing he trusted, his most faithful servant—Katar, the first pashan he had ever created in the furnaces of Imokoi, and the most deadly.

They tortured me, Kirin, for months and endless months. I lost count of the days as they cut, tore and pounded me. But I endured it all, taunting them, telling them I knew where Asroye was, but would not tell. While I lay there receiving their tender care, the greatest battle this world had ever seen was being fought in the plains east of Elaken. Dragons, rakshases, ravians, humans showered arrows and fire on one another. It was a battle no one won, Kirin—a battle where deaths gained nothing, that scarred the earth forever. Things might have gone differently had I not been in chains in Danh-Gem's Tower in the heart of Imokoi. Yet even as they pounded away at my body, breaking it in a thousand places, my mind was at peace.

As they inched me closer and closer to the painlessness of death, I prepared a great mind-control spell and cast it on Katar the pashan. To my joy—for his mind was as strong as any I have seen—he broke. He was in my power and would do my bidding. For in spite of all Danh-Gem's sorcery, he was a pashan, and pashans lack brains. Katar, the fool, slew my torturers and freed me.

And then came the stroke I was most proud of, Kirin. For Katar showed me an egg. A pashan egg—I knew nothing of such things. He told me, in his grating voice, that it was his own, his son, the egg would hatch forth a pashan as deadly as he, a pashan that would one day help bring back Danh-Gem. I was overjoyed—here was what I was looking for. For one of my chief fears had been—what if you were awakened at the right time and even had me to guide you, but could not even find Danh-Gem until it was too late? I asked Katar what else he knew about Danh-Gem's plan, but he said he knew no more. But at least I knew the egg was a part of whatever plan he had, and that his followers, two hundred years later, would come looking for the pashan that sprang forth from it. I decided I would make things easier for you—I would make the minions of Danh-Gem come to you.

Danh-Gem had hired a stork to throw the egg wherever it would hatch. While Katar stood blinking stupidly at me, I cast enchantments strong and deep on that egg, until it was glowing, red, green and beautiful, as Danh-Gem's powers worked in harmony with mine. I covered my face with a cloth, and pretended to be Danh-Gem himself—Katar and I gave the egg to the stork and he went away. This Spikes you speak of is the pashan that came from that egg, Kirin. He found you because I willed it so. Because I, Narak, your father, made it so.

Kirin looked at Spikes, crouching in the darkness at the mouth of the cave. Dropped by a stork, he thought. Son of Danh-Gem's most loyal servant, walking around with me. The slayer and the servant travel together. *Very* nice. The voice had not stopped.

And even as the stork flew away, trumpets sounded and Danh-Gem returned to his tower, running like a thief in the night. He had lost the battle, though the king of Asroye was no more. His very presence tore my spell off Katar, and while Danh-Gem climbed up to where we were—for he wished to torture the Demon-hunter personally and take his mind off the lost battle—Katar and I fought a bitter battle—a battle that I won. I threw Katar off Danh-Gem's tower even as Danh-Gem entered that chamber.

He was weak, for he had just returned from a battle, but I was even weaker—the torturers were very talented. He felled me with a single blow. He would have killed me right then, but suddenly the air was full of the sound of screams and he saw something that made him forget about me. I looked out of the great tower window, and at first I thought the sun itself was falling down to earth. Then my eyes cleared, and beyond the dazzling white light I saw the beautiful, resolute face.

I had endured the Tower of Danh-Gem for a year. Isara had come to avenge me.

She was on the most beautiful white carpet I have ever seen. She must have woven it herself, as she waited for me to return.

Danh-Gem forgot all about me. He threw great red balls of fire and summoned his flying dragons, but they burned away like scraps of paper when they hurtled towards the white flame she was bearing. Unnoticed, I crawled away, down the stairs to Danh-Gem's library. They had kept this book there, with his other books. I cast a spell of protection on the library, for I knew Isara's spell would destroy the tower, then there was a great scream, a blinding white light and I knew no more.

Kirin was silent for a long time. His breath was coming in deep, painful gasps. He suddenly realized his head was killing him as he pieced the puzzle together. So Narak's spell had protected the Untranslatables, and the asurs had brought them to Kol later. Spikes, guided by his father's spell, had wandered all over the earth looking for him, and had found him lying in the stone. Then they had come to Kol, met Maya and found the book. Was it chance, or was he really meant to slay Danh-Gem? And had his mother lived? And had Danh-Gem really died?

'I understand now, Father,' he said, shutting out the pain. 'Now tell me what I must do.'

I will soon have to go, Kirin, and it may be a while before I return to speak to you, for I have spent a lot of the power I put into this book already. But I will tell you now what you have to do.

First, I do not know what Danh-Gem's plan is, but I do know it must involve two things—the uniting of his former followers, and the pashan that serves you. The servants of Danh-Gem will find you, Kirin—you will not even have to look for them, they will hunt you. When they do come, you must control your anger and work with them.

'Work with them?' Kirin couldn't believe his ears.

Yes, Kirin. I do not want you throwing your life away rashly. You must wait till Danh-Gem actually does return and then you must slay him. No one knew more about Danh-Gem than Narak the Demon-hunter, and Narak the Demon-hunter tells you this—Danh-Gem always had an alternative plan. Therefore do not hinder his servants as they go about the process of restoring him to life—aid them if you have to. Your target is not Evil as a whole—it is Danh-Gem and only Danh-Gem. You must slay him, no matter what the cost. Gain the trust of his followers— pretend to be one of them. The pashan is your friend—use him. Use his loyalty. While they need him—and they do need him, I know not why—the followers of the rakshas will not harm you. Remember—if you fail, he will conquer all, for he will be more terrible and powerful than ever before. Wait for him to rise again, and then send him back to the pit he sprang from . . .

'Yes,' said Kirin, his head spinning.

And remember, Kirin—wherever you go, enemies will follow. Therefore I warn you—do not even go near those you trust, those who are dear to you. For if you do so, you will cast them into the very jaws of death. Trust no one. The ones who hunt you will arrive, I know it. They will arrive soon. Win them over, no matter how much hatred they arouse in you. A time will come later, I promise you, when you will have the power to decide whether they live or die.

'I will do what I can,' said Kirin. 'But I am not like you, or my mother. I am not a hero. And though you two may have been the most powerful mages in the world, I am afraid I do not have powers that even remotely measure up to yours. How will I slay Danh-Gem?'

Son, said Narak, laughing, and this time it was not the usual cold, dry laugh but a warm, affectionate one that made Kirin feel a new, strange, sinking feeling in a tight corner of his heart, *after the way I have treated you while I was alive, I would be far too ashamed to approach you empty-handed, even*

*in death. Do not despair! I will not be able to talk to you often
after this, but I will help you much more through other means.
I have four gifts for you. I will give them to you one at a time,
when I perceive you are ready to receive them. You are the son
of the two most powerful ravians who ever set foot in Asroye.
You have powers beyond your dreams, Kirin, son of Narak and
Isara. Would we send you to face Danh-Gem unarmed?*

*My first gift to you is memory, a light to shine on the
slumbering corners of your mind and awaken the ravian powers
that you have forgotten to use. Too long have you slept, son. My
friends and followers taught you how to fight beyond the muddy
dreams of the humans who rule the world today. And to succeed
in the task I set for you, you will need those skills. I will leave you
now—you and I both need rest, I have spoken too long. Rest in
peace for a while. But before that, to take my first gift, place your
hand on my face.*

Kirin put his hand on the page of the book, over his
father's face, the lines of which were breaking away, slithering
around like snakes, gliding over one another and forming a
hand, exactly the same size and shape as Kirin's. Kirin placed
his hand upon it. He was almost sure that the hand in the
book reached out and grasped his.

And then power flowed into him. The book grew
thinner, some of its pages seemed to melt away. Kirin was
shuddering and glowing as bright as the moongold on the
cover of the book as the awareness of his ravian abilities
flooded his mind. His body was shaking—a corner of his
mind, strangely detached, told him this was what being struck
by lightning felt like—and he saw, out of the corner of his
eye, through the strange colours that were flashing in front
of him, the towering shape of Spikes wrestling with something
that was growling and roaring at the mouth of the cave.

He opened his eyes and saw nothing at first. But he felt his senses singing. Suddenly he could see, hear, feel, as never before—there were new sounds in the air, new smells, new colours even in the darkness of the cave, as if different eyes had opened behind the ones he had been using all these years, showing him things right in front of him that he had never been able to see before. He fell to the ground, unconscious as the sudden rush of power overcame him. His hand fell limply to the ground, feeling the new, enriched texture of the earth. Then he was still, and saw no more.

27

It was the biggest hut on the island. They built it a little larger every time it fell in or exploded. It was a little distance away from the village where the actors lived. The door was wooden, and extremely battered. As Pygmy Lion opened it and entered, he saw the Badshah hunched over an extremely complicated-looking collection of glass vessels and tubes all connected to one another—a green liquid was bubbling fiercely inside. From time to time he was sprinkling a little of the liquid on a carpet that was struggling in a corner, held down by four large flowerpots.

Pygmy Lion was a pashan. There were no other pashans on Bolvudis—they usually sank the boats that tried to bring them (pashans were only suitable for land travel), so it was a mystery how Pygmy Lion got to Bolvudis in the first place. But there were two things driving him: he was an artist—the only pashan artist in the world, and therefore naturally drawn to the phenomenon that was Bolvudis—and every pashan in the world knew there was a substantial reward for his capture. For Pygmy Lion was a fugitive from justice, at least pashan justice, which usually involved heads rolling around without bodies attached to them.

Pygmy Lion had been a sculptor. Of course, since pashans are generally made of stone it would seem a little pointless to carve in stone, but Pygmy Lion had never cared about that. His Art was all that mattered to him. And there were many pashans who actually wanted statues of themselves made—some to beautify their caves and houses, others to fool their wives when they were busy having affairs.

And then Pygmy Lion had made a big mistake. He had fallen in love with one of his models.

Her name was Gelatina, and she was the daughter of a very important stalactroll, who'd kept his egg in his cavern instead of giving it to a stork, and brought up his daughter on his own. Pygmy Lion (whose name had been Basalto, but he had changed it after creating his first statue—that of a dead lion-cub) had been given the task of immortalizing her youthful good looks. Unfortunately, inflamed by passion, he had forgotten the difference between dead stone and live stone and had hacked off half of one of Gelatina's ears with his chisel, to make it correspond to the far prettier one on the statue. No one had been amused, and Pygmy Lion had fled for his life and ended up in Bolvudis. Now he made quite a good living acting, for there was always room for a killer troll in a Muwi-vision play. He'd also done good work recently in the emotional supernatural thriller, *There's a Soul in My Troll*.

The Badshah seemed to have forgotten the large, black cauldron that was steaming on the fire in the middle of the room. Pygmy Lion stomped over to it and peered at the pink, gooey mass inside. Bubbles were rising to the surface and exploding with loud, squelchy noises.

'Um, the cauldron's boiling over,' said Pygmy Lion deferentially.

'Duck!' yelled the Badshah, not even turning around to look as he dived beneath the table.

'What?' asked Pygmy Lion, not one of the world's quicker thinkers. It was as if two people had met inside his brain, were shaking hands and grinning uncertainly, wondering what to say.

The cauldron exploded. The inside of the hut was suddenly pink.

'Never mind,' said the Badshah a little later, emerging from under the table, unscathed. He closed his eyes and muttered for a while, and the pink slime began to slide off the roof, the walls and the instruments in the room and collect on the floor in a glutinous mass.

'There you go,' said Mantric happily, 'in a few hours it'll be cool enough to eat.'

Pygmy Lion said nothing. He was still pink.

'Interesting,' said Mantric, looking at him. 'It's sealed your mouth shut.'

Strange sounds began to emanate from Pygmy Lion. As he spoke, a large, pink bubble formed over his mouth. The Badshah, completely unperturbed, began to note down observations on a slate. Sweet gum that bubbles, he thought. I wonder what to call it.

Pygmy Lion blew hard and the bubble popped. 'How do I get it off?' he asked in a voice of thunder.

'I have no idea,' said the Badshah, returning to the glass tubes. 'Roll around or something. Or start a new Muwivision play while it's still there. *The Pink Pashan* . . . not bad. Or if you want a romantic twist to it, call it *Pashan in Pink*.'

After a while, he asked, 'Did you want to say something?'

'The island's being invaded,' said Pygmy Lion, still chewing on the gum. It was sweet and rubbery.

This time Mantric turned around. 'What?'

'I don't know. The giant crocodile's been attacked.'

'Is that it?' The Badshah looked relieved. 'Is it dead?'

'No. Stunned. We won't be able to see Tupshi, Queen of the Jungle wrestling today.'

There was a slight noise outside the hut. It sounded like a cough stopped mid-way. Mantric showed no signs of having heard it.

'Never mind. Go do something else. And don't worry about the pink stuff, it'll come off,' he said. Hopefully, he thought.

Pygmy Lion stomped off, pink and petulant. Mantric looked out of the window.

'I know you're there, I heard you,' he said. 'You could get killed, laughing like that. You might as well stop hiding and come in.'

'I wasn't prepared for what you've done to this island,' said the Silver Dagger as he walked in, looking a little sheepish. 'Pink pashans and imps, by the gods! This Muwi-vision business is sheer madness, Mantric. But it's a brilliant ploy. No one will suspect a thing.'

'Why did you attack the poor crocodile?'

'I didn't attack it, I was just trying to persuade it not to eat me.'

'I'm sure it was just being friendly, and you had to show off.'

'It surprised me, Mantric, honestly. I was reasonably gentle.'

'It's good to see you again.'

They embraced, laughing. They were old friends. Then

the Dagger stepped back and inspected his clothes. No stains, no burns, no strange wiggling creatures. Good. 'So, what do you think of our hero?'

'Definitely has potential. It doesn't matter what I think. We can't afford to lose this one.'

'Which is why I'm here. The Civilian isn't taking any chances this time.'

Mantric stopped smiling, suddenly. 'We'll have to make sure this one stays alive. There isn't time to train another one.'

'Which is why we have to get him the sword, Mantric.'

'I just don't see the reason for all this fuss about swords.'

'Heroes *have* to have swords, Mantric. It's *important*. It's the first thing about being a hero.'

'Well, if you insist—though I still think any sword will do—we will get Asvin the best sword in the world. The Durgan one, do you think?'

'My men are there already. The queen should not be a problem—not for Asvin anyway.'

'The carpet will need a little work, though,' said Mantric, looking at the carpet struggling in the corner. 'It's very headstrong.'

'The carpet's the least of our problems. I'm worried, Mantric.'

Mantric looked at him sharply. It was not like the Dagger to admit such things. 'Why?'

'The pashan I told you about—the friend of your daughter's. Disappeared, and so has the boy. Red Pearl will find them, but she's wounded, and the pashan is fast, as fast as a horse. I liked the boy, too—I wonder why he went. I wish I could go after them myself.'

'You could, you know.'

253

'No, I promised the Civilian I would stay. The vanars fight against us, Mantric. Even the Civilian had not seen that coming. And their leader—Bali—is, I hear, not a very nice sort of ape. And his soldiers are looking for the pashan. Something strange is going on, I can feel it.'

'But you will be needed here as well, believe me. This hero will need all the help he can get. I must speak to Maya about the pashan, though.'

'Let us see. When Asvin is strong enough, I will leave. There is so much work to do. Artaxerxia has to be taken care of, as well.'

'Strange, isn't it, that the Sultan was in Hero School with the Civilian.'

'Someone's coming,' said the Dagger.

I didn't hear anything, thought Mantric, but a few seconds later there was a knock on the door. Mantric opened it and went outside. It was Pygmy Lion, who said he had rolled around, but was still pink. To assure him that this in no way affected his masculine beauty was a minute's work for Mantric.

When Mantric returned, he didn't even bother to look around his hut. He knew the Dagger had disappeared.

28

When he awoke, the world was spinning in a mad rush of colours and sounds.

'Are you all right?' asked Spikes, shaking him gently.

'Yes,' said Kirin. 'I'm fine.'

He suddenly remembered vague images of motion at the mouth of the cave when he was sinking to the ground. 'Have you been fighting anyone? I thought I saw something.'

'It was nothing. Couple of bears. They seemed to think they owned this cave or something.'

Kirin smiled. 'Well, perhaps they did, you know.'

'Well, they don't any more.'

'I'm really hungry. Have you eaten anything?'

Spikes pointed to a little pile of fruits. 'Breakfast,' he said.

'What would I do without you, Spikes?'

'Die, probably.'

'I didn't know you liked fruits.'

'I don't.'

'Have you eaten anything, then?'

'Yes.'

Kirin knew better than to probe further. He quickly went through the pile of fruits, and soon there was no pile of fruits. He was thirsty, too, and he went out for a while, to the stream, and when he returned he was fresh, clean and ready to go—or wait, which was what he was supposed to do, he remembered.

He blinked a few times, because the sun was bright outside and the cave was dark. Then he stopped.

Spikes was sitting on the rock, holding the book in his hands.

He looked at Kirin. 'You haven't told me what you were doing last night,' he said.

Kirin sat down on the floor, at Spikes's feet, and told him Narak's story. When he reached the part where his father had allowed himself to be captured, and had met Katar, he faltered, and looked at Spikes. *Of course* Spikes was his friend. And no matter what happened, Spikes would be on his side. Wouldn't he?

'Tell me the rest of the story,' said Spikes. 'It involves me, doesn't it?'

His father had said pashans were stupid. He obviously hadn't met Spikes. Well, he had met the egg, but there is only so much you can say about an egg.

Kirin told Spikes the story of Katar and the egg of stone, and the coming of his mother and the death of his father and Danh-Gem.

Spikes was silent in the darkness.

Then he said, 'So your father killed mine.'

'Yes, and my mother killed Danh-Gem, who made your parents,' said Kirin, feeling a little uneasy. But pashans didn't care about their parents. Did they? How could they? They never even met their parents.

He suddenly realized that he had hardly ever met his . . .

'Shouldn't I be angry?' Spikes said softly.

'I don't know, Spikes,' said Kirin. Part of him was wondering whether to run.

'And now you will slay Danh-Gem, who created pashans like me. I am probably the only one of my kind left, just as you are the only one of yours.'

His eyes were glowing green in the darkness. Kirin watched him. This isn't happening, he thought. But Spikes was his friend . . . He'd probably lost Maya, and now . . . *Spikes*?

They were both quiet for a while, looking at each other.

Then Spikes laughed. 'So what do we do now?' he asked.

Kirin sat down on the rock beside him. He briefly considered hugging Spikes, but abandoned the idea because he would probably get hurt.

He grinned.

'Now,' he said, 'we do nothing.'

BOOK TWO

BOOK TWO

I

'**G**ood! A full twenty seconds this time. Now get the mud out of your eyes, and we will start over.' They were in the Square Forest in northern Bolvudis, where the trees were evenly spaced to allow voluptuous damsels clad in clinging saris to run from one tree to another in time to the music which would be played when the Muwi-visions were eventually shown to the public.

Asvin lay face downwards in a mud puddle and groaned. This was worse than the ashram. It was only the seventh day of his training, and he had already decided that he hated Gaam. Well, it was impossible to hate Gaam, but he didn't like him any more. The kind, friendly vaman who had told him stories about ancient heroes in the Bleakwood had disappeared, and he now faced a stern taskmaster who made his formidable kul-guru seem like a nurse.

He got up, and picked up the staff that Gaam had sent flying from his hands a moment before knocking him to the ground with a hard blow to his ankles. He had started swinging it warily, whirling it around, circling around Gaam, looking for an opportunity to strike.

'You needn't feel bad,' said Gaam kindly. 'Avrantics have always been hopeless at everything except archery. You are young and strong. It's just that your teachers so far must have been pathetic.'

Asvin, who had loved his venerable and terrifying old kul-guru, frowned and lunged. Gaam took a step back, tripped Asvin up and smiled as he went crashing into the same spot of mud as the last time.

Asvin got up fast this time, and attacked Gaam again. He was taller, quicker, heavier and stronger than the vaman, he told himself, as the staffs clashed. All he would have to do was concentrate.

For some time, only the sounds of wood hitting wood and swishing through air were heard.

'Much better,' said Gaam, panting a little, as he ducked and weaved to avoid Asvin's blows. 'You lack patience, but that is not a problem if the stars smile on you. And you have a natural aptitude for violence that will stand you in good stead. The other thing you lack,' he added, hitting Asvin on the knuckles and then on the back as he dropped the staff with a yelp, 'is technique. Which I can teach you.' He knocked Asvin down again.

'Again.'

This time Asvin didn't get up. 'How many weapons do I need to learn to fight with?' he asked wearily. 'Why can't I concentrate on the sword and the bow, and maybe the mace? My kul-guru said I could be the best swordsman in the world. Why do I have to learn to fight with these ungainly weapons?'

'Because you have to reach a stage where it doesn't matter what weapon you're using,' said Gaam, pulling him to his feet.

'Or even if you have a weapon at all. Most of single combat is fought in the mind. Of course, I cannot teach you all you need to know within this year. But you are learning fast.'

'Can we try something else now?' asked Asvin. He had been tired after the morning's intense yoga session to start with, and Gaam was anything but gentle.

'Can I have a go?' asked Maya. She had been leaning against a tree, watching, and smirking from time to time, annoying Asvin intensely.

'Weren't you supposed to be having magic sessions with your father?' he asked crossly.

'He's busy,' she said, picking up a staff. 'Come on.'

'I don't fight girls,' said Asvin stiffly.

'My family was from Durg,' she replied. 'Do they call Durgan warrior-women girls in Avranti?'

He picked up a staff. 'Very well, then.'

Gaam stood back, watching them with a benevolent expression. Ah, he thought, young love. Not that they were looking particularly loving at the moment.

They circled warily, and then started sparring. Asvin sent Maya's staff flying in a few seconds. He raised his staff to strike her down, but stopped.

'What happened?' asked Maya.

'Pick up your staff,' he said.

'That's unfair,' she said. 'Gaam hit *you* every time.'

'That's different.'

'Don't ever patronize me again,' she said.

Maya turned a cartwheel and picked her staff up. She's in good shape, Gaam noted. But then they taught gymnastics and unarmed combat in Enki. Spellbinders often found themselves in situations where they couldn't cast spells and people wanted to hit them.

Of course, no one meddled with them in Kol, but holidays in the country for spellbinders were generally fraught with danger. Anyway, if Maya had any Durgan blood in her she had probably spent most of her early years fighting.

'Come on,' she said. They clashed again, and soon Asvin disarmed her again. He stood in front of her, looking at her, his staff in the air.

'What? Are you scared?' she said. 'Strike!'

He closed his eyes and swung his staff.

He didn't hit anything. He opened his eyes, puzzled.

She was still standing in front of him. She hadn't vaulted back or ducked.

'Magic is very strong in Bolvudis,' she said sweetly. 'I couldn't have done this everywhere.'

Puzzled, he looked at his staff. It wasn't there.

He was holding out a rose. She took it from him.

'Why thank you, kind sir,' she said. In her hand, it turned back into a staff. She tapped him smartly on the head with it, and handed it back to him. Asvin stood staring at her, then dropped the staff with a yell. It was burning hot.

'We spellbinders prefer to use our hands when fighting,' she said. 'And our heads. We don't use weapons, because we generally don't need to.'

'That wasn't fair,' said Asvin, looking at the staff, now hissing and curling as it turned to ashes.

'Magic isn't fair,' said Maya, walking away. 'I'll see you at lunch.'

Gaam smiled again as he watched Asvin glare at her back. He'd asked Maya to perform this little stunt. Asvin might have to fight both women and magic-users later on, and it was important that he got some things clear right at the outset. Of course, she'd been more than willing.

It was important to hammer some of Asvin's Avrantic training out of him, Gaam thought. Most of it was good— Asvin was *very* good with the sword, the bow and the spear; a skilled rider, swimmer and hunter. Very strong, very quick, excellent reflexes, excellent stamina. And his education was coming in very handy—there would be no need to teach an Avrantic prince etiquette, dancing or the art of diplomacy. His tutors and guru had done most of Gaam's work for him. Of course some things would have to be unlearned— he had an extremely old-fashioned view of the world, but what did you expect from the Avrantics? And he was a little proud and arrogant, but that could be forgiven—that was always a problem with princes, and more days like today would cure him quickly. Lessons in humility were Gaam's speciality. He looked at the dashing young man sulking in the sunlight and was happy. All things considered, he was very good hero material.

'That's enough for now,' said Gaam to the glowering Asvin, and led him away. As they walked through the Square Forest, actors stopped singing and dancing just to watch them. Asvin has so much presence, thought Gaam, and the magic in the air enhances it. Since Asvin had come to Bolvudis, he had been inundated with offers from both imps and humans to act in the Muwi-visions. Gaam had instructed him not to accept, so Asvin had smiled at everyone regretfully and moved on.

But then Gaam, with typical vaman ingenuity, had thought of a way to keep everyone happy. Some boys from Xi'en had recently arrived in Bolvudis. None of them could speak Koli, but Mantric had been to Xi'en and spoke their language. They were all incredibly skilled in the martial arts, amazingly agile, supple and swift, and the imps were all swooning over them. Many new Muwi-visions were being planned for them to show off their skills in. Gaam found an imp named Atient who liked watching Muwi-visions at dawn, and every day, at dawn, Atient and Gaam would watch the boys from Xi'en teach Asvin Xi'en-style unarmed combat. Of course, these boys had probably learnt to fight before they had even learnt to walk, and it would be years before Asvin could match their skills, but he was learning fast.

Gaam had also started him off on endurance-training exercises, swimming underwater for hours and learning to control hunger, pain and fear. I will make him the complete hero, thought Gaam; Simoqin would have been proud of me. But I have to do something about the magic. We must get him some magic-resistant armour or something. And he has to be taught to fight magical creatures—belly-stabs for dragons, cold water for cherufes and so on. But all that can come later, once Mantric starts sending us on quests.

There is so much to teach him, Gaam thought. I must tell him more about the world—he knows astonishingly little about what lies beyond the borders of Avranti. And if he is to be a hero for the whole world, he needs to learn so much. Stupid Avrantics. The only nation more insulated and closed to the world is Xi'en. But do not worry, Asvin. I will make you as great a hero as the Seven Heroes of the Humans in the Age of Terror.

'As who?' asked Asvin.

Gaam realized he had said the last sentence out loud.

'The Seven Heroes of the Humans in the Age of Terror,' he said. 'Have you never heard of them?'

'No.'

'The band of heroes from all over the world who joined hands against Danh-Gem and won many battles? Remember?'

'No.'

'You must at least have heard of Anik of Avranti and Queen Raka of Durg.'

Finally Asvin's face lit up. 'Who has not? The greatest warriors in the world at the time, they single-handedly annihilated an entire Skuan army, and slew the notorious . . .'

'Hmph. Never mind,' said Gaam. 'I know about them, and there were five more heroes in their league, from Xi'en, Kol, Psomedea, Elaken and Ventelot. They were indeed the greatest of the mortals who fought Danh-Gem. The incident to which you allude is the storming of the dragon-citadel of Wurm in southern Skuanmark.'

'I thought it was just the two of them,' said Asvin, sadly, for of course seven people defeating an army and conquering a city is far less impressive than two people defeating an army and conquering a city. Three-and-a-half times less impressive, in fact.

'It was not just the two of them,' said Gaam, looking annoyed. 'It was not just the seven of them, either. It was the Chronicler, just like it always is.'

'The Chronicler? Who or what is that?'

'The Chapter of Chroniclers is a society in Kol that very few people in the word have heard of. Yet the deeds of the members of the Chapter would fill several books, and cause most of the epics of the world to be thrown away.'

'I don't understand.'

'Well, that is possibly because I haven't explained yet. Many of the tales of quests you have heard about, Asvin, are entirely untrue. Because it is not he who kills the dragon but he who returns with its head that gets to tell the tale of its slaying.'

'What?'

'Sit down, Asvin, and listen to me.'

Asvin sat on a tree stump and watched Gaam, who began to pace about. It was still morning, and birds were singing in the trees. On a little muddy patch to his right, Asvin saw the trail of paw prints and goat-droppings that meant Nimbupani had been there recently. Gaam cleared his throat and began.

'I understand your confusion. This is not something you are unaware of because of your Avrantic upbringing—it is a secret shared by very few people, a secret I am sharing with you simply because you may be Simoqin's hero, and I will be your Chronicler.

'Of course, there are some heroes who do all the things the epics speak of. They go out into the wilds alone, suffer bitter hardships and return after completing their quests. These men are brave and hardy, true, but the tales they tell are not very inspiring ones. Most of these men do not have a flair for story-telling, and speak most fondly of food found in unexpected places.

'Long ago, in the times when the great Ossus was alive, a certain knight of Ventelot had a bright idea—he asked his page to note down everything he did on the quest, so that when he returned, the world might know of his deeds. The page did so, and later, when the knight read the sordid story of robbery, murder and duplicity that was the true tale of his journey to slay a dragon, he was enraged, and he threatened to put his page to the sword. The page pleaded for his life and then changed the story completely, putting in distressed damsels, plundering dragons and many-headed ogres. The knight returned to Ventelot with gold he had stolen from a band of sleeping bandits and was rewarded with the hand of an extremely ugly princess—who was of course ravishingly beautiful in the tale.

'The page came to Kol, which was then a growing city

known only for the University of Enki—the Heart of Magic came to the city much later, in the Age of Terror—and founded the Chapter of Chroniclers. Because of Kol's central location, it was convenient for most heroes to travel to Kol and get a good Chronicler before setting off on their quests.

'The Chroniclers were the pages, squires, charioteers, mahouts and servants that no worthwhile legend speaks of, except perhaps as monster-food before the hero slays whatever or whoever he or she had set out to slay. They carried food, clothes, weapons and all the other things the heroes needed—and a lot of these heroes were princes and aristocrats who even in the wild demanded the comforts of their airy kennels. The Chroniclers wrote the tales of the hero's quests, which were often entirely fabricated, and gave them to the great poets, who in turn wrote the epics the world is so fond of. Of course, the Chroniclers maintained secret accounts of the truth, which are still preserved in the Chapter of Chroniclers' chambers in Kol. They make hilarious if occasionally sad reading.

'And sometimes, Asvin, the real heroes aren't the ones who appear in the paintings, or the ones who go to receive rewards from the king concerned. The Beast of Ukun was slain by an evil-smelling one-eyed hunchback, not by Hewgo the Handsome. Not all heroes are handsome, tall and strong. Some have atrocious manners, some are as ugly as an asur's nightmares and some have disgusting diseases. Some monsters are slain by accident. A blind old woman dropped a chicken on the head of the Basilisk of the Remorseless Taiga. Yet the legends sing otherwise. Here, again, the hand of the Chronicler is revealed.

'Of course, some heroes were all that they were made out to be, and the Seven Heroes of the Humans were mostly as brave and mighty as they are in the tales. But the truth about the storming of Wurm is that their Chronicler crept into the dragon-pen in the dead of night and put rotten mangoes in the dragon-food. In the morning, when the Skuan army were getting ready to charge at and mow down the Seven Heroes, who were standing outside the city, just out of bowshot, making rude gestures with their weapons, all the dragons had severe indigestion. Not unnaturally, this was too much for their fiery tempers, and they ate the army. The Chroniclers, however, speak of the Heroes slaying each and every Skuan who charged at them at dawn.

'You might ask why the Chroniclers, if they are indeed so bold and brave, did not claim to be heroes themselves. It is not that the Chroniclers minded the anonymity—they were often well paid and they didn't want the fame, (which always made impoverished family members and obsessed, swooning damsels appear out of thin air). They loved the adventure, the travel involved and the feeling of actually making history—making it up, as it were.'

'So all the legends are lies?' asked Asvin, shattered.

'Not at all. A lot of them are true. Besides, there are thousands of heroes whose deeds are not recorded. There might be a hundred Ossuses in the world, unknown, unsung. They did not have Chroniclers and were too shy or modest to brag afterwards. And there were some heroes who acknowledged the help they got from their Chroniclers, and the legends speak of every servant that went on the quests with them.

'But some of the legends are false. So many dragons have died, out of old age, indigestion or sheer boredom, and knights have come to empty caves, stuck swords in the corpses and posed for the portraits. And what of the heroes who are slain? No one sings about them. At most, there is the line in the epic that talks about the hundreds the monster has slain. That one of those hundreds might have removed a leg, a wing or even a head before dying is never mentioned. Remember, Asvin, many heroes may venture forth on the quest, but only one finishes it, and his is the tale that is told.

'So if you ever feel inadequate, and think you can never measure up to the heroes of the past, despair not! For I will be your Chronicler, and if you so wish, I will make you the greatest hero that ever walked the face of this earth.'

Asvin looked at him. 'Thank you, wise Gaam,' he said. 'But I think I would like the truth told. It is true that I want to be great, but I cannot bear the thought of lies being written about me. Whether I am the hero or not, whether I succeed or fail, you can tell the truth about me.'

'You pass the test,' said Gaam, smiling, 'but all the worlds' greatest heroes react similarly when they first hear about the Chroniclers. The truth, Asvin, is always told—it is told in the annals of the Chapter of Chroniclers. But people need more than truth from a legend. People need to believe in their heroes, to have something to look up to, some ideal to strive towards. If our heroes were not great and noble, fearless and bold, we would lose hope. Sometimes the truth is not what people need to know. There are many who would have left their homes and run at the slightest whisper of a rumour of an approaching monster, if they had not known that the dashing hero from a strange land, clad in shining armour, was waiting in their village, and that he would slay the monster, as he had slain so many before. They did not need to know that the hero was probably wishing he could run away as well, or perhaps that the monster was dying anyway and had made a secret pact with the hero so that its children would be looked after. Hope is important, Asvin. And whatever else heroes do, they bring hope to thousands. It is a precious gift, and one the Chroniclers are happy to give.

'Therefore do not insist that I write the truth. Instead, be brave and fearless, so that the legend I write is the truth. Nothing pleases a Chronicler more than having to write only one account of an adventure.'

'But what do the Chroniclers do now?' asked Asvin.

'The Chapter of Chroniclers now operates under the aegis of the Hero School in Kol. They write reports on the love lives of royal families, accounts of archaeological expeditions and mining surveys, but most of their money comes from making accounting tables. Thus they preserve their ancient skills, for all these are, again, mostly fictitious.'

'What was it like, teaching in Hero School?' asked Asvin. 'It must have been very thrilling.'

Gaam shuddered.

'Thank your stars you never fell under its evil influence,' he said. 'You would have learnt nothing there except the art of cloaking the meaning of whatever you say with high-sounding words. You would have returned to your country with ridiculous ideas about "modern methods of administration" and proceeded to ruin your nation's economy, turning Avranti into another warehouse for the merchant-guilds of Kol. And if your country did not want you back, you would have been picked up by explorers and sent to Artaxerxia, and you would have crossed the desert of Al-Ugobi and helped them conquer more lands in the west.'

'Never,' said Asvin, 'not the Artaxerxian thieves.'

Gaam looked at him sadly. 'In your words I see the work of Ventelot, and of Imokoi,' he said. 'I cannot understand the hatred the Avrantics and the Artaxerxians bear for each other.

I have been to both countries. You have so much in common, your languages, your food, even your race . . . When other countries were wandering tribes, Avranti and Artaxerxia were discovering advanced mathematics together. Yet even after Amrit the Great threw the colonists of Ventelot out of Avranti, the old hate remained. And Danh-Gem used it well in the Great War, promising Artaxerxia dominion over Avranti and using that bait to destroy the mighty armies of Elaken.'

He stopped talking and looked at Asvin. Asvin was looking completely blank.

'But you know nothing of the world beyond Avranti, and have been taught to hate Artaxerxia,' said Gaam, a little more kindly.

'I know very little,' said Asvin, sadly, 'about the wide world and the powers that rule it. When I returned to Ektara from the ashram in Shantavan and was taught the manners that court life demanded, I was told nothing about all that you have just said. My brother, Maharaja Aloke, said I need not concern myself with matters of state.'

'I understand,' said Gaam, 'and it is not a wholly bad state of affairs. For apart from Artaxerxia, you do not have any prejudices, and I am a patient teacher. Do not worry, Asvin. You will be an expert in international relations before I am done with you.'

And so, as the sun grew high in the sky and the shadows of the trees shortened, Gaam began to tell Asvin about the world he lived in; about the ice-wastes and cold forests of northern Skuanmark where he had saved Queeen from a pack of ravening wolves, of the great ocean to the east of Avranti, of the mysterious land of Xi'en where no outsider, good or bad, was really welcome (no one knew how large Xi'en was, for they would not show their maps to the world and their warships scared explorers away). Gaam spoke of Xi'en in a voice full of wistful longing because that strange eastern land fascinated him, with its ancient customs, skilled warriors, wise monks and beautiful, intricate works of art.

He told Asvin of Kristo Nalegamo, the Olivyan explorer who claimed to have sailed all around the world, sailing around the tip of the Ekera peninsula, the southernmost point of Elaken, where one could actually see the Vertical Sea. Nalegamo had claimed that there were huge uninhabited plains and great forests to the west of the Great Desert, full of strange beasts and pygmies. But no one had believed him because he had no proof that he had actually made the great journey, and everyone knew the seas were impassable and full of giant serpents.

Asvin listened, wonderstruck, and in his heart was born that very day a fierce, wild desire to see the whole world, to see the great white bears trudging across the ice-wastes in the north and to sail to the very edge of the Vertical Sea.

At five o' clock Maya appeared with Pygmy Lion, still tearing bits of the pink gum off his body and chewing them slowly and determinedly. He was carrying two large trays full of food.

'In lands far to the west it is now noon and time for lunch,' she said, breaking the spell of Gaam's words. Not that Asvin or Gaam minded—they both suddenly realized they were ravenous.

'I've learned more in this week than ever before,' Asvin told her.

'You seem to have forgotten a few things too,' she said, watching him tear into the food. 'For instance, in some cultures, people who have been rolling around in the mud wash their hands before eating.'

2

*T*he servants of Danh-Gem will find you, Kirin, you will not even have to look for them, they will hunt you. Kirin shuddered. He wondered what mysterious monster would seek him out, in this ancient forest. But he hoped that whatever it was, it would come soon. A week had passed, and he was bored.

He came out of the cave, and watched the sun shine through the leaves. The sound of the nearby brook seemed louder now. It had rained a few days before, not the miserable, thin, grey rain that fell on Kol in spring but well-fed, fat rain, when each drop landed with a splat—rain with personality. The ground was fresh and muddy, and the smell of rejuvenated leaves was in the air. It was good that they were not travelling now, thought Kirin, any fool could have followed their tracks.

He walked towards the pool, near the little waterfall, and stayed there for a while, watching a passing toad looking for flies. He was very comfortable in the forest. He thought of Maya, and how she would have been chafing in a similar situation, and smiled. How peaceful the Centaur Forests were. How long would it last?

He walked back to the cave, kicking a little pebble ahead of him. From time to time, he would point towards the pebble and pull with his mind, feeling slightly surprised every time it flew up to his hand. He tried holding it in mid-air, but couldn't for long. Practice, he thought, must practise this.

He was crouching to enter the cave when he felt it first.

It was nothing much, nothing alarming, just a sudden feeling of alertness, along with a hint of fear, as if danger was close, but not very close. Probably his new heightened senses, he thought. It would take some time before he grew used to them. Food tasted so much richer now, especially fruits. Even water had a subtle taste, fresher and more invigorating than he ever remembered.

But now was not the time to think about food. Now was the time to wonder whether he was being hunted.

Kirin turned around, his back to the cave, and looked around quickly, scanning the little clearing near the mouth of the cave with his sharp eyes. Nothing.

But he knew he was being watched. Watched by an expert woodsman.

Or a predator.

The feeling of danger was getting stronger.

Should he call Spikes? He was sleeping in the cave, but he was a very light sleeper . . .

At times like this, he found himself wishing he was carrying a weapon. It seemed so stupid now, being alone and unarmed in the wild . . .

Then he felt the movement. It was a very slight movement, a horsetail swishing to scare away an adventurous fly . . . It was a centaur.

'Red Pearl?' he called. 'Is it you? Come out!' He felt movement behind him, and knew that Spikes had opened his eyes. Good.

There was a sound of hooves stomping over mud, and Red Pearl emerged, a little distance to his left. Her arm was no longer bandaged, and she was carrying her bow. In her other hand, she held an arrow.

'I came out from behind this tree because I trust you, Kirin, and I know you won't do anything foolish,' she said, but he sensed wariness in her voice. Of course she didn't trust him, she was negotiating. Why should she trust him—he had run away with Spikes . . . Why had they let him come with them in the first place? Did they know something? Did they suspect anything?

He looked at her and tried to think of something to say.

'How long have you known I was here?' he asked.

'I have been watching you for three days now,' she said. 'But how did you know I was watching you? I didn't make any noise.'

Three days? That didn't make sense. He had felt her presence, that sudden chilling feeling that he was in danger, just now, not three days ago. Or had she come closer today? Was there a specific radius within which his senses were heightened?

'Well, now that you've discovered my presence and we're out in the open, perhaps you might consider telling me what on earth the two of you are doing,' she said icily.

Spikes came out of the cave. Kirin felt the sudden thrill of danger again. What was this? Red Pearl wasn't going to fight them, was she?

Was she?

'You stay in that cave,' she told Spikes. 'I'm talking to Kirin.'

Spikes didn't move. He looked at Kirin. Kirin looked at Red Pearl, who had moved back a little. Her bow was dangling loosely, but her muscles were tensed. She seemed to be measuring the distance between herself and Spikes.

Kirin nodded, and Spikes took a few steps backwards, disappearing in the shadows of the cave. Kirin looked at him but could see only his eyes gleaming in the shadows.

'Why did you run away, Kirin?' asked Red Pearl sternly.

'I don't remember taking an oath to stay with you,' replied Kirin, his mind discarding one fabrication after another. There was no point in making up a story—she would see through it.

'Don't play games with me, boy. I am not a patient person.'

'Put that bow away. I mean you no harm at all.'

'Why did you run away, Kirin? Why did you come with us in the first place? Who is Spikes, really?'

'Why do you need to know? We could leave the Centaur Forests, if you're worried about your kinsfolk. Don't follow us, Red Pearl. I cannot tell you why we left. You must believe me—I am on a . . . well, a quest of a kind. But I am on your side, on the Silver Phalanx's side. Trust me. You said you trusted me.'

'What is it? What is your quest, and how is Spikes involved? You must tell me.'

'It is something I have to do. I cannot tell you, Red Pearl. Believe me, I would if I could. But I cannot.'

'Very well. If this had been a standard assignment I would have shot you both by now, but there is something different about you, Kirin, I can feel it. Something about you that makes me want to trust you. Let me come with you.'

'No. I cannot do that. It will be dangerous.'

'Dangerous?' she laughed.

'Please, Red Pearl. Go away. Let us be. We are trying to help.'

The feeling of danger suddenly grew, sharply. Something was very wrong . . .

There was a very faint rustling sound.

'So you won't tell me what you are doing, you won't let me come with you, and you ask me to trust you,' said Red Pearl grimly. 'I'm afraid that's impossible.'

She brought bow and arrow together and aimed at Kirin. Then she stopped, surprised.

People reacted in different ways when Red Pearl pointed arrows at them. Some looked terrified, others fell to the ground and begged, the more foolish ones attacked . . .

She had never seen anyone look unconcerned before.

Unconcerned wasn't it. He seemed . . . distracted. He wasn't even looking at her.

Kirin's eyes stared into nothingness. And then he *saw* . . .

The servants of Danh-Gem will find you, Kirin. You will not even have to look for them, they will hunt you.

He *saw* the large black shape silhouetted in the tree, he *saw* the huge black arm set arrow to bow, he *felt* the tension as the bowstring was drawn back . . .

'Behind you!' he yelled.

'Oh, please,' said Red Pearl.

And suddenly there was a black arrow in her back. She stumbled, and almost fell, grasping Kirin to maintain her balance.

Then Red Pearl reared up on her hind legs, spinning around and fitting an arrow to her own bow in a blur. Before she could release it, a second arrow streaked down from the tree, aimed with deadly precision, striking her injured wrist. She dropped the bow with a cry and reached for the knife in a loose sheath bound across her bare waist, but she was a trained member of the Silver Phalanx and she knew she was dead even before the third arrow pierced her heart.

She sank to her knees, breathing heavily.

'Who is it that shoots me in the back, like a coward, without even issuing a challenge?' she called.

The huge black shape flew out of the tree and landed in front of her. There was a ring as a sword was drawn.

'My name is Bali,' said Bali, and his blade swung in a flashing arc.

A few birds flew out of a nearby tree, screeching.

Red Pearl's body fell to the ground softly. Her head rolled once, twice, and then was still in the soft mud.

Kirin felt a surge of pure hate streaking from his head to his fingers, as raw ravian power crackled and tingled in his hands. He suddenly knew that he wouldn't need a weapon . . .

When they do come, you must control your anger and work with them.

He stopped, and let his hand fall limply to his side.

'You can thank me later,' said Bali. 'Where is the pashan-lord?'

Spikes came out of the cave, claws out, head down, prepared to strike. He had never looked more menacing, Kirin thought.

'No, Spikes,' said Kirin, raising his hand, trying not to look at Red Pearl. He felt anger, deep and terrible anger, welling up inside him. He had to do *something* . . .

Remember—if you fail, he will conquer all, for he will be more terrible and powerful than ever before.

But he couldn't let Red Pearl die unavenged . . .

A time will come later, I promise you, when you will have the power to decide whether they live or die.

That time had better come soon then, he thought, hating his powerlessness. I will kill you one day, Bali, he promised himself.

'What do you want?' he asked, trying to keep his voice from shaking.

Bali said nothing. He picked up Red Pearl, and Kirin marvelled at his strength as he threw her inside the cave like a sack.

Then he bowed, and said, 'I apologize for the rather uncouth introduction. I am Bali, king of the vanars of Vrihataranya. I need your help, Spikes and yours, Kirin.'

'How do you know my name?' Kirin burst out.

Bali smiled, revealing glittering white fangs. 'We have a few common friends,' he said.

'*What?*'

'You can come out now, it's safe,' called Bali. A green creature crawled out from behind a tree and smiled uncertainly at them. Kirin looked at it and was speechless.

'*Hooba?*'

'Es elweys,' grinned the asur.

'But . . . how . . .'

'Let me explain,' said Bali.

Suddenly there was a sound of a horn blowing in the forest, and the distant sound of hooves.

'Curses!' roared Bali. 'The man-horses followed us!'

He turned to face Kirin.

'I am sure you know what I want,' he said in a low, urgent voice, 'and you know you must help me. Together, we can raise the Rakshas, I am sure of it. I would have explained everything, but we have no time—the man-horses will be here any moment. We should move north, fast.'

He gathered Hooba up on his shoulder.

'We must go *now*,' he said, and sprang up on to a tree.

You must control your anger and work with them. Win them over, no matter how much hatred they arouse in you.

'Get the bag, Spikes,' said Kirin. He looked at Red Pearl's body, lying in the cave. Your death will not be in vain, he promised her.

A time will come later, I promise you, when you will have the power to decide whether they live or die.

And Red Pearl had come out, exposing herself to Bali's arrows, only because she trusted him . . .

'Hurry!' called Bali.

Spikes and Kirin emerged from the cave. Kirin slung the bag with the book in it over his shoulder.

The horns of the centaurs rang out again, louder and closer. Hooves thundered through the Centaur Forests.

'Follow me,' said Bali, and streaked off, a black blur skimming from branch to branch, Hooba bobbing wildly on his shoulder.

Kirin looked at him, then at Spikes. Spikes shrugged his stone shoulders. Then they both took a deep breath, and began to run.

Bolvudis village, Griffinmonth 12th, 10 p.m.
Muwi-visions acted in 4, Number of times called beautiful many (strange, never happened before, anyway it must be my smart new clothes), Temptation to get out of smart new clothes and back into old rags severe, New spells learnt 2, Number of times worried about Kirin many, Attraction for Asvin 6/10, Magic 8/10.

Another good day. I love Bolvudis—this whole Muwi-vision business is brilliant. I never knew I could act before, but I'm getting offers left and right. Then again, it's probably because the imps think we're all actors, and I'm the Badshah's daughter after all. But it's huge fun. I've never really thought about clothes before, and the costumes they make here are amazing. Of course, they'll never get me to paint my face or put kohl around my eyes. Or wear jewellery, for that matter. I mean, at some point spellbinders have to draw the line.

Wonder what Kirin is doing—wish he were here. Very worried about him, actually, but he can take care of himself, and Spikes can take care of anyone who attacks them, so I suppose he must be all right. Red Pearl was following them—somehow I hope she and Kirin don't become lasting friends. I wish he'd told me why he had to go. Anyway, no point thinking about that, as I tell myself about once an hour. Which reminds me, I have to get the loose sheets I scribbled on for the last few days and stick them into this book—I'll die if Asvin finds them floating around.

Oh, Asvin! (Melodramatic sigh.) I don't think anything can ever happen between us. And I'll tell you why. It's because you're so caught up in the idea of being a hero that you can't love a damsel unless she's in distress. You can't accept the fact that I'm a lot smarter than you, and could probably beat you in a fight as well. And I won't make my eyes go big, or swoon, or whisper, 'My Hero!' in a pretty, high voice. I won't wander around naked singing in forests. I won't put myself in danger so you can rescue me and feel you've won me. I will flirt with you relentlessly, though, because you're unbearably nice and good-looking and your broad shoulders tell me you'll be an excellent hunter-gatherer and protector of our seventeen children. And every nice girl loves a hero, especially a hero with such a nice . . . There I go again. Why, o why must you take yourself so seriously? (Wistful sigh.)

Never mind. It's just a little attraction. And speaking of little attractions, I cornered Amloki a few days ago and asked him why he'd been avoiding me. To my complete astonishment, he went all red and muttered something about the demands of his art. I knew he was acting in Muwi-visions—why, only the other day I saw him in a horse-hair beard and a doublet stuffed with feathers, pretending to be a vaman—but that didn't explain why he would disappear whenever I was around and shuffle his feet embarrassedly whenever I pulled him out of his hiding place.

So I told him to tell me the truth and he said he had thought before that he was in love with me. I took care not to laugh at the funny little fellow, or say that it was impossible because he's a khudran and about as high as my waist, and told him that it would complicate matters, wouldn't it, if we went on quests together—so I was sorry, but it could never be. He said he knew, and that was why he was plunging himself into his work, and acting in at least a dozen Muwi-visions. He said it had happened before, and he knew he shouldn't be drawn to human women but he was so far from home, and very lonely, and I could do magic tricks and everything. And he knew he wasn't really in love with me, and it was perfectly all right now, and that he was very sorry. The poor, sweet little thing. I gave him a huge hug and kissed him, and he went brick red and practically ran. I haven't seen him since, though the imps have all been telling me he's rapidly becoming a big star. Anyway, I don't think he should come on quests with us—he's really smart and knows a lot, but being small and nice isn't going to get you anywhere with an asur, or a vanar. And he's done a lot of work already—I think he should just settle down and be an actor now. He can do all the vaman roles—they'll never get vamans to act.

Father's still busy with his tele-vision spell—he promised he'd teach me how to do it, it's simply amazing. But it'll take time to learn. He really is the greatest spellbinder in the world. I don't think I'll ever be as good as he is. I wish he would stop for some time, though, and teach me a little more. It's all very well, seeing through the eyes of seagulls or other animals while you lie in the comfort of your own hut, but it tends to make the conversation a little one-sided. And Irik and Stivin must be thoroughly tired by now, because they've been flying over the Centaur Forests looking for Kirin for a week.

When I told Father about Kirin, I swore him to secrecy too. He wasn't angry—he said he quite understood me not being able to tell anyone before. He was glad I told him, because the Civilian was quite concerned. It turns out the Civilian and Father send flying scarabs to each other all the time, and that this whole quest had been planned long ago. And there were two people in the last few years who were brought to Bolvudis because they suspected they might be Simoqin's hero, but they both died. Which is why so many people have been brought to take care of Asvin, myself included. And Asvin isn't supposed to know about the other two.

Father was very excited when I told him how Kirin made moongold glow and could move objects with his mind. He agreed that the moongold alone proved Kirin was a ravian. But he was really worried when I told him about Spikes, and said that vanars and crows were looking for a pashan who was the son of Danh-Gem's bodyguard, who would help them raise Danh-Gem. And they think it's Spikes. That's too strange for words . . . Why is he Kirin's friend, then? He would have killed Kirin long ago, because he knows Kirin's a ravian. Unless . . . unless Spikes doesn't know who he really is. Very complicated.

Father seemed most puzzled when he heard that Spikes had brought Kirin to Kol. And when I told him that Kirin was Narak the Demon-hunter's son and had a book that had told him he was supposed to kill Danh-Gem, Father got really excited and started writing to the Civilian at once. He told me that the Civilian would tell no one, except possibly the Silver Dagger. He said it seemed like Simoqin and Narak's rivalry had not ended with Princess Isara. And then we talked about how their different ways of preparing for Danh-Gem's return fitted everything the books said about them—one operating in the dark, in secret, and the other with humans, spellbinders, and a beautiful, mysterious prophecy that gave hope to the whole world. Well, the whole Danh-Gem-hating world, anyway.

Then he said it was imperative that we find Kirin and bring him here. If Spikes was the pashan that the vanars were looking for, and Kirin didn't know who Spikes really was, it could be really dangerous for him. I didn't agree. I said Spikes would never harm Kirin, and if it was indeed a coincidence that the pashan who is supposed to raise Danh-Gem and the ravian who is supposed to kill him are together, which seems impossible, then it's best that we do not meddle—Narak had always been scornful about humans, and obviously Narak's plan, whatever it is, shouldn't be tampered with. I think Kirin should be left alone, to do whatever he is doing. But obviously my father, who knows neither Kirin nor Spikes, did not agree with that. But he did accept that it was a great thing that there was a ravian in the world, and that his presence could only make the enemies of Danh-Gem stronger and possibly explain the rise in magic over the last few years.

He said that because of this new information, the Civilian would probably send the Silver Dagger after Kirin and Spikes, to follow them and find out what the vanars were doing. I thought that was quite a good idea, actually. But how come Father knows what the Silver Dagger might do? How close is *he* to the Civilian? The whole thing is very confusing, and I still think we should all leave it alone and trust Kirin. If the book is telling the truth—and it probably is, since Kirin would never have left without the proof he was looking for—

then I think we should just let Kirin be and concentrate on Asvin.

I always liked the stories about Narak better, though.

The very day I told him, a week ago now, Father showed me what tele-vision is about. He called Irik and Stivin, did a couple of very complicated mudras, fed them some fish and then they flew away. He lay back on his cot, eyes staring into nothing, and told me he could talk to me, but that he was seeing with their eyes. I talked to him for a while, but he wasn't replying, so I went away.

Then three days ago he told me that there was some kind of powerful cloaking magic in the Centaur Forests, and they had not been able to see Kirin or Spikes, because his vision had grown really clouded over a part of the southern Centaur Forests, which was probably where Kirin was. But Stivin saw three vanars moving into it. Father tried to look harder, but tele-vision is a great strain, and he's developed it only recently, so he couldn't. Not over so much distance, anyway. What was the vanar doing? I'm very worried. What, for that matter, are Kirin and Spikes doing in the Centaur Forests? And how quickly can the Dagger get there?

As for the problem of controlling the birds, I suggested that he use a bug of some kind—after all, they're smaller, so the strain would be less, and no one would notice them— I mean, why would a seagull be wandering around in the Centaur Forests anyway. Father was really happy with me, and very enthusiastic about the idea. He said the tele-vision bug would probably remove the need for spies some day, if the idea worked, and if the bug can be controlled over sufficiently long distances. It would probably make sense to use flying insects, but finding insects capable of really long-range flight will be difficult. But it's worth looking into.

Anyway, it might not even work on insects. Father said the spell would need considerable modifications, but we should definitely try. Why, if we could see through the eyes of trained bugs, we could find out all about Xi'en and Artaxerxia—especially what their secret sorcerers' schools have been up to all these years . . .

Asvin is coming this way. That's all for now.

4

They had run for a day without a pause, and then Kirin could run no more—he had collapsed on the ground, breathing in huge, ragged gulps, while Spikes stood and watched and Bali glared from a tree above. Then Spikes had picked Kirin up, and Bali and Spikes had run through the night and the next day and night, silently, swiftly. They were running northwards and eastwards, and the ground was sloping steadily upwards and getting rockier. Spikes was no longer leaving footprints, and whoever followed them would not be able to run at full gallop.

A few hours after they had started running, the sound of the pounding hooves of the centaurs had grown softer, and the blasts of their horns more remote, moving westwards. Later Bali had explained that he had brought two other vanars with him, and instructed them to kill the first centaur that approached and then move westwards, to draw pursuit away from him. Which was why, he said, Red Pearl's body had probably not even been discovered.

At dawn on the second day, they had heard the sounds of

many horns blowing loudly and fiercely, and being answered by horns in all directions. Far in the distance, they had seen a cloud of burning arrows flying into the sky. And then the Battle-Drum of the Centaurs had started beating.

They had stopped running at the first beat of the Great Drum, which tore the sky apart and sent every bird in the forest flying into the sky. For centuries, the Drum of the Centaurs had struck fear into the hearts of enemies—the Centaur Forests had never been conquered by invaders. Long and deep the Drum rolled, and they had started running again, spurred on by images of strong centaurs, long hair flowing in the wind, streaking through the forest with bright spears in their hands and bows slung on their backs. Every half-hour the Drum would beat once, a great *doom* that echoed from end to end of the Centaur Forests, from the Mountains of Harmony in the east to the Bleakwood in the west.

The beats of the Drum followed them, until, at midnight on the second night, there were two quick, thundering beats, a roll, and then silence. The centaurs had caught and killed Bali's soldiers at the edge of the Bleakwood.

Bali and Spikes ran on, Hooba and Kirin clutching on to them desperately as night turned into dawn. The Centaur Forests were green and dense, and they crossed many little streams that gushed from the hills and ran southwards, towards the ocean. Finally they came to one that was wider than most, and they ran along its western bank until they reached a roaring waterfall that plummeted from a sheer rock face into churning white rapids below. These, though they did not know it, were the Dawn Falls, where the centaurs and the Psomedean humans had made peace years ago.

Bali finally stopped and waited for Spikes to catch up

with him. Then, with amazing agility, he began to climb up the rock face, Hooba trembling and squealing on his back. Bali sprang from rock to rock, a few yards from where the roaring water gushed down, and Kirin watched the green dye on Hooba's back grow darker in the clouds of fine spray. Hooba was screaming shrilly but his squeals were lost in the roar of the waterfall.

Bali climbed until he reached a ledge, high above the rapids, which seemed to have been cut in the rock face. No centaur would ever be able to reach it, thought Kirin. The ledge ran up to the waterfall, and then there was a tunnel carved into the rock. Bali disappeared into it.

A little later, two other vanars appeared on the edge of the ledge, and started shouting to Kirin, who signalled that he could not hear them above the noise of falling water. They threw down a rope, and he climbed up, getting thoroughly drenched in the process. Then they tied two more ropes to rocks, threw them down and Spikes hauled himself up. In silence, they passed into the tunnel.

It led to a little chamber, lit up by torches, where three more vanars sat. Another tunnel let out of the chamber to a ledge right behind the waterfall, and light filtered through the white, falling water and filled the chamber. The torches on stands in the walls seemed unnecessary, as the light outside was growing stronger. Kirin marvelled at the smooth, round walls of the tunnel and the chamber. Bali pushed the stone door at the end of the tunnel leading to the ledge behind the waterfall shut. It closed with a click and immediately the roar of the waterfall was muffled and only filtered in faintly through the other opening. The light coming through the water-curtain was also shut off, and they looked at one another in the light cast by the flickering torches. The secret chamber had been made by vamans centuries ago for Psomedean archers who watched the river from behind the waterfall and shot enemies who were trying to cross. But none of those who now stood in the chamber knew that.

'The borders will be watched,' said Bali. 'It is only a matter of time until they return to the cave where I found you, and follow Spikes's trail. But they will lose us on the wet rocks, and they can never come up here. We have food, and can last for a long time even if they besiege us.'

'How did you find this place?'

'Chance,' grinned Bali, fangs gleaming red in the firelight. 'Chance, and good vanar eyes. We have made this a vanar stronghold in the heart of the man-horse realm. We are near the northern border of these paltry woods, but the border will be watched now, and we must travel east when we do, to the edge of the mountains, and then find our way north through the Peaceful Forest and thence to Vrihataranya and Vanarpuri. Travelling along the plains would be faster, but too many are watching the roads now. The ruler of Kol is a worthy adversary.

'But we will talk about our escape later. Tell us, who are you, Kirin? My friend Hooba here tells me you used to buy magical things from his shop, and that you are a powerful sorcerer but not a spellbinder. How is it that Spikes, lord of pashans, follows you?'

Kirin looked at Spikes. This was convenient. The little story they'd cooked up would probably work. If he was to stay alive, it had to work . . .

'Hooba has told you the truth,' he said, in the most sinister voice he could manage. 'I am indeed a sorcerer, and though modesty forbids me from saying so, I am probably the greatest sorcerer in the world. Spikes is the son of Katar, most trusted henchman of the great Danh-Gem himself . . .'

'I know,' said Bali.

What? You know? This is not good. Still, he can't know how intelligent Spikes is, he'll have to assume Spikes is as stupid as any other . . .

'No doubt that is why the great Spikes is as clever as a vanar,' smiled Bali.

Great.

'No,' ventured Kirin, 'his mental powers are a gift. A gift from me.' Spikes made a little menacing sound that would have sounded like a muffled laugh if anyone except Spikes had made it.

'But who are you really, Kirin?'

Well, monkey-man, I'm the person you, or someone who looked exactly like you, pushed into the wall when he was stealing the Untranslatable Books. But you didn't see my face, did you? You just pushed me into the wall and I fizzled out like an Alocactus. If you weren't one for the ladies, you might have remembered me.

'I am Kirin the Karisman,' said Kirin.

They looked puzzled, but suitably impressed.

Kirin tried to sound haughty. 'Of course, if you are a true servant of Danh-Gem, you will have heard of the Karismen.'

There was silence for a few seconds. This is where I die, thought Kirin.

'Of course, we have heard about the Krismen, who has not?' said Bali courteously. 'But do tell me a little more about yourself.'

I do believe I've got him. 'Karismen, not Krismen. Never lie to me again, Bali, lord of vanars. I will ask again—do you know who the Karismen are?'

'No, Kirin. The vanars were unfortunately not a part of the Great War, as I am sure you know.' Bali's tone was a lot politer now.

'It's all right, then. Anyway, the Karismen were—are— a secret society of sorcerers dedicated to assisting those who will bring the great Rakshas back to the world. Spike's egg,'— Bali nodded vigorously, he obviously knew about that too— 'was enchanted with a spell that made him seek me out.' This might actually work, he thought.

'I am the only one left,' he added quickly, before Bali could want to meet the other Karismen. 'The other members of the Secret Brotherhood were slain by the evil spellbinders of Kol. They were looking for me, too, but they did not know what I looked like—I used to roam in their very midst while they searched for me high and low. But they guessed I was a Karisman eventually, and to escape their clutches I was travelling south with a band of mindless circus performers. The orders given to me by the Chief of the Karismen—before he died a mysterious death—were to wait in the Centaur Forests until the servants of Danh-Gem found me.'

He paused for a moment, looking at the awestruck wonder on the faces of Bali's soldiers. This was fun. Unless they were going to kill him when he stopped, of course.

Bali was looking a little doubtful, though. He needed to be a little more convincing. But should he say it? He might as well—he was quite sure Bali was the one in the library.

'Where are the Untranslatable Books? Show them to me quickly,' he said.

Now Bali looked genuinely impressed.

'I was wondering whether you were lying,' he said. 'I apologize. You have powers beyond my comprehension, Karisman.'

He gestured to another vanar, who pulled out a little bag from under his seat. He drew the five Untranslatable Books out from under the bag. Kirin felt a little thrill of excitement.

'It brings my heart much joy to see them,' he said. 'The spellbinders had woven magic around their library that prevented Karismen from breaking in. So tell me, what do we do next? How are you planning to raise Danh-Gem?'

They looked at him in silence.

'What?' asked Kirin.

'Don't you know?' asked Bali.

'What?'

'We were basing all our plans on the hope that Spikes, or you, would know how to raise the Rakshas.'

Kirin stared at him blankly. 'I don't know.' They were amazing, wandering around the world, killing people everywhere because they thought a pashan might know things they didn't.

Bali looked back at him equally blankly. 'We were hoping you would tell us,' he said. 'I thought you said the Karismen would do that. I thought I had finally found what I was looking for.'

'I said the Karismen would *help*,' said Kirin. 'It is not for me to lead the forces of Danh-Gem, Lord Bali. The Karismen were advisers. I will help you, but a Karisman is never hungry for power. If there is a leader in these things, it must be you.' And if that doesn't make you like me, he thought, nothing will. 'I will study these books and see what I can do,' he continued. 'But have you done nothing so far?'

'Of course not,' replied Bali. 'Armies are being gathered all over the world. The night the next new moon appears there will be a great council in the heart of Vrihataranya, my great capital, where all followers of Danh-Gem will unite.

The asurs are gathering in Imokoi. Our allies in Skuanmark and the other northern lands are preparing for war. When Danh-Gem returns, we will be ready. But we do not know how to raise the Rakshas. I had thought Spikes would know. When you spoke, I thought you would. Perhaps the answer is in these books, I do not know. But I am not saddened, for somehow I think you will find a way. My heart is gladdened by the sight of you, Kirin, I know not why, but I take it as a sign of hope. I do not give my trust easily, but there is something about you.'

The last person who had said that had been Red Pearl, thought Kirin grimly. 'But I do not understand how Hooba fits into all this, or how you found out about me.'

'I used to hate asurs,' said Bali, smiling. 'I thought of them as pests, as maggots that should be stamped on. I still think that of the asurs of Imokoi—but Hooba is different, and he says there are others like him in Kol. Others who hate the asurs of Imokoi like me, and hold them in as much contempt as I do. Hooba and I, I found, have a lot in common.'

Hooba grinned shyly.

'I had told my friend, the Skuan lord Bjorkun, that we needed to find the most terrible pashan in the world,' continued Bali. 'He followed the wrong pashan, and had to flee from Kol—he set out east, to find me, in my secret hiding place, as we had decided. On the way, he found Hooba, who was also running away from Kol.'

'The blested northerners broke my emporium,' said Hooba, coming forward. Kirin noticed, for the first time, that there was a big black crow sitting in the shadows. 'End efter I hed told them ell ebout Spikes, too, end I hed let thet blested . . . good men, Bjorkun, stey es well!'

'Bjorkun knew he had made a mistake with the first pashan, and sent asurs out to look for Spikes, but you had already left the city by then. So Hooba here proved to be a great blessing. Bjorkun caught him and, in exchange for sparing his life, found out about Spikes—and a mysterious sorcerer named Kirin who we had never heard of before. Bjorkun gave Hooba to me, and I sent my soldiers out to find Spikes. And his mysterious master, if possible. Of course, if you resisted in any way they would have killed you.'

'But how did they find us? We were far away.'

'That was where my friend Kraken'—Commander Triple-Zero-One 'Kraken' croaked a greeting from the shadows—'helped me. His regiments of superbly trained crows combed the lands near Kol. They found you soon, on the road moving southwards—one of his crows had been following you since you left the city, in fact, since they had been ordered to track the movements of dangerous-looking pashans—and then my soldiers took over the pursuit, working with Kraken's crows. But they were killed, and then I took over the chase myself.'

'One day we shall rule the seven races of birds,' said Kraken proudly.

Kirin looked into Bali's eyes and saw laughter and scorn in them. Poor bird, he thought.

'The soldiers of Kol and Avranti are up in arms against the vanars,' said Bali. 'We must act fast. Three of my best warriors were slain in the Bleakwood. We will wait here for a while, and see if you can read these books. Whether you can or not, we will leave this place in three days—the sentries on the borders will be less vigilant then, and we cannot stay longer, for then I would be late for the council. Kraken, go to Bjorkun and inform him that I have found the pashan and the last of the Karismen. And that the council will be on the day we planned it.'

Kraken croaked harshly and flew away.

'I hope you can read the books,' said Bali. 'For if we cannot find out what arcane spells they contain, we may fail entirely.'

'The spellbinders of Kol toiled over these books for years, and found nothing. Yet I will try,' said Kirin. Now I'm deep in it, he thought. Of course, I won't be able to read the books. But let us see what Narak the Demon-hunter has to say about them. I wonder when he will return. Four gifts, he said. Perhaps a Danh-Gemish-to-Ravianic dictionary will be one of them.

He stretched out towards the books and pulled with his mind. The books slid over the smooth rock-floor and flew up to his hands. Everyone except Spikes gasped.

I'm getting good at this. Three days, thought Kirin. Let me see.

He opened the first book. It was the one about torture. Two other books were in the runic script he remembered, but he did not know what language they were in. The fourth and fifth books, however, were in the ravian script. But the words were not words Kirin knew.

I hope my father turns up fast, he thought. And I hope this Bjorkun doesn't know that the Karismen never existed.

He saw the look on Bali's face. Bali was trying to read his eyes. He was wondering whether he had made a mistake.

Of course you don't trust me yet, thought Kirin. But you will. You will.

Kirin smiled. It was not a nice smile. It was the smile he smiled when people who didn't want to pay for the Stuff pulled knives out and he knew Spikes was behind him, standing in the shadows in their corner of the Underbelly.

I am beginning to enjoy this, he thought.

'Well, I'd better catch up on my reading, then,' he said.

At that very moment, the Silver Dagger was standing in front of the cave that had been Kirin and Spikes's hiding place. Centaurs had been there—they had carried Red Pearl away and cremated her according to centaur custom. The Dagger had been chafing to leave Bolvudis ever since he had heard that Kirin was a ravian. But he'd had to wait for the message from the Civilian telling him that he could go ahead; as soon as he'd got it, he'd made his way back to the Bleakwood, and followed the secret signs Red Pearl had left for him, little scratches on trees which told him what he needed to know. He had entered the Centaur Forests the night after Red Pearl had been killed, and had just reached the cave. He had stopped to meet the centaurs, who knew him by sight and thought he was a messenger from Kol. He had learnt of Red Pearl's death and told them to make sure their northern borders were well protected, and followed her trail to the cave. A young centauress named Green Bow had come with him—to protect him from unknown dangers, he thought, smirking to himself.

His mind was working furiously. Though the ground was full of hoof prints, they'd left the spot where Red Pearl had died untouched. As he saw the old, drying marks in the earth, the whole scene was recreated in his mind. The centaurs had told him that they had followed and killed the vanars who had slain Red Pearl and that they did not know of any other intruders in the forest, though two more vanars had been seen in the northern parts. But no one had followed

Spikes's deep prints, which headed northwards; they had all rushed off to hunt the vanars. Of course, thought the Dagger, trust the centaurs to charge and not think.

He prowled around for a while, and found Kirin's footprints near the stream. Kirin had been here alone . . . where was Spikes? Kirin had come back to the cave, and Red Pearl had come down from the excellent vantage point she'd been in . . . three days, the notches on the bark had said. Kirin and Red Pearl had spoken for a while *here*, and then something had happened, and then two deep, huge footprints *here*—*vanar*—and then Red Pearl had fallen, where the earth was still stained with blood. He closed his eyes, and imagined the vanar, jumping down from *that* tree, and cutting her head off—he must have shot her first, she'd have fought him otherwise.

He looked in annoyance at Green Bow, who was watching him with an amused expression. Pretty young thing. Must be thinking I'm crazy, wandering around looking at the ground.

What had happened then? Kirin's footsteps, going into the cave, widely spaced, running, Spikes's prints, coming out, feet apart—the Dagger imagined Spikes coming out of the cave, crouching, ready to attack. Not a pretty sight. The vanar had turned, a broken branch *there*, back on the tree. Then Spikes and Kirin had started running—pausing to get their *bags* first? Why? And the vanar, judging by the line of twigs that lay on the ground *there*, heading northwards, where his body must have crashed through the tree, had followed them.

So there had been a third vanar. And Kirin and Spikes were running in the forest, and it was following them. And the other two must have been decoys. Clever, those monkeys. He looked around a little more . . . *asur* prints? In the Centaur

Forests, where asurs would be shot on sight? What was going on?

One thing was clear. He needed to follow them, and he needed to follow them fast. He had seen the vanars move, and he had seen Spikes running, and he knew even he could never run that fast. He needed transport. If only Mantric had finished that blasted carpet . . .

He looked at Green Bow and wondered. Of course, centaurs generally attacked people who wanted to ride them—and Green Bow was a centauress. Centauresses killed people who wanted to ride them, but he had no other choice. And he was good with animals, and he was brilliant with people, so . . .

He walked up to Green Bow and started talking to her. After what he deemed a suitable length of time, he used what he privately considered the deadliest weapon in his awesome armoury.

He smiled at her. It was his special smile, the most devastating smile in the world.

Green Bow's heart fluttered, and so did her eyelids. A little later, the Dagger was demonstrating one of the eighty different massage techniques he had learnt in Avranti and Xi'en. It was called 'The Kneading of the Horse's Flank.'

Green Bow stood in the forest, listening to his soothing murmurs and went weak at all four knees.

A little later, the Dagger asked her if she would carry him for a little while, for he had lives to save. Green Bow, smiling blissfully, pulled the Dagger up on to her back, and they set off at a furious pace.

5

The Sultan of Artaxerxia sat up and raised a thin eyebrow. 'What is it this time?' The young woman by his side adjusted her veil.

'I crave your pardon, O Exalted One, but something has occurred which I felt deserved your immediate attention,' said the Grand Vizier.

'Indeed? Tell me everything,' said the Sultan.

'One of our captains, Omar, has turned renegade. With a band of desperate cut-throats, he is establishing a rebel stronghold in the desert. Bandits from all over the Blessed Realm flock to him.' The Vizier tried hard to suppress a smile. He knew he had done well.

'This is sad news indeed. I remember warning you about this man. And now what I foresaw has occurred. If you would but pay the slightest heed to my wishes, these situations might be avoided,' the Sultan's thin lips curled into a thin smile. The little fat man was useful. The careless remarks about his daughter had been well timed.

'I crave your pardon, O Exalted One, I have been

negligent and deserve death,' said the Vizier, head bowed in shame.

'I spare your life, as you have served me faithfully for many years, but you have been warned.'

'A million thanks, O Exalted One.'

'But tell me more about this rebel Omar.'

'He calls himself Omar the Terrible. The very desert sands, it is said, weep at the rumour of his approach. The grains of sand in the Al-Ugobi, they say, cannot count the number of innocent virgins who have died by his sword.'

'Quite a threat to our peaceful country, then.'

'Yes. Of course, he does not have enough gold to carry on this reign of terror for long.'

'That is as it should be.' More gold for Omar the Terrible, noted the Vizier.

The Sultan thought for a while.

'You must see to it that Omar the Terrible never meets Bjorkun the Skuan, who, it is rumoured, is still roaming these lands in search of friends and gold.'

'Rest assured that meeting will never take place, Exalted One.'

'After all, our friends in Kol would be most aggrieved.'

'Yes, Exalted One.'

The Sultan put a thin finger to his forehead and thought for a while.

'Do you remember,' he said finally, 'the little lamp I gave you? The one that came from the desert?'

'It had slipped my mind, Exalted One,' said the Vizier, who was now seeing the jinn-lamp in his dreams even when he was awake.

'In case you find it lying around, as it were, wherever you have thrown it carelessly, keep it safely.'

'I will make sure no thief lays hands on it.' Who was supposed to steal the lamp?

'If a rebel leader obtained possession of a lamp, it could mean danger for the common people, who are my sole concern. And yes, if I remember correctly, the Chief Civilian of Kol, the gracious Lady Temat, who is said to be looking for powerful magical objects, would be saddened indeed if the lamp were stolen.'

'I will make sure that does not happen, Exalted One,' said the Vizier, as he began to rehearse the conversation with Omar in his head. 'You can trust me.'

'Oh, I do,' replied the Sultan, looking bored. 'I do.'

6

Kirin looked at the page in front of him, at the words he'd written, using a feather borrowed from a bird one of the vanar guards was eating and Hooba's green dye (he'd forced Hooba to stand in the spray in the chamber behind the waterfall). He could hardly believe it. The spellbinders hadn't been able to read the Untranslatables for two hundred years. And he'd read them in two days.

Well, he couldn't read the books written in runes, obviously. And he hadn't read the book on torture either, and had no intention of doing so. But he could have. He knew how. And he knew what he needed to know. He knew what to do to raise Danh-Gem.

It was in the other book in the ravian script, a little notebook with a red cover, that he had found what he was looking for. It was right on the first page. He'd written a translation in green ink, between the lines.

He looked at the page again, and at the words he had written. He'd written them in Ravianic, so that he would still be the only person who could read them. He didn't expect any of Bali's allies to know the language.

Of course, he thought, it was just coincidence that he'd been able to translate it at all. Or was it? Could it be fate, or karma or something? Rubbish. But, he suddenly thought, it wasn't all coincidence—if the spellbinders had been a little more tolerant of asurs, they could have found out for themselves. Why, even Maya looked down on the asurs, thinking they were little more than animals.

But someone must have considered the possibility that Danh-Gem, master of the asurs, might have written the book in Asurian. Was it the ravian scripts that had misled the spellbinders? Why had Danh-Gem written in Ravianic? Had he learned Ravianic to help him woo Isara? Well, the asurs had no written language anyway. And so Danh-Gem had used Ravianic. Clever touch, that, writing Asurian words in ravian letters. Had the spellbinders missed it completely, thinking it was some arcane language Danh-Gem had invented?

No, thought Kirin, the spellbinders must have thought the book could be in Asurian. But they'd probably read the words out to one of the Kol asurs who had brought the Untranslatables to them, who had either not known the language, or had pretended not to know. And the spellbinders wouldn't bother to dig any deeper—not with lowly, disgusting asurs.

The language the book was written in was Imokoi Asurian, the language of the danavs.

The spellbinders probably didn't even know that there was more than one Asurian dialect, thought Kirin. Considering I've been dealing with asurs for years, and I didn't know until the last time I went to Lost Street . . .

So it wasn't mere coincidence, he thought. It was open-mindedness. Either way, it doesn't matter. I know how to raise Danh-Gem.

Kirin had been poring over the words in the books for two whole days. He'd been getting nowhere, mumbling the strange, rolling words and flipping through pages. He'd picked up the red notebook in the morning—it was probably something Danh-Gem used to scribble in, he had thought, looking at the scrawled letters, unlike the neat handwriting of the book on torture.

Then in the afternoon, when he'd given up, he had been mumbling the first words on the first page—he knew them by heart, now—and suddenly something had sounded familiar. He'd heard one of the words before. Where? When?

Then he remembered. He remembered Lost Street, and a ring of danavs around Spikes, and the ugly leader, who had stepped forward and yelled the word that he remembered . . .

'Charge!'

And Hooba had translated . . .

He had then called Hooba, and read the words out to him. And when recognition and excitement had dawned on Hooba's face, he had dragged him out to the tunnel behind the waterfall and there, in the light of the afternoon sun through the roaring sheet of water, he had translated the first page of the book.

On whosoever would bring me back to my days of glory, I lay this charge—

When the moon is full in the month of Dragons, journey to the Circle of Darkness and in the pentagonal Altar Stone lay down five objects.

First, a claw from the hand of the son of Katar,

lord of pashans, my most faithful servant and adviser. For I will unite the pashans again.

Second, the most precious gem the humans know. For the strongest passion the humans feel is greed, and through greed and power-lust will I rule their hearts, minds and lands.

Third, a jinn-lamp from the sands of the west. For jinns, ifrits and rakshases are my siblings, and their world is my world.

Fourth, the iron crown of the asurs. For when the asurs are united, nothing can stand before them.

Fifth, and most important, bring me the Gauntlet of Tatsu, that I may ride the dragons again.

Bring me but these five things, and when my followers are united, and the moon is full in the month of Dragons, I will rise again, and give you all your hearts' desire, a world of truth and beauty, of power and wealth beyond your wildest dreams.

Of course, Hooba knew too. He was sitting next to Kirin and smiling smugly. But, thought Kirin, I could kill Hooba. I could throw Hooba out of the chamber, down on the rocks below. Then no one would know except me. Then I could destroy this book, and no one would ever know. No one would raise Danh-Gem. And I'd save a lot of people a lot of trouble.

Then he remembered—*No one knew more about Danh-Gem than Narak the Demon-hunter, and Narak the Demon-hunter tells you this—Danh-Gem always had an alternative plan.*

Well, he thought grimly, that's just great. But you're my father, and you and my mother spent your lives fighting this creature, so I'll take your word for it. And I'll tell the vanar. And help him get the things Danh-Gem spoke of.

He went back into the inner chamber with Hooba.

Bali was sitting there with one of his soldiers and Spikes. He looked up as Kirin entered.

He listened in silence as Kirin told him what to do.

Then he said, 'Thank you, Karisman. Words cannot express how much joy and hope you have given me. Now we will unite the followers of Danh-Gem, and we will get these five objects. But do not tell anyone about the Circle of Darkness. That we will keep secret until the time comes.'

So you don't trust your allies any more than I trust you, thought Kirin. But you will not be there when Danh-Gem rises again, Bali, lord of vanars. I owe Red Pearl at least that much.

They spoke for a while, and then the other vanar returned with bad news. Centaurs were patrolling the northern and eastern borders of the forest in great numbers. Getting out would be difficult. But Bali refused to worry about all that. He was in really high spirits.

Night came, and the vanars, who disliked closed spaces, went to the outer passage to keep watch in turn while the others slept. Kirin leaned on the rock wall in the inner chamber and shut his eyes. He was soon fast asleep.

You look like me, but you have your mother's eyes.

He was wide awake in an instant. He looked around. Hooba was sleeping in a corner, and Spikes was watching him. He took the book out of the bag, went to the tunnel behind the waterfall and pulled the rock door shut. There was a muffled thump as Spikes sat down next to it, on the other side. Good old Spikes, thought Kirin. He opened the book.

There was his father, and he was smiling.

Have Danh-Gem's vassals found you?

'Yes,' said Kirin, and quickly whispered the events of the last few days. He told Narak about the five things they had to get to raise Danh-Gem.

This is news indeed. And you translated this in two days, while the human spellbinders could not in two centuries? That was well done, son. Though I have always thought humans were sorry creatures.

'I'm a little worried about that, actually,' said Kirin. 'Everything seems to be far too easy. Bali seems to really like me now. I thought it would be far more difficult.'

You have been among humans too long, son. Let things be as they are—if they are less difficult and convoluted than you expected, be grateful, not uneasy. Remember this, it is important—most often the simplest solution is indeed the best one. As I am sure you will find out in time.

And as for the fact that these creatures appear to trust you, think nothing of it. Have you never heard of the ravian powers of mind control?

'I have,' said Kirin, 'but I don't know how to control minds.'

Mind control, sadly, is a thing that has to be taught. The power is within you, but it is too late for you to learn how to use it to deadliest effect. Even I could not use it fully, for when I was young I was too poor to pay for the training, and when I was rich I was too old. But remember this: creatures who have no magic in them will always like you, and want to trust you and believe you. Use this to your advantage, Kirin.

'Have I done the right thing?' Kirin asked. 'Should I have thrown the book away? Should I help them gather the objects they need?'

You have done very well. And yes, help them. Make sure you are deep in their trust. That will make it easier for you to fool them in the end. Because believe me, Danh-Gem will reappear. I do not think he even needs these things to be there. It might all be a ruse. Danh-Gem may simply be doing a lot of his foul work in advance—uniting his soldiers, getting the things he needs—so that he can start off his grand scheme to conquer the world immediately. For all you know, Danh-Gem may already be awake, and may be walking this earth even as we speak, waiting for his vassals to assemble, and then he will appear to them in all his glory. Throwing the book away would have been folly.

Now you will have to travel all over the world, and there is not much time. Let me tell you quickly, for my strength wanes with every word I speak and every new evil creature that appears in the world. Son, do you know the legend of the Chariot of Vul?

'Yes,' said Kirin.

Vul Kunpo was one of the most famous vamans in history. He had been the most skilled vaman craftsman who had ever come up to the surface of the earth, and many of the most marvellous tools, machines and buildings in the world were his creations. It was during the Age of Terror that Vul had reached the height of his powers.

Danh-Gem and the king of Kol had both wanted to win over the vamans. The vamans had been neutral until then—they had earned a lot of money providing weapons to both sides in the war, and they had no particular grudge against either side, since they were not very concerned with what happened above the surface, and no one threatened their vast cities deep underground.

According to the legend, Danh-Gem and the king of Kol

had both gone to Vul to plead for his assistance and his doughty soldiers, for Vul was also the chieftain of all vamans who lived above ground. They had reached his home on the same day, and the king of Kol had arrived first. Vul had promised weapons, armour and his small but mighty army of vaman warriors to him. Then Danh-Gem had arrived, and promptly killed the king.

Vul had no quarrel with Danh-Gem, but he had already pledged his allegiance. To appease Danh-Gem (and save his own life) he had promised to make him a chariot so wonderful that its powers alone would surpass all the gifts that he would give Kol. Vul made the Chariot of Vul, which Danh-Gem loved so fiercely that he took Vul prisoner, to ensure that he could not make any more such chariots for his enemies.

No one had ever seen the Chariot of Vul, but the legend said that Danh-Gem would disappear at one end of the world and reappear in a few days at another. And Danh-Gem could go to any part of the world whenever he pleased.

Before I let myself be captured by the slaves of Danh-Gem, continued Narak, *I roamed at will in the heart of his evil land, and even entered his dungeons and set free many of those he was torturing.*

Once, when I was in the heart of the dungeons of Imokoi, slaying guards and freeing prisoners, I found an old vaman hanging upside down, forgotten, in a deep, dark chamber. I cut the chains that bound him and healed him with a spell.

It was Vul. Years of torture had ruined his mind and body, but he rewarded me richly for rescuing him. He told me the incantation that would raise his Chariot from the bowels of the earth. I could not use it then, for the Chariot accepts only one master at a time, but I remembered the incantation.

I had said I would give you four gifts, Kirin. My second gift to you is the Chariot of Vul. Use it well.

'But you said the Chariot could have only one master at a time.'

That is true. And I want you to be that one master, Kirin, for no one else in the world knows the incantation. But let us see. If the chariot does not come when you call, it could only mean that Danh-Gem has already returned. Listen closely, for I can only tell you the incantation once. I grow weak.

'I noticed,' said Kirin, for the now familiar headache had returned. He leaned closer to the book. 'Tell me,' he said.

And then, ignoring the throbbing pain in his head, he listened intently as Narak told him.

As the first rays of the sun chased away the darkness under the leaves of the Centaur Forests, Kirin and the others climbed up the rest of the rock face to the bank of the stream, before it plunged into the rapids far below. Then Kirin looked around and found a relatively clear stretch of ground—a circle thirty feet across, Narak had said. Then, feeling incredibly self-conscious, he kneeled in the centre, put his hand on the ground, as Narak had instructed, and muttered the incantation, thankful that the dim roar of the waterfall muffled his words, because he thought it sounded really silly.

At first, nothing happened.

He hadn't told Bali what he was trying to do, and Bali was looking impatient and annoyed. The vanar soldiers were prowling around in the trees, bows in their hands, scanning the forest for prowling centaurs.

Did I say it wrong? Kirin thought. *But he said he could only tell me once—does that mean I don't get to use this Chariot? Or has Danh-Gem already returned?* He looked at the others, staring at him as he kneeled on the ground in the dawn sunlight.

Then, suddenly, the earth shuddered.

And Kirin's hand sank into the ground, as if it had been water.

Large ripples started flowing outwards, the grass bobbing up and down. The ripples extended across a circle, about thirty feet across, and then stopped abruptly. Kirin snatched his hand out of the earth, and heard many little popping noises as little air bubbles burst, leaving little craters in their wake.

'What are you doing, Karisman?' asked Bali, in a voice full of wonder.

'I am raising the Chariot of Vul, the chariot that Danh-Gem himself used to move at incredible speeds across the earth in the Great War,' said Kirin, as grandly as he could. 'Perhaps we should start getting ready to leave—unless you want to walk, of course.'

'Get the books. We're leaving,' snapped Bali. His soldiers disappeared.

The bubbles were getting larger, and the popping noises louder.

Then, as suddenly as it had started, it stopped. They waited in silence.

The earth shook again, and Kirin saw, to his alarm, that the centre of the circle was bulging, as a huge bubble, as big as the circle, began to rise slowly out of the earth. He saw the grass in the circle sliding off the growing bubble like rivulets and collecting at the edge of the circle, forming a thick green ring.

Kirin slid off the swelling circle of earth and watched silently. Bali fitted an arrow to his bow and pointed it at the bubble, which was now a thirty-foot-wide dome in the middle of the Centaur Forests.

Then the bubble popped, noiselessly, leaving a huge crater. Kirin looked down, and saw a deep, hemispherical, perfectly smooth basin.

There were two things in the basin. One was an earthen chariot, large enough for four people. It was unlike any chariot Kirin had ever seen—and he had studied many books about war. First of all, it had a wide seat. The front was open, and there were two huge parallel bars extending from under the seat.

This isn't a chariot, Kirin thought, this is a *rickshaw.*

The other thing in the basin was the rickshaw-puller, then.

It was a golem. None of them had ever seen a golem before, though Kirin had seen paintings of the clay servants of the vamans. He was huge, his black eyes burning in his impassive clay face, his hands folded together as he looked at Kirin.

'I am Mritik, Charioteer of Vul,' he said, 'at your service as long as you live. What is your name, master?'

'Kirin,' said Kirin. 'How long will it take you to get us to Vrihataranya?'

'Where in Vrihataranya?'

'Vanarpuri.'

'Three days.'

'Three days? That's amazing!' cried Bali.

Kirin stepped into the basin and slid down to the rickshaw. 'It's a pleasure making your acquaintance, Mritik,' he said.

'I am your humble slave, master.'

'Let's have no more of this master-slave nonsense. I think we are going to be friends.' Until I kill your last master, anyway.

'As you wish, master.'

'Tell me,' asked Kirin as Spikes and Hooba slid in and mounted the rickshaw while Bali handed his soldiers the glad news that they would have to make it to Vanarpuri on their own, 'did you drive Danh-Gem yourself? What was he like?'

'My last master forbade me to reveal anything about him. I cannot disobey.'

'Right.'

Bali joined the merry throng on the rickshaw seat.

'You amaze me, Karisman, again and again,' he said. 'For the first time, I actually think our schemes are going to work. And it is all because of you. It astounds me to think that I have only known you for four days. It seems like years.'

'Should we set off, master?' asked Mritik.

'Yes.'

Mritik pulled up the rickshaw bars in his giant hands. Above them, they saw earth rising in a dome, and the circle of light growing smaller and smaller, and then closing completely. Now they were sitting in pitch darkness. Kirin realized they were *inside* the bubble now, and Bali was fidgeting, uncomfortable in the dark, enclosed space.

A little shudder ran through the earth.

'Are we moving down through the earth, Mritik?'

'Yes, master.'

'So is it going to be complete darkness for three days?'

'No, master. When we reach the vaman tunnels, there will be light.'

The vaman tunnels, thought Kirin, this was amazing. He had heard of the tunnels of the vamans, which, according to rumour, ran under the earth, connecting the mysterious vaman cities to one another and the vaman mines on the surface. Huge loads of precious metals, probably drawn by golems, moved through these shafts every day, it was said.

The vaman mines were deep and vast, but they were nothing compared to the cities of the vamans, deep, deep underground, where metals were forged that no man had ever seen. How many vamans were there in the world, digging deeper, building strange machines that would never see the sky? What if they suddenly decided they wanted the lands above ground as well? But they wouldn't, thought Kirin. The things they love are all underground.

'We are now moving downwards,' said Mritik. 'This is the slow part of the journey. When we reach the tunnels, we will travel fast.'

A few hours passed. Then there was a little bump as their descent stopped. Then suddenly, there was light, bright, blinding light, as the bubble they were descending in popped open, and they were in the largest tunnel Kirin had ever seen.

The ceiling of the tunnel was as tall as the tallest tower in Kol, and the walls were hundreds of feet across, and were lit with dazzling crystalline vaman lamps. A double row of pillars, smooth and grey, ran down the middle of the tunnel— the rickshaw was next to the curving wall, and the pillars were at least a hundred feet to the left of the rickshaw, flanking a broad, white, perfectly even road running through the double line of pillars like a streak of silver on the grey-black stone of the tunnel floor.

The walls were grey and full of strange colours—green, red, blue, golden, streaks of precious ores. Kirin gasped as he thought of rows and rows of vamans, marching ant-like from city to city, or drawn by great golem-drawn carts.

'We are deeper in the earth than any human has ever

been,' said Mritik. 'This maze of tunnels extends nearly all over the world, from Skuanmark to Psomedea, from Xi'en to Artaxerxia. The vamans themselves have not explored further.'

'How long have these tunnels existed? How many are there? Can we go to the vaman cities?'

'I am forbidden to answer any of these questions.'

'By your last master?'

'No, by my creator, the great vaman Vul. Other beings are not allowed in the vaman cities. I cannot take you there unless a vaman instructs me to, and no vaman ever will.'

'But don't vamans use these tunnels? Won't they see us?'

'No, master. That is why the Chariot of Vul is the most wonderful thing ever made by vaman hand—at least, it was so, two hundred years ago. They could see us if we were standing still, but as long as I am moving all that can be seen of us by others in these tunnels is a slight shimmer in the air—and all those who travel in these tunnels travel on the road in the centre, and move very fast themselves. They will not notice us at all. Besides, we will be moving on the floor of the tunnel along this wall, and will not need to pass those who drive down the road in the middle.'

'Let's go, then.'

Mritik began to run, his great feet making pounding noises that echoed in the incredibly vast tunnel. There were other noises too—muffled, remote clangs and thuds, whispering echoes gliding through the tunnel. Kirin imagined huge mills, hammers and furnaces far away. He shivered— it was cold. They passed pillar after giant pillar on their left, and lamp after shiny lamp on their right, until it all became a blur, and it seemed to Kirin that they were sitting still in the rickshaw, the lamps had become a river of dazzling light and the pillars were running the other way, torn out of their places by the great wind blasting through the tunnel and forcing them back on to the clay seat. He would have loved to spend more time in the tunnel, simply looking at the beautifully crafted lamps and the strange colours in the walls, but a glance at his fellow passengers on the speeding rickshaw reminded him that now was probably not the best time. The rickshaw of Vul sped northwards.

Back in the Centaur Forests, Kraken had left for Vrihataranya, but the vanars weren't having much fun.

This was because they were both dead, lying in the rapids with centaur arrows in their necks. Green Bow was a good archer.

She had been confused in the morning, when Spikes's trail had disappeared on the rocks, but then she had seen the vanars jumping down into the rock chamber by the waterfall.

Above the waterfall, the Silver Dagger was prowling around. He found Spikes's footprints, and Kirin's, and the asur's, and *three* vanar tracks. Spikes's footprints led up to a strange, flat circle in the forest, around which grass grew in a thick ring. There were no footprints inside the circle, and no footprints leading out. Even the earth in the circle seemed to be of a slightly different colour, a little darker.

It was as if they had disappeared.

The plot thickens, thought the Dagger. What are Kirin and Spikes doing with the third vanar? And where are they? And wherever the vanar is taking them, is it by force, or are they working together? Do the others know Kirin is a ravian? *Is* he really a ravian?

Whatever it is, there's magic involved, and nothing I can do here.

He heard the sound of a horn. It was Green Bow, summoning her kindred. Well, I suppose there's no chance of a ride back, he thought.

He pulled a scarab, a quill and a parchment out of his Necessity Belt. Mantric had given him a special kind of magic paper. After the Civilian had read it, it would destroy itself in five seconds.

He disappeared into the forest, and began to write.

7

'Come in.'

Asvin entered Mantric's hut. 'You sent for me?' he asked.

'Yes. Gaam tells me your training is going well,' said Mantric, getting up and putting away the scroll he was reading.

Asvin smiled, but said nothing. He was a little scared of Mantric.

'Perhaps it is time for a little test,' said Mantric. 'To see how much you have learned in the last two weeks.'

He gave Asvin a piercing and thoroughly intimidating look. 'Sit.'

Asvin sat.

'Why do dragons lust for gold?'

'Dragons do not lust for gold. They hoard gold because they are often lazy, and do not like to go out in search for food. Rumours about their hoards ensure a steady stream of questing heroes, in other words, a staple diet. The dragon lust for gold should be called the dragon lust for gold-lusting food,' said Asvin.

'Correct. Have you seen the sirens of this island?'

'Yes.'

'Why are you still alive then, if those who hear the songs of the sirens rush towards them, blind with desire, and kill themselves in one way or another?'

Asvin was quiet for a moment, thinking of the singing girl in the forest. Then he remembered he was being tested, and quickly said, 'It's because of the perfume you've sprayed on them, to protect your actors and enable the sirens to add that touch of glamour to the Muwi-visions.'

'Elaborate.'

'Should I talk about the Eurekus Test?'

'Yes.'

'Very well. Eurekus, a powerful Psomedean king, once decided to find out more about the sirens, whose songs were destroying ships and forcing his mariners to take a long and complicated route around the Ossus Archipelago. He conducted what was called the Eurekus Test. He sent two ships to the island of sirens, each with a captain tied to the mast to report on the effect of the songs on the sailors. Neither returned. The sailors on the first ship jumped off the ship and drowned as soon as they heard the songs, and that ship was dashed to pieces on the deadly rocks around the island. The sailors on the second ship had wax in their ears, but when they saw the beautiful sirens they jumped off the ship too, and this ship was wrecked as well. This disproved the commonly held theory that it was the song of the sirens alone that drove men insane.

'Then Eurekus sent two more ships. Neither of these returned either. The sailors on the third ship were blindfolded, didn't have wax in their ears, and navigated through instructions the captain shouted. But this didn't work either—

when they heard the song, they jumped off the ship, and it was wrecked. The fourth ship never returned either, but it was not known whether this shipwreck occurred because the sirens had mysterious powers even beyond their beauty and music, or simply because the sailors on this ship had no idea where the ship was going, because these sailors were blindfolded *and* had wax in their ears.'

'Very good. You are doing well. Do you know who resolved the issue?'

'Yes. You did. You discovered in Kol that human attraction works not only through sight and sound, but through smell as well, as you described in your famous book, *The Nose Knows*. And you sent a ship with sailors with blocked noses past the island of sirens, and they were fine—they cheered and whooped when they saw the sirens, but stayed on the ship. Then you deduced that the sirens had a powerfully attractive smell, and that was the key to their charms. So you made a perfume that countered that smell, which is why Bolvudis is safe now.'

'Excellent. Gaam has taught you well. Now come with me, Asvin. There is something I have to show you.'

They walked out of the hut. They were heading for the caves at the other end of the island. The sun was rising over the sea, and in its light Asvin saw imps flying back from the Very Blue Lagoon.

They reached the caves after some time. Gaam and Maya were waiting for them.

They walked into the labyrinth of caves that ran under the island, in the light of a fireball hovering over Mantric's head. He led them through the damp, rocky maze, muttering under his breath. They followed him through narrow, downward-spiralling tunnels and deep caverns that were never used for the Muwi-visions. Asvin and Gaam spoke in whispers—neither of them knew where they were going.

'Do you know of the Seven Heroes, Asvin?' asked Mantric suddenly.

'Yes.'

'What was the mysterious thing about them?'

'No one knew how they travelled all over the world. It is well known that they routed the forces of the Hudlumm Revival in Ventelot and killed the Marauding Mummy of Mul-gharib in Elaken on the same day. Yet they could not have journeyed from Ventelot to Elaken in one day, even if they flew. There were many similar instances—the mystery was never solved.'

Gaam looked pleased. Asvin had a good memory. It always helped when pupils had brains.

'Well, today you will find the answer,' said Mantric. They had reached a dead end in a damp tunnel, and stood there, the flickering red fireball casting long shadows in the musty darkness.

He tapped on the cave wall, thrice, and muttered a few words. Immediately a section of the wall disappeared. 'Cloaking spell,' Mantric said to Maya, who nodded.

They walked into a little cave where, in a beautiful, ornate gold frame studded with rubies, stood a mirror, filling the cave with a soft silvery light.

'This is the Mirror of Icelosis,' said Mantric. 'This is the reason I have spent the last three years here, and this is why you have all been brought here.'

They stood in front of the mirror, and noticed that their reflections looked much cleaner than they did.

'This mirror, and six others like it, were made by Simoqin the Dreamer and Jaadur the spellbinder of Kol, one of the Seven Heroes,' Mantric continued.

'There were seven mirrors, one for each hero. This is the central mirror, the Mirror of Icelosis, the shape-shifting enchanter of Psomedea, chief of the Seven Heroes. In the early years of the Age of Terror it was installed here, on the forgotten island of Bolvudis, hidden from the eyes of the spies of Danh-Gem. When the heroes wished to assemble for their quests, they would simply walk into their mirrors, in their own lands, and be transported here, to this very chamber. Then they would travel together, through this mirror again, to the mirror nearest the place where they had to go. That is how they could travel from Ventelot to Elaken in a day, Asvin. And they could carry the mirrors with them if they needed to. It was a secret they kept well, a means of escape and travel unparalleled even by the legendary Chariot of Vul.'

'How did you find out about this?' asked Maya.

'A few years ago, I found the secret diary of Jaadur of Kol, in a dusty corner of Enki Library. It was a record of how he had made these mirrors. It was after that that I journeyed to Bolvudis, and found this mirror lying in this deep cave, uncared for, unused since the Great War.'

'And these mirrors, these gateways—could anyone use them?'

'No. Only the seven heroes could. But Jaadur, in his diary, said that after Simoqin's death, when he heard Simoqin's prophecy, he altered the fabric of the central mirror, to let any true hero pass. Which is why we are here. Because it is now that we will find out whether Asvin is truly the Hero Simoqin spoke of.'

'And are all the other mirrors intact?' asked Gaam.

'I do not know—I cannot travel through the mirror. I know the mirror in Kol cannot be used—it is lying at the bottom of the river Asa, cast there by Jaadur himself before he made the last entry in his diary, before the Last Battle. As for the rest—I do not know. All I know is that the Hero has to say the name of the hero whose mirror he wants to emerge from, and step into this mirror.'

'Are you sure the mirror still works? Have you tried passing through it?'

'No. This is not just a test for Asvin—it is a test for the mirror as well. I know it is still very powerful—it probably contributes a significant amount to the magic that runs wild in Bolvudis—but only a true hero can step through the mirror, and a true hero I am not.'

'How many people know of this?' asked Maya.

'The Chief Civilian, the Silver Dagger, and myself. We decided that we would find a hero, bring him to Bolvudis, and see whether he could walk through the mirror, and we would do this before the two hundredth year of the New Age.'

'Well, why did you bring Gaam and me, then? If only a true hero can walk through the mirror, we'd have to travel the old-fashioned way, wouldn't we?'

'I do not think so. I think only a true hero can open the mirror. Because the Seven Heroes travelled in style, accompanied by servants and Chroniclers, who were all sworn to secrecy about the mirror. Once a Hero has passed through the mirror, the gateway probably stays open for some time, allowing others to pass through. But they cannot come back without the Hero. I do not know—this is all conjecture. We will find out soon enough.'

'So if Asvin is the Hero, he will be able to pass through the mirror to one of the other six?'

'Hopefully.'

'And what then? We all train some more, and wait for Danh-Gem to turn up? That doesn't sound like much of a plan.'

'I agree, but we have to work with what we have. If he can pass through the mirror, I will be able to send him on a number of quests, and thus get powerful weapons, armour and magical objects—and prepare him for the battle against Danh-Gem.

'You are falling into common error here, Maya. Training the Hero is probably the most crucial part of the whole quest. Do you think Eurekus could have carried out his Twelve Labours if he had never been trained to wield a club by Black Oak, the centaur? And our plan has another purpose. Slowly, as Asvin's powers grow, rumours about a mysterious hero— who will save the world if Danh-Gem returns—will begin to spread. This will keep people from panicking, and ensure that sudden widespread chaos does not break forth at the slightest whispers of Danh-Gem's return.

'I will keep sending Asvin on quests, so that he may learn more about the world we live in and find many magical objects that may save his life, and yours, later. Then, if all goes well, when he is ready, or when Danh-Gem returns, whichever is earlier, we will return to Kol and the name of Asvin, Hero of Simoqin's prophecy, will be announced by the Civilian, and he will be the city's champion against the forces of Danh-Gem.'

'And when do these quests begin?' asked Maya.

'Why do you think I brought you here? These quests begin today. Today you will embark upon your first task. Today will be the day when Asvin gets his sword—a very important day for most heroes, I understand.'

Asvin's eyes shone with excitement. This was what he

had been waiting for. The Prophecy said he would bear the most powerful weapons in the world . . .

Gaam was looking excited too. 'You have chosen a sword for him?' he asked. 'You might have consulted me—I have some knowledge in these matters.'

'I'm sure you do, and that, begging your pardon, is precisely why I did not consult you, for I have strong views on the subject. The sword the Civilian and I have chosen for the Asvin is the sword of one of the Seven Heroes— the famous sword of Queen Raka of Durg, the most famous warrior-queen in history. It is the sharpest sword in the world, and all things considered, sharpness is what we look for in swords.'

'There are other swords,' said Gaam dubiously. 'I have heard of the sword of Raka, of course, but do you think that is the best possible sword for Simoqin's Hero? I mean, it doesn't even have a name. And magic swords should have names.'

'In the east, we do not name our swords—we consider it silly,' said Asvin, 'I would be thrilled to bear Raka's sword— I have heard of it. It rests in state in the palace of Queen Rukmini of Durg, our one friendly neighbour.' He looked thoughtful. 'To be fair, though, we do name our bows and arrows, which is just as silly. I never thought of that before.'

'There are a number of reasons why we have chosen the Durgan sword for Asvin,' said Mantric. 'First of all, getting the sword would not involve any danger—the Chief Civilian has known young Queen Rukmini since she was a child, and has already asked her to lend us this sword, and Rukmini has agreed. But it will be good practice for the rest of you— going through the mirror, and so on.'

'Where is the mirror in Durg?' asked Asvin.

'I do not know. Somewhere in the palace, probably. Perhaps it is lying forgotten in some storeroom. Or perhaps it is broken, in which case you will not be able to go to Durg and we will have to have the sword brought here.'

'Or we could get another sword,' said Gaam, looking dubious. 'Raka's sword may be the sharpest in the world, but it doesn't have any special powers.'

'I think the special powers of swords are really overrated,' said Maya. 'A sword that shines, or yells, in the presence of enemies could be a serious inconvenience, don't you think? It could draw enemies in the dark to you like moths to a candle. Or take the Talking Sword of Olivya—most of those who bore it died when they paused in the middle of a battle to ask it to repeat what it had just said.'

'Or the Invisible Sword of Icelosis,' said Mantric, 'which was never found after he dropped it in Danh-Gem's Wasteland. Perhaps it is lying there still. But the worst case is the Faithful Morning Star of Sir Speeralittle of the Almost-Perfectly-Circular Table. It always returned to its master when he threw it at an enemy—with so much enthusiasm that it would hurtle back at him even before it hit the enemy—and one sad day it beheaded him.'

'Oh, very well,' said Gaam, looking disgruntled. 'Let us get this sharp sword, then.'

Asvin was looking slightly downcast.

'What is it?' asked Mantric.

'Well, it's not really a quest, is it?' Asvin said. 'I mean, we just go to Durg, ask Queen Rukmini for the sword, and come back with it.'

Mantric smiled. 'Do not seek danger, Asvin, for if you do it will surely find you,' he said. 'If we are entering another age of high magic, as I suspect we are, I am quite sure that you will get all the danger and excitement you crave, and perhaps more than you can take.'

'But something puzzles me, Father,' said Maya. 'This reputation-building we are trying to achieve—well, couldn't we have just gone ahead with the Silver Dagger, whoever he really is? People all over the world know of him already.'

'Yes, but you forget we are looking for a leader who will give us hope. The Silver Dagger is famous, yes, but he works through fear, in secret. We need a hero, not someone who works for money, and often performs tasks which are— well, very necessary for Kol's well-being, but not entirely *heroic*. A hero is someone even the enemy admires, albeit reluctantly—not a known thief and assassin, however powerful he might be. And to oppose Danh-Gem we need a face to look at, not a shadow of fear. Besides, the Silver Dagger wants to retire.'

'Well, then, perhaps we should not wait any longer,' said Gaam. 'All this talk will be quite fruitless if we cannot pass through the mirror.'

'Very true,' said Mantric. 'Step forward, Asvin, and let us see whether you really are the hero Simoqin saw in his dream.'

The first rays of the rising sun tiptoed through the window of the fortress on Tiger Hill and fell on the serene and striking face of Queen Rukmini of Durg.

'Wake up, your majesty,' said Nidhi, shaking the young sleeper gently. 'The sun is rising, and it is time for the Dawn Water Ritual.'

Rukmini sat upright and blinked. 'Any news of Prince Chorpulis? Or the sword?'

'No, your majesty.'

Rukmini made an exasperated noise. 'The fool! What do I tell Temat's soldiers now?'

Nidhi frowned, more wrinkles appearing on her old, wizened face. 'I did not like the idea of you lending the sword to Kol in the first place.'

'Don't be silly, Nidhi. When Temat asks for something, you do not refuse. And what would we have done with the sword anyway? But that is irrelevant now. Do the soldiers of Kol know it is missing?'

'No. When did the Civilian say she would send for it?'

'She did not say,' said Rukmini, clambering out of bed. 'We had better find it fast, before she sends for it. I think some of the men of the Silver Phalanx are here, Nidhi.'

Nidhi shuddered. 'You poor child,' she said. 'I remember, when you were a little baby . . .'

'You've told me all the stories, Nidhi—let me think in peace now,' said Rukmini quickly. 'Also, the envoy from Potolpur will soon start making enquiries about Chorpulis. I must think of something to say.'

'Well, at least you won't have to marry him now,' chuckled Nidhi, 'pompous, arrogant little brat.'

'I wouldn't have had to marry him in any case, Nidhi,' said Rukmini icily.

'But it is time, Rukmini. You are young, and beautiful, and the Avrantic sage said you would have many children.'

'Forget all that—I'm worried about Potolpur, too, now. The prince was under Durgan protection, Nidhi. And one of the younger princes, Kumirdanga, is missing too. There could be diplomatic trouble.'

'That won't happen, your majesty. Nobody cares about Potolpur. And their feeble armies wouldn't last an hour against you. Besides, Shantavan is shared territory, and the incident occurred there. It's not your responsibility.'

Rukmini grinned. 'It's so ironic that it's called the Peaceful Forest, isn't it? Forget the tigers—we occupy most of the south and we are still the most warlike nation in the east, the Bandit King rules most of the northern ravines, whatever Avranti believes, and now that the rakshases have returned . . . you know, perhaps I should raise the army and find the rakshasi—the prince may still be alive. And we need the sword back for Kol.'

'Why? Let Potolpur rescue the prince! And if Kol wants the sword so badly, let them slay the rakshasi! Rukmini, child, these matters are out of your hands.'

'But it's an heirloom, Nidhi, and one of our most famous ones.'

'There are other heirlooms, and lives are more important. The times are changing, and our people need you. It would be foolishness indeed to venture off into the woods in pursuit of the rakshasi and needlessly put yourself in danger, when dark and doubtful times are ahead. Think of the throne—there is no heir, and you are so young. Find someone else to get the sword back. Come, now, we must hurry.'

'Very well.'

'Say the hero's name, Asvin.'

'Raka,' said Asvin, and prodded the smooth silvery surface of the mirror with a tentative finger. It was colder than ice. He drew his finger back. It left a black fingerprint on the mirror.

'It's working,' said Mantric.

Like ink thrown in water, the black spot was expanding

in swirling and flowing clouds, swiftly spreading all over the shiny oval surface. Soon the surface was completely black, and they saw little shining dots appear, twinkling on the dark bed like . . .

'Is that supposed to be the night sky?' asked Maya.

'Either that, or just a pretty pattern,' said Mantric. 'Step forward, Asvin.'

Asvin took a deep breath and walked forward. It was like walking into a silken curtain, he thought, as the soft folds of darkness swept over him. It was no longer cold, and suddenly there was a rush of wind. A second passed which seemed to stretch into years, and his foot fell on a marble floor. He stepped out of the mirror and looked around. He was in Durg.

'Well, he appears to be Simoqin's Hero, doesn't he,' said Gaam, smiling.

Mantric took a deep breath. 'I suspect you can pass through the mirror while it is black,' he said. 'It was probably Asvin's touch that brought about the transformation. You should hurry, who knows how long it will last.'

Gaam walked up to the mirror. 'Very well,' he said and put his hand into the mirror, watching as it disappeared into the blackness. He walked in.

'Nice,' he thought.

Then something hit him.

'What on earth was that?' cried Rukmini. 'Who was that man?' She grasped a robe and covered herself with it. 'Stop pouring water on me! Now you've got the robe all wet! Get my sari!' she shouted at the offending handmaiden, who stopped staring dreamily at the mirror and rushed off.

'He was very handsome,' giggled another handmaiden.

'It is a sign of evil times,' said Nidhi, in a voice of doom. 'Never before has the sacred Dawn Water Ritual been disturbed. That man must be found and killed.'

'Don't be ridiculous, Nidhi,' snapped Rukmini. 'Did you see the poor man's face? He clearly had no intention of walking in on me bathing. This is obviously a magic mirror.'

'I did not know, your majesty,' said Nidhi, trembling. 'The fault is mine. It was I who brought this mirror to the Chamber of the Dawn Bath thirty years ago, for your dear mother. I did not know—I merely thought it sad that such a pretty mirror should be lying locked up in a small room in the tower. I am the one guilty of violating the sacred Ritual. I should be executed immediately.'

'Oh be quiet for a minute, Nidhi,' snapped Rukmini, as the handmaiden rushed up with her sari. 'Personally, I'm quite glad this happened—now the Ritual cannot be held sacred any more and I can bathe alone, as I have always wanted to! But get a few spears,' she said to her maidens. 'If I know anything of men, he will be back.'

Gaam and Asvin came hurtling out of the mirror, nearly crashing into Maya. They rolled around on the floor for a while, and then got up, Asvin clutching his arm, where, in the heat of the moment, Gaam had bitten him.

'What happened, Asvin?' asked Mantric, looking concerned. 'You've gone all red.'

'Was there a monster? A rakshas?' asked Gaam.

'No,' said Asvin. 'Please do not ask me what happened. I cannot go back there.'

'Where? You did get to Durg, didn't you?'

'We must get another sword. The Durgan one is out of the question, now.'

'What did you manage to upset?' asked Maya. 'You were barely in there for ten seconds.'

'I cannot speak of it,' said Asvin.

'Unfortunately, you have to,' said Mantric.

Asvin turned various shades of red and purple, but finally the scorching gazes emanating from the others compelled him to blurt out: 'It was a bath-chamber. Queen Rukmini was not . . .'

'Say no more,' said Maya. 'It could have happened to anyone.' She didn't look happy, though.

'Don't make me go back,' pleaded Asvin.

'All right, I'll do it,' said Maya. The mirror had turned silver again the moment Asvin had emerged from it. 'Touch the mirror.' Asvin did so, and as soon as it went black Maya walked through.

As she entered the Chamber of the Dawn Bath, she noticed many things. The things were spearheads, and they were all pointing at her.

'I don't remember inviting you,' said Rukmini. She was not dressed for fighting, like the guards with the spears, but she was holding a long, curved sword.

'Sorry,' said Maya. 'Etiquette never was my strong point. You can put the spears down. I'm Durgan. Well, my parents were Durgan. You've heard of my father—the spellbinder Mantric. My name is Maya. You probably don't remember, but we met once, five years ago.'

The guards kept their spears at her throat, and looked at Rukmini.

'She's telling the truth, your majesty,' said a guard suddenly.

Maya looked at her, surprised. 'You won't remember me,' the girl said, 'but I used to study at Enki. I dropped out in two years—I was hopeless at magic.'

'Mantric is, of course, well known here,' Rukmini nodded. As the spears came down, she said, 'Spellbinders? I should have known. Who was the man?'

Gaam suddenly appeared through the mirror.

'Is the hero coming?' Maya asked him.

'Your father is still trying,' Gaam replied. He strode forward.

'Queen Rukmini? Greetings from Kol. My name is Gaam, and I have been sent by the Chief Civilian on an urgent errand. I apologize for the abrupt manner of our arrival—it was not planned thus.'

Rukmini and Nidhi exchanged glances. Rukmini dismissed the guards and handmaidens, and said, 'Did your people put this mirror in Durg?'

'No, your majesty. This mirror has been here for centuries, and its purpose was one that should remain secret. I believe you have consented to lend the Sword of Raka to Kol?'

'Yes, but Lady Temat has not yet told me why Kol needs this sword.'

'May I speak freely?' asked Gaam, shooting a wary glance at Nidhi.

'You may. Nidhi has cared for me since I was born.'

'We are training a hero, in case the rakshas Danh-Gem returns. You have heard of the Simoqin Prophecies? Well, we believe we have found the hero—it is a secret of course, but one that I am sure is safe with you.'

'Yes,' said Rukmini. 'And where is this hero?'

'He was the one who so rudely interrupted you a while ago.'

'I'll go get him,' said Maya, turning around and walking into the mirror.

She bounced off it and fell. Of course, it had closed, they couldn't go back without Asvin . . .

'We appear to be stuck here,' she said.

'We must seem really rude,' said Gaam. 'We were testing this mirror—we had no idea it would make us appear like this, I must apologize again.'

'It's really all right,' said Rukmini, looking amused. 'But can you not tell me any more about the hero, or the mirror?'

'I am afraid not. My lips . . .'

'Are sealed, no doubt. Very well. Well, I had indeed agreed to lend Raka's sword to Kol. But I am afraid I cannot now.'

'And why not, may we ask?'

'Because,' said Rukmini, 'Raka's sword is lost.'

The standard replies to such dramatic revelations are 'What!', 'How?', 'No!' or 'Then die, infidel!' but Gaam said, 'Oh, there you are.'

This was because Asvin, no doubt due to the uncanny knack that heroes have for making dramatic, perfectly timed entrances, had chosen the stunned silence following Rukmini's announcement to walk out of the mirror.

He looked at Rukmini sheepishly and said 'I, um . . .'

'She said it was quite all right,' said Maya sharply.

Rukmini was smiling. 'Is this the hero?' she asked. 'And does he have a name?'

'No,' said Gaam. 'Not yet.'

'I see. Well, welcome to Durg, nameless one. It is a beautiful land, full of beautiful sights.'

Asvin blushed, but saw she was still smiling, and breathed again.

Little sparks are flying whenever their eyes meet, thought Maya grimly. 'You didn't tell us about the sword,' she said abruptly.

'I will. I see you are as impatient as your father, Mala,' said Rukmini, smiling.

'Maya,' said Maya, smiling right back. And fine, so you have long, glossy black hair, but if you toss it around once more I'll singe it.

It was not until afternoon that they found out about the sword. The Durgans lived simply, but were generous hosts, and the biryanis they had for lunch made them forget all their troubles. After lunch, Rukmini took them to an empty hall and told them what had happened.

Queen Rukmini's most ardent and unquenchable suitor was Prince Chorpulis of Potolpur. Their fathers had been friends, and he had used that excuse to haunt the fortress nearly all his life, hoping to wear down Rukmini's defences through sheer perseverance. He had written her terrible love poems since they were both thirteen years old. His dubious poetic skills apart, he had many sterling qualities. It was just that no one knew what they were. He claimed the best thing about him was his sensitivity, but since, after seven years of courtship, he had still not realized that nearly everyone in Durg hated him, that seemed unlikely.

On his last visit, Chorpulis had decided that the reason Rukmini was not relenting and marrying him (the best and most eligible suitor possible) was not maidenly coyness as he had supposed so far but a typically (uncultured) Durgan preference for action over words. It was not that he was not a man of action—of course, he preferred the finer things in life—and if she wanted him to perform some crude task to prove his manliness and his courage, he was willing to do so.

Rukmini had laughed at him and told him to fetch her a hair from a yeti's beard. This had kept him quiet for a while, but soon he was back, telling her that he could not fulfil this request owing to an unfortunate shortage of yetis, but to prove his peerless courage he would walk (with her) through all the perils of Shantavan. He had pestered her for months, and she had agreed, just to be rid of him—for she knew that he would not even manage the walk.

Unfortunately, the prince had decided to take the sword of Raka with him—he had bored the guardians of the sword to tears, and borrowed it—to fight the nameless terrors they would meet in the forest and thus impress Rukmini, and the young queen had been completely unaware of this. South Shantavan was perfectly harmless for anyone accompanied by a Durgan, and they had passed through it peacefully, Chorpulis's servants riding behind at a suitably discreet distance.

It was when they had walked deep into the forest that things had changed. Suddenly there was less sunlight, and strange noises, and Chorpulis kept jumping in fright, hiding behind trees and then pretending he had only gone there to study paw prints, for the best woodmen knew that the best prints were behind trees.

The rakshasi Akarat, who had risen again, woken by the growing magic in the air and the earth, was prowling through the Peaceful Forest, and had seen Rukmini and Chorpulis. The terrible she-demon had either fallen deeply and immediately in love with Chorpulis or had simply thought he looked like a tasty snack.

Some time later, Rukmini, who had been walking fast, trying to ignore Chorpulis prattling away by her side, had seen the most beautiful stag ever. It was a dream-like beast, bright golden in colour, its antlers shining in the sunlight. Rukmini had immediately given chase, forgetting all about the Potolpuri prince. Chorpulis had trembled in fear and clutched her arm as she was springing off after the stag, so to calm him down she had drawn a big circle around him in chalk, and told him that he was safe as long as he stayed inside the circle and didn't wander around reciting poetry to the trees.

But the stag had outrun her. She had realized, too late, that it had been an illusion, probably the work of a rakshas, and had run back to where she had left Chorpulis only to find an empty circle in which lay a scabbard that she had recognized as the beautiful sheath in which Raka's sword had lain in state for years.

Rukmini had learnt it was Akarat the rakshasi who had abducted Chorpulis, from her friend Lalmohan the eagle, who had chased Akarat after she had abducted Chorpulis. Now Chorpulis was probably either in the rakshasi's den or in her belly, and the sword was missing too.

'I do not know what to do,' said Rukmini, pacing up and down the sunlit hall. 'If it is indeed Akarat the rakshasi, poor Chorpulis must be dead—she was one of the most terrible demonesses ever to walk the forest, and her return is terrible news. Though frankly, I am more concerned about the sword. I want to go to Shantavan and retrieve it—but my advisers are set against it. And I cannot risk the lives of my warriors over a sword, even if it is an heirloom.'

'It's painfully obvious what must be done,' said Gaam. 'We will get the sword back for you—after all, we are the ones who want it. We will slay this rakshasi, and bring back some token of the prince for those who wish to remember him.'

'I will come with you,' said Rukmini.

'No, your majesty, your advisers are right. Evil times may be ahead, and you must take care of yourself.'

'Very well. I will lend you horses and soldiers who will escort you to the circle where Chorpulis was taken. They will wait for you in southern Shantavan, and bring you back here when you return after slaying Akarat. I will send word to Lalmohan the eagle, and he will lead you to her lair. You cannot imagine what a burden you have taken off my shoulders. May the moon shine on your swords. And when you get the sword back—well, you may keep it. Consider it a gift from Durg, for Akarat had slain many great Durgan warriors ages ago.'

She looked at Asvin, and smiled. 'I know in my heart you will succeed, and I will see you again. I will make all the arrangements immediately,' she said, and walked out regally.

'Well, no point hanging around, is there. Let's go,' said Maya. To Asvin she said, 'This is what happens when you crave violence, and think the quests you are sent on are too tame. We get sent on a suicide mission.'

'Aren't you excited? This will be a great adventure! And of course I should go on a quest to get my sword—it's the way things should be. I have always wanted to fight rakshases. And I have heard and read so much about the terrible Akarat, and to think it is my destiny to slay her! I will cut off her nose and bring it to Rukmini. Isn't she beautiful? Rukmini, that is.' He looked really happy.

Maya and Gaam looked at each other, and shook their heads.

I will have to carry a club around with me, thought Maya.

I will have to give him a little advice about the perils of polygamy, thought Gaam.

Two days later, they met Lalmohan the eagle on the northern border of south Shantavan. They dismounted, and told

Rukmini's soldiers to wait for them. Lalmohan took them to the circle where Chorpulis had been taken and told them how he had seen the rakshasi approach Chorpulis in human form.

She had walked into the circle after talking to him for some time, picked him up and run back to her lair. Lalmohan had followed them—Akarat had seen him and knocked him out with a well-aimed stone, but not before he had seen where her underground lair was, its entrance strewn with the bones of her victims. She was a very powerful rakshasi, Lalmohan said—she could change her shape and size at will, and she had killed and eaten many noble beasts in the jungle, and humans too, whenever she could get them.

Lalmohan took them as far as he dared, which was within an hour's march of Akarat's lair. It was noon—rakshases were supposed to hunt at night—so they sat at the foot of a tree and argued about the best way to kill a rakshas.

Asvin wanted to challenge Akarat and fight her single-handedly, but Gaam reminded him that Akarat, if she grew to full size, could wipe out an entire army. Finally, they decided that Asvin and Gaam would sneak in and try to steal the sword as she slept, and would kill her in her sleep and rescue the prince if he were still uneaten. Asvin was quite violently opposed to killing her in this dishonourable way, until Gaam told him that whatever the legends said, this was how most rakshases and dragons had been killed, because it was simply impossible for humans to fight them face to face. Shantavan was throbbing with magic now that the rakshases had returned, and Maya was feeling very powerful, but she knew that human magic had never affected rakshases much and that she wouldn't be of much use.

'We must be very quiet—rakshases wake at the slightest

sound,' said Gaam, as they got up and started walking towards Akarat's lair. 'We must hope she is asleep, because she will smell our blood otherwise. We must attack every bird or beast we see now, because the really powerful rakshases were all excellent shape-shifters.'

The land was quite hilly. Further north there were deep ravines, where Pushpdev Rabin, the Bandit King, held sway over the passages through the jungle, robbing the rich and paying the poor for food and shelter.

They walked ahead stealthily. Shantavan was green, rich and beautiful. The sun was high in the sky, but the forest was growing thicker—it had been a while since they had felt sunlight on their faces, they were constantly covered in shadows as they passed under the great trees. An hour passed. They reached the twin boulders that stood in a little clearing, and the cleverly dug tunnel between them that Lalmohan had told them about—the entrance to Akarat's lair.

Maya had been feeling uneasy for some time. Little chills had been running up and down her spine—spellbinder intuition was very keen. She had whispered her fears to Gaam, and he had said it was the aura of the Rakshas. The jungle noises had ceased, and only the occasional sounds of the wind through the branches could be heard.

They crept up to the entrance. Loud snoring sounds were coming out of it. Asvin looked like he was going to say something along the lines of 'She sleeps' but Gaam put a warning finger to his lips.

But Maya still couldn't get rid of the feeling that something was very wrong. She conjured up a Thrillseeker. A Thrillseeker was a little green ball that bounced noiselessly towards the strongest source of magic within a particular area. She had learned how to create it recently, from Mantric, who had used a Thrillseeker to find the mirror. The Thrillseeker bounced off her hand, to the entrance of the cave. The rakshasi is inside, Maya thought, and reached out to grab the ball before it bounced down the tunnel.

Then the Thrillseeker stopped. It hovered in mid-air, and suddenly rocketed off into the sky, bouncing over their heads, going *behind* them.

It suddenly occurred to Maya that they were in a clearing in the middle of the jungle, so should have been standing in sunlight.

But they were still covered in shadow.

A large, woman-shaped shadow.

They spun around and saw two trunk-like, hairy blue legs, which led up to a crudely sewn tiger-skin tunic that barely covered the monstrous body of Akarat, who was standing quietly behind them.

She was as tall as the tallest tree, her fangs were gleaming white, her blood-red lips were dripping saliva. Her skin was dark blue, her hair was long and matted, and she wore a necklace of tiger skulls. Her small, cunning eyes were staring at them.

The Thrillseeker bounced up to her massive foot and exploded.

She laughed. The earth shook, and birds all over the forest took to the air, screeching.

Maya and Asvin looked at Gaam.

'Run!' he yelled.

He dived to his right as Akarat's foot came crashing down into the ground where he had been an instant ago. Maya fired a fireball into her eye, but Akarat didn't even seem to notice. With one fluid, sweeping motion, she picked Maya up with one huge hand and Gaam with the other. She kicked

Asvin, and he crashed into a boulder and fell unconscious to the ground.

She looked from Gaam to Maya, wondering which of them looked tastier.

Then a fat man came running out of the tunnel. He was clad in a tiger-skin loincloth, and looked as if he had just woken up. His bare flesh was jiggling as he ran, and he looked annoyed.

'Put them down, my love,' he said. 'You promised.'

'But I'm hungry, O sweet one,' grumbled Akarat in a voice of thunder.

'I have told you before, light of my life,' said Chorpulis. 'We shall feast on the fruits and wild honey of the forest, drink spring water and mead, and live in peace and harmony with the natural world around us. The Bard himself avoided meat.'

'But I'm a rakshasi, O eye of the moon,' pleaded Akarat. 'I cannot drink milk when I know there was a cow around it once.'

Chorpulis waved an admonishing finger. 'Now, now, my wilful little butterfly, who is your bouncing bunny?'

'You are,' said Akarat coyly.

She put Gaam and Maya, who had been watching this tender exchange with great interest, down on the ground, and patted their heads gently, almost cracking them open. Then she shrank until she was human-sized, and took human form. She was quite pretty, really, thought Gaam.

'All she needed was love,' said Chorpulis, holding the simpering Akarat's hand and looking at her with fond eyes. 'And I am tired of running after that cold-hearted swordswoman, who understands neither poetry nor the lofty heights my superior intellect dwells in. I grow weary of court life. Here in this idyllic setting, I will live, one with the trees, with my beautiful wild Akarat, and write poetry that will cast even the Bard's into the shade.'

'And I will be your apsara,' said Akarat, looking at him with loving eyes, 'but, my love, these barbarians have probably come to kill me and take you away.'

'Actually, no,' said Gaam. 'We just want the sword that you took with you . . . Prince Chorpulis, isn't it?'

'Yes,' said Chorpulis. He went into Akarat's lair and came back with the sword. It was covered with what looked like chewed-up hair.

'You can't give that away, I was using that,' said Akarat.

'Beloved,' said Chorpulis sternly, 'I will find you another toothpick.'

'Oh never mind,' grumbled Akarat. 'Take it.'

'It's all right,' said Maya to Asvin, who had sprung to his feet and was looking around for the rakshasi. 'Asvin, Akarat. Akarat, Asvin.'

'Sorry about the kick there,' said Akarat sheepishly. 'You know how it is—I'm sure you get a little cranky when you're hungry.'

'It's quite all right,' said Asvin, a little stiffly.

'I will tell you what we will do,' said Gaam to Akarat. 'We will go back and say that you ate Chorpulis, and that Asvin here slew you and retrieved the sword. Then no one will bother you afterwards, and you can live in peace here in this delightful haven.'

Chorpulis was ecstatic, but Akarat looked a little dubious—no doubt she had planned to eat a few avenging soldiers on the sly. But she nodded, and slipped a ring, cunningly carved out of ivory, off her finger. 'Go, and my blessings go with you,' she said, handing it to Asvin. 'No rakshas will attack you while you wear the Ring of Akarat. I hope this gift makes up for the injury.'

'It leaves me in your debt. This gift may prove invaluable,' said Asvin, bowing low. 'I thank you, and wish you both happiness. My friend Gaam will write a moving tale about your imprisonment, Prince Chorpulis—just make sure that you are never seen by humans again.'

'The earth will swallow me,' said Chorpulis. He put an arm around Akarat's slender waist and waved goodbye as they left.

Two days later, Rukmini and Nidhi stood and watched as Gaam and Maya passed through Raka's mirror. Then Asvin kissed Rukmini's hand, bid Nidhi farewell and disappeared.

'I wonder if I am destined to meet him again,' said Rukmini wistfully, as the mirror turned silver and reflected her beautiful face once more.

Nidhi looked at her and smiled. The young never saw it coming, she thought. 'I wonder who he really is,' she said.

'If you want to know what I think, I think he's Asvin, the Avrantic prince who died mysteriously,' said Rukmini slowly.

'He was about your age, wasn't he? Maybe a year older. And he has the favour of Lady Temat. And he may be Simoqin's hero,' said Nidhi. 'Why, he's almost perfect.'

'Don't be silly, Nidhi,' said Rukmini, but Nidhi, who was older and wiser, saw the smile Rukmini thought she had suppressed.

'But we will meet again, I think,' said the queen of Durg. And, obviously, she was right. Queens often are.

8

The great halls of Vanarpuri were throbbing with excitement. Vanar sentries stood on tall trees, ceaselessly watching for any signs of danger, as line after line of humans and asurs, blindfolded, led by a few armed vanars, trudged into the forgotten city. Parts of the great city were teeming with life again, and the air was full of tension, for the Great Council of the followers of Danh-Gem was going to take place tonight, the night of the new moon, the third night of Tigermonth.

No one had seen Bali for a week now, and Kirin, who had been introduced to the Parliament of Vanarpuri and had been given the right to free passage anywhere in Vrihataranya, correctly presumed that he was away organizing the Council, meeting leaders and chieftains from all over the world. Vanars had been raiding Avrantic villages near Vrihataranya, getting huge amounts of food and various other objects, for weeks now.

The clamour and bustle reminded Kirin a little of the streets of Kol. Instead of people on carpets there were vanars soaring from creeper to creeper, but on the streets of Vanarpuri the sheer variety of people was almost as mind-boggling as Kol. Barons from Ventelot, tribal chieftains from east Vrihataranya, rebel captains from Avranti, Durg and the Free States, and a few renegade daimyos from Xi'en mingled with Artaxerxians, Neo-Hudlumms, Skuans, asurs and vanars. Kirin noted there were very few pashans—they would not unite until Spikes called them—and no rakshases—they had probably eaten the messengers.

He had spent the week exploring the Great Forest with four old acquaintances—a troupe of asur musicians from Kol. 'The Sluggs' they called themselves, and they played hollow rocks that made an interesting range of popping noises. Jaan, Plop, Gojgoj and Stinko were the only Koli asurs in Vrihataranya, apart from Hooba, who was in hiding—they stood out among the white danavs from Imokoi, with their lurid skin dyes and strange, mop-like haircuts. They walked through the huge trees with Kirin, listening to strange monsters roaring far away and telling him they had invented an exciting concept—'interior decoration', they called it—and they planned to decorate Danh-Gem's castle when he returned. 'Dark interiors are so last Age. This time, we're going for light floral or pastel shades—cobwebs and bloodstained walls will get you nowhere, man,' Jaan had said.

But today he was with Spikes again, and they were talking to Angda, Bali's sister, who was ruling Vanarpuri in his stead. They were in a small temple, just outside the city.

He listened quietly as Angda spoke of the Sultan of Artaxerxia, and how he would not support them, but there was a desert chieftain, Omar the Terrible, who was on their side. The Xi'en Empire would not take part in the war against him, and could be overcome once the rest of the east was conquered. In the far north, the werewolves and the ice-giants had not yet responded to the call, but they would if Danh-Gem returned. The zombies of the islands near south Elaken could not travel so far, but they were ready to strike terror into the hearts of the living whenever necessary. She told him that great armies were being gathered in Skuanmark, Artaxerxia and Imokoi, and Xi'en assassins were being hired to kill many leaders in other lands, including Maharaja Aloke in Avranti and the Chief Civilian of Kol. Kirin didn't tell her that assassins tried to enter the Palace nearly every day.

'This Council will reveal many things, and I will preside over it,' said Angda proudly. 'But there are many leaders who could not come, as Kol and its allies are watching the roads, and the accursed Silver Phalanx strikes fear into those with feeble hearts. Omar the Terrible could not come himself, and neither could Bjorkun the Skuan lord, or the king of asurs. But many have come. We will make new allies, Karisman. War is coming. And you will have an important role to play in that war.'

'When is the Council exactly?' asked Spikes.

Angda, who had been speaking loudly so far, looked around and leaned towards them. 'That is what I have called you here to tell you,' she said, in a whisper. 'You will not be attending the Great Council.'

'What? Why?' asked Kirin, startled.

'Bali has told me to tell the two of you to stay outside the city tonight. When the Council begins, you should be waiting here, in this temple. There are other things in store for you tonight. I will say no more. The stones have ears.'

She sprang away, and disappeared into the city.

'They're all mad,' said Kirin, with feeling. They stood

there for a while, watching people file in through the gates, and then went for another walk.

At midnight, when the sky was dark and clear above the giant trees, the dull beating of great gongs announced that the Great Council had started. Kirin and Spikes were waiting in the temple, watching the torches of the vanar guards as they patrolled the city borders. The temple floor was made of great slabs of stone—some of the slabs, near the sacrificial altar had fallen in, and the whole floor was covered with fine, slippery moss. After the gongs stopped, there was a deathly silence. Even the night-song of insects could not be heard.

'This way, Kirin,' said a voice behind the great stone idol at the end of the temple hall.

It was Bali. He gave them white robes and capes, and they wore these, covering their heads with the great hoods. Bali led them through a passage behind the idol to a wide torch-lit chamber, where five other figures were sitting around a broad stone table. They sat.

'You are now members of the Brotherhood of Renewal,' said Bali. 'The identities of the other Brothers will be revealed to you, but you will not see their faces.'

He introduced Kirin and Spikes to Bjorkun, King Leer, the translator Tungz, Omar the Terrible, Abhishek, a minister from Avranti and a samurai from Xi'en who said he was a ronin, a samurai who owed allegiance to no liege-lord, and that his name was not important.

'I see no need for this secrecy. Every enemy of Danh-Gem knows of me, and this hood is uncomfortable,' said Bjorkun, throwing his hood back.

Leer and Tungz immediately did the same, but the rest remained as they were.

'You know why we are meeting here, and not in the Great Hall, I trust,' said Bali, sitting down.

'No,' said Kirin.

'The Hall will be full of spies and traitors,' said Bali. 'And the true-hearted folk who have come here have come here to join us—the speech Angda will give is a mere formality. And we do not want the matters we will discuss here to reach the ears of anyone outside this room—and you know what I speak of, Karisman. If the Civilian in Kol learns of our designs, some of the objects we seek will be destroyed, and our hopes will come to nought.'

Kirin nodded.

'I have told the Brothers about our discovery of the pashan-lord and you, Karisman. I have also told them about the wondrous chariot that you drew out of the depths of the earth, and they unanimously agreed that you should be a part of this secret Council, for we do not doubt your loyalty to the cause, or to the Rakshas. But I have not told them about the five objects we must procure to raise the Great Rakshas. I felt it would be more fitting if you told them, for it is your labours that have brought this matter to our knowledge.'

'You have aided us immensely already, Karisman,' said Bjorkun. 'And you will be richly rewarded, I assure you.'

Kirin cleared his throat. 'I do not ask for any reward, and there is much work left to be done. To raise Danh-Gem,' he said, 'we must get five objects. First, one of Spikes's claws.'

'Which we have,' said Bjorkun, his eyes narrowing into slits as he listened keenly.

'Yes. Do we also have the iron crown of the asurs?'

'It is in Imokoi,' said Tungz, 'but it is in our possession. It has been passed on from king to king, and no asur will deny its authority—not even the sewer-rats of Kol. The king can get it for you.'

Bali and Bjorkun exchanged a glance.

'The most precious gem the humans know,' continued Kirin.

'Which we do not have,' said Bjorkun. 'What is the most precious gem in the world? The Tear of the Sky?'

'Yes,' said Bali, 'and we will return to this one. Tell us the other two, Kirin.'

'A jinn-lamp from the western sands.'

'Strangely enough, that will not be a problem,' said Omar. 'It is a most puzzling coincidence, but I have a lamp in my possession. I do not have it here, but I know where it is. I take this as a sign that this venture will succeed.'

Bali and Bjorkun both smiled. 'We were grateful indeed when you chose to join the Brotherhood, Scourge of the Sands,' said Bjorkun.

'Not *join* the Brotherhood, Lord Bjorkun,' said Omar in a smooth voice. '*Lead* the Brotherhood.'

Bali flared up instantly. 'That is not possible,' he said. 'I am the one who has brought us all together.'

'Is that so, vanar-lord?' asked Bjorkun, smiling. 'Perhaps you do not know, but you would never have got anywhere without me. And Omar is the son of the Sultan himself, and was born a leader.'

'Now how did you find that out? Heads will roll in the sands,' said Omar, in the same calm voice.

'May I continue?' asked Kirin. 'The issue of leadership is not one I am interested in. I serve Danh-Gem, and no one else. Perhaps it is best that we work together as equals, and let Danh-Gem decide which one of you commands his armies. I am content to remain in the shadows.'

They looked at him, and nodded.

'Apologies, Karisman, do continue,' said Bjorkun. Kirin could feel the heat of Omar's gaze from under his hood.

'The fifth object,' said Kirin, 'is the Gauntlet of Tatsu.'

'Thank you, Karisman,' said Bali. 'The Gauntlet of Tatsu, needless to say, we do not possess. Yet hope lives, brothers. We have three of the five things we need for the spell, and we will merely have to find the other two. Which is why I invited you to this meeting,' he said, shooting keen glances at the ronin and Abhishek.

'Let us first deal with the Gauntlet of Tatsu, and how we are to obtain it,' continued Bali. 'Speak, my brother. Will you be able to get it for us?'

'I think so, if the spirits of my ancestors smile upon me,' said the ronin. 'I will journey to the Wu Sen Monastery, and endeavour to steal the Gauntlet. But it will be difficult even for me—and impossible for anyone who is not samurai. I will need two months.'

'You have two months, but no more,' said Bali.

Bjorkun shot a suspicious look at him, but said nothing.

'The Gauntlet of Tatsu was Danh-Gem's most prized possession,' said Bali. 'You should consider it an honour that the task of getting it is assigned to you.'

'I do,' said the ronin.

'That makes four,' said Omar. 'That means you, my friend, will have to get the fifth.'

Everyone turned and looked at Abhishek, who spluttered and said, 'I cannot do it myself! My position! The scandal!'

'You expected the Avrantics to help?' sneered Omar. 'That was not wise. All they can do is talk and drink tea.'

'I had asked Rabin, the Bandit King, to come,' said Bali.

355

'But he refused, for his quarrel is with Avranti alone, and after that this was the best I could do.'

Abhishek spluttered some more and said, 'Our unparalleled culture . . .'

'Tell us about the Tear of the Sky,' said Bjorkun. 'I have heard the name, and that the knights of Ventelot tried to steal it for the Crown of Ventelot, but that is all I know.'

'The Tear of the Sky,' said Abhishek, flustered, 'is, the legend goes, the tear of the Rain God when, seeing the parched earth, his grief . . .'

'I did not ask for its history,' snapped Bjorkun. 'And if you were planning to tell us that the city of Ektara was founded where it supposedly fell to earth, kindly do not. We want to steal this jewel. We did not offer you wealth beyond your puny dreams to hear you talk about your foolish myths.'

'Very well,' said Abhishek, 'then listen to me. The Tear of the Sky is impossible to steal, for it is fiercely guarded, except for one day in the year, when it is kept in the open, the day of the swayamvar of Maharaja Aloke's cousin, Princess Pratima. On that day, it is revealed to those who contest for her hand in marriage, and it is believed that the gods confer their blessings to them through this priceless gem.'

'Why would a princess's swayamvar be held every year? Does she change husbands once a year?' asked Kirin.

'No. The gem is supposed to be part of Princess Pratima's dowry, but it will never leave Avranti, I assure you. In any case, even on the day of the swayamvar, the gem is well guarded.'

'Why?'

'Because everyone knows that the swayamvar is nothing but an elaborate ruse to capture the Bandit King,' said Abhishek.

'I crave your pardon, minister. This is almost interesting. What on earth are you saying?' drawled Omar.

'The Bandit King is probably the best archer in the world,' said Abhishek, 'and it is well known that he and the princess are lovers. So for the last two years, the Maharaja has been trying to capture Rabin by making the swayamvar an archery contest, and offering the Tear of the Sky as a prize. For the last two years, the story has been the same—the Bandit King came to the swayamvar in disguise and won the archery contest, thus winning the hand of Pratima and the gem as well. And since the Maharaja knows the Bandit King is the world's best archer, he simply ordered his guards to capture the winner of the contest. But both years, Rabin managed to escape. This is why the swayamvar is held once every year, on the day of the full moon of the month of the Tiger— this very month, in fact. Everyone knows Rabin will come to the swayamvar this year as well—in disguise—and win the archery contest. In fact, the guards do not even challenge him when he enters Ektara in disguise. The Tear of the Sky will be laid on a cushion for all to marvel at, and when Rabin wins the archery contest, the guards will try to capture him again.'

'But what if someone else wins the archery contest?' asked Bali. 'Would he then win the gem?'

'Yes, but I suspect Maharaja Aloke has no intention of giving the gem away, and if Rabin does not turn up this year—he is ridiculously easy to identify as he is the only one in disguise and wears a silly green hood—the Maharaja will announce that this year the gem will stay in Avranti and the winner merely gets to marry the princess.'

'I thought the princess decided whom she wanted to marry, and that was the whole point of swayamvars,' Kirin said.

'There is much you do not understand about the world, boy,' said Abhishek loftily. 'Of course the princess has the final word. But we do not tell the world that, because everyone knows the princess wants to marry Rabin, and then no one else would even come to the swayamvar.'

'What if,' said Kirin slowly, 'someone else went to the swayamvar in disguise and won it?'

'Rabin is the best archer in the world,' said Abhishek simply.

'Well, what if someone removed him and went in his disguise?'

'What nonsense. That would be impossible.'

'True,' said Bjorkun. 'And that is why, Abhishek, you have to steal it for us. Vanars, pashans and asurs are not allowed in Avranti. I would be recognized, and Omar and the ronin have other tasks. We cannot hire archers now—the risk of betrayal is too great and the secret must not be revealed to anyone else. It has to be you.'

'But I am an important man,' gasped Abhishek. 'My reputation, my social standing . . .'

'Is there anything else you can tell us about the Bandit King or the gem?'

'No. That is all I know.'

'Very well, then. Omar?'

'Thank you,' said Omar. There was a hiss, a flash of steel and suddenly, Abhishek was headless.

Kirin looked at the blood-lust and excitement in the eyes of Bali and Bjorkun. 'Leave it to us,' he said. 'Spikes and I will go to Avranti, win the contest and get the gem for you. I know pashans are not allowed in Avranti, but I have a plan.'

'If it was anyone else but you, Karisman, I would have

laughed,' said Bali. 'But since it is you, I actually believe you can do it.'

He got up. 'Bjorkun and I will be travelling to the north,' he said. 'We will win over the werewolves and the ice-giants and return. Your tasks are clear, my brothers. King Leer gets the asur crown, the ronin gets the Gauntlet, Omar the lamp and Kirin and Spikes the gem. Two months it is, then. Bjorkun, Leer and I will now go to the Council, where the Civilian's spies must be wondering about our absence—our rousing speeches will reassure them. We will meet again, on new moon's night in Dragonmonth, with the five objects we need. Then we will see what is to be done.' He shot a glance at Kirin, who nodded quickly.

'The first meeting of the Brotherhood of Renewal is now over. Depart swiftly and secretly, and tell no one. Do not be late. If you fail, may luck be on your side, for I will not.'

He strode out of the room, followed by Bjorkun, the asurs and the ronin.

'You think you can get the Avrantic gem, sorcerer?' Omar asked softly.

'I will try,' said Kirin. 'Anyway, there is no one else.'

'A secret society of sorcerers called the Karismen, servants of Danh-Gem,' said Omar, getting up. 'That's strange—many of Danh-Gem's records are kept in Artaxerxia, and none of them speak of this.'

'We were a very secret secret society,' Kirin told him.

'I see. Most fascinating. And you have no desire to lead the Brotherhood.' He threw back his hood suddenly, and his shadow filled the room.

'I have never heard of the Karismen,' he hissed. 'And I have shown you my face. Very few people alive have seen my face. I hope you come back with the gem, sorcerer.'

Then he cast his hood over his face, turned and was gone.

'I don't see why you had to volunteer,' Spikes told Kirin as they left the chamber, stepping carefully over the large pool of Abhishek's blood.

'Didn't I tell you?' said Kirin, managing a smile. 'I'm helping them. I want to see this through. And as I said, I have a plan.'

9

*B*olvudis village, Tigermonth 4th, 5 a.m.
Muwi-visions acted in 7, New spells learnt several,
Warrior skills 3/10, Magic 8/10, Attraction for Asvin
don't know.

It's been a month now since Kirin disappeared. I wonder
what he's doing, and where he is. I hope he's thinking about
me sometimes, because I miss him terribly.

I don't believe I'm waking up this early voluntarily. But
before I go for the back-breaking yoga and martial arts session
that has become a part of my routine (alas!) I'd better write
down what happened last night. Really strange.

Asvin and I were walking across the cliffs, listening to the
sirens singing on the rocks. I had spent the evening trying to
teach him elementary spell-casting, which was not such a
good idea. Anyway, it was very romantic and everything and
Asvin was throwing several soulful glances in my direction,
so I was quite pleased. We were cutting through the Square
Forest, and Asvin suddenly said he had something to tell me.
Just then I realized how perfect the setting was, just right for
a hero who wanted to make passionate declarations, and just

dark enough for him not to see if I grinned in the middle. So I said, What is it, Asvin?—as innocently as I could.

Then he suddenly stiffened, like a dog on a scent, and started plodding through the forest. Panic attack, I thought, and ran after him, asking him what was wrong. He said he could hear the song again. I listened carefully, and I heard it too—it was a very sweet sound, coming from inside the Square Forest. A song, in some northern language. I liked it, but Asvin was completely enchanted—he just kept walking towards it, I almost had to run to keep up.

After a while the song grew louder, and we saw something glowing in the forest. I remembered the girl Asvin had talked about in the Bleakwood—and yes, it was her again. I saw her, and realized why Asvin had been raving about her. Tall, slim, blonde, looked like a Skuan goddess. Flowers at her feet, discreet vines around her.

Trust my luck. When I'm really attracted to someone, I get, for competition, beautiful raven-haired Durgan princesses and mysterious naked singing maidens. I suppose I should be grateful the rakshasi Akarat was taken.

Asvin made a complete fool of himself. He burst out of the trees saying, Nightingale! And the girl saw him and fled. What a figure—I must get more exercise. Asvin threw himself down on the ground and kept saying, Not again, not again. I wonder why.

Who is that woman? Is she some spirit of the forest who has followed Asvin here? Is she a northern siren of some sort? Is she dangerous?

We went to Gaam's hut and told him. Asvin was still in a daze—while he was busy tripping over Queeen, I told Gaam the singing naked girl was back. He looked worried.

Well, Asvin's here, I have to go. In a few days we'll finish preliminary training and start going on more quests.

10

The sun was bright in north Shantavan as a man walked along a narrow path running through the forest. He was tall, broad and handsome, clad in tight green clothes. A long yew bow, a shabby pack and a full quiver were slung across his back, a weather-stained sword in a ragged scabbard hung from his belt and a merry song was on his lips. A fine figure was Pushpdev Rabin, the Bandit King.

A few years ago he had been the Raja of Oodh, a peaceful little country west of Avranti, before Maharaja Aloke had annexed his lands unjustly. The young king had barely escaped with his life. He had fled to Shantavan, and he ruled the northern half now, with his faithful and ever-increasing band of followers.

Rabin of Oodh had studied in Hero School in Kol, and was implementing in the forest many of the theories he had learned there. Economics was his favourite subject; he had even written a book—*On Economic Inequality: Redistribution of Income in a Hypothetical Forest Economy*—which was now a standard text in Hero School. He aimed to rob the rich and pay the poor until perfect economic equality and social justice were achieved in a transformed, classless society.

'Three days, my love,' he said to a passing squirrel. 'Three days, and I will steal you away, and you will be my merry queen, and I will bring you fresh flowers every morning.'

The squirrel ran away, unimpressed. A boy emerged from behind a tree. Not dangerous, Rabin thought, releasing his sword-hilt. Pleasant looking boy. 'Hail, my merry lad!' he said jovially. 'And what brings you to this peaceful wood?'

'You,' said Kirin. 'I've been watching you for three days now. Are you the Bandit King?'

'Why?' said Rabin, drawing his sword. 'Who wants to know?'

'He does,' said Kirin, and Rabin turned and saw a face, very close to his. A very ugly face.

Spikes was leaning against a tree, inspecting his claws casually.

'See, you are going to answer my questions,' said Kirin quietly. 'But we can do this my way, or we can do this *his* way.'

Common sense and bravado wrestled for a moment inside Pushpdev's head. Common sense won.

'I am the Bandit King,' said Rabin proudly.

'Very pleased to meet you. How quickly can you get the disguise you are planning to wear for Princess Pratima's swayamvar?'

'*What?*' said Rabin, stunned.

'Well?'

'I'm carrying it right now. What is going on?'

Kirin knelt, put his hand on the ground and muttered the incantation. The earth quivered, and began to bulge.

'This time, you are going to bring Pratima back with you,' said Kirin. 'I'll tell you how on the way.'

Two Avrantic guards stood, spears crossed, in front of the Hall of Fire in the Ektara Rajprasad, where the swayamvar was going to take place a few hours later. Their uniforms were shining and their moustaches were gleaming with oil, the ends honed to razor sharpness by patient rolling. They knew the princes who would start arriving any minute now would not even notice them when they parted their spears and saluted them, but you had to look your best for the swayamvar. The guards of entrance to the Hall of Fire were held in great esteem by the other guards—the royals, of course, never even looked at their faces.

A young man came rushing down the corridor. 'Pashan loose in the palace!' he gasped. 'Two guards are down already, and it's coming this way!'

'Run tell someone else, lad,' said one of the guards. 'We can't leave our posts.'

'But there isn't anyone else! The other guards haven't come yet! You have to come with me!' said the young man urgently, and ran back down the corridor.

'I suppose we'd better follow him,' said the guard, shrugging.

'We should send word to the Senapati,' panted the other as they broke into a run.

'There's no time now!' yelled the man. He opened the door at the end of the corridor, and the guards ran in past him and stopped abruptly when they saw Spikes standing over a fallen man, fangs gleaming, in the middle of the empty hall.

The young man slammed the door shut. The guards raised their spears as Spikes charged at them. Before he could reach them the man stepped forward, and extending two long fingers, jabbed one guard sharply behind the right ear, and then the other. The guards turned and looked at him, puzzled.

Then their eyes glazed over and they swayed and fell.

'You should have let me take them,' said Spikes.

'How did you do that, Kirin?' asked Rabin, getting up.

'Nerve endings,' said Kirin, dragging one of the guards behind a heavy curtain. 'They'll sleep for hours. Now get the other one. We must hurry.'

It was straight out of *The Standard Book of Swayamvar Surprises*, Chapter Four. They had stopped thinking of new ones.

Target: A fish.

Attach to bottom of a rotating disc far above the floor. Use sharp instrument.

Disc should be spinning on a pole that stretches from the floor to the ceiling.

Seven crescent-moon-shaped blades, spinning on the pole below the disc, at different speeds.

At the bottom of the pole, a circular tank filled with water.

On the floor of the tank, a mirror.

The candidate has to shoot the eye of the fish, seeing only the reflection in the tank.

Arrow must pass through all seven blades.

All candidates have to use the same bow and organizers must provide identical arrows. Breaking of bow is punishable by death.

Kicking of pole and dirtying of water to disadvantage other candidates not allowed.

All candidates to be given one chance only.

If more than one candidate shoots fish the bride-to-be chooses from among the successful candidates.

(Note: Keep spare fish)

The Hall of Fire was huge, one of the largest in the Rajprasad. It was a closed hall, but so brightly lit that the absence of windows was never noticed. The only entrance to the hall was the huge door at one end, which was mostly left open, letting the sunlight in from the corridor outside. At the other end, facing the door, was the Throne of the Tiger on a wide dais. There were hundreds of huge torches on the walls, and one roaring fire in the centre, which had been burning ever since Avranti had been founded, in front of which the wedding ceremonies were performed when more conventional swayamvars took place. Many beautiful paintings hung between the richly carved pillars along the walls. Servants manning huge fans kept a constant refreshing breeze whispering through the hall. Fifty guards stood, wielding spears, at regular intervals, behind the large seats where the princes from all over the world sat, in a long line on either side of the Hall of Fire.

Maharaja Aloke sat on the ornate throne, wearing the Crown of the Sun, with the Maharani to his left and the Senapati to his right. The princess Pratima was sitting on another throne, next to the Maharani. Beside her stood her bodyguard, a Durgan warrior-woman, whose principal duty was to keep an eye on her and see that she did not run away to Shantavan.

In front of the throne, just below the steps that led up to the dais, on a scarlet velvet cushion, lay the Tear of the Sky, a huge, sparkling diamond, that seemed to shine with a white fire of its own. It was the most precious jewel in the world.

Like all such gems, there was a long history of murder and hatred behind this one. As it lay in the hall, every eye turned to it from time to time, to simply soak in its brilliance, and in every mind was born a fierce desire to possess that brilliance, to snatch the gem from the cushion and run.

Which was why there was a special regiment of guards, kelaripayattu warriors from the Sambar Plateau in south Avranti, whose sole duty was guarding the Tear of the Sky.

Four warriors, bare-chested, their dark oiled skins glowing, stood around the gem, never even looking at the princes who, one after another, were walking up to the spinning pole further down the hall, beyond the fire in the middle, and trying in vain to shoot the revolving fish.

Already there were about thirty arrows in the ceiling, and everyone in the hall was growing impatient. These princes weren't *expected* to shoot the fish. Where was the Bandit King?

Aristocrats from all over the world sat sullenly in the seats on either side of the hall. Many of them had come directly from Vanarpuri, and were pretending hard that they had never seen one another before. They made a fine spectacle, with their brilliant raiment, their shining armour and their glittering array of deadly weapons, with or without runes and complicated names. Kirin, standing in a guard's armour beside a pillar, looked at the many proud, haughty faces all over the hall, the result of so many centuries of selective breeding, and was strongly reminded of a troop of Artaxerxian camels he had once seen entering Kol. Many of these princes have seen me wandering around in Vanarpuri, he thought. Luckily, I didn't exist in their universe even then, because I didn't have a name to go with my face. And I'm safe here—none of these overbred morons would ever look a mere guard in the eye.

A loud murmur ran down the hall. A tall, broad figure, completely covered in a dirty green cloak and hood, shuffled into the Hall of Fire. The guards at the door gave each other meaningful looks as they parted spears and let him pass. The words 'The Bandit King' flew around the hall, and whispers climbed on the shoulders of other whispers and peeked as the green-clad one sat on a seat that had thoughtfully been left empty at the far end of the hall. It was one of those unbreakable Laws of Nature making its presence felt.

The mysterious stranger shoots last.

As he sat, everyone in the hall stared for a few seconds, and then the swayamvar continued, everyone in the hall gallantly pretending they weren't perfectly aware that it was Rabin of Oodh under the faded cloak.

What an idiot Rabin is to think he is fooling everyone, thought Kirin. He comes here every year, and sits in his shabby clothes among these princes, who are nearly all dripping with jewellery. As if the guards would even let him in if they hadn't been told he was coming. Just because he hides his face, he assumes no one can see him. And look at the princess—her eyes are glowing, and she's all excited. My sweetheart is here, and he's going to carry me away. The only thing missing is the white horse.

Well, Father, you said you had given me a lot of power. I'll find out today, he thought. The first time I'm really trying to flex that ravian mental muscle.

Well, just two to go before him. I'd better get moving.

He began to move silently towards the far end of the hall, closer to the Tear of the Sky. No one looked as he walked behind the seats. Some of the other guards threw questioning looks at him, but said nothing.

The swayamvar was drawing towards a close—there were just three contestants left. A daimyo from Xi'en stepped up, picked up the bow, took his arrow, and pointed it upwards, looking down into the tank.

The old kul-guru, now sadly senile, was sitting near the pole, giving the contestants streams of useless advice. As the daimyo pulled the bow-string back, he jumped up and said, 'Wait!'

Annoyed murmurs ran through the hall. The kul-guru said, 'What do you see when you look into the water?'

The daimyo said, 'Seven revolving crescents, and a fish.'

'Hopeless,' said the kul-guru. 'Anyway, shoot, for what it's worth.'

The daimyo let the arrow fly. It glanced off a blade and shuddered into the ceiling.

A ripple of excitement ran through the hall. One more to go, and then the Bandit King.

Lukochuri, last of the Potolpuri princes, stepped up. 'What do you see?' asked the kul-guru.

'I see only the fish,' said Lukochuri, peering into the water.

'So close,' said the kul-guru, shaking his head. Lukochuri looked harder.

'Wait a minute, Venerable One,' he said, 'I see only the eye of the fish.'

'We have a winner!' announced the kul-guru. 'For his aim will surely be true!'

'Thank you,' said Lukochuri, and shot.

And missed completely.

There was complete silence in the Hall of Fire as the last archer stepped up. How broad his shoulders are, thought the beaming Pratima. Well, this is it, thought Kirin. Every guard in the hall gripped his spear a little tighter.

The green-cloaked archer picked up the bow and took an arrow. 'What do you see?' asked the old kul-guru.

'I see a foolish old man who will get an arrow in the heart if he doesn't shut up,' replied the archer in a sinister whisper.

The rattled kul-guru sat down.

The man in the hood took aim carefully, waited until the blades were almost perfectly aligned and then shot. There was an excited gasp as the arrow left the bow. And a huge 'Oh!' as it shot through the blades and pierced the eye of the fish.

'The Bandit King has done it again!' someone shouted.

Maharaja Aloke stood up. He's done this before, thought Kirin, as he moved up between two seats. Well, this is it.

'Well done, stranger,' said Aloke, as several guards moved forward. 'But should not my fair cousin see the face of the man who has won her hand?'

The figure in green said nothing.

'Oh come on, Rabin,' said Aloke. 'This is ridiculous. We've got you this time. Even your own men have not bothered to show up. Just surrender quietly. Show me your face, and let us finish this.'

Silence. Some of the princes drew their swords.

The figure in green slowly lifted a gloved hand to his face. Then threw the hood back in one swift motion. Pratima screamed.

It was Spikes.

At that precise moment, when each and every eye in the hall was fixed on Spikes's magnificently ugly face, Kirin reached out and the Tear of the Sky flew to his hands. He slid it into a pocket and stepped back. The kelaripayattu warriors, like the rest of the people in the hall, gasped as Spikes said, 'I win the contest. I claim the bride, and the prize.'

Every eye swung to the cushion where the Tear of the Sky had been a second ago. Another gasp, an even louder one, echoed from floor to ceiling. 'It's gone!' yelled someone who believed in pointing out the obvious. (There's *always* one.)

There were two seconds of stunned silence.

Then Aloke cried, 'Seize him!'

The fabric of the cloak was ripped apart as Spikes's spikes burst through it. With one great hand he swept aside the spears of the nearest guards. He turned and ran towards the door, pushing aside the few who managed to reach him. He was moving very fast—only the two guards who stood at the gate had any chance of stopping him now. They stood their ground as Spikes hurtled towards them, and pointed their spears at him.

Then one of the door wardens stepped back, and swung the handle of his spear, bringing it down on the back of the other's head with a mighty crack. As the guard fell stunned, the assailant threw off his helmet.

It was Pushpdev Rabin, the Bandit King. He blew the assembly a kiss as Spikes ran past him, and then they slammed the great hall doors shut. A second later a hail of arrows and spears shuddered into the mighty doors and stuck there, quivering.

'There's magic in this!' yelled Aloke, springing down from the throne, sword drawn. 'Get them!'

Every guard save one ran towards the door and pounded on it, but it was barred from the outside.

And now for the real test, thought Kirin. He threw his arms into the air, and muttered a spell Maya had taught him.

There was a *whoosh* as every fire in the room went out, plunging the Hall of Fire into complete darkness.

There was pandemonium in the hall. A few guards ran to re-light the torches, but they couldn't. Someone wailed, 'Never before has the sacred fire gone out! The end of the earth is come!'

Princess Pratima's Durgan bodyguard suddenly felt a sharp pain as someone poked her behind the ear. She turned angrily, but her limbs seemed to have fallen asleep and she crashed to the floor.

'Do you want to marry the Bandit King?' asked a soft voice in Pratima's ear.

'Yes,' she replied.

'Then come with me.'

Twenty minutes later, when the great door was finally broken down, the palace was searched from end to end, but no sign of the princess, the pashan or Rabin could be found.

The city gates were watched ceaselessly for weeks, but fruitlessly—they seemed to have vanished off the face of the earth. It was concluded later that the Bandit King had been working with evil spirits.

But the most mysterious thing, everyone agreed, had happened in the Hall of Fire. For when sunlight had flooded the great hall, they had seen, on the dais where Aloke's throne had been, the marble slabs had been mysteriously ripped up, and right in the centre of the dais was a perfectly smooth brown earthen circle, stretching thirty feet across. A few hours later another circle, exactly like the one on the dais, was found in a derelict stable, where no well-bred horse had ever been housed.

antric had told Asvin that the time had not yet come for him to go through the mirrors in Xi'en and Elaken, and Asvin had found that the mirrors to Avranti and Ventelot didn't work—try as he might, he could not go through them. They were either broken, or blocked, Mantric had said. And the next two months passed so fast for Asvin that he never even found the time to ask Mantric what was so dangerous about the mirrors in Xi'en and Elaken. The mirror in Kol, of course, was out of the question—since it was underwater, if he opened it the cave would be flooded in an instant.

When Mantric had heard about their adventure with Akarat in Shantavan, he had looked pleased. If Akarat had risen again, he had said, it meant that the level of magic in the world was strong enough for the old Psomedean monsters to reappear, which meant that Asvin could go on a number of quests. And so as Tigermonth passed, and then Seahorsemonth came and went, Asvin went for quest after dangerous quest, and reached a point where a normal day of rigorous training began to feel like a holiday.

Every day, the mer-men or the imps would come and tell Mantric about a new monster that was ravaging an island in the Ossus Archipelago. Then Mantric would call Gaam, Asvin and Maya to him and send them to fight the monster, borne on dolphin-drawn boats. They were never very far from Bolvudis, and often Irik or Stivin Seagull would come and call them away from one quest because they had to go on a more important one.

The good thing about this whole exercise was that Asvin was gaining not only invaluable experience but also a large number of extremely valuable magical items. Some of these had belonged to heroes of days long gone and had turned up in the bellies of reappearing monsters—some others were lying in forgotten caves in one Psomedean island or another. And more were being sent to him from Kol.

In two months, he had achieved more than any hero had ever done in the past. Of course, this was largely due to Gaam and Maya, and the fact that so far they had known how to deal with every monster they came across and had not had to work it out for themselves.

And they chose their quests carefully, not attacking monsters in uninhabited islands unless there was something to be gained from it.

Of course, some adjustments had to be made. For example, when a giant sea serpent had been spotted idling in the ocean, no doubt scouting for a pleasant coastline to ravage, they had known it would attack a maiden tied to a rock. The only problem had been getting a maiden to volunteer to be tied to a rock. No one in Bolvudis particularly wanted to end up inside a sea serpent's stomach. Asvin had been very surprised, until Gaam had explained that it was not always the case that a hero's mere presence would cast all damsels in the area into perilous predicaments he could rescue them from. Most of the rescues in the legends were, Gaam said, either fictitious or pre-arranged, and hardly ever sheer coincidence or fate. In the end a grumbling Maya had let herself be tied to a rock while Asvin, sword in hand, prowled the beach.

The fact that the serpent's arrival had created a huge wave that had swept Gaam and Asvin far away and Maya had had to burn off her ropes and kill the monster on her own was, they all agreed, best kept secret. From the serpent's scales Gaam concocted a brew that he made Asvin and Maya keep in goatskin pouches tied to their belts at all times—it was a vaman secret, an All-Weather Potion. Once you drank it, you would be affected neither by Skuan cold nor by Artaxerxian heat. It was because the vamans drank this potion every day—they made it from the scales of the giant serpents in the underground seas—that they could withstand the immense heat underground, and could wear thick armour even in the heat of the Al-Ugobi desert. They were the first humans to drink this sacred potion, Gaam told them, and they felt suitably honoured.

Asvin collected many magical swords, bows, shields and spears on his quests. He even had an amulet that protected him from stomach ailments, a ring that prevented baldness, a bracelet to ward off earthquakes, boots that made no sound and earrings to prevent insect bites. But the most wonderful thing he found in the Ossus Archipelago was a magical helmet that let him see in the dark. This he had won after cutting open a hydra that had reappeared in the swamps of one of the islands in the Archipelago.

They had known from the tale of Eurekus that if they cut off any of the heads of this nine-headed monster, they would have to burn the stump really fast, or two heads would grow in the place of the one they had removed. After thinking for a whole day, Maya had had an inspiration. She had asked Mantric to create three huge cauldrons of really glutinous Gum That Bubbles, and they had fought the hydra with these. They had sloshed about in the swamp until the monster had attacked them, and then they had thrown Gum at it for a few hours, until all its nine heads were completely preoccupied in chewing maniacally, and all its sharp fangs were stuck together. Then Asvin had advanced and slit open its belly neatly, and found the helmet.

It was on that very day that Asvin realized that he had been in love with Maya for some time. He also knew that his chances of winning her in a typically heroic manner were very slim indeed; that he could not surpass her in wit, knowledge or skill, and she was just as brave as he. So for the first time in his life, Asvin found himself in a situation where he badly wanted to woo someone, but could think of absolutely nothing to do. So he dealt with it in the easiest way possible, telling himself that it was mere infatuation and it wouldn't work, because after all they had to work together and romance would complicate matters.

But when, on one clear dark night in Bolvudis, he heard the song of the wood-nymph again, he resolved not to go looking for her even if she was the most beautiful woman in the world.

And when, a minute after deciding this, he found himself running out of his hut towards the mysterious maiden in the Square Forest, and drawing closer and closer to her wondrous song, he felt very guilty indeed. And when Gaam, who had also heard the song, caught up with him in the forest, admonished him sternly and made him return to the village, a part of Asvin was grateful.

Slowly, but surely, rumours about Asvin's deeds had begun to spread. Whispers had flown to every corner of the world—there was a mysterious Hero in the world, the Hero of Simoqin's prophecy, and hope was not all lost.

And the followers of Danh-Gem heard rumours too—of the slaying of the great Akarat and many other powerful monsters, of a nameless, faceless hero who was performing deeds as great as those of Ossus or Eurekus of old.

The month of the Dragon began. One morning, Maya and Gaam watched Asvin match the young fighters of Xi'en step for step on the cliffs of Bolvudis. As he battled them in the gusting morning wind, radiant, handsome and fearless, they knew he was almost ready for whatever Danh-Gem and fate would throw in his way.

'There is just one more thing,' said Gaam, 'and then we can take him to Kol, and wait for Danh-Gem to arrive, and when he does, reveal Asvin to the people.'

'And what is that one thing?' asked Maya, watching Asvin, enraptured.

'The most powerful armour in the world,' said Gaam. 'The Prophecy said he would wear it.'

'Where is it?'

And he told her, and saw the fear he felt reflected in her eyes.

Meanwhile, the Silver Dagger was in Kol, gathering news from all over the world. From time to time, the men of the

Silver Phalanx brought him little magical items they had found or won, and he would send them to Bolvudis.

He heard that Princess Pratima of Avranti was now happily married to the Bandit King. But the members of the Silver Phalanx who spied on Rabin told him that the Bandit King had not revealed even to his own men how he had brought Pratima to Shantavan—he would only say that he had been sworn to secrecy.

Then he heard of the earth circles in Avranti and thought of the one he had seen in the Centaur Forests.

Where was Kirin? Had he worked with Rabin? He knew that vanars had come to Rabin and Rabin had refused to go to Vrihataranya—so was Rabin working with vanars now, or with Kirin? And why had Kirin stolen the Tear of the Sky? Or had he?

Was he even alive?

This was the first time that the Silver Dagger had failed. But though it left a bitter taste in his mouth, he accepted defeat with a shrug of his shoulders, because he knew he could not fight magic. Magic was growing in leaps and bounds every day now—he had seen the waters of the Fountain of Enki, and they were rising every day. The Civilian had sent divers down to the bottom of the River Asa to find Jaadur's mirror. But so far it continued to elude them.

The Dagger also heard of the mustering of armies in the north and west, and made sure that the rift between the Koli asurs and the Imokoi danavs remained wide. His men were busy too. Certain barons in Ventelot had already disappeared, and there were four members of the Silver Phalanx amongst the troops of Omar the Terrible. They had orders to kill him on sight. But he never showed his face even to his own men.

The Dagger knew there was a lot he didn't know. He

knew everything that had happened in the Parliament of Vanarpuri, and what the leaders who had assembled there had done after that—but the vital clues were missing, the leaders' movements were still shrouded in mystery. He had still not found Omar the Terrible, though he had discovered that the Sultan was his father. And though he knew that Bali and Bjorkun were somewhere in the north—one of his best men were following them—he had no idea what they were trying to achieve. An Avrantic minister who had gone to Vrihataranya had not been there at the Council, and had not returned. And in Xi'en, a ronin trying to steal the Gauntlet of Tatsu had been killed by the Wu Sen monks. The Civilian had sent many messages to Xi'en, asking that the Gauntlet be brought to Kol, where it would be safer, in secret—but it was unlikely that Xi'en would let that happen. There was a pattern somewhere, he knew it, they knew his spies were among them. They were trying to do something in secret, something that could be stopped. But he didn't know what it was, and neither did the Civilian. And there were new assassins coming to Kol every day. Mercenary ninjas from Xi'en, young, untrained fanatical boys from Artaxerxia, even a vanar in disguise or two.

How many more would he have to kill?

He was getting tired of everything. In a world of rakshases, the Silver Dagger was just another mortal.

Maybe I should write that letter, he thought, because if I lose interest I'll get killed in a day.

Maybe I should write that letter now.

12

'Thank you, Karisman. You have repaid my trust by returning. The next meeting of the Brotherhood of Renewal will take place as planned tomorrow night,' said Angda, her dark face shining with excitement in the light of the torch she was holding.

And then we have two weeks to go until Danh-Gem reappears, thought Kirin. It's hard to believe this is actually happening. Two weeks. I'm not getting any sleep tonight.

'Where are the others? Are they here? Have they got the things?' he asked.

'The asurs have arrived with the Iron Crown, Karisman. Crows have been coming regularly, and I know that my brother and Lord Bjorkun are on their way and within a day's march of Vanarpuri—they will be here by tomorrow night. But there is no news of the ronin, or of Omar. I will tell them of the amazing speed with which you completed your quest. You must take me for a ride in this amazing chariot of yours.'

'I will,' said Kirin, who quite liked Angda. I wish I knew whether it's ravian power that makes her trust me, or whether

I'm worth liking for myself, he thought. At least I know I wasn't controlling Maya. I'm so glad she's a spellbinder. But there are other things to think about now.

Bali had told Angda not to allow Kirin and Spikes to leave Vanarpuri until he returned, 'for their own safety', but she had let them wander as they willed for the last two months. And in the course of his journeys through the darkness of Vrihataranya Kirin had made a new friend.

His name was Mr Djongli, and he was a man who lived with the vanars, a huge man generally seen in a leopard-skin loincloth with a huge hunting-knife in a sheath slung over his shoulder. He swung through the creepers of the giant trees like the vanars and would occasionally stand on a large branch, pound his chest with his fists and scream loudly, issuing a fierce challenge to the whole jungle. And all through the jungle, animals would scream in response. Kirin had asked Djongli whether he was the king of the jungle and whether the animals were responding to his call, but Djongli had replied rather sheepishly that the animals were screaming at him to shut up. He generally kept away from Vanarpuri, but when he had seen Kirin wandering through the jungle he had come down from his tree-house to say hello and soon they had become fast friends.

His parents, Djongli said, had been famous scholars in Kol, and had always been fascinated by issues such as evolution and the study of extinct animals. They had found the city of Vanarpuri after years of study in Vrihataranya. Bali's father, who had been king at the time, had spared their lives on the condition that they taught the vanars about the rest of the world. It was Djongli's parents who had taught the vanars to speak, read and write Koli. They had enjoyed their new roles and had stayed on in Vanarpuri—Bali's father had grown very fond of them, and when they had died, he had adopted their infant son. The only reason he was still alive, Djongli told Kirin, was that he and Bali were supposed to be brothers, though they hated each other.

Kirin learnt a lot from Djongli during his stay in Vrihataranya. He got plenty of exercise, wrestling with animals and skimming through the trees—he could pull creepers with his mind, and it grew easier every day, because his powers were growing. He read the books Djongli's parents had written about the vanars and the plants and animals in the forest, and saw many savage and beautiful creatures. Once they had even seen a manticore padding through the jungle—Djongli had dragged Kirin away, because the manticore was dangerous and had killed many vanars without any provocation.

Djongli took Kirin to deep, hidden valleys and caverns, and showed him gigantic caves with strange, primitive drawings on them, and gigantic bones that he had dug out of the earth and arranged with the help of his parents' books—they were the bones of incredibly huge lizards that had walked the earth millions of years ago. He took Kirin into parts of the Great Forest unseen even by the vanars, and showed him the dwellings of the Jajbor tribes, the last remnants of a once mighty civilization—most of their ancestors had migrated to the unknown lands that now lay south of the Vertical Sea. These tribes had a very strange sense of humour—they would often leave masks, pots and weapons near the edge of Vrihataranya, so that explorers from all over the world could find them and think they had discovered new civilizations. And the Jajbors made many different kinds of masks . . . Kirin wondered if all the thirty-odd little tribes whose artefacts were proudly displayed in the museums of Kol existed only in the minds of the Jajbors.

A few asurs had started trickling into Vanarpuri from Imokoi, bearing weapons and news. Kirin, who'd always had a sneaking fondness for the asurs of Kol, found that the danavs weren't really all that different. He also found that with asurs, his mind control powers worked really well—now that he was stronger, he could actually make them do things he wanted them to do. No wonder Danh-Gem stopped sending asurs to attack ravians, he thought. They probably ended up attacking one another.

With this newfound power over asur minds, Kirin, inspired by the example of Djongli's parents, started trying to teach the asurs about the world. He ended up learning much more than he taught—he learnt a great deal of asur history, picked up the rudiments of the danav language and most importantly, learnt that the asurs didn't want to learn anything about anything. Kirin was not a patient teacher, and he had given up after three days. I'm doing enough to change the world, he had thought. But I wish someone could teach the asurs that there's more to life than money, food and fighting. Actually, I wish someone could teach the humans that too. Vanars are different. They don't want money.

So Kirin had gone off into the forest again with Djongli and Spikes, and wandered far and wide. But Angda had told him to return to Vanarpuri before the old moon died, so when Dragonmonth arrived in Vanarpuri, Kirin did too.

One thing that was worrying Kirin was that his father had not said anything to him since that night in the Centaur Forests. Sometimes the book had flipped open in the night, and he had rushed to it, but nothing had happened, the book had just glimmered dully in his hands. He wondered if Narak had lost the strength to summon him, and whether he would be able to give him the other two gifts he had promised him.

Kirin, with his new heightened senses, could actually feel magic growing, as his own powers increased—and sometimes when his sharp ears had caught strange humming sounds coming from the book, he had wondered if his father was in pain. But the book had remained stubbornly silent—perhaps his father was just conserving his strength, Kirin had hoped.

For two months now, a nameless fear had been growing in Kirin's heart, a feeling of growing danger, a feeling that he was being watched by someone close to him, but nothing had happened—there were no enemies hiding in the trees, no panthers springing at him from the thick undergrowth. Or maybe, he had sometimes thought, Danh-Gem's powers are growing stronger, as he prepares to rise . . . or maybe I'm just overreacting, and being tense and nervous, and generally behaving like an idiot.

But none of his fears had been unfounded before, sadly, and he wondered if some other power was preventing his father from speaking to him . . .

And as he watched Angda tear away through the branches that served as streets in Vanarpuri, he wondered how he was expected to kill Danh-Gem if his father could not find the strength to show him the way.

He lay down on his rug on the cold temple floor and drew the book out. Now would be a good time for you to come, he thought.

Were you worried?

He opened the book and saw a strange, twisted smile on his father's face.

'Where were you? Are you all right?' he whispered breathlessly.

Apart from the fact that I've been dead for two hundred years, I'm fine. Narak laughed drily.

'Is it getting difficult to talk? Are you in pain?'

That is irrelevant. There is not much time. When is Danh-Gem supposed to rise?

'Full moon, Dragonmonth—fifteen days away.'

Now tell me, son—what weapon do you use?

'I don't carry any weapons. I never needed any in Kol.'

And did you think you could slay Danh-Gem with your bare hands?

'No.'

Narak said nothing.

'I thought you would guide me,' said Kirin after some time.

And so I will.

When I made this book, I wondered—Danh-Gem cannot be slain with any weapon made by mortal hands. I do not know what form he will rise in. What weapon should I give my son? A sword? A mace? But what if the form Danh-Gem assumes makes that weapon unsuitable? And what if my son is unskilled in the use of that weapon? Days I spent dwelling on this matter, and finally I reached a solution. I would give up the weapon that had taken me ten years to make. I would give you the weapon I had carved out of the living shadows of Elaken and tempered once a year in my own blood. I would give you the Shadowknife.

'You gave up your own weapon?'

It was necessary. The weapon, like the task I have set for you, is not a gift but a burden, Kirin. So you need not thank me. It is your forgiveness I should ask for.

'What is this Shadowknife? How did you put it inside the book?

It is not inside the book. It is on it.

'The moongold?'

Put your hand on the cover of the book, Kirin.

'All right.'

What, in your opinion, is a good weapon?

'Well, a sword, I suppose.'

Then imagine a sword, Kirin. The sharpest, subtlest sword in the world. Are you seeing it in your mind? Close your eyes if you have to. Can you see it?

'Yes.'

What are you holding in your hand, Kirin?

Kirin cried out in amazement. The black cover on the book had melted away, and the whole book was glowing— the whole cover was shining moongold now. But the blackness hadn't disappeared. It had melted off the book and on to his hand, and there it had formed a long, double-bladed sword, completely black, so black it made the darkness seem grey.

It was the Shadowknife.

The Shadowknife served me faithfully, Kirin. Take good care of it, for it is living shadow. It will take any shape you desire, and will become whatever weapon you desire to wield. This is the weapon that will pierce the hide of the Rakshas— the weapon of Narak the Demon-hunter, returned to haunt Danh-Gem in his hour of glory.

Kirin wasn't even looking at Narak. He was staring at the black shape in his hands, which was changing shape as fast as his mind could think. As Kirin saw weapon after weapon in his head, the Shadowknife melted and became a spear, a bow, an axe, a dagger, a lance, a shield . . .

It melted and grew, it dissolved and hardened and Kirin could not take his eyes off it.

Do not use this weapon until Danh-Gem rises. Every asur has been told tales of the Shadowknife of Narak, and you will be revealed to the servants of Danh-Gem as an enemy. Do not try to find a sheath for it, for no sheath can hold the Shadowknife.

'Where do I put it, then?'

Think of a ring.

Kirin watched as the black crossbow twisted and shrank until it was a bright black circle on his finger.

'This is amazing,' he said.

Not anyone can wield this weapon, Kirin. To wear it, immense magical powers are needed. Powers that you have. You can face any enemy on this world, Kirin, and defeat him, because the power to mould the Shadowknife lies not in the Shadowknife, but in you. Never forget that.

'I won't.'

I will leave you now. I have just enough strength to speak to you one more time, Kirin. I will give you my final gift then. After you have slain Danh-Gem.

'Wait, please. I want to ask you something,' said Kirin.

Hurry, then.

'What happens to me after I slay Danh-Gem?'

Now is hardly the time to think of that. Concentrate on the task ahead, Kirin.

'Did you even think of that? Or did you only consider how Danh-Gem was to be killed?'

Did I not say I would give you another gift after you killed Danh-Gem? Narak sounded angry. *Do not judge me solely by what I did to you two hundred years ago! I loved your mother, and I love you, Kirin. I will not tell you what the fourth gift is. I will only say that you will be given a choice if you succeed. I will not force you to do anything, ever again. You will decide where you belong.*

'In the ravian world, or here?' asked Kirin softly.

But Narak said nothing. He was still frowning. The lines faded, and he was gone.

Kirin put the shining book away, lay back and started to think.

13

'I hope you're not tired or anything,' said Gaam as he led Asvin towards the mirror, 'because tonight is going to be a long night. Did you bring everything?'

'Yes,' said Asvin, gripping the hilt of his sword. 'Where are we going this time?'

'Elaken,' said Gaam. 'We're going to get you some armour.' Gaam was in full armour himself, and carrying his huge battleaxe.

They reached the cave where the mirror stood. Maya and Mantric were waiting for them. Queeen was there, too. She gave Asvin an enthusiastic welcome as he entered.

'The Simoqin Prophecy,' said Mantric, 'said that the hero would wear the most powerful armour in the world. Tonight, Asvin, you will go to get that armour. It is the most dangerous quest you have attempted so far, and if you succeed, you may rest assured that your powers are as great as any of the Seven Heroes in the Age of Terror. For one of the Seven Heroes—Anik of Avranti, in fact—was slain while he was attempting to get this very armour.'

Asvin's face turned white. 'The armour of the Scorpion Man? But does that really exist?'

'You will find out tonight, Asvin. For tonight you will go to Elaken, through the mirror of Zinat, which, if Jaadur the spellbinder spoke true, lies inside the Pyramid of the First Pharaoh.'

The Book of the Scorpion, an ancient Elakish tome, spoke of the legend of the First Pharaoh, who would one day return with the armies of the dead and destroy all evil in the world. The Pyramid of the First Pharaoh was the first and greatest of all the pyramids of Elaken. It was rumoured that priceless treasure lay inside the Great Pyramid, treasure worth more than all the treasure that had been plundered from the rest of the necropolis, but no one knew how to enter the Great Pyramid, and even if they knew, few thieves would have dared to walk its secret pathways. For the First Pharaoh did not sleep alone. He was guarded by the dead and by his immortal servant, the Scorpion Man.

No living person had seen the Scorpion Man, and no one who had seen him had returned to tell the tale. But the scribes of ancient Elaken had written in their sacred tomes of the armour that he wore, the shining armour that no weapon or magic could pierce.

The Scorpion Man, the legend said, stood in a trance, talking to the gods, in a vestibule near the Pharaoh's burial chamber, and would wake if any thief went near the sleeping Pharaoh. But the Scorpion Man would also wake once on every moonless night, and if anyone asked him for a gift then, he would grant it, as long as it did not involve the Pharaoh or his treasure.

Through the ages, this legend had inspired heroes to try to enter the Great Pyramid and simply ask the Scorpion Man for his magical armour. But every hero who had entered the Pyramid had been slain by the forces of the dead that guarded it. No one had even managed to reach the Scorpion Man. It was said that Danh-Gem himself had tried to enter the Pyramid. He had not found the entrance and had tried to break down the walls, but the magic inside had proved too strong even for him.

'In Avranti, our records say that Anik left the palace saying he would not return without getting the Scorpion Man's armour. And he never returned,' said Asvin. 'So he did go to the Great Pyramid, through Zinat's mirror. But how could Zinat's mirror be inside the Great Pyramid? All I know of her is that she was one of the Heroes. Gaam told me very little else.'

'Zinat of Elaken was much like the Silver Dagger of today,' said Gaam. 'She was an accomplished thief and assassin, and her movements were always shrouded in secrecy. But it is said in the Chronicles that the belly dancer who slew the Sultan of Artaxerxia was none other than Zinat in disguise.'

'Zinat was the best thief in the world,' said Mantric, 'and Jaadur writes in his book that she managed to find a way into the Great Pyramid, because she sought the armour herself. She even took her mirror in there with her, to escape through if she failed. But after entering the Great Pyramid, she did not dare to go further. The entrance she found closed as soon as she entered and it had taken her more than a day to get through—the Scorpion Man would not awake again for a month, on the next moonless night, and she could not possibly survive a month fighting the undead in the Great Pyramid. So she left the Pyramid through the mirror. Which is convenient for us, because the mirror stands there to this very day, I hope, and tonight you are going through it to get the armour. Of course, if the mirror is broken then Gaam can steal a vaman-made armour for us, but I do not think the mirror will be broken.

'Be very careful, all of you. And though the Prophecy seems to demand that you get the armour, remember, your lives are much more valuable than any metal, even if it is the most powerful in the world.'

'One question,' said Gaam, turning to Maya. 'Why have you brought Queeen here?'

'Well, you told me she was very good at solving mazes, and I'm pretty sure there'll be one in the pyramid—at least, the Book of the Scorpion speaks of "the twisting tunnels of the dead", which I thought must mean a maze. That's why,' said Maya, surprised because Gaam sounded annoyed.

'That is true,' said Gaam, 'but I don't think she should come with us tonight.'

'Why not?'

'Well, it will be dangerous in the pyramid,' said Gaam, looking at his dog, who was busy licking Asvin's hand noisily.

'Oh come on, you old soft-heart,' said Maya. 'You know as well as I do that the undead don't attack animals. Besides, Queeen's been of no use whatsoever so far, and it's time she justified her existence.'

'I suppose so,' said Gaam, but he looked unhappy.

'You might as well get started,' said Mantric. 'The sun's already set. If you do succeed in getting past the traps in the pyramid, remember—do not under any circumstances touch the Pharaoh's tomb, or the treasure! That will guarantee a slow and painful death—at best.'

'Thanks,' said Maya, as Asvin stepped forward, said 'Zinat' and touched the mirror. Black clouds billowed over the silver surface, 'Now we feel so much better.'

She stepped through the mirror with Queeen, and Gaam followed, looking disgruntled.

The mirror was about to turn silver again, when Mantric turned and saw a white blur streaking into the cave, past his feet and jumping into the mirror.

From a hole in the fabric of space-time (which looked like a mirror) in the Great Pyramid of Elaken emerged two humans, a vaman, a dog and a rabbit. Steel-Bunz had had enough of being left behind.

Zinat's mirror was behind a huge pillar, it seemed. They fumbled about in the darkness.

'Do I make a light?' whispered Maya.

'Wait,' said Gaam, 'Asvin, spy around a bit.'

Asvin put his magic helmet on and saw a huge hall. He could see clearly enough, but the helmet turned everything he saw green. What they'd thought was a pillar was actually the back of a huge statue.

Asvin stepped up to the middle of the hall and saw a double line of statues leading up to a door on one side and a sarcophagus on the other. The statues were all identical—a woman's body with a cat's head, sitting on a throne. In the deathly silence the sound of Queeen panting was obscenely loud.

Some of the statues were headless, the others looked arrogantly across the hall. The floor was mainly smooth, but sometimes there were great cracks in it. Asvin walked up to one and looked down. He could not see the bottom of the chasm.

'You'll need light, I think,' he said. 'There are cracks on the floor.'

An instant later a cold blue light shone behind the statue, casting long, threatening shadows across the room, as a fireball appeared above Maya's head. It seemed to Asvin that the eyes of some of the statues blinked, and the arms shifted. You're imagining things, he told himself. He looked upwards, and could see the ceiling, far, far above. He'd always thought the passages in the pyramids were narrow and constricting. But then this Pyramid was like no other, he reminded himself.

The others walked up to him and looked around the hall.

'This place is full of magic,' said Maya. 'Very old, very powerful.' She closed her eyes, and the fireball above her head grew brighter, and they could see the whole hall, every statue staring silently into nothingness. 'That hardly took any effort,' she said.

'Which way do we go, Gaam?' asked Asvin.

'The door, I think,' said Gaam. 'I don't like the feel of this hall.'

They walked to the door, jumping over the wide cracks in the floor, Asvin leading the way.

But just as he was about to reach the door, it slammed shut. Echoes reverberated through the hall and died out. There were several creaking noises, one long, loud hiss, and then silence.

'We woke someone up,' said Maya.

Asvin drew his sword.

Suddenly, with a roar, the cat's eyes of the statues sitting nearest the door burst into flames. And then, two by two, the eyes of the statues on either side of the hall lit up with ancient magic fire. When the statues were headless, there was a gush of flame at the statues' feet, as the eyes on the severed heads lit up, throwing fiery beams of light across the broken floor. Finally, the two statues nearest the sarcophagus woke. All the heads turned, creaking, towards the intruders, and they were caught in the glare of hundreds of fiery eyes.

They froze, looking at the expressionless feline faces and the burning stone eyes.

The room was filled with light and smoke, and the sound of a roaring flame. The fireball above Maya's head withered and went out.

'Is this the part where we die?' she asked Gaam.

'A quick dash towards the mirror might be a good idea,' he replied.

The lid of the sarcophagus at the other end of the hall suddenly flew up into the air, and crashed on the ground. There was a sudden stab of bright white light.

'Who disturbs the sleep of the servants of the Pharaoh?' asked a voice. A woman's voice, rich, purring, deep and seductive. Something white and shining jumped out of the sarcophagus. There was a flash of light, and then a small white cat was standing in front of Asvin. Its skin was shining brightly and its eyes were pools of utter darkness.

Every statue in the hall lifted its head and screamed. Asvin, Maya and Gaam cowered to the ground and covered their ears, terrified.

'Silence!' yelled the voice. It was the cat speaking. 'Sleep now, sisters. The Pharaoh still rests, and our day has not come yet.'

With a thundering crash, the statues resumed their original positions, and the fires in their eyes went out. The only light in the hall now was the glow of the talking cat. It padded around them slowly, looking silently at them. It stopped again, in front of Asvin.

'You do not look like grave-robbers,' she said. 'What are you, and what do you seek?'

'We are not thieves,' said Asvin. 'We do not come here seeking riches or glory. Great danger threatens the world outside, and we believe the Scorpion Man's armour can help us overcome the dark tide. But who are you, tomb-dweller?'

'I am called Erkila, soul-guide and tomb-guardian,' said the cat. 'And the dangers that you face, human, mean nothing to me. For those dangers are nothing compared to the danger you are now in—for I am dangerous, little one. Many have sought the armour of the Scorpion Man—all have failed. They have played my Game. And they have lost. But do not be disheartened! It has been many a year since heroes of the world outside came to play the Game with me.'

Erkila stood on her hind legs, and suddenly grew. Now she was a woman, incredibly tall, towering over them, and her head was the head of a vulture. The smooth, purring voice disappeared, and was replaced by a harsh screech.

'In the beginning, I used to release my warriors as soon as intruders entered the Pyramid, to kill them instantly. But as the centuries passed, that grew boring. So I devised the Game. You will play with me tonight, children, and if you win, you may ask the Scorpion for his armour. And if you lose, you will have the honour of joining the Pharaoh's army. And when the dead rise, the skies break and the oceans burn, you will march under my banner to eternal victory.'

'Run,' whispered Gaam.

Maya nodded, and tried to move to tell Asvin, but found she was rooted to the spot.

'Do not struggle, my love,' screeched Erkila, floating up to her. 'I know you are eager to play with me, but be patient. I have millions of games to play, and I must decide which ones you will enjoy most.'

She suddenly flew up and hovered over their heads. Wings stretched out from her back, huge wings that spanned the breadth of the hall, statue to statue. Large claws appeared and fastened on to Gaam's head, lifting him, struggling and kicking, into the air.

'You are the oldest one, yes?' asked Erkila.

'Yes,' croaked Gaam, wrestling hopelessly in the giant vulture's grip.

'And so you should be the wisest,' said Erkila, flapping her wings and rising higher and higher. 'We will see.'

'Don't run away, children!' she called as she soared and disappeared. 'I'll be back for you!'

Asvin and Maya found they couldn't move. They stared at each other helplessly. A little while later, Asvin felt something on his foot. It was Steel-Bunz, and he was clambering on to Asvin's cloak.

'What are you doing here, Fluffy?' asked Asvin in amazement.

'Shh,' said Maya. 'She's coming back.'

'I forgot to tell you all the rules,' screeched Erkila, landing heavily on the floor. 'All of you will have to succeed in the little games I will give you. If any of you fail, I win, and your souls are mine. Now then, little man, you look like a warrior. I have something that you will like.'

She grabbed Asvin with her huge claws and flapped away. Steel-Bunz clung grimly on to Asvin's cloak, closing his eyes and flattening his ears as the wind rushed on to his face.

Maya tried spell after spell, but she couldn't break the one Erkila had cast on them—she seemed to be rooted to the floor. She gave up and waited. Soon the sound of giant wings flapping told her Erkila had returned.

'Two little mortals are playing the Game. As for you, pretty one,' she croaked, 'you need to be taught a lesson in patience. I see you can do magic. But can you solve puzzles? And can you fight, pretty one?'

The doors creaked open, and the invisible bonds that held Maya disappeared.

'On you lies the burden of finding the way to the burial chamber,' said Erkila. 'If your friends succeed, I will bring them to you. You may keep the dog—I have no use for it. If you grow hungry, I advise you to eat it.'

Queeen flattened her ears and looked at Maya beseechingly. I know just how you feel, thought Maya. She walked out of the door.

'I will be watching,' screeched Erkila. 'You will make a fine slave, my little love. Now run along.'

Then the doors slammed shut again and Maya was alone with Queeen.

She lit a fireball and began to walk down the tunnel that stretched out in front of her. Looking around, she saw graffiti on the walls—strange signs and scrawls made by the workers who had built the Great Pyramid. After a while the tunnel narrowed drastically—it was just about wide enough for her to walk through and quite low, so she had to stoop a little.

She tripped on a raised stone and fell. There were several sharp clicking noises. She noticed that the tunnel was sloping gently downwards, a thin, square passage into the depths of the earth. She got up, dusting her robes, and heard a rumbling sound behind her. Queeen yelped. Maya turned.

And saw a huge stone sphere, as wide as the tunnel, rolling towards her. If I stay here it'll crush me, and the only way to go is down, she thought. Queeen dashed past her and raced down the tunnel. Clever dog, thought Maya, and began to run.

Asvin rolled over and sprang to his feet. His shoulders were very sore where the vulture had seized him but he still had his helmet. He looked around in the green light.

A long corridor, with lines of statues down either side. Standing figures with animal heads. The bodies were human, and male this time, arms folded, often holding rods or ankhs across their chests. Some of the heads were vultures, some jackals, and some crocodiles. He half expected them to turn and glare at him, but they sat still, ignoring him.

'Well, Fluffy, it's just you and me,' said Asvin to Steel-Bunz, who was doing an investigative nose-twitch.

Far away, at the other end of the corridor, there was the sound of a door creaking open.

'Or maybe not,' said Asvin.

Gaam shouldered his battleaxe and trudged along the tunnel where Erkila had dropped him. There was a faint glow ahead of him. He saw what it was, moving towards him gracefully on padded feet.

'No wonder she wanted the wisest,' he said wearily. He looked around in the growing light and saw hieroglyphs on the walls. People hunting, fishing, cutting crops. A simple life, he thought. I could have tried that out.

She walked up to him and sat down. Her beautiful cruel eyes met his. 'Who are you?' she asked.

'I am a vaman, a teacher, and my name is Gaam,' said Gaam.

'And I,' said the Sphinx, 'am the Sphinx.'

Maya and Queeen stopped running and darted to one side as the tunnel suddenly widened. The stone sphere thundered past them as they flattened themselves against the wall. They heard the sound of the sphere rolling down the slope, and suddenly there was silence. Probably a pit or something, thought Maya.

'Well, Queeen,' she said, 'she said we had to find our way to the burial chamber. I knew there would be a maze somewhere. But first, a little rest, I think.'

But Queeen snarled at her, and began to run fast, down the tunnel. 'Wait! Queeen! Not so fast!' called Maya, but Queeen was gone. Maya started to run. This is not good, she thought. What on earth is wrong with the dog now?

She soon caught up with Queeen. The sleek wolfhound was snarling, crouching at the end of the tunnel, where it emerged as a hole in an endless wall that must have taken thousands of years to make. Probably not the work of the living, thought Maya with a shudder. She ran to the edge and looked down, and couldn't see the floor. She suddenly remembered that she'd not heard the sound of the sphere hitting the bottom. If there was a bottom.

She made her fireball brighter, and saw, ahead of her, a stairway, apparently suspended in mid-air, leading down into the chasm. The light was not bright enough to see where it ended, but there was nowhere else to go—she couldn't see anything except empty space ahead, below or on either side. There was a five-foot gap between the edge of the tunnel and the beginning of the stair, probably made by the sphere when it hurtled downwards.

She turned and looked at Queeen, who was bristling all over, and growling continuously. 'What's wrong, Queeen?' asked Maya. She held out a hand, meaning to pat Queeen's head, and snatched it back as Queeen snapped at it.

Queeen rushed back, upwards, into the tunnel. Maya had had enough. She hurled her fireball, and it flew over Queeen's head and blocked the tunnel, creating a wall of fire just ahead of Queeen. Queeen howled in anger and then turned. She looked a little different—her eyes were blazing and her fangs were bared. From her throat emerged a low, warning growl.

'We're going to have a little girl-to-girl chat now,' said Maya, advancing.

Then she stopped in amazement, and stared.

Asvin gripped his sword hilt tightly.

'Come on, then,' he said.

The undead warrior charged. He was practically a skeleton, though some dead flesh still clung to a few of his joints. There was a pinpoint of light in each gaping eye socket, and his bony fingers clutched an ancient sword and a shield. His fleshless mouth grinned horribly at Asvin as their swords met.

The skeletal warrior was strong and fast, but Asvin's sword was the sharpest in the world. Asvin ducked, whirled and struck at the shoulder. His sword cut through bone, and hacked the warrior's shield-arm off. The round shield fell with a clatter, but the warrior continued to fight as if nothing had happened. But a few seconds later, Asvin cut his head off. The skull bounced on the floor a few times, and lay still.

'Was that it?' called Asvin.

Then he looked at the line of skeletons standing silently in front of him, and realized that it wasn't.

The next undead warrior charged.

'If you answer my riddle correctly,' said the Sphinx, 'I will let you live. If not . . .'

'You won't,' finished Gaam. 'I understand. I've read about Sphinxes.'

'There is only one Sphinx,' said the Sphinx, 'and that is me.'

Gaam opened his mouth to argue, but shut it with a snap. 'Well, what is the riddle?' he asked instead.

The Sphinx looked at him regally. 'Are you in a hurry?' she asked.

'Yes, actually,' said Gaam.

'It's been a long time since I played this Game. Anyway, here is the riddle, mortal. Answer it, or die.' She cleared her throat. 'What walks on four legs in the morning, two . . .'

'Man,' said Gaam.

'What?' said the Sphinx incredulously.

'Man,' repeated Gaam. 'The answer is Man. Can I go now?'

'How did you know?' asked the Sphinx suspiciously. 'Did Erkila tell you?'

'No,' said Gaam. 'I've heard it before, actually. Now can I go?'

'No.'

'*No?*'

Something was very wrong with Queeen.

She stopped snarling and lay down. She started to whimper, as if she was in immense pain.

Some kind of spirit's got into her, thought Maya, some sneaky little undead spirit. She cast a healing spell on Queeen, but the wolfhound continued to writhe on the floor, howling loudly and mournfully.

As Maya watched, horrified, Queeen's fur began to grow shorter. Her head began to change shape and her claws began to melt, with horrible screeching noises. Her muzzle grew inwards, her tail began to sink into her back. She thrashed around in agony, and then suddenly her back was lengthening, and so were her legs. Long hair began to sprout out of her scalp, and her fangs shortened and flattened. Her tongue disappeared into her mouth and cherry-red lips sprouted and grew.

Gods protect her, thought Maya, she's turning into a human.

And as the fur all over Queeen's body disappeared, revealing fair, soft skin, and her long golden hair framed her perfect face like a halo, and her beautiful, lithe, naked body lay motionless on the stone floor of the narrow passage, Maya thought, she looks like a Skuan goddess.

Then it hit her. And she laughed aloud.

'No wonder Gaam didn't want you to come!' she said. 'You were Asvin's forest maiden, Queeen!'

Queeen looked at her beseechingly.

'I'm not angry at all, so there's no need to look at me like that,' said Maya, grinning. 'But do tell me what was going on.'

Queeen said many things, but they were all in Skuan, and Maya couldn't speak Skuan. 'But you do understand Koli, right?' she asked Queeen, who nodded.

'Well, we'd better get on with finding the burial chamber, then, if you can't talk to me,' said Maya briskly. 'Can you solve mazes in human form?'

Queeen shook her head mournfully.

'Of course you can't,' said Maya. 'I do hope we get through this. Because Gaam has a lot of explaining to do. It's all right, you needn't look so scared, Queeen. Come along now. And stay behind me until you find some clothes. You make me feel fat.'

They jumped across the gap on to the staircase, and began to climb down.

Fifteen skulls lay on the floor of the corridor, at the feet of the statue. Asvin leaned on his sword and sighed.

The first five had come one at a time. Then they had attacked in twos.

'I don't know if I can keep going much longer,' he muttered. His arm was wounded, and his side was bleeding freely. There was a gash on his forehead as well, and a slow trickle of blood was clouding up the helmet.

Three skeletal warriors marched forward this time.

'Well, might as well go down fighting,' said Asvin wearily. Then something moved near his foot. 'What is it, Fluffy? You know, I'm glad you're here. Well, at least I won't have to die alone.'

The undead soldiers began to run towards him.

I promised myself I wouldn't help you again unless you asked me to, thought Steel-Bunz. And you don't deserve my help, after leaving me behind so many times. But if I don't save you now, you'll probably die. So I suppose I have to. I wish I could tell you I'm doing this not because I think you're this great hero, but because I'm a Red Phoenix Guard, and for the Red Phoenix, Duty comes first.

'Fluffy! No!' cried Asvin as Steel-Bunz shot forward. He bit the skeleton in the middle hard, under the knee-cap, dislocating the bone completely.

The skeleton tried to hop forward on one foot, but lost its balance. Its sword flailed wildly in the air, and it crashed to the ground, tripping up the other two. For a while the three undead warriors crashed around in a wild tangle of bones. Then Steel-Bunz sank his teeth into his victim's neck vertebrae and one skeleton stopped thrashing around.

Asvin leapt forward and with two well-placed strokes removed the heads of the other two.

'That was brilliant, Fluffy!' he cried. 'Just keep tangling them up like that and we'll finish them off in no time!'

Steel-Bunz gave him a withering look. Really, he thought. Is that what you'll do. Inspired.

Three more skeletons stepped up.

Just follow my lead, boy, thought Steel-Bunz, and leapt forward. Asvin, his eyes shining with sudden hope, brandished his sword and yelled, 'For the Sun!' and charged.

Oh, *please*, thought Steel-Bunz as he streaked towards the undead soldiers.

'Well, say *something*,' said Gaam. The Sphinx had been looking at him ferociously for some time.

'I will ask you a riddle, mortal,' said the Sphinx, finally. 'If you can answer it, you live.'

'But I already answered your riddle!'

'Well, you'll have to answer another one!'

'That's not fair!'

'Besides,' said the Sphinx, 'you cheated.'

'I did not!'

'You did.'

'This is ridiculous!' said Gaam, throwing his arms upward in despair. 'Look, just ask me another riddle, then.'

The Sphinx was silent.

'Do you mean . . .' said Gaam after some time, 'that you don't know any other riddles?'

'Silence, mortal!'

'Right.'

Maya's fireball was trying its best, but the darkness of the Great Pyramid had been there for thousands of years and no upstart fireball was going to chase it away. In the dim blue light, Maya could see only the staircase—even the wall behind them had faded away. She had lost all sense of time and space—it seemed as if they had been descending for hours. Of course, time doesn't run normally here, she thought. Everything in this Pyramid thinks in terms of centuries.

They reached the bottom of the staircase. It was a circular platform, apparently suspended in mid-air. There were two more floating staircases attached to it, one to the left and leading up, and one to the right, leading down.

Maya walked to the stairway leading down and looked down. She could see only stairs in mid-air, fading into darkness. She looked harder—it seemed as if there was a platform below, just like the one she was standing on, with more stairs leading in different directions.

Well, it's a maze all right, she thought. And apart from the fact that it's a multi-level three-dimensional stair-maze floating in the air in some strange magical dimension, and it's completely dark, and my maze-solver is a naked woman I've known as a dog for months, everything is going according to plan.

She suddenly realized that the thumping noise she had been hearing for some time was not, as she had supposed, the sound of her own heart but the sound of heavy footsteps on stairs.

Then Queeen screamed.

'What,' said the Sphinx, 'has sixty-seven legs, forty-two heads and two tails?'

'Have you ever asked anyone this riddle before?' asked Gaam.

'As a matter of fact, I have.'

'And were all the people you asked this riddle to people who had answered the first riddle correctly?'

'Yes, they were. Stop playing for time.'

'Just one more question—has anyone managed to answer this question?'

'No,' said the Sphinx smugly.

'Well, the answer to your riddle is very simple. What has sixty-seven legs, forty-two heads and two tails? Nothing. It's just a trick question you've made up to kill people who knew the answer to your riddle. Because you don't know any other riddles, do you?'

The Sphinx was silent.

'Well? Was my answer correct or not?'

'It was,' said the Sphinx sullenly.

'Let me go, then.'

'You're making me look bad. If you pass me, Erkila will never send me the good ones again.'

'I'm sorry, but I had no choice. Now please let me go.'

The Sphinx looked at him for a while, and made up her mind.

'No,' she said.

'Get off her!' shouted Maya.

Queeen was struggling wildly in the grip of a man. Well, he would have been a man if he hadn't been very dead. He was an interesting shade of purple-green, and bits were falling off him as Queeen squirmed in his grasp. He obviously had no intention of letting her go, so Maya hurled a fireball at him. The thing let go of Queeen, and danced around the platform, burning in the angry red flame. He fell off the edge and hurtled downwards, finally landing with a *thump* on a platform far below. The burning undead being lit up the maze of stairs much brighter than Maya's fireball. In the red glow from below, Maya saw that they were in the middle of a cobweb of floating staircases, straight and spiral, connected by platforms or ending in mid-air. It was a mind-boggling, dizzying spectacle—a mesh of stone that would make ordinary people stumble and fall off the platform at the very sight of it.

But Maya and Queeen stayed on their feet, because they had lived in Kol for years, and no three-dimensional maze could be as terrifying as Kol traffic. The only difference was that if the spectacle of Kol overwhelmed you, you could sit on the footpath for a while, but here you would go hurtling to your death in the yawning chasm or break your neck on a staircase.

Another dead man leapt off a staircase above them, groaning, and met another fireball. He slumped down and lay burning and screaming on the stairway they had just descended, lighting up the network of stairs above them. In the light they saw two more undead stomping slowly down the stairs to the left. The light draws them, thought Maya.

'Stay back!' she yelled, advancing, twin fireballs appearing on her hands.

One of the undead held his palm out in a gesture of parley and stepped forward. 'Do not throw that fire, child!' he groaned, stepping forward. 'We mean you no harm.'

He was now somewhere between green and grey, but he had once been handsome. His hair had fallen off in clumps, and one of his eyeballs was dangling from its socket near his rugged jaw. He wore rusted Psomedean armour.

'It has been a long time since I saw a woman,' he wheezed, 'and a pretty one at that.'

'Not one more step,' said Maya quietly. The fireballs hissed, wanting to be released.

'Not all of us speak the language, dear, so do not kill me,' said the newcomer. 'For I can help you.' But his other eye kept stealing glances at Queeen, and his grey tongue started dribbling green slime on the platform. 'I am Thoseus, hero of Psomedea. Treat me well, for soon you will join our ranks, and it would serve you well to have me as a friend.'

'I've heard of you!' said Maya. 'You went out in search of a minotaur centuries ago, and were never seen again! How did you end up here?'

'Wrong maze,' said Thoseus. 'And I lost the thread with which I hoped to solve it. If you enter the Maze of the Great Pyramid, you can only escape if you find the Pharaoh's burial chamber, and if you fail, you do not leave—you cannot see in this accursed darkness, and now you are doomed to stay here forever. When your body dies, the spirits will take over, and you will guard the maze with us. Your pretty blue light will not shine forever, child. Soon weariness will take over, and we can wait forever for you to get tired. One day, you will sit down. Then one of us will take you, child, and you will die, and dying you will join us and walk this maze for all eternity. But I could make things so much easier for you.'

'How many of you are there?' asked Maya, seeing more dead men lurching slowly along the stairs that zigzagged around the platform.

'None have counted our ranks, but there are enough,' said Thoseus, taking a step forward. 'What is your name?'

'Stay back,' hissed Maya.

'Do not resist me, child,' said Thoseus, his eye gleaming. 'Let me bring you into the shadow-world. For I retain my sanity even here, as I entered with noble intentions. Others have not been so lucky. There are many who came here looking for the Pharaoh's treasure and could not get out. Gold-lust drove them mad. If they take you, you will suffer forever!' He jerked his head at the figure behind him and one of his ears fell off. 'The one behind me is not so friendly, child. If he takes you, you will regret it, believe me.' His eyeball fell off and bounced off the platform. 'Much, much better to let me do it, child. Then you can sleep in peace before you walk with us.'

'Stay back. And what do you mean, take me?'

'One kiss,' said Thoseus, 'and I will tell you.' He lurched forward again, and grabbed Queeen. 'Perhaps your friend is more reasonable.'

'Men,' sighed Maya. She released the fireballs, and watched Thoseus burn as he fell far below.

The next undead stepped on to the platform.

'Good form, I say!' he rumbled cheerfully. 'Never liked that old blighter. Rambling on about missing bulls—all Psomedean to me, of course.'

'You *are* mad,' said Maya. 'Stay back, please.'

'Oh come on, love, play fair! Let's not have any of this fire business, what? Oh, I forgot to introduce myself.'

'No need. You're from Ventelot.'

'Oh, bally good guess, love! But I'm more than that— I'm a Level Two Paladin, and I've got more than half my Hit Points left!'

'What on earth are you saying? Stay back!'

'I'm asking you not to start a Deathmatch, love, because I don't want to eat you. I mean, I know I'm dead, but I'm frightfully hungry, to tell the truth. Let's team up! I'm due for a level rise any day now. And cooperative games are so much more fun.'

'Do you understand what he's saying?' Maya asked Queeen. Queeen shook her head. Maya shrugged her shoulders and sent the Level Two Paladin flying backwards in flames.

'This maze opens to the burial chamber, somewhere,' she

said. 'But that horrible thing was right—we cannot search forever in the darkness. We need a plan.' She looked down and saw that the undead she had burned were still glowing, and a good portion of the maze was lit up. 'Of course, if we removed the darkness . . . You know, if we could just manage to see the whole maze, we could actually solve it, find the right route and walk through, instead of climbing thousands of stairs hunting pointlessly. In that sense, this maze is easier than walking through hedges and tunnels—all we have to do is light it up, and then we can work out how to escape. But how do we light it up? We could keep burning these corpses, I suppose, but how do we get past burning undead on the staircases?'

She thought for a while. Then she looked at Queeen. 'I know it's rude,' she said, 'but you're related to werewolves in some way, aren't you?'

Queeen shuddered, but nodded. Maya smiled.

'Which is why fire doesn't affect you much, right? The first thing was pawing you all over when I blasted him, and you weren't even hurt.'

Queeen nodded again.

'Well, there's our answer!' said Maya.

Queeen stared at her blankly.

'I burn them, you kick them off or something, and then we get out,' said Maya, practically skipping around on the platform in excitement, 'But this maze is rather large, so we need a direction to start working in—we need to know where the tomb is. And if you, my friend, are wondering where the tomb is, why, I have an answer for that as well. The best mazes have their starts and ends marked, yes?'

She conjured up a Thrillseeker and threw it up into the air. It flew towards the right and disappeared.

'Correct me if I'm wrong, but the Scorpion Man is probably the most magical thing in this Pyramid, and if my Thrillseeker is to be believed, we will find him if we walk *that* way. And now for some light.'

She threw fireballs around randomly. Some disappeared into the darkness and fizzled out, but a large number caught random undead lurching around on platforms and staircases. Soon the entire maze to their right was alight, and burning corpses stumbled up and down the staircases all around them. And whenever other undead crossed the burning ones, they would burst into flames as well. Spellbinder fire burned almost anything.

'They say I'm the most brilliant young spellbinder in Kol,' said Maya, whipping out a chalk and sitting on the platform with a satisfied grin. 'You know, Queeen, sometimes I think they're right.'

She looked around, ignoring the undead falling in flames everywhere, and began to draw.

'Well, ask me something else, then,' said Gaam.

'I don't have to,' snarled the Sphinx. 'I could just kill you here, and no one would ever know.'

'What would no one ever know?' asked Erkila. She trotted up to them, cat-shaped, and sat. 'Why are you taking so long?'

'I haven't asked him the riddle, Erkila,' said the Sphinx, bowing.

'Well, go ahead.'

'Just ask me anything you can think of,' said Gaam kindly.

The Sphinx leaned forward. 'What have I got in my pockets?' she asked, an insane glare in her eyes.

'That's not a riddle, that's a question!' said Gaam indignantly.

'Well, you said she could ask you anything,' said Erkila smoothly. 'So you have to answer her. But I admit it's a little strange. Where did you get this riddle?' she asked the Sphinx.

'I don't remember. Possibly from someone I ate,' murmured the Sphinx. 'Well, mortal?'

'Are you sure you want me to answer your riddle?' asked Gaam.

'Of course.'

'And you will let me go if I answer correctly?'

The Sphinx shot a look at Erkila, watching them calmly. 'Yes,' she said.

'Very well. When I saw you first, I noticed that like all Sphinxes, you are half woman and half lioness. Also, like all Sphinxes, you do not wear clothes. Since you do not wear clothes, you have no pockets. Therefore, you cannot possibly have anything in your pockets.' He bowed. 'A somewhat impulsive question, if I may say so.'

'There's no need to gloat,' grumbled the Sphinx. She padded off, leaving Gaam with Erkila.

'You pass the test. I will take you to the burial chamber,' said Erkila, turning into a vulture and seizing Gaam by the shoulders. 'You may await the rest there.'

Forty-six skulls lay on the floor of the corridor. Asvin trampled over them, looking desperately for Steel-Bunz.

'Fluffy!' he yelled. 'Fluffy, please, come out!' But he called in vain. Tears sprang to his eyes.

Together they had vanquished five columns of the undead soldiers, and then the skeletons had started coming in fours. There were twenty left, five columns of four each.

Asvin and Steel-Bunz had fended off the first three attacks, but in the last charge, Steel-Bunz had disappeared underneath the pile of bones that had accumulated during the fight. A huge skeleton had crashed down over him, sword in hand.

He had not come out.

The last four skeletons were the tallest of them all. They advanced on Asvin, who could barely stand up. But he waved his sword defiantly at them, ignoring his wounds.

'I will avenge you, sweet Fluffy,' he said through his tears. 'Your death will not be in vain.'

He swayed where he stood and almost fell, but then gathered himself up and charged.

The burial chamber of the First Pharaoh was the most magnificent room Gaam had ever seen. The Pharaoh's sarcophagus lay in the centre, the solid gold death-mask shining in the light that burned in the eyes of the statues of the gods. There were beautiful paintings and carvings on the walls, showing the Pharaoh giving gifts to the gods, playing *senet* and conquering other lands. The ceiling showed the sky, and the birth and death of the sun. The air shaft, through which the Pharaoh's soul was supposed to rise to meet the gods, was inlaid with gold.

By the tomb of the Pharaoh stood richly decorated canopic jars, where the internal organs of the ruler were preserved, precious jewel-studded magical amulets and *shabti* figures representing the workers who had built the Pyramid. In one corner stood a golden boat, which would carry the Pharaoh to the land of the dead, where the gods would weigh his heart against the Feather of Truth.

Gaam noted the deeply engraved hieroglyphs that recorded the Pharaoh's name. Speaking the name aloud would, according to the legend, bring him back to life. Gaam wondered if one day the Scorpion Man would truly stop his prayers, come to the chamber and wake the Pharaoh up.

A trapdoor set in the floor opened suddenly and Maya and Queeen walked up into the burial chamber. Queeen ran over to Gaam and stood by him, head bent, crying silently. Maya followed her in, walked up to Gaam and folded her arms.

'Explain,' she said.

'In a minute,' said Gaam. He gave Queeen a small vial, the contents of which she drank. Gaam patted her on the head. 'It's all right, Queeen, I don't blame you,' he said gently. 'There was nothing you could do.'

They watched in silence as Queeen fell to the floor and started writhing again. Her shape changed, fur sprouted, her tail reappeared and soon she was a dog again. She ran up to Maya, barked and licked her hand.

'You obviously knew all along. Now tell me everything,' said Maya to Gaam.

'Queeen is a werewoman.'

'What?'

'A werewoman. You know werewolves are humans who turn into wolves when they see the moon. With Queeen it's the other way around. She's a wolf, but when there's no moon, she turns into a woman.'

'Where did you find her?'

'I saved her from a pack of hunting wolves in Skuanmark. She has been my companion ever since.'

'Your companion?' Maya raised her eyebrows.

'I see Queeen as a wolf who is sometimes ill. Nothing more,' snapped Gaam.

'But isn't it a problem? Hasn't something like this happened before?'

'No. The potion I gave her always turns her back into a wolf. We've never had a problem—she would just stay indoors with me on moonless nights, and drink the potion whenever she felt the change coming. Unfortunately, when we were in the Bleakwood, Asvin saw her. It was partly her fault— she went far away to change, as I had trained her to do, but she was singing, and Asvin heard her.'

'Does she always sing? Don't people hear that?'

'No. The poor girl was singing because she has been in love with Asvin since the day we left Kol.'

'Of course.'

'I was afraid you would find out,' said Gaam. 'Fortunately, neither of you followed her tracks in the woods—and Asvin never noticed how he would always meet me and Queeen after he saw the girl. I will make sure Queeen never runs wild again—she always listened to me in the past, but after she saw that Asvin was obviously enamoured of her as well, she broke out of the hut in Bolvudis, twice, so that he could hear her singing in the woods. But he never made the connection, and I thought I was safe. When I saw you had brought her to the cave, I knew it would all go wrong. Maya, please don't tell Asvin about this—it would break Queeen's heart.'

'Your secret is safe with me, Queeen,' said Maya solemnly to the wolfhound, and she wagged her tail happily.

There was one skeletal warrior left, and he was the worst of the lot. He had already injured Asvin several times. Asvin's feet were dragging, his sword-arm was racked with pain and he could hardly see through the haze of blood.

The last warrior threw him down to the ground, and raised his sword to deliver the killing blow.

Here it ends, thought Asvin, and heard a sickening crash

as bone hit bone. Then everything turned black, and he saw no more.

When he opened his eyes and sat up Erkila was perched on a statue, watching him gravely with her black eyes. She has won, he thought. I must be undead. I will have to spend the rest of time losing weight and standing on guard in this corridor. He looked around, and saw that the last skeletal warrior was lying on the floor. I suppose I must congratulate him, thought Asvin, if we are going to be brothers in arms. Well, brothers in bones, anyway.

He suddenly noticed that one of the skeleton's legs was missing.

And its neck was bent oddly, as if someone or something had snapped it.

He was aware of a moist nose pressing into his hands.

'Fluffy!' he cried as joy and realization flooded through him. 'You saved me!'

At least you have the grace to admit it. There's hope for you yet, lad, thought Steel-Bunz.

'You know,' said Asvin, 'the name Fluffy doesn't suit you. Together we have slain fifty undead soldiers. Fluffy and Asvin? It doesn't sound right. I will have to think of another name for you.' He knitted his brows and thought.

That's it, thought Steel-Bunz. He names me something like Mr Snuggles, and I break his neck.

(Far away, somewhere in the gambling dens of the heavens, Petah-Petyi, the Goddess of Chance, sat alone at a table, because no one would play with her—she always won. She held two million-sided dice in her hands, and threw them on the table.

The dice rolled for an eternity, then finally settled. She

looked at them. 'Double One,' she murmured. 'That almost never happens.')

'I think,' said Asvin, 'that I will rename you Steel-Bunz.'

It was the happiest moment of Steel-Bunz's life.

Moments later, Erkila dropped Asvin and Steel-Bunz in the Pharaoh's burial chamber, and Maya began to cast healing spells on Asvin.

'You are mightier that I thought,' said Erkila in her low, melodious cat-voice. 'You have passed the tests of the Great Pyramid, and the treasures of the Pharaoh are now yours. Take as much as you want—there is enough there to make your wildest dreams come true.'

'Why do you still try to trick us, spirit?' asked Gaam angrily. 'We know as well as you do that a potent curse lies on that gold, and the Scorpion Man himself will hunt down all those who touch it. Tell us no more lies, please—we are weary, and we would like to see the Scorpion Man.'

'It was a last test, my child,' said Erkila. 'Your pardon! I will not seek to deceive you again. Follow me to the vestibule, and you may speak to the Scorpion.'

She walked out of the burial chamber gracefully, her white paws not even stirring the fine layer of dust. They followed her down a narrow, dark tunnel to the chamber of the Scorpion Man.

'These mortals seek an audience, Master,' said Erkila in a hushed voice as they stood outside the chamber.

'There is no moon tonight, and the world is free of evil dreams,' said a voice inside the room that sounded like a thousand snakes hissing together. 'Who are these mortals, Erkila? Why do they not sleep? Bring them in.'

After seeing the magnificence of the Pharaoh's tomb,

they had expected the Scorpion Man's chamber to be richly decorated. But it was completely bare, and the only thing in it was the Scorpion Man himself. He filled the room, towering over them, looking down at them with a mixture of sorrow and weariness in his eyes.

From the waist down, he was a scorpion, black, translucent and terrible. His curved, venomous tail was the deadliest weapon they had ever seen, or would ever see. Above the waist, he was human-shaped. His arms, neck and head were grey, and his torso was shining silver. His body was taut and rippling with muscles, his hair was steel-grey, and his eyes, like Erkila's, were infinite pools of darkness. But where Erkila's eyes were sinister and forbidding, his were wise and sad. His arms ended in huge, curving pincers, and there were six legs under the scorpion part of his body.

'Make your wish, and if I can, I will grant it,' he said as Asvin entered, head bowed, palms clasped together.

'Gracious one,' said Asvin, 'I wish to save the world from a terrible rakshas that threatens it. I have come here tonight to beg you for the gift of your armour. With it, I think I have a chance to play a part in the vanquishing of the forces of evil, which grow stronger every day in this diseased world.'

'A smooth tongue and strong arms will get you far, my son,' said the Scorpion Man, bending forward and looking deep into Asvin's eyes. 'I am bound by my sacred oath to give you what you crave, and to ask you no questions. Yet I can see inside your heart, and it is pure. That is a good omen. But do not use my armour for evil purposes, son—this I beg of you.'

'I will not, I swear it,' said Asvin reverently.

'Bare yourself above the waist, hold out your hands, and close your eyes,' said the Scorpion Man. Asvin did.

The Scorpion Man cupped his pincers together and held them a little distance above Asvin's hands, as if he was about to pour water from his hands to Asvin's.

Maya and Gaam watched as a thin silver stream flowed down from the Scorpion Man's pincers to Asvin's hands. From Asvin's hands the silver liquid flowed to his waist, and the Scorpion Man's shoulders turned the same grey as his arms. They realized suddenly that the silver liquid was the armour, and it was slowly passing in a thin stream to Asvin. It was collecting near his waist and rising upwards, covering his skin and moulding itself perfectly to his body. When the armour was wholly poured, the Scorpion Man's chest was completely grey and Asvin looked as if his torso was covered with mercury.

'Of course, the rest of your body is still vulnerable,' said the Scorpion Man, 'so this armour does not make you invincible, son. But know this—no weapon, no curse, no power of nature can pass through the material of this armour. You can never take it off, as it is now a part of your very skin, but you can conceal it with clothes. When you die, it will vanish, and return to me.'

'Thank you for this invaluable gift,' breathed Asvin. 'I promise you I will use it well.'

'That is as it should be,' said the Scorpion Man. 'Now leave, children, for I must return to my meditation. Show them out, Erkila.'

'Yes, Master,' said Erkila. 'Follow me, little ones.'

She led them out of the Scorpion Man's chamber and towards her own.

14

'**M**y king wants to know why we are sitting here in silence. He orders you to start the council,' said Tungz, slightly nervous as his eyes met Bali's.

In the chamber behind the idol in the temple outside Vanarpuri, the second meeting of the Brotherhood of Renewal had not exactly got off to a flying start. Bali, Angda, Leer, Tungz, Kirin and Spikes were sitting at the great table. Conversation was not flourishing.

'The rest are coming,' growled Bali. 'Tell him to shut up and wait.'

Tungz spoke to Leer in hushed tones, and Kirin, understanding a few of the words, smiled. Tungz was obviously more of an interpreter than a translator.

'My king graciously accedes to your request, but warns you that time is pressing, and his patience is drawing thin,' said Tungz.

Angda put a warning hand on Bali's arm, but it was unnecessary; Bali smiled, and said, 'I'm touched.'

'I hear you met my brother, Karisman,' he said, turning towards Kirin. 'Let me tell you something about him.'

But Kirin never heard what Bali had to say about Djongli, because just then Bjorkun entered the chamber.

'Omar is here,' he said in a low voice.

Omar, wearing a cloak and hood over his white robes, swept past him into the room, pearly teeth glinting in a brief smile as he sat down. 'The roads were watched,' he said. 'There are spies in your jungle as well, Bali. I hope your soldiers are doing something about it.'

He drummed his fingers on the table. 'Where's the samurai?' he asked.

'Dead,' snapped Bali.

'Indeed. But no doubt the mighty Bali has already thought of a hundred solutions to this trifling problem. Are we all here? Let us begin.'

'No, we're not all here,' said Bali.

Heavy feet stomped down the stairs. Bali threw a questioning look at Bjorkun. Bjorkun nodded.

A rakshas entered the chamber. His fiery red eyes swept the room and settled on Bali.

'I used to think monkeys were only good for eating. Now the king of the monkeys is bringing back my cousin!' he shouted. He laughed, a deep belly laugh that made them all flinch.

'The Brotherhood of Renewal?' he roared. 'That's good, that's very good. Danh-Gem would have laughed his head off.'

'We're glad you could come, mighty Aciram,' said Bali. 'Please take a seat. There is much to discuss.'

'Now, which one of you do I eat?' yelled the rakshas,

ignoring him. 'It was a long walk, and my belly is empty!'

He looked around at their stunned faces for a few seconds, as if weighing them in his mind.

Then he drew his red lolling tongue back into his mouth and smiled, his fangs shining horribly.

'Obviously one of my better entrances,' he said quietly. He turned himself into a man, sat down and looked around the table, grinning as relieved expressions flooded their faces. 'Don't I get a nice white hood?' he asked Bali.

'Aciram? *The* Aciram?' asked Omar.

'That's me,' said Aciram. 'Don't bother telling me who you are, westerner. I won't remember.'

'There is one in this room who you will rejoice to see,' said Omar smoothly. Kirin's heart sank. He knew what was coming. 'We have a Karisman among us!'

'What's that?' enquired Aciram.

'You know, a Karisman,' said Omar. 'The human sorcerers who were Danh-Gem's closest advisers?'

'Never heard of them,' said Aciram irritably. 'As far as I know, I was Danh-Gem's closest adviser. Who is this Karisman?'

Everyone's eyes turned to Kirin. Bali and Bjorkun looked stunned. 'What is this, Kirin?' asked Bali.

'No one knew about us except Danh-Gem himself,' he said, trying to keep the panic out of his voice.

'Rubbish!' roared Aciram. 'We have an imposter in our midst!'

Bali and Omar stood up and drew their swords. Kirin jumped backwards and stood against the wall. His hood fell off and the fear on his face was clear to all of them.

'I think, Kirin,' said Omar, 'that you owe us a little explanation.'

'Why would Danh-Gem tell other rakshases about us?' said Kirin. 'They would obviously disappear when the magic levels fell. That's why he chose humans in the first place. And we were dedicated to bringing him back—nothing to do with the War at all. Besides, this was a secret best kept very secret—there was always the risk of betrayal. Not that I'm implying the great Aciram was untrustworthy.' He shot a look at Aciram, and noticed with satisfaction that the rakshas was looking shocked.

'Besides,' continued Kirin, 'if I was working for Kol, I would have killed Spikes long ago—you would never have found his claw. I would have not translated the book. I would not have raised the chariot.'

'Gaining Bali's trust,' snapped Omar. 'Looking to seek out and betray the whole Brotherhood.'

'Oh please,' said Kirin, getting into his stride. 'I could have told the world about the Brotherhood long ago. I am too deep in your counsel, Bali. You must know I am not a spy. Besides,' he said, putting a hand in his pocket, 'when you left me alone, free to go wherever I wanted to, when I could have gone straight to Kol and told the Civilian everything about you, would I have risked my life in Avranti to get *this*?'

He took the Tear of the Sky out of his pocket and held it up in the firelight. They gasped in awe as the magnificent gem sparkled like living flame.

'Are you satisfied, Aciram?

'Yes,' said the rakshas, never taking his eyes off Kirin. 'I am very satisfied.'

Kirin looked at him. The rakshas actually winked at him.

'So Danh-Gem kept secrets even from me!' he said. 'A

424

humbling thought, but an amusing one. I beg your pardon, Karisman. Your enemies are my enemies.'

He smiled again.

Omar looked disappointed. He turned towards Bali. 'I am still not happy with this,' he said. 'My heart tells me the Karisman is concealing something from us. I agree he has served us well, and when Danh-Gem rises he will surely be rewarded richly, but I propose we remove him from the Brotherhood.'

'Why are you so eager to remove him?' asked Aciram. 'Is it because he has done all he can do for you, and you do not need him any more? I do not think you and I will be friends, westerner.'

'The Karisman stays in the Brotherhood,' said Bali with finality. 'My apologies, Kirin.'

'Whatever you say, Bali,' said Omar softly.

'In any case, Omar, you do need me,' said Kirin. 'Unless you want to go and steal the Gauntlet of Tatsu yourself.'

'We seem to have forgotten why this council was called,' said Bali. 'Five objects are required. The ronin has failed. But do we have the other things?'

'My king has the Iron Crown,' said Tungz. Leer took the asur crown out and put it on the table.

'And I,' said Omar, 'have the jinn-lamp.'

He put it on the table. Kirin placed the Tear of the Sky beside it.

'You have done well, mortals,' said Aciram. 'The rakshases, for their part, are finally ready to unite. But there is only one banner that will unite us, and that is Danh-Gem's. When he rises, we are one.'

'Accursed Ventelot is not with us,' snapped Bjorkun. 'The Civilian of Kol has been at work. And our journey to the

North was not a success, but we achieved some things. The ice-giants and the werewolves will not venture from their lands. But they will not fight against us. The werewolves at least would have joined us if we had reached earlier. But the Silver Phalanx had been there before us. We spoke to the werewolf chieftain, and he said he would hunt with us if Danh-Gem rose again.'

'If Danh-Gem rises,' snarled Bjorkun, 'half the world will stand by us. But until then, we must soldier on against the forces of evil.'

'If Danh-Gem rises,' repeated Omar in his most gentle voice. 'And when will Danh-Gem rise? Does our friend the Karisman know?' But his gaze was fixed on Bali.

Don't look at me, Bali, don't look at me, please, thought Kirin. But it was too late. Bali had already sent a conspiratorial glance in his direction. Under the hood, Omar's thin lips curved into a smile.

'We will come to that,' said Bjorkun gruffly. He shook his head impatiently, his long mane of yellow hair swishing in the firelight. 'There is one matter I want to clear up first, a matter we touched upon last time—the issue of leadership. Bali and I discussed this at length during our journey to the North. We decided that the Brotherhood of Renewal should have no leader—we should work side by side, as equals. I want everyone to accept this.'

'I admit I find that a little difficult to digest,' said Omar. 'I am used to being in command. But I will accept it. For the good of the Brotherhood.'

Aciram, Kirin and Spikes nodded their assent. Leer mumbled something.

'My king says this is ridiculous,' said Tungz. 'It is obvious that he and no other should lead this Brotherhood, as the asurs are not only the most faithful of Danh-Gem's servants but also the most numerous, and hence the most powerful. My king, as the most powerful leader here, assumes his natural right to the leadership of this Brotherhood.'

Bali smiled. 'You were right about them, Bjorkun,' he said. He leaned forward, his shadow covering the asurs. 'Tell me then, Powerful One,' he said, 'why is it that the asurs of Kol, with their cunning brains and full pockets, do not come to our aid? For of all asurs they are the most useful.'

'My king laughs disdainfully,' said Tungz after a little frenzied muttering. 'The rats of Kol are merchants and thieves. We do not need them. They will tarnish the glory of the asur nation.'

'Of course,' said Bjorkun, fingering his axe. 'But tell me, do the danavs follow Leer, or the Iron Crown? For I have heard that they will follow even a human if the crown is on his head.'

'Lies and blasphemies,' hissed Tungz, without bothering to consult Leer. 'It is true that the Iron Crown is the supreme symbol of royalty and one does not have to be a danav to wear it, but we will never follow a human.'

'But you might follow a Koli asur, yes?'

'It could never be,' replied Tungz. 'The Koli asur would have to challenge King Leer and wrest the crown from him. And King Leer is the strongest asur walking the earth. No snivelling Kol-maggot could defeat him in a fight.'

'But let us pretend,' said Bjorkun, standing up, 'that one did.'

He hurled his axe across the table at Leer. The axe cut into the middle of Leer's skull and carried him to the wall, where he hung like a butterfly stuck on a pin, his limbs thrashing uselessly.

'I quite enjoyed that. He was annoying me,' said Aciram, watching Leer's death throes. 'But did that serve any purpose?'

'You can get up,' Bali said to Tungz, who was grovelling on the floor. 'We're not going to kill you now.'

'What did you do that for?' asked Kirin.

'We need the support of the Koli asurs,' said Bali. 'And the Imokoi asurs will follow the Iron Crown. Under a Koli king, the asurs will finally be united.'

'And who is to be this new king, and what has he done to earn your favour?' asked Omar.

'He helped the Karisman solve the riddle that revealed what we had to do to raise Danh-Gem.' said Bali. 'Hooba!' he called. 'You can come in now.'

Hooba entered the chamber. 'You are now the king of asurs, and a member of the Brotherhood of Renewal,' Bjorkun told him. Hooba was quiet for a few seconds.

'Ell right,' he said, and grinned at Kirin.

'This is your prime minister, Tungz,' continued Bjorkun. 'He will help you in all matters concerning kingship, and tell your fellow asurs how you defeated Leer in a duel. Is that not so, Tungz?'

Tungz looked around the room for some time. 'Yes,' he said finally. 'I will serve you faithfully, King Hooba.'

'And Hooba speaks their language, too,' said Bali. 'It was a good idea, my friend.'

'That's settled, then,' said Bjorkun.

'Wait a moment,' said Omar. 'Did you say the asur found out about the five things we need to find?'

'With the Karisman,' said Bali, but the slip had been made. Bjorkun smiled grimly.

'I was under the impression that the Karisman knew everything about this,' drawled Omar. He looked at Bali. 'It seems, vanar-lord, that you and he are holding something back.'

'And do you blame me, human?' snarled Bali, finally losing his temper. 'We are surrounded by spies and traitors! Who can be trusted?'

'Who exactly are you accusing?' hissed Omar. 'What is your game, vanar?'

'Peace!' said Bjorkun, pounding on the table. 'I confess, Omar, that one day in the North, when Bali told me when Danh-Gem is supposed to rise, my initial reaction was anger, too. But he has a point. Could he have revealed it to you two months ago, when the Avrantic minister, Leer and the ronin were sitting here? And, for that matter, did you really expect him to trust you with this most crucial piece of information? He had just met you.'

'There are such things as private conversations, Bjorkun. And you did not tell me either,' snapped Omar.

'This is the first time I am meeting you since I learnt.'

'What are you all talking about? When is Danh-Gem going to rise?' thundered Aciram.

'Two weeks from now,' said Bali, 'full moon night of Dragonmonth.'

'Where?'

'The Circle of Darkness, in Imokoi.'

'And we have to get the Gauntlet of Tatsu from Xi'en to Imokoi in two weeks! That is impossible!' shouted Omar. It was the first time Kirin had seen him lose his composure.

'I think this running around to get things to lay down for Danh-Gem is quite ridiculous,' rumbled Aciram. 'I knew Danh-Gem. If he wanted to rise, he would rise on his own— he would not depend on anyone else.'

He always had an alternative plan, thought Kirin. We

can't let this go—I can't lose control. Not when I'm so close. 'There is no other way. That is why the Karismen were trained,' he said.

'So what do you propose to do? Do you actually think you can you get the Gauntlet to the Circle of Darkness in two weeks? That is madness!' roared Omar. His hood fell off, and his eyes were blazing. 'Do you have any idea how far away the monastery is? You think you can climb the Mountains of Harmony! Stealing from the fools in Avranti is one thing, the Wu Sen monks are quite another! Did not the samurai say it would be impossible for anyone else?' He sat down, fuming.

'Do you think you can do it, Karisman?' asked Bali quietly. 'You have not failed even once yet.'

Kirin smiled at him. 'I can do it,' he said evenly. 'I know I can. Spikes and I will leave tomorrow at dawn.'

'No,' said Omar. 'You cannot take the pashan with you, he is too valuable. And if you are killed, we will lose his claw as well. You can go get the Gauntlet, or die trying, but you will not take away one of the four objects we have. Otherwise,' he clutched the lamp to his chest, 'the lamp disappears too.'

'Omar is right, Karisman,' said Bjorkun. 'Besides, it will take us two weeks to travel to the Circle of Darkness. We must at least lay four things down and see if that brings Danh-Gem back. We cannot let Spikes go with you—by the time you return, it will be too late.'

'That's all right,' said Kirin, unable to think of any reason why Spikes should come with him—apart from the fact that he would feel very lost without Spikes.

'I could go with him,' said Aciram. 'I could storm the monastery and bring out the Gauntlet.'

'No, Aciram,' said Omar. 'You cannot defeat the Xi'en

monks with force. Their puzzles can never be broken—the more force you use, the more convoluted they become.'

'I will come with you, Karisman,' said Bali. 'The rest of the Brotherhood can take these four objects to Imokoi. My work here is done—Angda can represent the vanars in the journey to Imokoi.'

'We will use the path through the forest, and over the mountains to Imokoi,' said Angda, her eyes shining. 'The open roads are full of evil soldiers.'

'Yes. It is a good thing that we will be travelling underground, Karisman,' said Bali. 'All roads to Xi'en are being watched. Kol is evidently doing its own bit to protect the Gauntlet. I wonder what the accursed ronin said before dying! What if I had told you all about the Circle of Darkness, Omar? You would have reached there to be welcomed by the Silver Phalanx. The Silver Dagger himself would have helped you raise Danh-Gem, no doubt.'

'After this dazzling display of wit, do we have anything to discuss?' asked Omar.

'Not really. We will leave at noon, brothers, for the last lap of this long race. Get ready. It is beginning,' said Bjorkun. 'Our labours are going to bear fruit at last. This council is over. Let us get some rest.'

'Get some of our best soldiers to take you part of the way, Angda,' said Bali. 'At least up to the mountains of Imokoi. After that, you can travel by yourselves, unless the roads of Imokoi are no longer safe.'

'Nothing is safe any longer, but there are fewer spies in Imokoi than anywhere else, and they will not be ready for all of us together. In any case, we will have the crows flying ahead to warn us if danger approaches or lies in wait,' said Bjorkun. 'We will get there in time, if we stick together—

already there is too much discord in the Brotherhood. But time will sort that out.'

'And if time does not, Danh-Gem will,' smirked Aciram.

'This council is over,' repeated Bjorkun. 'The Brotherhood will not meet again in full strength until Danh-Gem walks the earth. I wish you and Kirin luck, Bali. If truth prevails, we will meet in Imokoi. It is dawn, let us get some rest before our journey.'

'I wish you luck, Karisman,' said Omar as he followed Bjorkun out of the chamber. 'Maybe when we meet again you will earn my trust.'

The asurs and the vanars left. Aciram rose and looked at Kirin. 'Is there anything you want to say in private to me?' he asked. 'Anything you could not say before the council?'

'No, not really,' said Kirin, wondering what on earth was going on.

'I see. Well, good luck,' said Aciram, smiling. 'My heart tells me I will see you in Imokoi.'

He left the room. 'What was that?' Kirin asked Spikes.

Spikes shrugged. 'I have no idea,' he replied. 'So I'm not going to see you for a couple of weeks at least.'

'No,' replied Kirin, 'unless you want to run away to Xi'en with me, which might not be a good idea.'

'Are you going to kill Bali?'

'I think so.'

'Good luck. But why are you so sure you can do it? You sounded as if you already have the Gauntlet in your pocket.'

'Remember how you said learning the danav language wouldn't get me anywhere?'

'I said you would never teach the asurs anything.'

'Which was true, I admit. But it helped me in another way, Spikes. I translated a bit more of the red notebook—

the one where I found the list. And I did it without anyone's help, which is why only I know what I read.'

'What did you read?'

Kirin waited for some time with his head to one side. 'I thought I heard someone outside,' he said. 'Something's wrong with me, I've been feeling very uneasy, especially when I'm alone.'

'What did you read?'

'Everyone seems to have forgotten that the Gauntlet of Tatsu has already been stolen once, by Danh-Gem. Of course, they may have changed the way they guard it, but I know a great deal about the monastery now, and I know a secret entrance that Danh-Gem made. Because on one of the pages of Danh-Gem's red notebook, the heading was "How I Stole the Gauntlet of Tatsu". There were maps, Spikes, maps, and descriptions of the monastery. And there was an answer to a question, an answer I wouldn't have thought of, simply because it was so obvious . . . which is why I know I can steal the Gauntlet. Don't say anything. Someone's coming.'

It was Bali.

'Do you need sleep, Karisman?'

'Yes, actually.'

'Well,' grinned Bali, 'you can sleep in the Chariot. I've brought everything we need. Food, water and furs for the mountain. Come on, let's go.'

'See you in Imokoi, Spikes,' he called out as they left the chamber. 'Kill Omar if he gets too annoying.'

'I was thinking about it,' said Spikes.

15

As the sun set over Kol, the Fragrant Underbelly was beginning to fill up. A young woman walked in and looked around. Behind a crowd of grimy vroomers, sitting at Kirin's old table, was a grey-clad figure, perched on a high stool.

She walked up to him and said, 'They found the mirror. It's in the Palace now.'

Triog walked up with a tray of drinks and greeted the two people at the table.

'Hello, Triog,' smiled the beautiful young woman whose real name was Roshin. 'Remember me?'

'Of course I do,' said Rightog. 'You've been in the sun, I see. Holiday?'

'Yes,' smiled Roshin. 'I went to Amurabad.'

'That's a dangerous place,' said Middlog, setting the drinks down on the table. He looked at her companion and looked puzzled. 'I didn't know you two were friends. Where did you meet?'

'Under the tables of the Underbelly, in fact,' grinned the Silver Dagger.

There was a fever of excitement and near panic running through the Free States. People were expecting Danh-Gem to turn up any day, and even the rumours of the mysterious Hero of Simoqin could not calm them. The asurs were leaving the city in large numbers, and more and more vamans were coming in. Magic had grown visibly stronger—the power of the Heart of Magic had grown, and it was a very good time to be a spellbinder—first-year students were suddenly finding themselves capable of performing very strong magic.

People from all over the world were coming to Kol, and the more daring of them inevitably drifted into the Fragrant Underbelly. Hence no one was surprised when the newly formed Guild of Superb Heroes declared that the Underbelly would be its headquarters.

The Guild of Superb Heroes was a group of people from all over the world, who had gathered in Kol to unite against the forces of Danh-Gem. Dressed in outlandish costumes, they would tell tall tales of their own exploits, and proudly proclaim that Kol was safe even if the Hero of Simoqin never actually turned up. Led by the Man of Reinforced Iron, a former champion of the WAK, and his brother, a trapeze artist named The Skimmer, they gave the people of Kol occasional hope and frequent mirth. Children ran home and told their parents about the mighty Thog the Barbarian, and a sumo wrestler from east Xi'en who painted himself purple and called himself the Unbelievable Bulk.

Who could feel fear in a city under the ceaseless vigilance of Supper-Man, who could eat anything, the scythe-wielding Jax the Reaper and the rubber-jointed and sweet-smelling Minty Python?

Of course, the spellbinders, inspired by these heroes, had formed their own group of crime-fighters—a dashing band of final-year students who called themselves the Hex Men, who were presently at the Underbelly, sitting around a large table debating noisily over the advantages and disadvantages of black uniforms. In the din they made, the soft words of the two leaders of the Silver Phalanx were inaudible to anyone else.

'Asvin's training is complete,' said the Dagger. 'The mirror couldn't have been found at a more convenient time. Now I can enjoy a life of peace and quiet, and you can run the show.'

'I can't believe you've retired,' said Roshin. 'I refuse to believe it.'

'Well, I have,' said the Dagger simply.

'But you can't quit now. We need you more than ever. It's just beginning.'

'There's always something just beginning. I've really had enough of this. And I've trained you for years. It's time for me to go.'

'Well, it's your decision, I suppose, but it won't be the same without you. You gave the Phalanx that touch of glamour.'

'Well, if it's glamour you want, I'm sure you can provide more of it than I can, Roshin . . . or should I say Rupina.'

'Don't call me that,' said Roshin sharply. 'I still have nightmares about the Sultan leering at me. You should have let me kill him while I had the chance.'

'The Civilian wants him alive. If Omar becomes the Sultan it will be far worse, believe me. You did very well to find out about him, by the way.'

'It was nothing. What cuts deepest is that I actually saw the lamp. But they took it out of the palace and gave it to Omar before I could get my hands on it. What else did the samurai say before they killed him?'

'They need five things to raise Danh-Gem,' replied the Dagger. 'Four they have. The Gauntlet is the last.'

'Who's leading them?'

'Omar, Bjorkun, the vanar Bali, a sorcerer called Karisman and Spikes.'

'Spikes? He's joined them? I thought he would. What happened to that boy, Kirin? Is he on their side, too?'

'I don't know,' replied the Dagger. 'Chances are he's dead.' Unless he's calling himself Karisman and working with them, he thought. Too bad the ronin hadn't seen his face. But why would a ravian work with them? To wait for Danh-Gem to rise and then kill him? Possibly. How sure can we be that Kirin really is a ravian? Well, if Mantric says he is that's good enough for me. Nothing I can do about it either way. It's all in the past. I must stop asking these questions if I want to stay sane.

'So it all hinges on the Gauntlet,' said Roshin, looking thoughtful. 'And Xi'en won't let us have it. To be fair, why should they just give it to us? I mean, it is theirs, isn't it? This is the first time I've seen the Civilian lose an argument.'

'I evidently didn't train you well enough,' sighed the Dagger.

'The Civilian never expected Xi'en to hand over the Gauntlet,' he continued as she stared sharply at him. 'But the theft of the Tear in Avranti shows us that we cannot allow it to remain in Xi'en, because there are strong magical forces at work. It needs to be hidden somewhere else, and where better than the treasure room of Kol? And if Xi'en will not give it to us, we will steal it.'

'But when some of us volunteered to steal it you forbade it.'

'Of course I did,' said the Dagger. 'The Wu Sen monks are not just experts at martial arts. They are powerful sorcerers as well. If they were left alone to guard the Gauntlet, even I could not steal it. Which is why the Civilian went on a diplomatic offensive. She went on asking the emperor to ensure the Gauntlet was safe, until the emperor had to increase security. He sent a few of his best soldiers—the Green Serpent Guards—and now they have taken charge of the Gauntlet, much to the annoyance of the Wu Sen monks.'

'And how does that help us? The Green Serpents could beat us in combat,' said Roshin. Then her jaw dropped. 'Wait a minute—the Green Serpents—you mean Chen is in the Wu Sen monastery now?'

The Dagger smiled smugly. 'Yes. We now have our man on the inside. And we also have a complete map of the monastery, and a list of the guards' schedules. And when we are ready, Chen will help us steal the Gauntlet.'

'But if Chen is in the monastery, who is spying on the emperor?'

'No one. But some sacrifices have to be made. The Gauntlet is more important now. Besides, after it is stolen I am sure the Imperial Guards will return to the court.'

'So when do I start?' asked Roshin, her eyes shining.

'You're not stealing it,' said the Dagger. 'Yes, you're very good, but even I couldn't get to the monastery now. Because the Wu Sen monks are patrolling the foot of the mountain. And if anyone passes them, they will be aware of it. Skill will not help—they are using magic.'

'How are we going to steal it, then?'

'We aren't. It's going to be stolen by someone who can appear on the mountain without climbing it.'

'I don't understand.'

'I said, didn't I, that the mirror couldn't have been found at a better time? It saves me the trouble of sending you to Bolvudis with the maps and loads of equipment. The Civilian wants Asvin to steal the Gauntlet of Tatsu. Because he can go to the monastery without crossing the foot of the mountain. One of the seven mirrors is high up on the mountain, in a hidden cave near the Wu Sen monastery, according to Mantric—the hero it belonged to was a Wu Sen monk. And now that Jaadur's mirror has been found, Asvin can come to Kol and learn everything he needs to know before going to Xi'en. I will send a scarab . . .'

The Dagger laughed. 'Old habits die hard,' he said, shaking his head. 'I won't be sending any more scarabs. You will tell the Civilian to send a scarab to Mantric, to tell him that the mirror has been found. And Asvin should come to Kol, with Mantric preferably, some time around the sixth. It's time he learnt what it's like to be in the Civilian's service.'

They sat in silence for a while.

'You know,' said Roshin, 'I just had a thought.'

'Tell me.'

'Remember, long ago, I told you I couldn't get involved with my employer?'

'Yes. I remember very clearly.'

'Well, you're not my employer any more, are you.'

The Dagger leaned back and smiled. This certainly opens up a new range of possibilities, he thought.

Roshin leaned forward. 'Of course, I totally understand if there is someone else—or as is more likely in your case, a queue.'

The Dagger waved a self-deprecating hand coyly.

'I was talking to Captain Rupaisa yesterday,' continued Roshin blandly. 'We agreed that now that you had retired, you should settle down—maybe start a family.'

She saw the Dagger's smile vanish and a horrified expression take its place, and laughed aloud.

16

The Wu Sen Monastery was mostly carved into the side of Mount Laoye, one of the highest peaks of the Harmony range. It was a seat of ancient wisdom, and protected by thick walls and fierce guards. Savage snowstorms lashed at it all through the year, even as the rest of the world squirmed in the grip of summer, but the power of the sorcerer-monks kept the monastery safe.

Asvin, Mantric and Maya passed through the mirror into Kol and met the Civilian on the sixth of Dragonmonth. The Civilian gave them the maps and timetables her spy in the Imperial Guards had sent, and they sat together for three days and worked out a plan.

Maya also went to her room in Enki and found, to her immense relief, that the matchbox containing Prince Kumirdanga was safe. She put the slug out in the middle of a field, because bright sunlight would make the spell wear off in a day or so.

On the morning of the ninth, they returned to Bolvudis with the papers the Civilian had given them and a trunk full of vaman explosives that made Gaam's face break into a huge smile. The Civilian had been strengthening Kol's ties to the vamans in the form of trade benefits, and had got, in return, many wondrous pieces of vaman craftsmanship to add to Kol's awesome armoury. There was no doubt whose side the vamans were on this time—Kol had the money.

Gaam was overjoyed to hear that Mantric was going to come with them. Stealing the Gauntlet of Tatsu would involve using magic stronger than Maya could create alone. The spell they were planning to use was called the Blur, and normally it took at least five spellbinders to cast it. But Maya and Mantric were very powerful.

The Blur made whatever it was cast on difficult to see, and if it was cast with sufficient strength, it could make a person or an object invisible. But this spell could only be cast when it was very cold, and the spellbinder casting could not move while the spell was working. The spellbinder casting the Blur had to be able to see the person it was cast on, and the spell could only remain while the person was visible to the spellbinder. Mantric and Maya could not practise the Blur in the heat of Bolvudis, but they had done it before.

At sunset, they all gathered in the cave and passed through the mirror to Mount Laoye through the mirror of Yong-gan, the Wu Sen monk who had secretly become one of the Seven Heroes. Even the Grand Lama of the Wu Sen monks had not known how or why Yong-gan mysteriously disappeared from the monastery from time to time.

Yong-gan's mirror was in a cave he had hollowed out magically in a little rock-cleft on the western spur of the mountain, about ten minutes' march below the monastery in clear weather. It was well above the snowline, and they were in no danger of being discovered by the sorcerer-monks who, annoyed by the clamour the Imperial Guards made, were meditating in little huts below the snowline, aware of every bird and beast that prowled in the forest below them. No intruder would pass their stern vigil. They had not dreamt that four would-be thieves could suddenly materialize out of a mirror above their realm of awareness.

Gaam gave the rest some All-Weather potion to drink. Then he and Asvin rolled aside the rock that blocked the mouth of the cave. The entrance was covered by two hundred years of snow, but it took Mantric and Maya only ten minutes to burn through it. They set a cloaking spell on the hole they made in the snow, so that that it would look like the rest of the mountainside. Putting on white cloaks, they walked through the white illusion on to the flank of the mountain and began to climb towards the monastery.

The Phalanx spy in the monastery, Chen, had written that the Gauntlet was hidden in a chamber underneath a courtyard in the south-west corner of the monastery. No one was allowed to enter the chamber apart from the Grand Lama, and Chen had never seen what was inside it, guarding the Gauntlet. The key to the chamber was kept in a small room outside it, with one guard. There were stairs leading up from that room which led to a small trapdoor that opened right in the middle of the courtyard. The courtyard was empty and well-lit with hundreds of Alocacti, and closed in with high walls on all four sides. At regular intervals along these walls were small rooms where skilled archers sat day and night, their bows aimed at the empty courtyard, ceaselessly watching and listening for the slightest shadow or whisper that would tell them that an intruder was entering.

The emperor's guards, the fearsome warriors called the Green Serpents, were guarding the monastery on a rotating basis. Every hour they would shift positions, and one guard would march to the trapdoor relieving the guard inside of his duty. Before the shift in the room with the key, the guard would be patrolling the south wall of the courtyard. Here the wall was thickest, because outside was the snow-covered mountainside. It was towards this wall that they were heading.

'Remember, we can't start before eight,' whispered Mantric as they reached the wall and huddled together beside it. 'That's when Chen will be by this wall.'

'I know,' grumbled Gaam, quickly unpacking the bag that held the explosives. But his frown changed to a gleeful smile as he tucked a few sticks of the explosive in the snow against the wall. 'I love blowing things up,' he cackled.

'What's the explosive called?' whispered Maya.

'This is no ordinary firework-powder,' said Gaam. 'It's a new vaman invention, called Implosive. I don't think it's ever been used above ground before—it's really powerful, I'm only going to use a little bit.'

'Won't anyone hear the bang? And won't there be bits of the wall lying around?'

'It's supposed to be completely silent. And it's not really an explosive—it makes rock implode, sucking it inwards into a vacuum. What they do is . . .'

'Quiet,' hissed Mantric.

Gaam nodded apologetically. 'Stay back when I light the fuse,' he whispered.

The others nodded. They waited in silence.

When the faint sound of a gong somewhere inside the monastery announced it was eight, Gaam lit the fuse and they scurried backwards and waited. They watched as the little flame burned its way down the fuse. Then there was a soft plop and a huge dent appeared in the wall, as if someone had scooped the stone out with a spoon. Gaam ran up to it, placed more Implosive in the dent and scurried back. A short while later, there was another plop, and the hole in the wall grew deeper.

The stone wall around the Wu Sen Monastery was at least twenty feet thick and it took quite some time before the tunnel they were creating ran right through it. The tunnel was just wide enough for two people to crawl through, side by side.

As the last little bundle of Implosive imploded, the tunnel was flooded with light. They had burrowed right through the wall, and the white Alocactus light from the courtyard was shining in Gaam's face. Mantric quickly rushed into the tunnel and set a cloaking spell on each end. Then they sat in the dark tunnel, waiting for a signal from Chen.

A few minutes later there was a scraping sound outside the mouth of the tunnel, and a little whistle. Chen had been waiting for them, and had seen the mouth of the tunnel suddenly appear in the wall before Mantric closed it with the cloaking spell. They did not dare to look outside in case anyone else saw them.

Gaam crawled out of the other end of the tunnel and started back towards the cave where the mirror stood. They had agreed that he would stay near the mirror, to warn the rest in case there was unforeseen danger on the mountain.

'Chen doesn't know we're using the Blur. When he walks

to the trapdoor, walk with him. Don't talk to him until the trapdoor closes,' whispered Mantric to Asvin.

Maya and Mantric cast the Blur on Asvin. At first Maya cast her spell, and Asvin's shape became hazy and blurry. Then Mantric added his power, and Asvin vanished altogether.

Maya and Mantric took out small hollow tubes and stuck them through the wall-illusion that Mantric had created when he had cloaked the end of the tunnel that opened towards the courtyard. They would have to be able to see Asvin for the Blur to stay on—there would appear to be two holes in the wall, but that was a risk they would have to take. They peered through the tubes at the courtyard, and saw Chen standing outside the tunnel.

Asvin crawled through the fake wall out of the tunnel, stood up and tapped Chen lightly on the shoulder. Chen looked stunned for an instant, but he had been trained to never show emotion, and quickly regained his composure. He looked straight ahead, then nodded his head slowly.

Mantric and Maya slowly got used to keeping the Blur on Asvin. They could see him, wandering around Chen, looking impatient, because Chen would not go to the trapdoor until nine o'clock, when it was his turn to guard the room with the key. They waited.

At nine the gong rang again. Chen started walking towards the trapdoor as another guard walked out from the room underground, and went to a room at the opposite corner of the courtyard, where he would be thoroughly searched, to see if he had stolen the key. The Green Serpents did not take any chances.

Chen marched up to the trapdoor. He lifted it up, and waited for a second. Asvin, correctly interpreting this as a sign that he was to descend first, quickly walked down the stairs. As soon as he passed out of the spellbinders' sight, he became visible again. Chen closed the trapdoor behind him quickly, and climbed down the stairs after Asvin.

They reached the bottom of the stairs. There was nothing in the room except a single torch on the wall, and a golden key that lay in the centre of a marble table. There was a richly decorated door on the south wall of the room.

'You don't look like a spellbinder,' said Chen quietly. 'You gave me quite a shock there, tapping me on the shoulder suddenly. How did you manage to make that tunnel?'

'I'm not a spellbinder,' said Asvin, 'and I did not make the tunnel. What happened was . . .'

'Whatever it was, I'm sure it was very interesting. But we don't have time for this,' said Chen. 'Sorry, I shouldn't have asked in the first place. The key on the table is the key to that door. I think the Gauntlet is inside.'

'Stop!' he hissed, as Asvin strode forward and reached for the key. Asvin froze.

'You aren't very bright, are you,' said Chen, looking annoyed. 'You almost gave the game away. You can't just take the key. It's protected. Look at the ceiling.'

Asvin looked up and saw a creeper entwined around a square wire on the ceiling, the dimensions of which were the same as the table on which the key lay.

'Those are mewlips,' said Chen. 'There are silk threads connecting the table to the wire. They're very thin, which is why you can't see them. The slightest touch on a thread will make the mewlips scream their bulbs off, bringing every guard on this mountain running to this room.'

Asvin looked harder and saw the thin threads shimmering

very faintly in the firelight. There was enough space between the threads for a hand to slip through, though.

'I'll get the key,' said Chen. 'My arms are slimmer than yours.'

He gingerly put his arm through the threads and extracted the key.

'If you could get the key all along,' said Asvin, 'why didn't you steal the Gauntlet?'

'Because I'm a guard,' snapped Chen, 'and guards are searched thoroughly after coming out of this room. I would never manage to smuggle the Gauntlet out, even if I managed to pass whatever peril resides in that chamber. It was hard enough sending the maps to the Civilian. Besides, she needs me to be in Xi'en. Just go through the door and try to get the Gauntlet—this is not the time for conversation. Go.'

Asvin put the golden key in the keyhole in the door. It slid open, and he walked in, drawing his sword. The door closed immediately after he entered. In the outer room, Chen saw the key disappear from the keyhole and reappear on the marble table. He grimaced. The Silver Phalanx didn't like magic.

Asvin looked around the little room as the door closed. There didn't seem to be any monsters crouching in hidden corners—in fact, there were no hidden corners. The room was completely bare except for a golden statue of the Shanti-Joddha, which was smiling benignly at him. Its eyes were glowing with wisdom and understanding, and Asvin, suddenly feeling embarrassed to be standing in front of the holy man's statue with a naked sword in his hand, sheathed the Sword of Raka. There was no sign of the Gauntlet.

He walked around the room, tapping the walls, but found nothing.

'What you seek is hidden,' said a voice suddenly.

Asvin snapped around but saw no one.

'Sit down, my child, and lay down your burden. You seem to be carrying the weight of the world on your shoulders.' The voice was calm and soothing. It was coming from the statue of the Shanti-Joddha.

As if in a dream, Asvin sat down in front of the statue in the lotus position. A part of his mind was screaming at him to hurry up, to tear the room to shreds and find the Gauntlet, but the voice of the Shanti-Joddha's statue was impossible to resist. Asvin closed his eyes and listened to the voice.

It spoke of peace and harmony, of wisdom and truth, of karma and salvation. Asvin slipped deeper and deeper into a trance. He felt ready to renounce everything, to spend the rest of his life here in the monastery listening to these wonderful words. After some time the words blended into one another, and it seemed to Asvin that he was listening to celestial music, and beautiful lights were shining in his eyes. He would stay in this room forever, he would be one with the universe, he would give up his foolish and violent quest . . .

The voice in his head shouted, Your Quest!

Asvin's eyes opened with a start. I was under a spell, he thought. This must be a trap. I've been here for half an hour at least. Poor Maya, waiting in that cramped tunnel.

He stood up and looked around wildly.

The voice stopped speaking and sighed. 'But you will not listen to reason, will you?' it said.

Asvin looked hard at the statue. Something about the calm eyes scared him. He felt as if the walls were closing in on him.

'Very well,' said the voice. 'If you will not listen, you will not listen. You must feel you are ready to make your own decisions. The paths are clear to you, and you know which one you wish to walk. Very well.'

The statue's hands were laid on its lap, palms upwards and open. A white stone, tear-drop-shaped, appeared in one palm. A black stone, similarly shaped but inverted, appeared in the other.

'Tell me, then. What do you want?'

Asvin looked from black stone to white stone to black stone again. What does it mean? He wondered. Black or white? Which one do I choose?

He stared at the two stones. What was he supposed to do? Black or white?

Perhaps white signifies light and black darkness, he thought.

'The white stone,' he said.

The Shanti-Joddha smiled.

'Hasty,' said the voice. It sounded smug.

Asvin felt sudden terror as the room turned white around him and disappeared. There was a flash of light, a feeling of being dragged through space, and then silence. He opened his eyes.

He was standing in the middle of the courtyard, on top of the trapdoor.

He was visible.

Time seemed to slow down for Asvin. The sound of the clanging alarm gongs seemed to last for hours. He heard each individual bow twang above him, he saw each arrow sail slowly across the air towards him; he felt them shudder, one after another, into his armour.

His magical armour.

On the other hand, time was moving very fast for Mantric and Maya. They saw Asvin a few seconds after he materialized above the trapdoor—they were expecting him to come up with Chen. They quickly set the Blur on him and he disappeared. In the few seconds that he had been visible, Asvin's chest had begun to bear a startling resemblance to a porcupine.

Startled cries rang out across the courtyard. Green Serpent guards came running into it, swinging their swords wildly. But Asvin dodged the swishing blades and ran straight to the tunnel.

'Did you get the Gauntlet?' asked Mantric as Asvin entered the dark tunnel and they stopped the Blur.

'No.'

'Are you hurt?'

'No. Scratch on the arm.'

'Let's get out before they start searching the mountainside,' hissed Maya. 'How long will the cloaking spell last?'

'A day or so,' replied Mantric as they ran out of the tunnel into the night, 'but we'll be back tomorrow before it fades. Chen's timetable will come in very handy.'

They entered the cave without further incident, and returned to Bolvudis through Yong-gan's mirror.

'I still don't understand why you have to choose the black stone,' said Mantric as they walked out of Yong-gan's mirror into the cave. 'But if it asked you which one you wanted, and you picked the white one and it was the wrong one, it's pretty clear what you have to do tonight.'

'Are you sure it didn't give you some clue? It spoke to you for half an hour, it must have said something,' said Gaam to Asvin.

'For the twenty-fifth time, it didn't give me any clues,' said Asvin crossly. He had spent the whole day trying in vain to remember what the statue had said.

'Is it eight o'clock again tonight? But we won't have to

make the tunnel again, yesterday's one is still there, right?' asked Maya.

'No, Chen is coming to the wall at nine tonight, not eight. He's got the ten o'clock watch in the room with the key. And we can't assume our tunnel is still there. They might have found it and filled it up,' said Mantric. 'These aren't standard spell-casting conditions; I don't know how long the cloaking will last.'

The snow-illusion at the mouth of the cave was still there, though. They climbed up to the monastery again and discovered that their tunnel had not been discovered. The gong rang out at nine, which meant Chen would be arriving at the wall soon.

'I think I should stay here with you tonight, in case there's fighting. In any case, the cave is well shielded and I got really bored last night,' whispered Gaam. Mantric nodded.

At that precise moment, on the western spur of the mountain, a little distance away from Yong-gan's cave, the snow suddenly rose in what looked like a gigantic bubble. It swelled up on the mountainside, thirty feet across. Then it popped, noiselessly.

'Well, we're here,' said Kirin.

He jumped out of the rickshaw.

'We need to find three rocks arranged in a perfect triangle,' he told Bali. 'Danh-Gem's secret passage is there.'

He watched Bali skim around over the snow. For the last five days, Kirin had been thinking just one thought, and he was thinking it now.

When do I kill Bali?

I should just go ahead and do it now, he thought. Before

he does anything I should feel grateful for. No, that's not logical. Let me be sure I can get the Gauntlet on my own. Then.

Ten minutes later, he found the three rocks he was looking for and began melting the snow between them. But when the snow had gone he found, to his dismay, that there was no tunnel underneath. The monks had found it and filled it up with loose rocks. Now he had no idea how to get to the chamber with the Shanti-Joddha's statue that Danh-Gem had written about. He sat down on one of the stones and tried to clear his head and think of a plan.

Maya and Mantric cast the Blur. Asvin walked out of the tunnel and tapped Chen lightly on the shoulder. This time Chen was expecting him, and didn't twitch a muscle. As Maya and Mantric settled down with their seeing tubes and got used to keeping the Blur on, Asvin sat down on the floor and waited for ten o'clock to strike.

'I,' said Kirin, 'am an idiot.'

He summoned Mritik. I need a tunnel, he thought, and I have a golem with me, and I'm sitting around and wasting time.

'Can you dig me a tunnel, Mritik?' he asked.

'Yes, master,' said the golem. 'Where to?'

'The south-west corner of the monastery,' said Kirin. 'No, wait.'

I don't know how they're guarding the Gauntlet now, he thought. But Mritik won't know how to find the chamber with the statue.

'There's a tunnel here filled with loose rocks. Can you clear it up?' he asked.

'Yes, master.'

'Well, clear it up, please.'

The earth closed over the Chariot of Vul. Minutes later, the rocks that sealed the mouth of Danh-Gem's tunnel flew into the air, and Kirin saw the massive shape of Mritik. He had dug sideways into the tunnel with his huge hands, parting the rocks of the mountain like a man walking through tall grass.

Without saying a word, Mritik began to walk deeper into the tunnel, pushing the rocks aside, compressing them.

'Should we follow him?' asked Bali.

'No. We'll wait until he finishes the tunnel and then I'll go and get the Gauntlet.'

'Whatever you say, Karisman.'

Kirin and Bali sat on two of the three rocks. Bali watched the mountain, looking for guards. Kirin watched Bali.

Well, I'm going to get to the Gauntlet now, thought Kirin. I don't need Bali any more. And his back is turned to me. I should stab him now—it would be perfect revenge for the way he killed poor Red Pearl. No point wasting time thinking about it.

Now is the time for Bali to die.

He looked at the Shadowknife on his finger, and it slowly turned into a sharp, wickedly curved dagger. He crept forward until he was right behind Bali. Then he raised his dagger, ready to strike.

Up in the monastery, the ten o' clock gong rang out. Chen and Asvin started off towards the trapdoor.

I can't do it, thought Kirin. I simply can't do it. He trusts me. I *know* him. He depends on me. I can't kill him. He thinks we are *friends*.

The Shadowknife turned into a ring again just before Bali turned around.

'What is it?' he asked sharply.

'Master?' came the voice of Mritik from the tunnel.

'Yes?' said Kirin gratefully.

'There is a slight problem.'

After what had happened last night, Asvin had expected more security. The courtyard wasn't empty tonight. There were six Green Serpent guards marching up and down it. But Chen and Asvin reached the trapdoor safely.

'There is some power guarding the other end of the tunnel, master,' said Mritik. 'I could not break through.'

'Probably the Shanti-Joddha's statue,' said Kirin. 'There is another room beside the one where the tunnel ends, Mritik. Dig around until you find it. But don't break in until I join you.'

'Yes, master,' said Mritik and disappeared.

Kirin looked at Bali, who was still staring at him with a puzzled expression on his face.

I know I promised I would kill you, he thought. And if I were a hero, I would keep that oath or die in the attempt. The word is sacred, once spoken, and so on. But I'm not a hero. And I'm breaking my promise. I won't kill you, Bali. You were doing what you believed was right, and I do not have the right to judge you. But I do not want to become like you. And if I had killed you a moment ago, I would have been no better than you.

'Is something wrong, Kirin?' asked Bali.

But, thought Kirin, you're not going to the Circle of Darkness. I owe Red Pearl at least that much.

And he remembered Red Pearl's head falling to the ground and felt the same surge of hatred he had felt then. Ravian power welled up inside him, flowing through his veins.

He suddenly realized that he wouldn't have needed the Shadowknife to kill Bali . . .

'What is it, Kirin?' asked Bali. 'Should we go down the tunnel?'

'No, Bali,' said Kirin, his voice as cold as the snow around them. 'You are not going down that tunnel. This is where we part.'

'I don't understand,' said Bali, looking at Kirin, amazed. It seemed to him that Kirin was burning, in a flame blacker than night. 'What do you want me to do, then?'

'I want you to run away, Bali,' said Kirin. 'I want you to run away as fast as you can. Because I am a ravian, Bali.'

His voice grew stronger.

'I am a ravian, the son of the two greatest ravians that ever walked this world.'

Bali, face frozen in a mask of horror, drew his sword.

'You cannot touch me Bali,' said Kirin, as power filled him. 'I am beyond you now. I possess powers beyond your feeble imagination. But I am not going to kill you. I am sparing your life, because you believed in me. You have lost, Bali. Your plans and your dreams have failed. You will never reach the Circle of Darkness in a week. I will take the Gauntlet and the Chariot to Imokoi. When Danh-Gem rises, I am going to slay him. And there is nothing you can do about it.'

'Traitor!' roared Bali, lunging at him. But Kirin raised his hand, and Bali's sword snapped in half. Bali flew back through the air and crashed down on the snow twenty feet away.

'You cannot fight me, Bali,' said Kirin. 'I am too strong for you.'

Bali snatched his bow from his shoulder and fitted an arrow to it.

'Don't make me break your bow, Bali,' warned Kirin. 'You will need it if you are to have any hope of getting off this mountain. Go now! Don't try to follow me down this tunnel. Because I will be aware of your presence before you can strike me, and my patience is not infinite. The next time you trouble me, I will not let you live.'

Bali's arms sagged limply and the arrow fell to the ground.

'Do you understand me?' asked Kirin sternly.

Bali's eyes were burning with hate, but he nodded. He knew he was beaten.

'You may slay Danh-Gem, Kirin,' he said. 'But you will not live to gloat about it. My labours have not been in vain. The armies of Danh-Gem are united. And they will hunt you down. Farewell.'

He shouldered his bow and took a great leap down the mountain. Kirin turned and walked into the tunnel.

Dark clouds covered the moon. A storm was coming.

As the wind started howling loudly, Bali turned and climbed back up the mountain, a maniacal light in his eyes. He crossed the tunnel and leapt upwards, towards the monastery.

'Welcome once again, my child,' said the statue as the door slid shut. 'Sit down for a while, and listen.'

Asvin tried to keep his mind clear but the statue's voice droned on, drowning his senses and soothing him into a state of unreal calm. He sat down, cross-legged, and listened.

Chen was watching the trapdoor when he heard a noise behind him. He turned around and saw two gigantic hands thrusting out of the wall behind him. They grasped the solid rock and tore it apart like paper. A monstrous clay man entered the room.

Chen was about to raise the alarm when he remembered—the hero was inside, trying to steal the Gauntlet. He whipped out his killing sword and struck at the clay man, who caught it and bent it like a blade of grass.

Mritik grabbed Chen with his other hand and would have crushed him, but Kirin ran into the room and hissed, 'Don't.' Mritik let Chen go and Kirin knocked him out with a well-placed jab.

Kirin's ravian eyes saw the silk threads dangling from the wire fixed to the ceiling. He put his hand between them and pulled with his mind, and the key came flying to his hand.

'Go to the Chariot and wait,' he told Mritik.

He put the key in the keyhole and turned it. The key turned all the way but the door didn't open. Kirin pushed at it but nothing happened. He put his ear to the door. It sounded as if someone was talking inside.

He tried the key again, several times, but the door didn't budge. Exasperated, he threw the key down on the ground.

It broke.

That was probably not a very smart thing to do, he thought.

Bali soared into the air and landed by the wall of the monastery. He crouched there for a while, wondering how foolish it would be to jump right over the wall and see what lay inside. Very foolish, he thought. But he *would* find the Gauntlet or a way to get to Imokoi by full moon night. The ravian would die a grisly death.

Snow was beginning to fall, but through the whirling flakes Bali saw something that made him stop dead in his tracks.

Four sets of footprints, leading into the wall.

He walked up to them and looked at the wall. He put his hand on it. The wall sank in, and he almost fell into it.

Bali jumped back. Sorcery everywhere! But whoever had made these prints and gone into the wall wasn't a guard.

Whoever it was had found a secret way in.

And would know a secret way out.

He sat down in the snow and waited.

A few minutes later, he heard whispers. There was someone *inside* the wall. Whispering very softly. No human would have heard those whispers, especially when the wind was howling so loudly.

But then Bali was no human.

'I'm telling you, something moved back there,' said Gaam.

'Well, we can't look,' replied Mantric. 'We have to keep our eyes on the courtyard, remember? If Asvin fails again, he'll be appearing above that trapdoor any minute.'

'It's dark anyway,' said Maya. 'And we heard nothing. You're imagining it.'

'I'm going out,' said Gaam. 'I probably imagined it, but I'm going to stay near the mirror. If there are guards prowling around outside, our escape may be cut off. I don't fancy climbing all the way down this mountain, with or without the Gauntlet. I don't want to escape guards only to be caught by monks.'

He walked through the wall into the growing storm outside.

He crouched and walked down the slope to the cave,

looking around for any sign of life, but saw nothing. Ten minutes later, he reached the cave and went inside, through the snow-illusion.

He was still feeling uneasy, but everything seemed to be all right. The mirror was shining softly. He sat down on a rock and began to hum a mining song.

'No!' said Asvin, standing up and shaking his head. 'I will not listen any more!'

'Very well, then. I see it is time for you to take sides again,' said the statue.

The white stone and the black stone appeared again on its palms.

'What do you want?' asked the voice.

'The black one,' said Asvin.

The Shanti-Joddha smiled.

I wonder why they never found this mirror, or whether they found it and let it be, thought Gaam, looking at Yong-gan's mirror.

There was a soft twang behind him.

Gaam didn't bother to look around. He dived, clutching his axe.

The black arrow that would have pierced his heart from behind grazed his neck, spilling blood, but not wounding him seriously. But the next arrow, shot a second later, bit into his left arm.

Gaam rolled over and sprang up as the huge vanar lunged at him. He plucked the arrow out of his side and threw it away. But Bali was too fast for him. The vanar's fist crashed into his face.

'My name,' said Bali, standing over him, 'is Bali!'

'And mine,' replied Gaam, bringing his axe-blade down, hard, on Bali's foot, 'is Gaam.'

'Hasty,' said the statue. It sounded smug.

Asvin felt sudden terror as the room turned white around him and disappeared. There was a flash of light, a feeling of being dragged through space, and then silence. He opened his eyes.

He was standing in the middle of the courtyard, on top of the trapdoor.

He was visible.

Again.

He closed his eyes and waited for the arrows.

Kirin, who had tried every spell he knew on the door, was sitting on the floor of the outer room, deep in thought, when he saw the door suddenly outlined in a flash of light. He put his ear to the door. The voice wasn't speaking any longer.

He put his finger, the one bearing the Shadowknife, on the keyhole. He felt the Shadowknife melt and pour into the keyhole, filling the grooves inside. Then it hardened, and he twisted it.

The door slid open.

'It's a busy night,' remarked the statue as he entered. 'But sit down, my child, for there is much I can teach you.'

And Kirin found, to his surprise, that it seemed like a good idea. He sat.

Mantric and Maya had been watching closely this time, and they cast the Blur on Asvin almost immediately. He dodged the swinging blades and raced to the tunnel.

'Where's the Gauntlet?' asked Mantric.

'I don't have it.'

'What?'

'Let's get out of here,' said Maya. 'Some of the guards are running out of the courtyard—they might be planning to search outside.'

They ran out of the tunnel on to the mountainside. Mantric was asking Asvin many questions, but Asvin couldn't hear anything over the sound of the wind, so he ran on.

'What happened?' asked Mantric as they entered the cave.

'Well, I went in, and it talked to me again,' said Asvin, entering the cave and walking towards the mirror, 'and when it asked me what I wanted, I said the black one, and then it put me out on the courtyard again.'

'Why is the cave empty?' asked Maya, but neither of them paid any attention to her.

Asvin touched the mirror and said, 'Icelosis.'

'Did it say what do you want, or which one do you want?' asked Mantric.

'It said what do you want.'

'But you told me yesterday it had asked you which one of the stones you wanted!'

The mirror turned black.

'So? What's the difference?'

'When people talk to you,' said Mantric, 'you should listen.'

He stepped into the mirror and vanished.

'Come on, Maya,' said Asvin. He looked at her.

She was standing over a frozen puddle of blood.

There were huge, bloody footprints leading out of the cave.

'I think,' she said, 'that we need to find Gaam.'

'I will ask you once again, slowly,' said Bali, tightening his iron grip over Gaam's throat. 'How were you planning to use the mirror to escape from the mountain?'

Gaam looked down into the sheer precipice Bali was holding him over. At least four hundred feet, straight down, he thought. Not a nice prospect.

He looked up, into Bali's eyes.

'You will not get off this mountain alive,' he told the vanar. 'I have broken your bow, and wounded your foot. You cannot jump, you cannot shoot. Your only hope is to let me go.'

'You fought well for a midget,' said Bali. 'But if you do not tell me, I will kill you. I need to get off this mountain. How do I use the mirror? Tell me, dwarf!'

'That's vaman, not dwarf,' said Gaam through clenched teeth. 'Would you like it if I called you a monkey?'

'Maybe your friends will prove more talkative,' said Bali. 'I am not joking. This is your last chance.'

'I would have thought of good last words, but you wouldn't understand them,' Gaam told him solemnly.

Then Bali let him go and he fell.

Asvin and Maya raced across the slope, ignoring the stinging snow. Maya was conjuring up fireballs, but the wind was blowing them out. But they were moving fast in spite of that. They followed the blood trail in the flickering blue light, though they knew that sentries in the monastery would see the fireballs soon, if they had not done so already.

Maya was tired after casting the Blur, but anxiety about Gaam spurred her magical powers on to new heights. She finally succeeded in making a white fireball that resisted the wind. The snow shone around them.

Then they heard a terrible roar that echoed across the

mountain, and saw the huge form of the vanar standing on the edge of the precipice.

He was holding Gaam's axe.

'If you're looking for your little friend,' he shouted as he saw them, 'it's too late! I don't want to kill you two as well. Just tell me how to get out of here. Tell me how to use your mirror!'

Asvin said nothing. He ran on grimly towards the vanar, sword shining in the white light.

'I gave you a chance!' yelled Bali. 'If you wish to die, so be it! Death to all humans!'

It's him, thought Maya, it's the one I set on fire in the city.

Asvin and Bali circled for a while, and sprang forward. Sword and axe came together with a horrible clang.

'Thank you for the advice,' said Kirin, 'and I would love to listen to more, but I'm in a bit of a hurry.'

The statue sighed. 'Very well. If that is the way you wish it to be, if you feel you are ready to make your own decisions . . .'

A white stone appeared in one of its palms, a black stone in the other.

'What do you want?' it asked Kirin.

Kirin looked into its calm, shining eyes and grinned. At least they hadn't changed this part.

'I want the Gauntlet of Tatsu,' he said.

The Shanti-Joddha smiled.

Then it split down the middle like a walnut shell, breaking in half. Inside the statue, on a small marble block, was the Gauntlet of Tatsu.

It was made with bright red dragon-hide, fiery and leathery. The fingers had claws attached to them, steel claws

463

glowing bright. Kirin picked up the Gauntlet and saw his own face in the claws. He was smiling.

Without thinking, he slipped the Gauntlet on.

And the world changed.

The room faded in front of Kirin's eyes, and he did not know whether it was real or a vision, but suddenly he was standing on an immeasurably tall black pillar, far above the ground, in the middle of a cloudless night sky, and he could see the whole world all around him. He looked around him and saw pinpricks of light appearing on the ground, far below, like stars twinkling in the sky. Fiery orange dots. He looked harder at one of them and suddenly there was a rush of wind and everything blurred around him, then cleared. He was now standing in a swamp, and the mud in front of him was bubbling. He looked to his left and everything faded again. He felt as if he was being thrown across the world, and then suddenly he was in a long tunnel, and a red glow was growing slowly at the other end. He looked to his right and again he felt as if he were flying forward. When the wind stopped roaring he was standing on an ice-lake and a huge crack was appearing in the middle. Steam was coming out from the crack in the ice. I must be dreaming, thought Kirin. I'm having a vision of some sort.

Then he looked up and saw huge lizard-shapes with bat-wings silhouetted against the moon. He suddenly noticed that the Gauntlet on his right hand was burning and crackling, but he felt no pain. Then he looked down and saw his reflection on the ice.

He gave a startled cry as he looked into his own eyes.

His brown eyes had vanished. His eyes were now completely red, glowing like lava, with a reptilian vertical slit down the middle, like Spikes had.

He heard a hissing voice.

We hear and obey, master, it said. *We are coming.*

Then Kirin suddenly realized what was happening.

He was waking the dragons.

He pulled the Gauntlet off.

There was an angry hiss inside his head as the world swam back into place. He was back in the room with the broken statue. The vision, or whatever it was, had ended. He was shivering, but his skin was burning hot.

He heard the dragon's voice again.

We wait, master, it said. *We sleep in silence. When you are ready, we will come to you.*

Kirin shuddered.

His head was spinning. Not because he had been standing high above the world in his dream, or because he was afraid. He was feeling dizzy because for one moment, when he had realized what was happening, he had felt insanely happy.

With this Gauntlet, I could rule the world, he had thought.

He had felt a rush of power quite unlike the ravian power he was learning to control. He had felt the magic of the dragons, and it was still beating inside him.

I almost gave in there, he thought. So this is what happened to Danh-Gem.

Will I be able to kill Danh-Gem? Or will I fail in the end? When the time came to strike I could not kill Bali. But Danh-Gem is different. If I let him live, people all over the world will die.

Maya would be in danger.

And that's not even the main reason. I have to finish my father's task. And even though Danh-Gem didn't kill my parents himself, he was responsible for their deaths. He's the only reason I'm here. When the time comes to kill him, I will be ready.

He looked at the Gauntlet, glowing red in his hands. Danh-Gem must not get his hands on this, he thought. Because, unlike me, he doesn't think conquering the world is a pointless thing to do. And with this . . .

He walked out of the room and into the tunnel. The world was slowly returning to normal, and he suddenly heard, through the tunnel, the sound of the wind howling over Mount Laoye.

Well, that's it, he thought. Just one more thing left to do.

Then he heard a voice over the wind. A voice screaming, 'No!'

A familiar voice.

In fact, his favourite voice in the whole world.

'*Maya?*' he said. 'What on earth . . .'

He ran out of the tunnel and into the storm.

Gaam had wounded Bali, and though Asvin was a skilled swordsman, the vanar was winning. Asvin was beginning to look tired, his breath was coming in ragged gulps, and his sword-arm was almost wilting.

Maya was hovering around them, sending fireballs flying at Bali whenever Asvin was far enough to be safe, but the wind and the snow were turning her missiles aside.

Bali was losing a lot of blood. But his eyes were gleaming with malice, and a horrible smile was fixed on his lips, for he was happiest when fighting.

He dropped his guard. Asvin lunged forward, and realized too late that it was a trick. Bali stepped to one side, ducked and swung Gaam's axe with all the strength in his mighty body. The axe sliced through the air and landed horizontally across Asvin's chest with a sickening thud. Asvin looked at the axe buried in his chest. He looked mildly surprised. He took a step backwards and fell heavily.

He stayed down.

'No!' screamed Maya. She was too tired to throw any more fireballs.

'No more fire from you, my dear,' snarled Bali, leaping at her and pinning her down on the snow. He held her hands in a crushing grip. 'Now I threw one down the mountain, and cut the other in half. I think you are going to talk.'

He dragged her to the edge of the precipice and made her look down.

'You don't want to join your friend down there!' he roared. 'Show me how to escape through the mirror!'

'I can't,' she said, watching his gleaming fangs inches above her face. 'I can't make the mirror work.'

'You lie!'

He stood above her fallen form, his foot on her neck.

'I will tear your limbs apart with my bare hands if you cannot show me the way off this accursed mountain,' he snarled.

Behind them, Asvin got up, rubbing his chest.

He was not even bleeding. The armour really was unbreakable. He should have been sliced into two pieces by that mighty blow.

He saw Bali holding Maya's head over the edge of the precipice. He sprang to his feet.

Seconds later, the blade of his sword was sticking out of the front of Bali's head.

Asvin sank to the ground, completely spent.

Bali looked at him, then at Maya. He lurched forward, and toppled over the edge. And fell like a stone into the great precipice.

They lay silently on the snow for some time, listening to the wind blowing over the mountain and the sound of their hearts pounding. Then Maya got up and pulled Asvin to his feet.

'You saved my life,' she said.

'Finally,' said Asvin, smiling. 'I've lost count of the number of times you've saved mine.'

'Your sword! You've lost your sword. The most powerful sword in the world.'

'As Gaam said, there are many other swords. Do you seriously think I could have kept the sword and let him kill you?'

'Well,' said Maya, grinning as she cast a healing spell on him, 'heroes are supposed to be obsessed with their swords. And you're so obsessed with being a hero.'

'If I had anything else to hit him with, I would not have used the sword.' He locked her hands in his.

'You could have hit him with Gaam's axe,' she pointed out, pretending she hadn't noticed.

'I could have. That's true. Has it ever occurred to you that you might be very important to me?' He pulled her to him.

'I could never be a hero's consort,' she said.

'No one's asking you to be one.'

She looked genuinely puzzled. 'Does that mean you see me as an equal, or does it mean you're not in love with me?'

'You're more intelligent than I am. Decide for yourself.' He kissed her.

She pulled away after a while. 'Asvin, Gaam's dead,' she said. 'I just remembered.'

It hit him then. Tears sprang to his eyes. 'I can't believe I forgot,' he said bitterly. 'All I could think about after killing the vanar was how much I love you.'

But Maya wasn't looking at him. She was looking over his shoulder with a shocked expression on her face at someone standing a little distance away from them, watching them intently, something red glowing in his hand.

'Kirin?' she said.

Kirin stood there silently, looking at her face in the white light, not even noticing the storm.

Asvin looked at her, stunned. 'My name is Asvin,' he said coldly. Up in the monastery, the alarm-gongs were ringing wildly.

'Kirin!' yelled Maya, shoving Asvin aside, and started towards Kirin.

But Kirin didn't reply. He had seen enough. He turned and ran into the howling wind.

'Kirin, wait!' yelled Maya, running blindly behind him, snow lashing across her face. Behind her, Asvin realized what was going on and gave chase too.

I bring death and danger to those I care about, thought Kirin as he sped across the snow. We weren't supposed to meet. It's better this way. She'll be happy with him. He's a hero. She's probably in love with him too. Look at me! I'm not even human. I don't even belong in this world. But I'm glad I got to see her again before the end. And if I do kill Danh-Gem, I will not stay, he decided. I'll go wherever my people are, and make things easier for everyone in this world. I'll make things easier for her. She can forget all about me and be happy with her hero.

He raised his arms and the fireball above Maya's head went out.

Kirin disappeared behind a rock ledge.

When Maya managed to light a fireball again, Kirin was gone. She ran to where she had last seen him, jumped over the ledge and reached a strange flat circle in the rock, rapidly disappearing in the snow.

'It was Kirin!' she yelled as Asvin caught up. 'He had the Gauntlet, too! He disappeared! What's going on?'

'Come away,' said Asvin, grabbing her arm. He was feeling a wild surge of jealousy, an emotion that was completely new to him.

Above them, there were shouts. The Green Serpent Guards had seen Maya's fireball. Bows twanged and the air was suddenly thick with arrows. They were coming down the slope, firing at the light.

Maya put out her fireball and they ran in silence to Yong-gan's cave. But as they disappeared into the snow, one of the Green Serpents saw them and shouted. Arrows flew into the cave entrance as Asvin turned the mirror black. Then they dashed through the mirror, and cannoned into Mantric, who was waiting anxiously in Bolvudis.

'What happened? Where's Gaam?' he asked, but they said nothing, falling to the floor and panting as they recovered their breath.

On Mount Laoye, the mirror turned silver just before the first guard fell into the cave and fired an arrow into it. As other guards fell through the snow-illusion, Yong-gan's mirror broke into a thousand pieces. The storm howled on outside.

It's almost over, thought Kirin, as the Chariot of Vul sped away from the mountain. Just one more step. And I'm not going to think about Maya any more. She probably never even missed me.

But he thought of nothing else for the next eight days, while the rickshaw sped through the long tunnels from Xi'en to Imokoi.

17

The full moon shone down on the Circle of Darkness. It shone down on a huge circle of flat earth, at least five hundred feet in diameter, in the centre of a huge, barren plain, where grass had not grown for years, where no bird or beast lived, where no sound disturbed the eerie silence except the mournful whistling of the dry summer wind. A wide ditch ran around the circle with an entrance to the west. No one knew whether some ancient power lay on that circle, or whether it had been filled with earth carried from somewhere else, because the earth in the circle seemed a shade darker than the rest of the plain.

It shone down on the ring of megaliths that stood in the centre of the circle, huge menhirs of bluestone, eight feet apart, forming a circle that was a hundred feet across. These giant blocks were connected by more blocks laid horizontally on their tops, forming an elevated circle of stone that had once been continuous, but was broken now—some of the horizontal blocks had fallen off and lay outside the circle, dull and grey in the moonlight.

It shone down on the pentagonal Altar Stone that lay in

the middle of the stone ring, where the druids of Ventelot of old had carried out their mysterious rituals in the light of the moon centuries ago.

And it shone down on a giant bubble that was rising silently from the depths of the earth just outside the Circle of Darkness.

Kirin climbed out of the crater and looked around. The first thing that struck him was the silence. There was no wind, and no sign of life anywhere. He looked up, and saw the stars glittering in the clear sky, and the full moon shining coldly on the stones ahead of him.

He walked into the Circle of Darkness, and as he crossed the ditch he heard a harsh croak. Startled, he looked around, and saw a large black crow sitting in the moonlight, on top of a fallen menhir.

'He's here,' said Kraken.

Out of the deep shadows cast by the giant pillars of rough-hewn stone walked Bjorkun and Angda.

'Get the others, Kraken,' said Angda. Kraken flew off.

'Welcome, Karisman,' said Bjorkun. 'We have been waiting for you. The others are hiding close by, they will be here soon. But where is Bali?'

'Dead,' said Kirin.

As Angda cast herself on the ground and wept, a cold wind from the mountains to the west began to blow across the plain.

Asvin, Maya and Mantric walked out of Jaadur's mirror. The Chief Civilian was waiting for them.

'You will stay in Kol from now,' she told Asvin. 'Because your time has come. My spies tell me that the forces of Danh-Gem are united, and they wait for his call. Our forces are waiting, too, in case my efforts to stop a war fail. As I suspect they will.

'As for why I have brought you here tonight, there are two reasons. First, since Danh-Gem was killed on full moon night in Dragonmonth two hundred years ago, I thought it would be an interesting idea to go to Enki University and look at the Fountain. Let us see how much magic is flowing through the air and the earth tonight. And second, there is someone I want you to meet.'

She led them down long corridors to a small room where a vaman was standing, a battleaxe in his hand. He was richly dressed, and when he turned towards them they cried out in joy, because his face was a face they knew well.

'Gaam!' cried Asvin, springing forward to embrace him.

But the vaman raised a hand. 'I am not Gaam Vatpo,' he said. 'But the error you make is a common one, for even vamans cannot tell us apart at times. I am his brother, Mod.'

Their faces fell. 'We are one with you in this time of grief, Mod,' said Asvin. 'Gaam was with us when he died.'

A strange smile played across Mod's face. 'I will not mourn yet,' he said. 'We vamans do not consider a vaman dead if he was lost anywhere near the earth. Not until Gaam's body is found will I believe that he is dead.'

'Mod is the ambassador of the vaman king in Bhumi,' said the Civilian. 'As you probably know, Kol and Bhumi have signed a treaty of alliance. If there is a war, the vamans are with us.'

But they were not interested in politics just then. 'Is that just a custom, or is there some reason to believe Gaam may still be alive?' asked Mantric.

Mod smiled again. 'I have lived in Bhumi most of my life,' he said. 'I am telling you this only because you were his friends. There are vaman mines hidden under the Mountains of Harmony. If Gaam survived the fall, he would go underground to these mines, for he knows where they are.'

'How?' asked Mantric, startled.

'The vamans have ways of going home,' said Mod. 'I cannot reveal them. Of course, chances are he is dead, but do not despair just yet.'

The full moon shone down on the Circle of Darkness.

It shone down on the faces of the eight members of the Brotherhood of Renewal, standing around the Altar Stone.

Omar unsheathed his sword and saluted the sky. 'Brothers,' he said, 'this is our hour of triumph. We are all here tonight . . .'

'We are not all here,' snapped Bjorkun. 'You may not care about Bali's absence, but I do. Let us not have any speeches. Karisman, tell us what to do.'

'Bali may not be here, but Angda represents the vanars tonight,' said Omar smoothly. 'They have served us well, and deserve our gratitude.'

'Served us?' said Angda incredulously.

'It seems to me that you forget your place, westerner,' rumbled Aciram.

'Can we get on with this?' asked Kirin.

'First,' he said, as they subsided, glowering, 'we need your claw on the stone, Spikes.'

Spikes said nothing. He unsheathed the claws on one hand, laid it down on the stone, and brought his other hand down upon it with a mighty crack on one finger. The claw broke off. Spikes walked back and stood beside Kirin. If he felt any pain, he did not show it.

A mild tremor ran through the earth.

'The Tear of the Sky,' said Kirin.

Bjorkun set it on the Altar Stone beside Spikes's claw.

None of them saw the dark clouds that were gathering in the west, heading towards the Circle of Darkness faster than the wind that was whistling through the stones.

'The jinn-lamp.'

Omar set it down beside the gem.

'The Iron Crown.'

King Hooba held it in his hands for a moment, looking at it longingly. Then he put it down on the pentagonal stone, beside the lamp.

The clouds shut out the stars to the west. Thunder rumbled far away.

Then, there was darkness. They looked up and saw the clouds speeding over to the east, shutting out the stars.

'It is time,' said Bjorkun, in an awed voice, his long hair flying about in the strong wind sweeping across the Circle.

'And finally,' said Kirin, feeling the earth tremble, and trying to keep his own voice from shaking, 'the Gauntlet of Tatsu.'

He took the Gauntlet out from the folds of his cloak and they gasped as it shone fire-red in the darkness. He looked at their faces, red and black. He looked at Spikes, and tried to smile but couldn't. He stepped forward and set the Gauntlet down between Spikes's claw and the Iron Crown.

The red light went out.

The wind stopped abruptly. He could see nothing.

No one said anything.

He stood there in the darkness for a minute, and then couldn't bear the silence any longer.

'Well, we've done our bit,' he said feebly. 'What do you think happens now?'

No one replied.

'Well?' he asked. 'Say something, someone!'

He reached out and touched Spikes. 'What is it?' he whispered. Spikes said nothing.

Sudden terror, deep and silent, struck Kirin. He ran to where Angda had been standing on his left, and felt for her in the darkness.

He found her, touched the smooth muscles on her back, but something was wrong.

She was as hard as Spikes. 'Angda?' he said, loudly, but she didn't reply.

Then it hit him suddenly. Angda had turned to stone. He ran past her, feeling along the edge of the Altar Stone, and found Bjorkun. He'd been turned to stone too.

He looked around wildly, but saw nothing. The Shadowknife turned into a sword and he swung it around, tentatively.

The silence was killing him. He wanted light, sound, anything, any sign of life.

As if in answer, thunder rumbled again, very close. A huge bolt of lightning forked through the sky outside the Circle, splitting the plain where it landed.

Then the clouds above Kirin shifted slightly, and a single, incredibly bright moonbeam shone through, falling gently on the Altar Stone, lighting up the five objects Danh-Gem needed. Kirin heard the splatter of raindrops, and whirled around. Torrents of water were stinging the plains all around him, but inside the Circle of Darkness no rain fell.

There was a loud crack, and the Altar Stone split in half. And Danh-Gem rose.

The Altar Stone crumbled to pieces. The five objects scattered on the ground.

A small cloud slowly formed above them, wispy at first, but growing stronger and taking shape. It grew darker and thicker, whirling and solidifying, until edges and lines appeared, and Danh-Gem stood in the moonlight.

No one had ever seen a painting of Danh-Gem, but Kirin had expected a giant creature wielding terrible weapons, a rakshas man-shaped, black or dark blue, red-lipped, white-fanged, dressed in skins and skulls, awe-inspiring, death-dealing.

But Danh-Gem was man-sized and grey-cloaked, a little shorter than Kirin. A large hood covered his face. Yet Kirin could feel the power of the eyes under the hood; he could feel them darting around, looking at the stone figures around him, searching for something. Danh-Gem's movements were quick and cat-like. He stepped lightly off the rubble of the Altar Stone and looked at the objects lying on the ground.

The Shadowknife twisted and writhed in Kirin's hand, sensing the rush of power that was flooding through him.

Then Danh-Gem saw Kirin. He turned towards him. His eyes were hidden under the shadow of the hood, but Kirin saw his mouth. A strong jaw, and even white teeth, smiling coldly.

It was as if Kirin's blood had been turned to ice. Danh-Gem's gaze hit him like a cold slap, and for a moment he felt as if he was rooted to the earth. But he summoned all the power that lay within him, the power that ran through his blood, the power his parents had left him. And suddenly he was free.

Kirin lunged forward and plunged the Shadowknife into Danh-Gem's heart.

'I think,' said Mantric slowly, 'that Danh-Gem has returned.'

They were in a great hall in Enki, looking at the University Fountain, at the water brought from the Vertical Sea.

'It's never been this high before,' said Chancellor Ombwiri. 'Never. And as for what just happened—it's completely unprecedented. Not even in the Age of Terror did the water ever rise this high.'

The Fountain was empty.

The water was on the ceiling.

The Unkissable Toad, who lived in the Fountain, was croaking in astonishment.

'This means the dragons are awake,' said the Civilian. 'And if Danh-Gem has the Gauntlet . . .'

'But Kirin has the Gauntlet,' protested Maya.

'And your friend Kirin, the other missing link,' said the Civilian slowly. 'The last of the ravians. No doubt he is involved in whatever is going on. I only hope his designs succeed.'

'Unless he's a traitor. Unless he's working for Danh-Gem. Unless he was lying to you all along,' said Asvin harshly.

'You have no idea what you're talking about,' snapped Maya. 'I don't understand how you can be so stupid.'

'This is not the time for arguments,' said Mantric. 'Do you not realize what has happened? Danh-Gem has risen again. Now whatever it is that Kirin is doing, if humans are to solve this problem, the solution lies in Asvin's hands. We must get ready for whatever is coming. Difficult times lie ahead. I see great deeds ahead, for both of you. For all of us. Exciting times lie ahead. Dangerous, yes. But interesting times. Very interesting indeed.'

'If Danh-Gem has indeed risen tonight, we will get to know by tomorrow,' said the Civilian. 'In that case, Asvin, tomorrow will be a big day for you. Tomorrow you will be revealed to the world. You will become its greatest hope. If anything can bring hope to the people when the dragons of Danh-Gem attack, it will be the knowledge that the Hero of Simoqin is on their side.'

'I will not fail you,' said Asvin solemnly.

'I know,' said the Civilian. 'In this at least we have succeeded, this battle at least we have won. This may be one of the most important nights of your life, Asvin. A chapter is closed for you, and a new one is beginning. Your training is complete. Soon the world will know a new hero.'

They stood in silence, watching the water as it rippled in the dome on the ceiling.

The Shadowknife passed right *through* Danh-Gem.

The seconds turned into hours for Kirin. He felt the knife pass into the grey cloak, not even tearing it. He stumbled, fell forward, and passed into Danh-Gem.

He felt coldness, numbing, bone-chilling coldness as their bodies came together. Then a sudden, gladdening gush of warmth, of life as he passed *through* Danh-Gem, tripping, falling, landing on the ground heavily. He rolled over, his mind working furiously.

I struck too soon! He hasn't materialized fully yet!

He groaned as he rolled over and prepared to spring to his feet. Now Danh-Gem would be aware of him. He would have to fight Danh-Gem. The element of surprise, his chief weapon, had gone.

He looked at Danh-Gem. The rakshas was not charging at him, hands raised, to deliver a killing blow. He had turned, and was looking down and smiling at Kirin, a mildly amused smile.

Then he laughed. Aloud.

A cold, dry laugh.

Danh-Gem lifted a hand to his hood and threw it back, uncovering his face.

And Kirin froze to the ground and stared in stunned silence.

It was the face of someone who looked very like Kirin.

There was a scar on the left side of the face, from beside the eyebrow all the way down to the jaw. The face looked older than Kirin, the jaw was stronger, the eyebrows were a little thicker and the lips a little thinner than Kirin's.

It was the face of Narak.

Hero finds book, apparently by coincidence. Book contains apparently trustworthy character, with strong resemblance to hero. Hero trusts book. But book turns out to be villain. Surprise, surprise. Fight. Hero battles all odds and wins the day. Not my own idea. Got it from a book. A human book, funnily enough, written by a young woman in Ventelot whom I subsequently ate. Humans do have their uses, said the cold voice in his head, the voice that Kirin knew so well. *But there's a vital difference in our story, Kirin. Because I am not a villain.*

'And I,' said Kirin, standing up, 'am not a hero.'

He jumped forward and swung the Shadowknife, but it passed through Danh-Gem again.

You can't hurt me, Kirin, said Danh-Gem. *The Shadowknife is my own weapon. Calm down, sit down, and listen to me.*

'No,' said Kirin. 'You fooled me completely, I admit. I've lost. I feel absolutely no desire to sit here and listen to you gloat. You shouldn't have pretended to be my father. Just kill me quickly and do whatever it is you want to do with the world. I have nowhere to go, no one to go to. I don't want to hear how you fooled me. You've won. Just kill me.'

Danh-Gem laughed. *So you deny me the pleasure of the Long Explanation. You really aren't a hero, Kirin. Any hero worth his sword and his big boots would know that the part of the story where the villain holds him captive and tells him every minute detail of his master plan is the part where he gets the time to think of a miraculous means of escape. But you know there is no means of escape, there is no one to save you, and you ask me to kill you so you don't have to hear me go on and on about how clever I am. But I won't kill you, Kirin. And if you think I'm alive again, you're wrong. If you really want to know the truth, I can't kill you. I don't have enough power. You can walk away from here, and I won't harm you. You are free to go.*

But where would you go? No one in the world outside will believe you, Kirin. And you cannot use my chariot until I let you do so again. So sit down and listen. Simply because you will learn a lot if you listen.

Kirin couldn't see a flaw in Danh-Gem's reasoning. He sat down and listened.

I am dead, Kirin. Your mother killed me. No one comes back from the dead, Kirin. Not even me. I can't take over the world. I am, as they say, history.

'Why all this, then?' asked Kirin. 'What was the point of all this?'

The point to all this was to give you a choice, Kirin. To give you a chance to rule the world.

'Me?' asked Kirin. 'Why would you want me to rule the world?'

Because I love you.

He's mad, thought Kirin, but suddenly he didn't care any more. He laughed aloud. 'Of course you do,' he said. 'It all makes sense to you, no doubt. But may I ask why you love me?'

I love you, Kirin, because I am your father.

The clouds parted, and the full moon shone down again on the Circle of Darkness. Kirin saw the other members of the Brotherhood standing stone-stiff, with horrified expressions on their faces and awe in their unseeing eyes. Danh-Gem followed his gaze.

They will wake later. I felt the need for a private conversation.

'What do you mean, you're my father?' said Kirin. 'Even if I forget all the lies you told me when you were pretending to be Narak, I still remember my parents' names. I am the son of Narak the Demon-hunter and Isara. All your lies cannot change that.'

True. You are the son of Narak and Isara. The thing is, I am Narak the Demon-hunter.

'What are you saying?' asked Kirin incredulously. 'You're a ravian?'

No. I'm a rakshas.

'Well, it looks like I'm going to listen to your Long Explanation after all. But you'll lie to me again, won't you?'

No. But this time, it doesn't matter to me whether you believe me or not. Because I will never see you again after tonight. The power I used to make the book you found is almost drained. I am here only because I could never care for you as much as I should have when I was alive, and I want to make up for that now.

'You're growing weak again? But my head isn't aching.'

The headaches were my excuse for disappearing whenever I didn't want to answer your questions.

'I see. Anyway, that's the least of my worries now. So I'm a rakshas, not a ravian?'

No. I told you, Kirin, rakshases and ravians can both have children with other species. Remember the tales of the half-rakshas heroes? I even told you about half-ravians, how it was dangerous for them to travel between worlds. In fact, the spell that turned you to stone when the ravians departed probably saved your life as well. How could you pass through the portal to the next world? You're not wholly ravian.

Of course, no one could imagine a rakshas and a ravian getting married and having a child, so I don't blame you for being amazed. You are half rakshas and half ravian, Kirin. That is why you have a few powers of each, and lack some of each as well. You cannot control minds completely, like true ravians could—that power is there within you, but it is weak. And you cannot change shape like rakshases can. But you have mental power over objects, like ravians, and you can play tricks with fire and with light and darkness, like rakshases.

'But I was casting human spells then. The spells I learnt in Kol, the spells a spellbinder friend of mine taught me.'

Human spells! Danh-Gem laughed. *There is no such thing as a human spell, Kirin. Humans have no magic in their blood.*

'That's not true. The spellbinders are very powerful.'

What the spellbinders do is rakshas magic, Kirin. That is

why you can do spellbinder magic, too. The spellbinders have rakshas blood in them.

'I don't believe you.'

What do you know about rakshases, Kirin? Nothing. You know nothing except the things foolish humans write. There was a time, long before I came into power, when rakshases roamed freely among humans, in human cities. You forget that rakshases can change shape. Not all rakshases live in forests and eat humans. Many of us spent thousands of years living amongst humans, disappearing when people began wondering why we didn't die.

'So if magical creatures are reappearing now, I suppose it means that rakshases in human form are walking the streets of Kol. Eating people.'

I myself think humans serve only two purposes—food and sport. But not all rakshases are like that. Very few of us eat humans, in fact. Most rakshases didn't like the idea of eating things that talked. They were the rakshas equivalent of human vegetarians. Many even married humans and had children with them. Many humans spent their lives not knowing they were married to rakshases or rakshasis. Spellbinders, sorcerers, druids and mages were the results of these marriages. They were mortal, but could do magic. Of course, the blood was diluted when the pure rakshases disappeared—today's spellbinders are weak in magic, and their life spans are as short as those of ordinary humans. The spellbinders, of course, know nothing of this—they just think they are extraordinarily gifted. Typical human behaviour—ignore things that stare you in the face.

'Why didn't you tell me all this before? Why did you lie to me?'

You wouldn't have believed me. You don't believe me fully even now. And there is no reason why you should. But you would have simply thrown the book away if I had told you in the library that I was Danh-Gem. Because you have spent years among humans, Kirin. You believe that all rakshases are evil. Just as you believe that all ravians were noble creatures.

Kirin was silent. For some strange reason, he was sure Danh-Gem was telling him the truth. But he was far from convinced.

'Tell me more,' he said. 'Why did my mother marry you? How can you be Narak *and* Danh-Gem at the same time? How did you really die? Nothing makes sense.'

It is a long story, Kirin. A story I have waited two hundred years to tell.

First, let me make one thing clear. I am not evil. Neither, of course, am I good. I am a rakshas. I do not feel apologetic for anything I have done. I make no excuse for who I am. Everything I did, I did knowingly.

Kirin nodded. 'Go on. I have the time, and I'm supposed to be immortal. But if you're really dead, and you stand to gain nothing from this, don't lie to me.'

I am telling you the truth this time, Kirin. Now listen to my story.

The story begins centuries ago when a young rakshas, hunting in Vrihataranya, saw a shining light a little distance away, and went closer to look.

When I reached the place where I had seen the flash of light, I found a young man lying on the ground. I was hungry, and charged at him in tiger form, but even though he could not have seen me, he sprang up and out of the way.

Long I chased him, but he was quick, and he had mysterious powers. He brought branches crashing down on my head— sometimes he flung me back by just pointing at me. Try as I might, I could not catch him.

I chased him deep into the forest and he was lost. I knew he could be no human, that he was not of this world. I took human form, spoke to him and befriended him.

His name was Narak, and he was a ravian. A low-caste apprentice warrior-mage who had been sent from the world the ravians were planning to leave, to see if this one was inhabitable. As we walked through the jungle, I questioned him skilfully— he revealed all he knew about the ravians and their customs.

I knew right then that a new power was going to enter our world, a power that would change the world even if it did not seek to dominate it. And I was worried. I had to know more about this power. I killed Narak and ate him, and then took his shape. Days later, when more ravians came to our world, they found me. I told them the world was not fit for ravians to live in. But they were not convinced. They looked around, liked our world and decided to stay.

'And you stayed with them, as Narak.'

The city of Asroye was founded in the heart of Vrihataranya. I helped in its making. My six brothers lived in Vrihataranya, and I would divide my time between them and Asroye. At that time I had no plans of conquering the world. The rakshases do not unite easily, Kirin. They are not hungry for power.

In the beginning I was fascinated by the ravians—I idolized them, and considered myself incredibly blessed because I lived among them. Of course, that changed later.

Their magic in particular amazed me, and I decided to learn it. My toys, made with rakshas magic, fascinated them, and they paid me good money, money which I put to good use. And then, one day, I saw the princess Isara.

I forgot everything else, and was consumed with love. I tried to abduct her in rakshas form, and she defeated me with magic but did not kill me. I returned to Asroye with a new mission in life—I resolved to win her hand. I resolved to be worthy of her.

My family was powerful amongst rakshases even then—we were waging war against the armies of Ventelot, who were trying to clear Vrihataranya to set up their foolish cities. As my power grew, so did our might. I learnt all about politics and war from ravian books, and put my new knowledge to good use. We began to expand our territory, and our power grew. Slowly rakshases from all over the world began to flock under my banner.

Kirin looked at the figure of his father as he paced from stone to stone, a distant glitter in his eyes.

One day, my brothers brought me news of a magical Gauntlet in Xi'en. A Gauntlet that would let its wearer control the dragons. As soon as I heard of it, I desired it madly. I journeyed to Xi'en, and after great hardships, dug through the mountain and stole the Gauntlet. The dragons bowed to me, and I was drunk with power. Then for a while I lost control, and did many cruel things that I bitterly regret now.

In the years I had spent in Asroye, I had managed to meet Princess Isara a few times—she often bought toys from me, and we became friends. Every day I fell deeper and deeper in love with her. And I thought she returned my love but was afraid to acknowledge it. When I had the Gauntlet, I decided I would conquer the whole world and present myself as its ruler to the ravian king. That, I thought, would make me worthy of her even in his eyes.

And then I found allies all over the world. The asur-vaman wars had just taken place, and the vamans had established themselves as rulers of the underworld. The asurs had nowhere to go. Humans hated and feared them. And when they heard of the ravians, who had begun to venture forth and meet the rest of the world, they thought the ravians would give them the shelter they so badly needed. Ignorant fools.

The ravians thought the asurs were the most despicable creatures they had ever seen. They hunted them like animals, Kirin, and filled the plains south of Vrihataranya with asur carcasses, for the ravians were mighty sorcerers and wielded terrible weapons. So where did the asurs go? They came to the new rakshas-lord whose fame was beginning to spread all over the world, the only ruler who cared not that they were ugly and barbaric. They came to Danh-Gem.

And I don't blame them, thought Kirin. Or the pashans, for that matter. The way the Avrantics sneer at them even today . . .

With the asurs, we rakshases conquered Imokoi and set up a rakshas kingdom there. I learnt the secret of pashan birth, and I made the asurs build giant furnaces in Imokoi. There I raised my elite pashan soldiers, and was delighted by their strength and cunning. The first pashan I created, Katar, became my closest friend and companion.

The whole world realized that war was coming, and it was time to gather armies and build armouries. The humans and I happened to go to the vamans on the same day for help, for vaman craftsmen have always been the world's finest.

The few vamans bold enough to come to the surface fought for the humans, but I gained a treasure as priceless as the Gauntlet—the Chariot of Vul. My problems were solved. I could go anywhere in the world at incredible speeds, and no one would suspect a thing.

I found allies in Artaxerxia and Skuanmark—I fanned the age-old hatred that lay between these two kingdoms and Avranti and Ventelot, and used their armies to overrun Elaken and Ventelot. But I had no intention of harming the ravians. Neither did I attack Kol then, for they already had the ravians' favour. Lord Simoqin used to travel to Kol often, and the power of the spellbinders was stabilized by his gift, the Heart of Magic.

Even so, I had become the most powerful ruler in the world.

I returned to Asroye. I had been missed there, but no one suspected who I really was. I met Isara in secret, and our meeting was joyous, for she loved me dearly too.

One day, in rakshas form, I caught a ravian in the forest and sent him to the king with a letter, formally worded in flawless Ravianic, begging for his daughter's hand in marriage. Fool that I was.

The king was enraged. I realized the depths of my idiocy— I had realized long ago that he would not even let her marry a low-caste ravian and I had actually thought he would let her marry a rakshas!

The ravians hunted down one of my brothers, Kirin. They killed him. He had done nothing to them—they simply killed him because another rakshas had dared to presume to ask for the ravian princess' hand. And on his body they scrawled the most arrogant, the most humiliating message possible. Pacing through the jungle anxiously, waiting for word from the king, I found the mutilated body of my brother.

My fury knew no bounds. I now knew I had wasted all those years—taken so many lives, destroyed so many families—chasing something that would never be mine.

It was then I found out that my love was betrothed to Simoqin, Lord Simoqin the Dreamer, high-caste, gentle ravian-lord, handsome, noble, brave. I could not bear it.

I took ravian form, entered Asroye, and lured Simoqin out. Then as a rakshas, I fought him in the forest, summoned Mritik and bore Simoqin back to Imokoi.

He was stronger than I thought. Long we fought under the shadows of the trees. He wounded me—Danh-Gem ran a long finger along the scar on his cheek—*but I was stronger.*

But when we were back in Imokoi, I realized I had made a mistake. Of course, the ravians started the quarrel with the rakshases, but bringing Simoqin to Imokoi was not a wise move. For I knew in my heart that if the ravians fought against me, I would lose. They were too strong for me.

It was from Simoqin that I found out that the ravians were planning to leave this world, that some of them thought they were harming it with the great infusion of magic they had brought into it. And then a thought struck me—what if I could return after they had gone? What if I could avoid their trap?

'And so you made the Prophecy on Simoqin's chest,' said Kirin.

Yes. Of course, as you may know, I did not believe in prophecies, so the silly rhyme I scrawled on Simoqin's chest was a savage joke—revenge, if you will.

'The Prophecy was a joke?'

Initially. But then the idea was born in my head—why not make my own Prophecy come true? If the ravians fought me, I would disappear, and I would return when they had gone. The Prophecy, if it were made known throughout the lands, would ensure that my followers remembered me when I returned from hiding, and that they would be ready to obey my commands.

I wanted the ravians to read what I had written, for only then would my brother be avenged. So, as Narak, I returned to Asroye, with Simoqin. The fool was barely alive, and quite mad. He kept babbling about some dream he had seen, of a mirror and a hero. He repeated this to Isara, and died.

'The hero Simoqin spoke of does exist, actually,' said Kirin. 'He is a very brave and noble young man.'

We need not bother with Simoqin's hopes. They were all doomed to failure. Let me return to my tale.

After my return to Asroye, I dwelt there for a while, ruling

Imokoi from afar. I became Asroye's greatest hero. The ravian-rakshas war had started, and my blows struck deeper than any other. The ravians did not follow their own noble battle rules— they fought as dirtily as the most desperate rakshases. They used bribery, treachery, deceit, traps—as did we, I confess—it was war. I was a part of the councils of the ravians—I would know which of the asurs, humans and rakshases were turning traitor, and would have them killed. At the same time, I would venture forth to battle with other ravian heroes, and I would be the only one who returned.

A year after Simoqin's death, your mother and I were secretly betrothed.

Even my own forces did not know the truth behind Narak the Demon-hunter. None save my brothers, none of whom survived the war, and my wily cousin, Aciram.

So that was why he was looking at me strangely, thought Kirin. He thought I was my father.

When I knew that all the ravians looked up to me, I asked the king for his daughter's hand. Once again I was refused, as I have told you before. It mattered not that I was the greatest of the ravian heroes—my caste alone made me unworthy of her. But this time, many of the king's most powerful generals were on my side, and so was the princess herself. We were married, and were banished from Asroye. But even in exile, we were famous.

But the more I witnessed the might of the ravians, the more I knew that my days were numbered. And I knew I could not tell Isara the truth—like all ravians, she hated rakshases. I realized that the only way to defeat the ravians was to outlast them, to lie in wait until they left—to make my own Prophecy come true.

Danh-Gem stopped walking around, and sat down. He looked at Kirin, and smiled suddenly. A gentle light shone in his eyes. He was silent for a few moments. Then he spoke again, louder, because the rain was falling hard outside the Circle.

Then you were born. You cannot imagine how happy I was that day, Kirin. But I could not spend time with you, as I wished to—there was always some battle, some hero to dispose of, some traitor to eliminate. And no matter how long I studied magic, ravian or rakshas, I could not find a spell mighty enough to wake me up after two hundred years. So I decided it would be you. If the ravians won, I would save you from the dangerous portal and somehow guide you, somehow ensure you were the most powerful being walking this world.

As I told you, I always had an alternative plan.

'And that's why I'm here today, is it. Because I was your alternative plan.'

I decided that whether I survived or not, you would have the chance to rule the world; you would have the chance to do what your father could not—utterly defeat the stratagems of the ravians. I began to look for spells that would keep me preserved in some form for two hundred years, and at the same time I started writing the book as Narak. If I won the Great War, I thought, if I destroyed the ravians, I would give you all the love any father could ever give. If I failed, however, I wanted to be sure that you would have everything I had struggled for—that your life would be extraordinary.

The War was at its peak, then, and my brothers were sending me messages urging me to return to Imokoi and lead the dragons into battle against Kol. I left Vrihataranya, to prepare for the Last Battle, knowing I might never see your mother again. I bade my love farewell for the last time. It was then that she revealed that she had secretly prepared a spell, a spell mighty enough to slay Danh-Gem. I was shocked, but I persuaded her to wait for a year, to give me time to find out about Danh-

Gem's warning. It would take me that much time, I thought, to either annihilate the ravians or create a spell that would make me sleep for two hundred years, like the one I had made for you.

'Did she never suspect that you were a rakshas?'

No.

'You must have been a very good actor, then.'

I did not have to act, Kirin. To Isara, I was a loving husband, a powerful sorcerer and a strong warrior. All of which were true.

'I suppose so. Go on.'

I returned to Imokoi and immersed myself in preparation for the Last Battle. It was then that I made my greatest mistake. I completely forgot about Isara's spell—the War filled my mind.

I finished the book that would guide you, and decided that Katar's son would be the one who would wake you.

'So that story about controlling the mind of Katar was entirely untrue. I thought at the time it seemed improbable, but I had started trusting you long ago. You simply cast your spells on Spikes's egg.'

I did not need to cast any spell on Spikes—I knew that your very presence in this world would make him hunt for you until he found you, and the pull of my power in the books I was leaving behind to guide you would draw him to whatever city the books were in. But I put strong magic on the egg, so that it would hatch whether or not the stork that was carrying it delivered it to a suitable place.

The year passed incredibly quickly. The Last Battle was fought, and it was lost. But the books that would guide you were all finished, and after I returned from the Battle, I sent off a stork with Katar's son's egg. I decided to go into hiding, to somehow stage my own death, so that the ravians would leave.

'I was wondering about that. If you had managed to do that, all this wouldn't have been necessary, would it?'

I do not know. It is possible that I might have disappeared, like the other rakshases, when the ravians left. Turning you to stone at that time ensured that you did not vanish like the others, and when Spikes woke you up, magic started rising in the world again.

'I see. And Spikes isn't magical anyway. Go on with your story, then.'

I gave the books to the asurs, and told them to give them up to human sorcerers when they surrendered. I knew that human curiosity would ensure that the books, being sources of knowledge, would not be destroyed. I wrote them in Ravianic, in the language of the danavs, the language I had created myself, and hoped that somehow you would understand them one day. I gave the book to the asurs just in time—if I had kept it in the tower, Isara's spell would have destroyed it.

My work in Imokoi was done, and as I prepared for the last part of my plan, I heard my soldiers screaming. I went out on the battlements and saw your mother flying towards the tower, and realized my great mistake.

'Couldn't you have stopped her?'

I do not know. I could have tried. But to succeed, I would have had to kill her, and that I could not do.

'So you did nothing.'

I tried to stop her. I took ravian form and she saw me and would have stopped, but it was too late. Even as our eyes met, she released her mighty spell and I knew I was dead. I knew that my only chance to defeat the ravians was you.

'And casting the spell killed her as well.'

Danh-Gem looked shocked. He sat down on the ground, as if his knees had given way.

I did not know that. Are you sure?

'I remember being told that my parents were dead, by the ravians before they left.'

But were they sure?

'Does it matter?'

Danh-Gem looked at him silently for a while, then took a deep breath and continued.

I guessed the ravians would leave, and you would be brought up amongst humans. I also hoped you would discover either that you were ravian or that you were rakshas. I knew the former was more probable, and that is what happened, is it not?

Kirin nodded.

The spell obviously worked. You were turned into stone, and Spikes brought you to Kol.

I did not know how long it would take for Spikes to find you, or how long it would take for you to find the black book, so I turned my Prophecy to good use. I made up a list of five things you would have to get to restore me—five things that would ensure my followers were united, and you could wield their combined power if you wanted to. I kept one of Spikes's claws in the list of five simply so that my followers would need Spikes on their side, and you as well. The lamp and the crown ensured that the Artaxerxians and asurs would be behind you. Your translating the red book was smart work, but if you had not managed to translate the Asurian tongue I would have told you what the five objects were. But you managed on your own.

'And you helped me get the Gauntlet as well. And the gem?'

It will look good on the crown.

'That was the only reason?'

No. I kept it there as a test for you, a chance for you to have faith in your own powers, a chance for your allies to accept you as a leader and a chance for you to use the Chariot of Vul. By the way, only you can summon the chariot, because you are my son. The incantation was a little trick. The chariot will come whenever you want it too.

'It doesn't feel very nice, you know, hearing you tell me what a fool I was, and how easily you manipulated me. So far, my life was full of things I didn't understand. Now it all fits, but I don't like it at all. Making me think I was avenging my father's death—it worked, but I wish you had found another way.'

I pretended to be Narak simply because I knew that you would not listen to a rakshas. Besides, I was Narak, and a lot of the things I told you were completely true. And I suspected you would not be hungry for power, or be driven by greed, because neither of your parents was. I knew, therefore, that making you think you were avenging your father would be the surest way to make you follow my instructions. I wish I could have found another way, too. It was not pleasant for me either.

There were many flaws in the plan—you might easily have killed—or been killed by—any of my followers. I told you to wait, to be patient, and fortunately you listened. I hoped you would find some story to explain your powers to them, and you did. You are much like me, son.

'I don't understand one thing, though,' said Kirin. 'Were you awake all the time? Could you have risen whenever you wanted to?'

No. I was awakened by your touch, in the library in Kol. After that, I watched you all through. I spoke to you whenever I felt you needed it.

Of course, you made things difficult for me. From your talk with the girl you were in love with I understood that you were going to see the most powerful human spellbinder in the world. That was dangerous for me. The human might have told you not to trust me. Besides, I was sure by then that my followers all over the world were looking for Spikes, and if they found you with the spellbinders there would have been deaths—probably their *deaths—and then you would never have won their trust. When I told you that you would lead those you loved into danger I was telling you the truth—the vanars were following you.*

'Did you make that giant panther attack us?'

No. That was a fortunate coincidence. But the Bleakwood is a dangerous place. The rest of the tale you know. You gathered the objects and my followers, and here we are.

'Here we are, indeed,' said Kirin. He sighed. 'You are telling the truth, aren't you?'

Yes. Lying would not help me here. I cannot come back to life.

'So all I've done for the last few months has been a huge trick.'

Do not say that, Kirin. You have discovered your past, you have discovered who you are, you have discovered what you are capable of. You should be proud. I admit I brought you here by deceit, but what happens here tonight will determine the future of the world.

'Then tell me,' said Kirin. 'What happens now?'

He looked around at the stone figures of the Brotherhood of Renewal standing silently around them, then at Danh-Gem, who was watching his son with keen eyes.

I have another gift left to give you, son, said Danh-Gem. *I told you if you succeeded I would give you a choice. You have succeeded. As I said before, I will not force you to do anything, ever again. You will decide where you belong.*

The wind and the rain had stopped. The sky was clear. Father and son stood as still as the stones around them.

'Tell me,' said Kirin.

But before I tell you, Kirin, answer me. Do you hate me for what I did? Do you think I was wrong? Would you have done differently?

'I don't know,' said Kirin. 'I don't want to think about it. Does it matter?'

No.

'Tell me, then. What are these choices you wish to give me after two hundred years, that you evidently feel will set everything right?'

You will decide your own destiny from here, Kirin. You are my heir, the heir of Danh-Gem, and probably the greatest power alive on this earth. Soon I will wake your companions. The choices before you are very simple. You may leave, or you may stay. If you decide to leave, Mritik will take you wherever you want to go, and then disappear. And if you decide to stay—if you decide to stay, all my power will come to you. You will lead your companions down whatever road you wish to travel.

I do not ask you to choose between good and evil. I ask you to choose between awareness and ignorance, between action and inaction, between affirmation and denial. Now you know who you are. What you choose to do with that knowledge is for you to decide.

And you must decide. Now.

'Don't make it sound so simple,' said Kirin. 'You offer me armies, you offer me supporters. As you said, you offer me the chance to rule the world. But I don't think you understand a very simple thing. I don't want to rule the world. Yet if I go away . . .'

If you go away, it is likely that your former comrades will join forces anyway. War is coming, Kirin. Will you take part in it, or will you stand aside? The Brotherhood of Renewal seeks to dominate the world—with or without you. Will you let their powers combine and wreak havoc? Or will you step forward and decide what road they will take? Because you have the power to do so, Kirin. They will follow you blindly when they learn you are my son. You alone can unite all my followers of old. You alone can rule the rakshases.

'I don't want to be followed blindly. I don't seek power. I don't want to control people's lives.'

Danh-Gem didn't reply.

Kirin sat down on the ground and thought.

If I don't lead his followers, the world will be plunged into war and thousands will die. And I will end up thinking it was my fault—that I could have stopped the war. But even if I lead his armies, will I be able to stop the war?

And people all over the world will hate the son of Danh-Gem, whatever I do, simply because I'm half rakshas. I will be known as the Dark Lord, or something like that, and even if I try to set things right half the world will hate me and the rest will follow me out of fear.

And I'm not cut out to be a king.

But could I live with the knowledge that I could have stopped the war?

Actually, I could. Very easily. I'm sure I could convince myself it wasn't my fault. I'm clever enough to do that.

And I'm not above temptation, not at all . . . So much power . . . I would be lying to myself if I said it didn't tempt me. But will I be able to handle it?

What if I lose control? What if I go mad with power, as I suspect he did?

So rakshases weren't evil after all. And I would have died if I'd gone through the portal.

Of course, he could be lying.

I could set a lot of things right. I could stop the war. I could stop asur persecution. I could stop people from capturing magical creatures and killing them for their skins and horns. I could make sure all the non-human creatures in the world are treated better. There's a lot of injustice in the world and I could set things right.

But I could also set a lot of things wrong. Will I know where to stop?

It really is up to me, isn't it?

So I belong to this world after all. Well, part of me does, anyway. The ravian world, wherever it is, is closed to me now.

This means I'll probably see Maya again. What will she say? What will everyone say?

They'll all think I'm evil. Is anyone evil, really? Was my father evil?

Why? Because of his rakshas blood? What will the spellbinders say when I tell them the blood of rakshases flows through their veins too?

It's going to be fun.

No. I think I should walk away from it all. Even if I leave, I will still have my powers. I will still be myself. Besides, I'll have given up the chance to be the most powerful ruler in the world. Self-sacrifice and rejection of greed and temptation are what make a hero a hero.

That settles it.

Kirin looked into his father's eyes.

'I'll do it,' he said.

I was hoping you would.

'The other choice would have been too heroic.'

And you aren't a hero, are you. Neither was I.

Kirin smiled at the Rakshas. 'Yes,' he said, 'I'll do it.'

Of course, you do realize you're going to be extremely unpopular in certain parts of the world. I was not very nice to a lot of people.

'But tell me, if you could have come back yourself now, would you have tried to conquer the world?'

I've thought about that often, and I don't think I would have. After all, the ravians are gone, and I don't feel the n eed for revenge. I was very bloodthirsty before, but your mother changed that to a large extent. I might not have started another war. But then again, I might have. Old habits die hard.

'Well, what happens now?'

Now I tell you I think you made the right decision. And that you've made me very happy. Now I can depart knowing that my son knows the truth, that I have been able to give my son a great deal of power and the freedom to decide what he wants to do with the rest of his life.

'I'm touched,' Kirin smiled.

I must be getting old. I was never this sentimental before. But I can't get any older, can I? I'm dead.

Be that as it may, son, I still have one more gift to give you. Put on the Gauntlet.

'I don't want to control the dragons. Besides, the last time I put the Gauntlet on I almost lost my mind.'

You have already woken the dragons. You did that on the mountain. It is too late to turn back now. I know the feeling you speak of—the first time I put on the Gauntlet it happened to me too. The power of the dragons goes straight to your head. But it happens only once.

Kirin picked up the Gauntlet and put it on slowly. Nothing happened.

Then the earth trembled and shook, and the stone slabs that connected the tops of the rings of menhirs exploded into thousands of tiny fragments. It seemed to Kirin that the stones were burning.

Then the ground near the Altar Stone split in two, and the head of a dragon burst out into the night.

She was a Xi'en serpent-dragon, the most beautiful and terrible creature Kirin had ever seen. Her smooth scales were blacker than the night, her body was shining and incredibly long, her eyes were wise and shining white. Her sleek, sinuous body slid out of the earth, and she looked at Danh-Gem fondly. She wound herself around the ring of menhirs, and throwing her head upwards, let a stream of white fire up into the sky.

My last gift to you, son, said Danh-Gem, *is the Queen of Dragons, Qianzai, Mother of Darkness. The Gauntlet does not control her—no power on earth can tame her or enslave her. But she was my friend, not because I forced her to be, but because she chose to be. And years ago, we decided that if my great plan succeeded, she would be your guide after my departure. It is good to see you, Qianzai.*

'Your son looks like you,' said Qianzai, her beautiful eyes meeting Kirin's. 'You need not worry about his safety, my friend. Go in peace.'

Kirin smiled at her, and heard more dragon-voices in his head, for he was still wearing the Gauntlet.

We are coming, master, they said.

Kirin did not take off the Gauntlet this time. He knew he was ready.

It is time for me to go, son, said Danh-Gem. *My work is done, and my labours are at an end. I cannot expect you to mourn for me, and I have no parting words of fatherly wisdom to give you. The power is in your hands now, use it as you will.*

And when the time comes, you will unite the rakshases, I can feel it. Your story has reached a turning point—mine, though, is over. And I am glad to say it had a happy ending.

And Danh-Gem smiled at Kirin, turned around and disappeared.

There were creaking, groaning noises and the Brotherhood of Renewal awoke.

'What happened?' asked Omar. Then he saw Qianzai and fell silent.

'Why are you wearing the Gauntlet, Karisman?' asked Bjorkun.

They looked at Kirin again and saw for the first time the power that lay within him.

'Danh-Gem has returned!' shouted Aciram. 'I knew it all along, master! I knew you were but testing us! Look at him, and rejoice, brothers! Danh-Gem is reborn!'

But Kirin shook his head and Aciram fell silent. He looked at each one of them in turn.

He smiled suddenly, for he was beginning to enjoy himself.

Dark Lord? Well, he was a lord now, and he had always been dark . . .

And then, though his lips did not move, they heard his voice in their heads.

I am Kirin, son of Danh-Gem, he said, and they looked at him, and awe and terror were in their eyes. *Do not bother to kneel. We have work to do.*

He looked at them, and saw the fear they felt.

You don't trust me yet, he thought. But you will. You will.

Epilogue

It was almost dawn when the Silver Dagger walked into the Fragrant Underbelly.

Of course, they say every day has twenty-four hours, but that can't be true, he thought. Some days are definitely longer than others.

Tomorrow was going to be one of those long days. The people of Kol would have to be told that Danh-Gem had risen, and that they had a new Hero.

And tomorrow he would set off on his new mission.

For he was back.

It was annoying that no one in the Silver Phalanx would even be surprised. They'd told him he'd never be able to lead the quiet life. And they were right, which was annoying.

He looked at the little piece of paper in his hand. There were a few names on it. Big names. Soon the same names would be on tombstones.

So I can't do magic. That doesn't really matter. I'm still the best there is. And my decision to come out of retirement has nothing to do with loyalty or patriotism, he thought. It's simply that the Civilian offered me double pay. That's a *lot* of money.

He had just met the Civilian, and heard the news. The dragons were awake, and Danh-Gem had probably returned.

And so had the Dagger. The Silver Phalanx would not need a new leader after all.

Tonight is an important night for Kol, he thought. An important night for Asvin, too—tomorrow his life will change. I hope he survives it all. Nice boy.

I wonder where Kirin is. He obviously hasn't killed Danh-Gem. He's probably dead. I mustn't jump to conclusions, though. Time will tell.

He looked around, and smiled and waved at a few people.

If they knew who I really was they would probably die. In fact, they would definitely die, I would probably have to kill them myself, he thought.

What had the Civilian said? Interesting times lay ahead. Very interesting times.

He looked at the pretty Elakish crooner, and she blushed. Life was very good sometimes . . .

A new Age is coming. The world has changed. Maybe war lies ahead. But the Civilian and I will stop it if we can. And we can, too. Yes, interesting times lie ahead. The Age of Heroes? Or the Second Age of Terror? Who knows?

The Silver Dagger walked up to the bar and sat on a high stool, swinging his legs about. He smiled his most dangerous smile at a few pretty women, and watched with satisfaction as they responded. They always did.

Triog ambled up to him. 'Drink?' asked Middlog.

'The usual,' said the Dagger.

'Dragonjuice, well-shaken?'

'Stirred, not shaken,' replied Amloki the khudran.